IRON COMPANY

'TAKE UP YOUR guns!' cried Magnus, lifting his own to his chest and cradling the all-important cord. 'Follow me!'

At last, the men had some direction, something to get their teeth into. With a roar of aggression and rage, they rose up as one and charged across the broken stone. Magnus was at the forefront, eyes wide, sweat starting from his skin, expecting to hear the blast and whine of gunfire at any moment. He muttered a quick prayer to Sigmar. All there was now was luck, or grace. The light had almost gone entirely, and every black shape against the earth looked like an enemy soldier. His heart banged in his chest, his lungs laboured. Battle had come at last.

They kept running. No shots echoed. The bugles rang out again. Some of the knights had overshot, and were cantering back. The air was filled with the shouts and war cries of the defenders, but no guns fired. It was as if the enemy had never existed.

A cold shiver passed through Magnus's stomach. They should have been hard upon them by now. They were being drawn out. The snipers had withdrawn. It was a trap.

A WARHAMMER NOVEL

IRON COMPANY

CHRIS WRAIGHT

To MD. With thanks and admiration always.

A BLACK LIBRARY PUBLICATION

First published in Great Britain in 2009 by
BL Publishing,
Games Workshop Ltd.,
Willow Road, Nottingham,
NG7 2WS, UK

10 9 8 7 6 5 4 3 2 1

Cover illustration by Clint Langley.

Map by Nuala Kinrade.

A CIP record for this book is available from the British Library.

UK ISBN: 978 1 84416 778 4
US ISBN: 978 1 84416 779 1

See the Black Library on the Internet at
www.blacklibrary.com

Find out more about Games Workshop
and the world of Warhammer at
www.games-workshop.com

Printed and bound in the UK.

THIS IS A DARK age, a bloody age, an age of daemons and of sorcery. It is an age of battle and death, and of the world's ending. Amidst all of the fire, flame and fury it is a time, too, of mighty heroes, of bold deeds and great courage.

AT THE HEART of the Old World sprawls the Empire, the largest and most powerful of the human realms. Known for its engineers, sorcerers, traders and soldiers, it is a land of great mountains, mighty rivers, dark forests and vast cities. And from his throne in Altdorf reigns the Emperor Karl Franz, sacred descendant of the founder of these lands, Sigmar, and wielder of his magical warhammer.

BUT THESE ARE far from civilised times. Across the length and breadth of the Old World, from the knightly palaces of Bretonnia to ice-bound Kislev in the far north, come rumblings of war. In the towering Worlds Edge Mountains, the orc tribes are gathering for another assault. Bandits and renegades harry the wild southern lands of the Border Princes. There are rumours of rat-things, the skaven, emerging from the sewers and swamps across the land. And from the northern wildernesses there is the ever-present threat of Chaos, of daemons and beastmen corrupted by the foul powers of the Dark Gods. As the time of battle draws ever nearer, the Empire needs heroes like never before.

CHAPTER ONE

There are many who pour scorn on the engineers. They call us madmen, fools, or worse. We have no honour in the Empire, nor in the lands beyond. And yet I foresee a great change coming. When the sword fails and where the spell miscasts, iron and blackpowder will still retain their merit. Our time has not yet come. But as the days grow darker, it surely will. Only when all the Emperor's companies are Iron Companies will the future of our race be secured. Then we shall no longer be scorned, but lauded and justly appraised as the mightiest and most learned of men.

The Notebooks of
Leonardo da Miragliano

IT WAS THE end of winter, and the worst of the ice had retreated north at last. The ground still lay as hard as bone, and the trees were bare. Their black trunks rose starkly into the grey air. Men wrapped themselves heavily against the chill. The countryside was silent but for the echoing croak of ravens. When the sun rose, it was weak, its light watery. When it set, the cold came creeping back from the mountains, and families huddled around meagre fires, watchful of the flickering shadows.

The streets of Hergig were almost empty. In the faint light of dusk, the narrow houses clustered together tightly, rising from the filth of the streets in uneven, jagged rows. The most elaborate of the buildings were roofed with slate and had frames of oak. The poorest looked tired and stained with age.

Hochland was not a wealthy place, and there were more poor places than rich. The elector count and his court preferred to dwell for most of the year in their private estates near the southern borders. Only in the deep winter did they trail back to Hergig, sheltering in the massive Kristalhof in the centre of the city. The vast keep ensured they were isolated from the worst squalor of their subjects. Those who could afford it constructed their town houses around the prestigious Hofbahn district, as close as they could get to the keep. Those who couldn't took their chances in the lower town, where the squalid dwellings were rammed up against one another and the militia patrolled in teams.

Magnus Ironblood took a look around him. He felt tired and grimy. Of all the houses before him, only one was lit. A hand-painted sign hung on battered hinges:

The Boar. There were a thousand inns with that name in the northlands. This one looked no different to the rest. The light coming from the doorway was dim. There was no sound of carousing from inside, just a low, surly murmuring.

Still, the place served beer, and that was the important thing. Magnus walked towards it, his long leather overcoat swirling as he went. The expensive garment marked him out in such places. He no longer cared. Fitting in had never been his principal strength.

He pushed the door open. The inn was little more than the lower room of a private house. Old straw lay on the floor, reeking. Tallow candles burned in alcoves, leaving black streaks against the daub walls. There was no bar, just a long table on which dusty bottles and kegs of beer had been piled. A shrewish woman sat behind it, counting copper coins into a jar. There were a few more wooden tables in the centre of the room, and long benches against the walls. As Magnus entered, some of the drinkers turned their heads towards the door. There weren't many of them. They were all men, all old, all clothed in heavy cloaks and jerkins against the cold.

Just like me, thought Magnus, dryly. This is what I've become.

The drinkers went back to nursing their flagons. One man looked at Magnus for a little longer. He had a sparse grey beard and glittering eyes, and hunched over his drink protectively. He kept up his gaze for a few moments, before turning back to his beer.

Magnus ignored him, and walked over to what passed for the bar. The old fool probably lusted after his coat. He could try and get it if he wanted. Better men had failed.

'Beer,' Magnus said to the woman, curtly.

She gave him an irritated look, as if serving customers was something to be avoided, and put her coins down.

'Keg, or bottle?' she asked.

To have beer from a glass bottle was a rarity. Magnus looked at the ones on show carefully. The glass was deep green and thick, with long corks protruding from the neck. They had foreign characters on the labels, angular and unreadable. Plundered stock, then. Anything could be in them.

'Keg,' he said, throwing a single coin onto the table.

The woman got up and filled an iron tankard with a dark brown liquid. There was virtually no head on it. It smelled almost like beer. There was more than a hint of the drain about it too.

Magnus took it up and wandered over to one of the benches. He sat heavily. As he did so, he noticed that the man with the beard had left. None of the other patrons paid him any attention. He took a sip of his drink. It had a sour finish, but he'd had much worse. It was wet, it would take the edge off his mood, and nothing much else mattered.

He pushed himself back against the wall, letting his legs stretch out against the floor, watching the furrows his heels made in the dirt. His boots had once been something to be proud of. Expensive leather, expertly sewn. Now they were just like him, faded and battered. He looked down at his legs. Though it was hard to remember, Magnus had once been considered tall.

Handsome, even. Now he just looked big. The muscles that had pounded hammers on anvils were still there, but lay under an unwelcome covering of fat. His features had become lined and hard from the elements. His dark hair, jet-black when he'd been in Nuln, was now ragged and flecked with grey. At least they matched his eyes now. Just like his father's, pale grey irises like the flank of a Middenheim wolf.

The beer went down well. Before he knew it, the flagon was nearly empty. Magnus left the dregs where they were. You never really wanted to know what was in them. He gestured to the woman for another. She brought one over, grumbling as she came.

'And?' she said, holding out a grimy palm.

Magnus paused. His payment should have been good for more. His were rare coins, minted in Nuln, almost the last remaining from his final cache. He thought about protesting, but the beer had sunk deep into his body, making him lethargic. Who cared if he was being cheated? The money would be gone soon enough anyway.

He pressed a second coin into her hand, and the woman skulked off. Magnus took a thoughtful sip. For what he was paying, he might as well try and enjoy it.

As he lowered the rim of the tankard, the door opened again. A gust of frigid air sighed into the room. A man entered. He looked nothing like the others. His flesh was smooth and clean, his robes expensive. Aside from the thin layer of mud lining his soft boots, little of the street clung to him. As his fingers moved, the weak light caught on metal. He was wearing rings on his pale, effeminate fingers. Walking around Hergig like that was dangerous. He was either very stupid, or very powerful.

The man pushed his long cloak back, revealing a sleek, rounded stomach. Everything about him was self-satisfied, from his grooming to his pink, fleshy face. The woman hurried up to him, her earlier irascibility swept away.

'Herr Grotius,' she said, handing him a bottle of beer. 'You do us honour.'

The man looked at her distastefully, and reached for some payment.

'Not necessary, not necessary,' the woman said. 'Will you have anything else?'

The man Grotius looked around him. His expression seemed to imply that nothing, absolutely nothing in this miserable place could possibly be of the slightest interest to him.

'No,' he said. His voice was syrupy, and conveyed a casual disdain with a minimum of effort. 'I won't be here long.'

The woman withdrew, looking back at the newcomer nervously as she did so. A few eyes around the room were raised in his direction, but flicked down again as soon as he looked around. Magnus suddenly felt a chill run through him. Grotius was walking towards him.

'Herr Magnus Albrecht Ironblood?' he said.

Magnus nodded warily. The man pulled a chair from a nearby table, wiped its surface with the corner of his cloak, and sat down carefully.

'May I join you?'

Magnus looked at the man with suspicion. The rest of the drinkers seemed to know who the newcomer was, and went back to their low-voiced conversations.

'Do I have a choice?' asked Magnus.

Grotius smiled thinly.

'Of course you do. But I'd recommend spending a few moments in my company. We have something of significant mutual interest to discuss.'

Magnus took a deliberate swig of his drink, weighing up the situation. The man had the air of an official, a court flunky. If that were true, it boded badly for him. He had never had a good experience with officials. They were parasites, paid gold to administer the affairs of their benefactors while the masses starved.

'Is that so?' said Magnus. 'Then you won't mind telling me who you are, who sent you and how you knew I was here.'

The man raised an eyebrow.

'You really don't know who I am?' he said, musingly. 'They told me you were new to Hergig, but still.'

The man took a sip from his bottle, and winced. He put it down as if it was full of wasps. As he did so, the doors of the tavern burst open. They slammed against the walls heavily, and a group of men burst in. Three or four of them, plus a slovenly woman with a painted face. They called out for beer. Their red cheeks and bleary eyes indicated they'd already had a lot.

The woman frantically tried to calm them down, but one of them broke into a song. Magnus sat back, smiling. The lyrics were enlightening, something about a miller's daughter and an oversized grindstone.

Grotius, however, didn't see the funny side. He stood up, and fixed the ringleader with a cold stare.

For a moment, the man kept going. But his friends saw the danger. He was dragged into the shadows and hastily quietened. As realisation dawned, Magnus saw the man's face turn ashen. He slumped into the corner and was given a dirty flagon to cool his spirits. They clearly knew who Grotius was. It was only him, it seemed, who was at a disadvantage.

Grotius's gaze swept the rest of the room. All eyes were lowered. The hum of conversation returned. The man sighed irritably, and looked back at Magnus.

'My name is Valerian von Grotius. I'm an agent of Count Ludenhof. My duties are many. You should know from the outset that I'm in the complete trust of the elector. That may inform our discussion, since you're clearly new to Hochland.'

Magnus maintained his sceptical expression. This was getting worse.

'As for how I found you,' said Grotius, 'it was a simple matter. The name Ironblood still carries some weight in the Empire, no matter how much you've tried to extinguish it. Even now, despite your lamentable fall from prestige, you don't much resemble the scum from around here. When news reached me that you'd ended up in Hergig, I was able to draw on a few outstanding debts. In that, as ever, I was ably served.'

Magnus inclined his head sardonically.

'Glad to hear it,' he said. 'Your sort never seem short of willing helpers.'

Grotius ignored Magnus's tone.

'A happy consequence of office,' he said, looking down at his rings absently. 'I've been waiting to meet you for several days. I'm glad to finally have the honour.'

Magnus belched loudly.

'So now we're all happy,' he said. 'Suppose you tell me what you want, and then leave?'

A flicker of annoyance crossed Grotius's features for the first time.

'I'll be pleased to leave you to your many pressing affairs,' he said, looking at Magnus's stained jerkin with faintly veiled disgust. 'Do you think I enjoy coming to such places?'

He collected himself.

'You're unfamiliar with the politics of Hochland,' Grotius said, settling against the creaking back of his chair. 'Let me illuminate you. Much as we might wish it otherwise, the benign rule of Count Ludenhof is not as universally appreciated as it might be. As with all the states of the Empire, there is discontent, there is envy, and there are rivals to the sovereign office. Through the enlightened policies of his advisers, the count has maintained the security of his position with considerable efficiency. But there are always issues, always the threat of strife.'

As he spoke, Grotius looked genuinely pained by the spectre of disloyalty to the count. Magnus sighed, took a deep swig of his drink and slumped further against the bench.

'There is a woman of noble birth, the Margravine Anna-Louisa Margarete Emeludt von Kleister,' continued Grotius. 'She's the mistress of several familial estates to the north of the province, bordering on the Hochland Mittebergen, the Middle Mountains. The source of her wealth has never been entirely clear, but she has deep pockets. Among her possessions are several mines. It's possible she's discovered a hidden source of precious metal, maybe even gold. If so, that gives her substantial independent means. She could mint coinage, even hire mercenaries. It is a situation which has proved increasingly intolerable.'

'Sounds like some woman,' said Magnus. 'Maybe we should meet.'

'I'd like nothing better,' said Grotius. 'But you might find it difficult. For over a year, she has rebuffed any attempt to draw her back within the fold of legitimate government. Reasonable requests for a tithe of her wealth have met with no reply. Repeated embassies have returned with no response. She has, in effect, become a rebel.'

Magnus sighed deeply. Grotius looked in the mood to spin out his tale. Magnus was tired, and the potent ale was beginning to generate a low throb behind his eyes. The murky business of Hochland's internal politics was no concern of his.

'So bring her to heel,' he said. 'Ludenhof will have to learn to control his women.'

Grotius looked awkwardly at him.

'The thought had occurred to us. Sedition is not tolerated here any more than it would be in Nuln or Altdorf. When it was clear the margravine had ceased to fall within the writ of the state, an armed delegation was sent to her estate with orders to arrest her. She was not there. According to reports, she had raised her own troops with gold and promises, and set up court in a remote citadel in the mountains. The implication of this is clear. She intends to resist arrest, and build up her strength over the winter. In the spring, she may have gathered enough men to move against the elector. Obviously, this situation could not be tolerated. One of our agents reported that she had amassed a considerable store of arms which could only grow. On my advice, an army was mustered and sent to bring the rebels to heel.'

Grotius's sense of awkwardness seemed to increase. Some of his easy self-assurance had dissolved.

'That was over a month ago,' he said, quietly. 'They have not been heard of since. We have no idea of their fate. There are many, myself included, who believe them destroyed.'

Magnus let out a low whistle. Despite himself, he was beginning to become intrigued.

'You lost an army?' he said. 'Careless. If you ask me, heads should roll. Right at the top.'

Grotius gave him a withering look.

'And so we come to the present situation,' he said. 'There is a rogue margravine hidden in the Mittebergen, gathering fresh troops to her side with every passing week. No attempt to contact her has been successful. The integrity of the state is compromised. The count is greatly troubled, and has sworn to bring the affair to a speedy conclusion. Funds have been transferred from his personal account in Altdorf for the raising of a second army. He is determined to crush the rebellion before it can blossom further. Hochland will not be divided.'

Magnus drained his tankard, and looked at Grotius. 'Fascinating,' he said, licking his lips. 'But I'd listen a lot better if…'

Grotius snapped his fingers irritably, and the woman at the table instantly began to pour a fresh flagon of ale. The drunkards in the corner were getting steadily louder again. One man was gnawing at a chicken bone in the shadows, the pink juices running down his chin. Another had brought out a scrawny fighting cockerel and was showing it to the woman proudly. All across the Empire, in every squalid hole and cranny, similar scenes were being played out. It was a dreary thought.

'So now we come to it,' said Grotius, watching as the beer was delivered. 'The army is gathered and is nearly ready to march. All is in place, save for one element. Our master engineer, Marcus Frölich, was on the first campaign. His machinery, his crews, all are lost. We have guns in Hergig, but no one to operate them. We could send for a replacement from the college in Nuln, but our request would take days to arrive, and weeks to respond to. So when I discovered that an Ironblood was in Hergig, you can imagine my satisfaction. You are here, and, despite everything, your name still means something. Or at least it does to those who know about such things. There is money in this, Herr Ironblood. Money, and a chance to recover yourself.'

At that, Magnus let slip a long, bitter laugh. He looked at Grotius, a wolfish smile playing on his lips.

'Ah, my friend,' he said. 'You've been badly advised. If you need a master engineer, look elsewhere. There are good reasons for my leaving the service. Yours was

20

a nice story, and I feel for your loss, but you'll need to find someone else to be your gunnery captain.'

Grotius maintained his equable expression, and placed his hands comfortably across his broad stomach.

'You would do well to consider the proposal,' he said, weighing his words carefully. 'The count himself has been told of your presence here. Matters have been set in motion. Decisions have been ratified. I trust you know what that means?'

Magnus felt his anger rising. He placed his tankard down roughly on the bench beside him. This would have to be cut off before it could go any further.

'Sigmar damn you!' he hissed. 'You have some guts to come here and talk to me like I was some boy of your master's. I've served in armies larger than you've ever seen. I've commanded batteries of a hundred guns and answered to Marshal Helborg himself. If I had a weapon…'

Grotius's eyes went flat.

'But you don't, do you?' he said, acidly. 'Even I've heard of the Ironblood pistol. Where is it now? In the hands of some strumpet witch hunter? You've squandered everything, Ironblood. Whoever you used to be, whatever you used to command, now you're just another feckless wanderer, ripe for nothing but the press or the poorhouse.'

Magnus's eyes blazed, but the words died in his throat. Despite it all, the accusations hit home. Grotius had done his work well, and knew where his vulnerable points were. The agent's lip curled slightly in a sneer.

'I began reasonably, in the hope that you might be persuaded to see the gracious opportunity the count has extended you,' Grotius said. 'He's a man who's used to having his wishes granted. I suspect he would be extremely disappointed to learn that his offer has been turned down.'

Magnus felt his anger sink into a kind of dark resignation. He was new in Hergig, and the few friends he had here would be no protection if he made enemies of the authorities. He knew just enough of the ways of the Imperial hierarchy to appreciate the position he was in.

'Now that you put it like that,' said Magnus, not bothering to hide the scorn in his voice, 'I'm inclined to listen further. Tell on.'

Grotius let his vicious expression slide, and the benign air of satisfaction returned. The man had all the deceit and silky manners of a career diplomat.

'The resources at your disposal would be considerable,' he said, matter of factly. 'There are several big guns, many smaller pieces, and the crew to man them. There are also companies of handgunners, some equipped with the famous Hochland long guns. They'll all need close supervision. The commander of the army, General Scharnhorst, is not a believer in the new sciences. That is to be regretted, and is also why we need you. Since you're so proud of your prior experiences, I cannot believe a man such as yourself would have much of a problem with our requirements.'

Magnus found himself only half-listening. The evening had gone from merely bad to terrible.

'I suppose you have the plans all prepared?' he said, looking at the thin foam on his beer grimly.

'The place the margravine has chosen is called Morgramgar,' he said. 'I will arrange for our charts to be sent to you. It is a citadel, high up in the mountains, reputedly built on a single spur of rock. She has not chosen the location idly. Morgramgar was built to withstand a siege. It will be hard to reach, and even harder to storm. I won't lie to you, Ironblood. The task will be arduous. There is much about the rebellion we don't know. And if tales of Kleister's riches are to be believed, we cannot be sure how many men she has bought. We need commanders of calibre, not hired swords.'

Magnus drank again, feeling the sour liquid slip down his throat easily.

'You paint an attractive picture,' he said. 'No wonder you're having trouble recruiting. What of this Scharnhorst? Is he good?'

Grotius couldn't conceal a slight flicker of discomfort before his face resumed its habitual smoothness.

'He's one of Hochland's most decorated soldiers,' he said, lowering his eyes. 'He has commanded many of the elector's armies.'

Magnus leaned forward, and placed his tankard on the table roughly.

'Look,' he said, his eyes glinting. 'I don't care what you think of him. This whole province is a backward hive of peasantry. Commanding a Hochland battalion is about as impressive as organising a village fayre. You may have a few decent handgunners up here, but that's it. I'm going to need more than that. Sending an army into the mountains with a provincial hick at the helm will be suicide, for all of us. You'll have to do better than that.'

Grotius's eyes went flat.

'If we're so backward here,' he said, slowly and deliberately, 'then it was a poor choice you made to live amongst us. You may not have appreciated it yet, being so new, but we are a proud people. You would do well to remember that. Not all Hochlanders are as tolerant as I am.'

Magnus snorted with derision.

'You need me,' he said. 'If you didn't, you'd have dragged me to the gaol already. I know where we stand here, Grotius. If I refuse, I'll suddenly find my every doing a matter of interest to the local sergeant. I'm too old and weary to play that game.'

He fixed the agent with a dark look.

'I can do your work for you,' he said. 'You know that. But I want payment up front, and I want the money to do it properly. My own team, and funds to hire whatever I think I need. And I want full command of the engineer companies. This Scharnhorst can do what he wants with the halberdiers and the archers, but I don't want any interference with the guns.'

Grotius returned the glare coolly.

'You'll get money,' he said. 'For yourself and for your company. The gunnery crews will answer to you. But don't attempt to cross Scharnhorst. He's the general, and he's in command. I warn you, he won't tolerate any attempt to undermine that. You've served before. You know how it is.'

Magnus drained the last of his tankard. Three flagons' worth already. How had he become so accustomed to it, so quickly?

'And I command the heavy iron,' he said. 'I won't tolerate any attempt to undermine that, either.'

He placed the empty tankard on the bench beside him.

'I'll have to meet this Scharnhorst,' Magnus said, wearily. 'Perhaps we can come to some arrangement.'

Grotius shrugged, pulled his cloak about him and looked over to the door. As he moved, all eyes around the tavern turned to him. The conversations ebbed again. The desperation to see him leave was palpable.

'That's your business,' he said. 'Now I must go. There's much to arrange. Where are your lodgings? I'll have the documents sent to you.'

'Above the blacksmiths on Karlfranzstrasse,' said Magnus. 'There's a coaching inn on the corner of the street. Get your man to ask for directions there.'

Grotius nodded, and rose. As he did so, he threw a couple of coins onto the bench.

'I'm glad you saw the opportunity here, Ironblood,' he said, failing to keep the edge of disdain from his voice. 'That concludes our business. I'll be in touch. In the meantime, enjoy a drink, courtesy of the count.'

Magnus bowed ironically, leaving the coins where they were.

'I'll be sure to thank him when we next meet.'

Grotius turned and walked back towards the doorway. A few of the drinkers raised their heads slightly, but kept their eyes low. The cockerel squawked, and was silenced. The door opened, and the chill of the night rushed in once more. It slammed shut with his passing, and the flimsy wood shivered.

The room relaxed. Conversations became more animated, and furtive glances were shot in Magnus's direction. The slovenly woman began to cackle. Magnus ignored her and looked at the coins before him. They shone dully in the dirty light. The sum was derisory. He'd been suborned so cheaply, with so little struggle. Even a year ago he might have laughed off a man like Grotius. The coins would have been hurled back at his preening, prancing face. He could have resisted the commission, taken his chances with the militia, broken free of Hergig and laughed in the faces of his pursuers.

Not now. When the spirit had been broken, the carrion crows began to circle. With a heavy sense of futility, he picked up the coins. Magnus looked up at the serving woman, who was glaring at him with suspicion and hostility.

'Another,' he said in a thick voice.

CHAPTER TWO

Is there anything which embodies the might of the Empire of man more than the cannonry it can bring to bear? What other nation of the world has mastered such dread science? What other race can deploy the lines of death-dealing iron as we can? With every passing year, our metallurgists discover more, and our alchemists distil purer and more potent strains of the blackpowder. Though the lost souls of Chaos may sweep down from the Northern Wastes, and the savage greenskins assail us from their foul holes in the mountains, we have nothing to fear as long as we remain true to the sacred lore of the machine. In it lies our salvation, our redemption, and our one true hope.

Address given by Solomon Grusswalder
Master of the College of Engineers, Nuln

THORGAD GRIMGARSSON WAITED silently in the shadows under the trees. Glamrist felt light in his gnarled hands. It always did, when the time came. A thin reflection of moonlight gleamed along the blade. The edge was as sharp as the High King's own. He'd ground it himself. The only way to get it done properly.

Ahead, the faint light pooled in the narrow clearing. There was movement. Thorgad narrowed his eyes. Years of living in the lamplit halls of his ancestors had made them almost as good in the dark as they were under the sun.

'Grobi,' he mouthed, letting his lips curl with disgust.

He ran a finger lightly along the axe blade. Even in the weak light, the runes were visible. They gave him comfort. Soon they would be drenched in black blood. It had been too long since Glamrist had drunk deep. The spirit of the weapon was taut with readiness.

There was a low chattering. The grobi were careless. Too rarely were they disturbed in the heart of the forest. This was their realm, a world of throttlings and chokings, a miserable life of preying on the unwary and the foolish. Even if he had not been schooled to hate the race from birth, Thorgad would still have despised them. There was nothing in the world more deserving of death than a goblin.

One of them shuffled into full view. It was wearing a dark cloak. A hooked nose poked out from under it, and there was a quick flash of curved yellow teeth. Others scuttled into the clearing. They were excited. One of them had picked up a trail of something. They clutched their weapons in scrawny hands. Gouges, sickles, nets, twisted scimitars. The chattering grew louder. They were moving off.

The time had come. Thorgad made a final assessment of their numbers, then hefted Glamrist expertly.

'Khazuk!' he bellowed, and burst from the undergrowth.

In a second he was amongst them. The axe whirled in the air. A slick of blood splattered across Thorgad's beard and breastplate. The stench of it clogged his nostrils.

The goblins broke like animals, squealing and squawking. Some leapt up into the trees, scrabbling at the bark. Others darted into the foliage. Thorgad went after them like a hunter after rabbits, swinging the heavy blade with abandon. The muscles in his powerful arms responded instantly. It had been too long since they had done anything but hammer iron. The change felt good.

The slowest of the grobi were soon cut down. Their twitching bodies lay amid the bracken. Tattered cloaks hung from briars. The sound of their screams echoed from the tree trunks.

But then it changed. One of them must have noticed Thorgad was alone. A series of barked orders ran through the forest. The dwarf stood in the centre of the clearing, panting. Silvery light limned the open space. Beyond, the shadows clustered, as dark as nightshade. The squawking stopped. The rustling branches fell still.

Then, one by one, points of yellow light appeared. Dozens of them.

'Grungni's beard,' muttered Thorgad. 'More than I thought.'

He spat on the ground, turning slowly, watching the sets of eyes multiply in the gloom. He was surrounded. Still they waited. He let his breathing return to normal. His eyes narrowed. They would have to rush him to have any chance. Who would be the first to try it? He found himself grinning.

'Come on then!' he roared, breaking the eerie silence.

They came. A wave of chattering, snickering hate. In the half-light they looked like rats, swarming across the ground. The first of them reached him. One leapt up, its thin face distorted with fear and malice. A second later it fell to the ground, nearly sliced in two.

More came at him. Thorgad felt something grasp his ankle. A scimitar whistled past his neck. Fingers as hard as iron rods scrabbled at his cloak. He kept moving. Glamrist was working quickly now. He hurled it in wide arcs, smashing apart any grobi that got too near. The shining blade was soon as black as pitch, stained with a thick layer of gore. He could feel his own blood trickle across his right arm. One of the grobi knives had hit home. In his activity, he'd hardly noticed it. The axe sang. The squawking rose in volume.

Still they came. More were arriving from the deeps of the forest. Thorgad swung round, looking for an escape route. There was none. Much as he hated to admit it, he might have been a little ambitious. A vicious-looking grobi leapt up towards his face, teeth snapping. Thorgad felt the spittle on his skin, smelt the putrid stink. With a snarl of disgust, he brought his left fist up. Bone crunched, and the cloaked horror crumpled. Thorgad spun around again.

Too late. He felt the sharp pain of the gouge as it bored into his thigh. Glamrist flashed, and the grobi staggered backwards. Its entrails spilled, gleaming in the starlight.

Thorgad grunted as the pain radiated up his leg. This was getting difficult. More grobi fell. His arms were streaked with blood, his face spattered with it. Still they jumped towards him. He felt something grab hold of his cloak again. The grip held. Two more sprang towards him, flails spinning. In their hateful eyes, there was the glint of victory.

Thorgad roared with frustration. He jabbed and hacked the axe head into the attackers. He wrenched his arms around, trying to dislodge the clutching hands. He could feel himself losing balance. The axe was ripped from his fingers. From somewhere, he heard a high cackle of glee. Even as he was dragged down into the undergrowth, he managed to take two more with him, smashing their brittle heads together until their eyes popped and the skulls fractured. As he felt them clamber over him for the killing blow, he had time for one last curse.

'Grimnir take you all!' he spat, watching the scimitar blade rise above him.

It never fell. Something spun across the narrow clearing, flashing in the starlight. There was the whine of crossbows. Bolts thudded into their marks. The blade fell uselessly from the goblin's hands. It tumbled back to the ground. The squealing broke out again. More shafts found their targets.

Then the dwarfs came, charging across the clearing, axes swinging. The grobi broke and ran. These odds were less to their liking. They were pursued, driven back into the endless shadows of the forest. From the depths, the sound of killing began again.

Thorgad pushed the limp body of the dead grobi from him. He shook his head to clear it. That had been too close. Painfully, feeling the deep wound in his thigh, he hauled himself back onto his feet.

'What are you doing here?' came a gruff voice.

Thorgad looked up. The dwarf before him was almost entirely encased in ornate armour. His helmet was engraved with the likeness of Grimnir, and he carried a heavily decorated warhammer, already running with goblin blood.

Thorgad grimaced as he leaned on his wounded leg.

'Heading east,' he said, retrieving Glamrist from where it had been dropped.

'You almost lost your blade,' the armoured dwarf said, disapprovingly. 'That would have been a great shame on your family.'

'My family already bears shame,' said Thorgad. 'It's why I'm here. But you have my thanks.'

The armoured dwarf took off his helmet and extended a gauntlet. His hair was ivory-white and his beard was long and pleated. A venerable warrior, then.

'Snorri Valramnik,' he said. 'And you owe me nothing. Killing these vermin is its own reward.'

Thorgad grasped the dwarf's hand.

'Thorgad Grimgarsson,' he said.

Valramnik raised a bushy eyebrow.

'Grimgarsson?' he said. 'That explains why you're here. You should be more careful.'

Thorgad didn't reply. He tore a strip from a dead goblin's cloak, and begun to wind it around his wound. The bleeding was already slowing. It would heal soon. The dawi were made of strong stuff.

Valramnik looked over his shoulder. His warriors were returning to the clearing. The last of the grobi were either dead or driven far off.

'We can't stay long,' the old dwarf said. 'A debt of honour takes us south. But this meeting may be more than chance.'

He leaned towards Thorgad, and his voice lowered.

'I know what you seek,' he said. 'Your time may be at hand. The umgi are fighting over the Morgramgariven. War will come soon. A good dawi knows how to take his chance.'

Thorgad looked at Valramnik steadily. He gave nothing away.

'How do you know this?'

Valramnik laughed, and his barrel chest shook.

'Never you mind how I know,' he said. 'I speak to many folk, dawi and umgi. You can listen and profit, or ignore me and your grudge will never be erased. The Empire is no place for you, Grimgarsson. You should listen to advice when it finds you.'

Thorgad grunted, trying not to show his interest too much. He began to clean the gore from Glamrist. Inwardly, however, his heart had begun to race.

'If this is true,' he said carefully, 'I will be in debt to you twice over. A chest of gold would be too little reward.'

Valramnik laughed again. His warriors had all returned, and he put his helmet back on.

'Don't incur debts you can't pay!' he said. 'But if you wish to clear them, look for me in Karak Hirn. Until then, Grimnir be with you.'

With that, he turned back into the shadows and stalked off. His entourage went with him, and soon they were lost in the darkling trees.

Thorgad stood silently for a while, pondering the strange ways of fate. After some time, he collected himself, and slung Glamrist across his back. His face gave little away. Despite the grobi, despite the unexpected reprieve, despite the tantalising news, his expression remained stony. With a halting limp, he turned west, and began to plough through the forest once more. The coming days would determine the truth of Valramnik's news. But it was worth following the lead. At least it gave him some purpose. After weeks in the wilderness, now Hergig awaited him.

MAGNUS CAME ROUND. The world gradually made its presence felt. It was cold, pale and unpleasant.

He half-sat up in bed, and took a look about him. He was in his garret above the blacksmith's. It was filthy. Dirty linen was strewn across the bare wooden floor. Harsh light fought its way through the narrow, grimy window ahead of him. In the corner of the room, a pile of heavy, huge chests sat, covered in rumpled sheets. They were the only items of any worth in the chamber. The wood was oak, dark with age. All were banded with iron, and there was a strange rune on the lock. Dwarfish make. Despite hundreds of years of artistry in the Empire, still nothing could compare to them when it came to making things to last.

Magnus pushed the sheets from him, and carefully rubbed his chin. It was thick with stubble. A line of drool ran across one cheek. His breath was foul. The room stank. His temples began to hammer.

Shakily, mindful of his eggshell-weak head, Magnus staggered to his feet and headed for the chamber pot. A wave of nausea lurched across him. When done, he shuffled to the window, shoved the rotten frame outwards and hurled the contents into the street below. There was an outraged curse, followed by raucous laughter.

Magnus smiled grimly. He still felt sick. Most of his clothes from the night before had been thrown across a rickety chair. He pulled them back on. Their stale aroma blended artfully with the other malodorous smells in the room. The icy morning air, now rushing into the bedchamber through the open window, did little to dent the seamy atmosphere.

There was a metal bowl on a shelf next to the chair, and a chipped pitcher of water. The surface was lined with scum. Magnus poured it into the bowl, dipped his head towards it and splashed his face. The chill water brought a rush of blood to his face, and his head thumped more strongly. He shook it, and his unruly hair whipped across his cheeks.

Magnus took a deep breath, feeling himself gradually come back together. He looked out of the open window. The sun was still low in the sky, but it must have been at least mid-morning. His room was on the second floor of the blacksmith's rambling house, and he could see a landscape of sloping roofs in every direction. Mud-coloured smoke rose lazily into the pale sky.

The chatter of the street filtered up towards him. It was lively, vital, obscene, good-natured. Everything that Magnus wasn't.

He opened the draughty door to his humble chamber, and stomped down the creaking stairs. Two storeys below, the forge was clearly at work. With each clang of the blacksmith's hammer, the veins in his forehead gave a sympathetic spasm of pain. Wincing against the hammering, Magnus entered the wife's private domain in the floor above the forge.

As he stumbled in, Frau Ettieg turned to greet him. She had been cooking, and her cheeks were crimson from the heat of the oven. She wiped her hands on her grease-stained apron, and frowned.

'Drunk again?' she asked.

The blacksmith's wife was a solid, heavy-boned woman with a face like a man's. She rarely lost her frown, which made her look even more masculine. Magnus felt sorry for her. Her husband, the swarthy, violent Herr Ettieg, had been enjoying the favours of the maid Brigitta for some time. It was common knowledge in the neighbourhood, especially since the plump, bright-eyed Brigitta was pretty indiscreet about the whole thing. In Frau Ettieg's situation, Magnus wouldn't have looked his best either.

He ignored her comment, and sat heavily at the table. The smell of oily pancakes wafted from the oven.

'Anything to wet a man's lips?' Magnus said. Even he was surprised at how gravelly his voice sounded.

Frau Ettieg shook her head disgustedly, but got him a cup of small beer from one of the cupboards. She put it down in front of him, still shaking her head.

'It's not good for a man to drink all day and all night,' she said. 'You'll end up in the gutter. And you owe Pieter a month's rent. He won't wait forever.'

Magnus took a swig of the weak, foamy beer. It tasted more like dirty water than ale, but he felt his body respond almost instantly nonetheless.

'I'll be fine soon,' he said, without much conviction. 'I'm waiting for something to come in. Trust me.'

As he spoke, Magnus dimly remembered something about last night. Some promise of money. He frowned, and pushed his hand through his oily hair. What was it?

Frau Ettieg sighed, and went back to the oven.

'A man came for you this morning,' she said, absently. 'He left you a message. It's on the table.'

Magnus winced. People calling for him was never a welcome sign. He looked across the table. There was a roll of parchment lying on it, bound by a leather cord. There was a seal. Count Aldebrand Ludenhof's seal.

His stomach gave a sudden lurch, and the small beer rose uncomfortably in his gorge. It all came rushing back. Grotius. The assignment. That was why he'd got so drunk.

Magnus reached for the parchment and unrolled it. There were letters of commission from the count's private office, all signed in sweeping flourishes of black ink and stamped with the official marks. Grotius had written him instructions. The Hochland Grand Army's store yards in Hergig had been alerted to the situation. He was expected to pay them a visit at noon. General Scharnhorst was also down to meet him in the afternoon.

Magnus rolled his eyes. Grotius had been nothing if not efficient. The little worm.

'What time is it?' he asked Frau Ettieg, leafing through the dense roll of orders and instructions.

'Late,' she replied, keeping her attention on her cooking. 'You've been snoring like a pig for hours. Do you want a pancake?'

Magnus shook his head, and rose from the table.

'I've got to go,' he said. 'You should have told me about this earlier.'

Frau Ettieg turned, placing her hands on her barrel-like hips crossly.

'And go up to that pile of filth you call your room?' she asked. 'Not likely. If you're going out, I'll get that little slut to clean it.'

Magnus swallowed the last of the beer, spat into the corner of the room and brushed his clothes down casually.

'Tell her to keep away from the chests,' he said. 'I'll be back at the end of the day.'

Frau Ettieg came up to him. She frowned, and flicked some of the detritus of the night from his leather overcoat. She could be strangely maternal at times.

'Take this,' she said, pressing a steaming pancake into his hands. 'You're a disgrace. Your father would weep to see you.'

Magnus shrugged. Once so many people told you the same thing, it lost its power to shock.

'Thanks,' he said, munching on the cake. It tasted of fat and curdled milk. 'I'll enjoy it on the way.'

* * *

THE VAST MASS of the Kristalhof loomed into the pale grey sky. Its enormous walls sloped slightly inwards as it rose from the chaos of the streets around it. Its dark flanks were brutal in their simplicity. There was no adornment, no decoration. It had been built for war. The towers at each corner were broad and squat, banded with lines of granite. If the count and his court were inside, there was no visible external sign. A few crows flapped lazily above the keep. They were mere specks against its bulk.

Magnus looked up at it grimly. In an ugly town, it was the ugliest building. It might have even been the ugliest building in the entire Empire, although there were plenty of contenders for that crown. He was glad he was not going inside. The store yards of the Hochland Grand Army were in a compound under the shadow of the Kristalhof.

The 'Grand' Army was nothing of the sort. Unlike the drilled perfection of the Reiksguard or the massed ferocity of the Middenheim regiments, the Hochlanders were slipshod and slovenly. The store yards were a case in point. Piles of halberds and pikes lay across the muddy yards, their tips gently rusting in the damp. Blackpowder kegs were left next to bales of dry straw. Rows of cannons had been left exposed to the elements with not so much as a sheet across them. As he toured the yards, Magnus's temper worsened. By the time he came across the quartermaster, his mood had become black.

'Who're you?' said the quartermaster, a thick-set man with weasely eyes and a broken nose. He looked hostile and dishonest, much like quartermasters across the whole Old World.

Magnus handed him his letters of warrant from Grotius.

'This place is a disgrace,' he said, looking sourly at the chaos around him.

The quartermaster looked back at him stupidly. Despite the letters of warrant, he looked deeply suspicious of Magnus.

'You're an Ironblood?' he asked, leering with his tiny eyes.

Magnus glared at him.

'I am,' he growled. 'If you knew anything of your trade, you'd know that. Look at those guns! You're a damned fool.'

Magnus walked up to one of the great cannons. It had a long iron barrel, about six feet. It was functional rather than decorative, but well made. He ran his finger across the pitted outer surface. A Gottekruger, a minor marque from Nuln. Solid, dependable, accurate. It deserved better treatment. The rim of the gun had corroded, and the axle had rotted almost entirely away. It would need a week's work before it would fire again.

Looking insulted, the quartermaster limped after him.

'Begging your pardon, sir,' he said, disingenuously. 'We don't get the funds we need. What are you after?'

Magnus gave him a withering look.

'Everything that works,' he said. 'Which I'd say is about half of what you have. We need as many heavy cannons as you've got. The bigger the better. They're for breaching walls. I was told you have rocket batteries and volley guns too, though Sigmar only knows what condition they're in. Is this true?'

The quartermaster looked evasive.

'You mean the Helblasters?' he said. 'We might have two left. I'd have to look in the sheds. It'll take time. Of course, I'd go a lot quicker if you could see your way…'

The man squinted at Magnus, and didn't finish his sentence. Magnus felt his heart sink even further. The quartermaster was as corrupt as a Tilean. On another day, Magnus might have paid him something, just to oil the wheels of business. But the quartermaster had picked the wrong time to angle for payment. Magnus's headache had settled into an acute, stabbing pain behind the eyes. He needed another drink.

His temper snapped. Magnus suddenly swept down on the quartermaster and grabbed him by his collar. He pushed his grizzled face into his, knowing that his breath would still be as foul as a gnoblar's crotch, and bared his teeth.

'I don't know what kind of peasants you've been used to dealing with,' Magnus hissed, keeping his gaze locked on to the other man's irises, 'but fool around with me and I'll tear your eyes out for shot. My papers are from Valerian von Grotius. Give me any trouble, and I'll be straight on to him. He'll be glad to deal with any parts of you still remaining alive after me and my lads have given you a proper going over. Is that understood?'

The quartermaster's eyes were now filled with fear.

'Yes, sir,' he squeaked, and his body went limp.

Magnus let him go, and brushed his coat lapels down.

'I'll leave the list with you,' he said, coolly. 'You have until sundown to prepare an inventory. I want everything specified on the list to be ready for when the army leaves. If you have to get help in, that'll come out of your own fat pocket. You'll get your fee when I'm happy, and not before.'

The quartermaster looked at him with an expression of pure loathing.

'Yes, sir,' he said once again, bowing unsteadily.

Magnus turned away from him imperiously, and walked back past the lines of decaying ordnance. The quartermaster looked spiteful enough to do something to the guns in revenge, but hopefully his fear of Grotius would put some speed into the man's work. For the first time that day, Magnus felt something approaching pleasure. His blood was pumping, and his head was clear. He still had it, despite everything.

'Herr Ironblood!' came a gruff voice from close behind him.

Magnus froze. The pleasure evaporated immediately. Whoever that was, it didn't sound good. He turned to see a tall, raven-haired man in a long dark green cloak looking at him coldly. The top of the man's head was bare, and his bald pate glinted dully in the pale sunlight. He was wearing a fine jerkin and cloak. A broadsword rested against one thigh. An exquisite blade. An iron star hung from his breast, bearing the crest of Ludenhof.

So. This was the general.

'Herr Scharnhorst,' said Magnus, and bowed. 'I was on my way to see you.'

Scharnhorst raised an eyebrow.

'Our appointment was an hour ago,' he said. His voice sounded like iron scraping across ice. His face was lean and angular. A long, old scar bisected one cheek. 'I saw you having a discussion with my quartermaster. Is anything amiss?'

Magnus paused. This was their first meeting. Diplomacy was normally a good plan. But the man clearly knew nothing about gunnery. There was no point in hiding the truth.

'This yard is not up to scratch, general,' said Magnus bluntly. 'The ordnance is rotting away. We have a long trek to the Mittebergen. If I'm to deliver you guns capable of breaching the walls of Morgramgar, your man will have to do his job better. And not for a fee.'

Scharnhorst didn't respond at once, but his thin lips pursed. A crow cawed in the far distance, and for a moment Magnus could imagine the general's head transposed with it. They were remarkably similar.

'I see,' said Scharnhorst. 'You're to be commended on your diligence. I'll have a word with Gruber.'

Magnus bowed.

'That would be appreciated, general.'

Scharnhorst remained stony.

'Walk with me, Ironblood,' he said, and began to amble towards the yard entrance. Magnus fell in beside him.

'You've chosen to be blunt with me, Ironblood,' said Scharnhorst. 'I admire that in a man. I'll be similarly blunt with you.'

He turned to look directly at Magnus. The scar made his face look almost like a death mask.

'There is a great schism at the heart of the Empire,' he said. 'There are those who place their faith in the tools of Sigmar. The sword, the axe, the warhammer. You know the sort. But there are also those who have departed from his teaching. They look to the ways of the sorcerer, the scholar and the–'

'The engineer,' said Magnus, finishing his sentence for him. A deep weariness had settled within him. He'd heard this speech a thousand times, and from a hundred different soldiers.

Scharnhorst let slip a wintry smile.

'Quite so. And, in the name of honesty, you must know that I am in the former camp. You people kill as many of our own kind as the enemy. On every campaign I have conducted, some disaster has befallen our engineers. If it were not for the urging of Herr Grotius, I would not have taken a master engineer at all. The cannons would have been under my command. That you should know.'

Magnus bit his lip. That was idiocy. There was probably no one left in Hergig besides him who knew how to transport and deploy the heavy guns properly. Leaving it to a man with ice in his veins and lead in his head would be a disaster.

'Grotius made the better choice, I'd say,' said Magnus, keeping his voice just on the right side of insolence. 'With respect, these things aren't toys. They can win you a war, but only in the right hands.'

Scharnhorst looked at Magnus doubtfully. His eyes crawled across his mud-streaked coat, and seemed to linger on every patch of grease, every tattered hole.

'And you have the right pair of hands?'

Magnus could well imagine how he looked, with his ragged clothes and unkempt hair. Scharnhorst couldn't be blamed for underestimating the command of his art. Only the night before, Magnus had been little better than a vagrant. A commission didn't change that. It would take time to get back into his old role.

'I'm an Ironblood, general,' he said. 'Ask anyone. Grotius had to search for me by name.'

Scharnhorst looked doubtful.

'They told me Ironblood was a famous name in your trade,' he said. 'They also told me you were washed up. I don't know about the first of those, but I can see the second is true. You should get yourself cleaned up. You're a mess.'

Magnus absorbed the insult without flinching. He was getting used to it. Being labelled a disgrace had become almost second nature.

'This has all happened quickly, general,' said Magnus. 'Until last night, I didn't know I'd be travelling with you at all. You have to make some allowances.'

Scharnhorst gave him an icy look.

'Don't tell me when I may or may not make allowances,' he said. 'I'll be the judge of that. And I don't care about your problems, Ironblood. You can drink yourself to death in as many inns as you like, just as long as you're not under my command when you do it. You are now, so you'd better get yourself together. Next time I see you, you'll have shaved, and at least tried to look like an officer worthy of respect from the men. And do something about your stench. Even the flagellants don't smell as bad.'

Magnus tried to look as deferential as he could.

'Very good, general,' he said. 'I'll get right on it.'

Scharnhorst nodded.

'You do that,' he said. 'We don't have much time.'

With that, he turned on his heel and left as abruptly as he'd arrived. Magnus watched him walk up towards the Kristalhof. No doubt he had some banquet to attend or audience to conduct. The life of a member of the noble classes would always be different.

He left the store yard and began to head back towards the blacksmith's house. He'd have to tell Frau Ettieg that he'd be away for a while. She'd miss the rent money, but little else. As he walked through the streets, Magnus caught sight of a promising-looking sign. *The White Hart.* It even looked pretty clean. He stuffed his hand in a pocket, and was pleasantly surprised to find a few coins. That improved his mood. Scharnhorst was right: if he was going to try and pull an Iron Company together he would have to pull himself together first. But that could wait. Right now, he needed a drink.

SILVIO MESSINA REGARDED the man before him coolly. The drunkard was a vast, hulking brute. Ill-shaven, stinking, poorly clad. Like all the inhabitants of the Empire, he didn't know how to look after himself. It was pitiful.

Silvio ran a finger through his own elegant jet-black mane of perfectly glossy hair, and sighed. Hergig was a tiresome place, and this episode was more tiresome still. He certainly knew how to pick the wrong tavern. It just wasn't his night.

Lukas edged towards him, looking anxious.

'Do you want me to call for the militia?' he hissed in a worried whisper.

Silvio irritably gestured for him to withdraw. It was bad enough getting into bar fights in such a hole. Having a wide-eyed youngster to look after too was almost too tedious for words.

'So keep out of this, *ragazzo*,' Silvio said. 'It'll be over in a moment.'

As he spoke, the brute came at him, arms flailing wildly. There was an appreciative roar from the rest of the drinkers in the tavern. The animal was clearly well known here, and fancied himself as the cock of the walk. The fact that this knuckle-headed ass was the best on offer was another damning indictment of the provincials and their backwardness.

Silvio waited until the last moment before slipping to one side. He evaded the cartwheeling fists of the drunkard easily. As the thick-set man reeled at him again, Silvio stuck out an impeccably crafted leather boot, and watched his assailant career into the beer-soaked floor of the inn. A roar of laughter broke out around the room, and tankards were thumped against tables.

The man thumped his fists on the ground with frustration. Slowly, cumbersomely, he got up, and turned to face Silvio once more. As he did so, his eyes went wide. The rage left his face, and his hands fell to his sides. He stood, stupidly.

Silvio allowed himself a dry smile of victory. His pistol, an exquisitely crafted gun from the studios of Salvator Boccherino of Luccini, was pressed lightly against the fat man's forehead. Even in the dull light of the candles around them, its silver shaft glistened. The intricate engravings of the famously beautiful courtesans of Luccini graced the chamber, while the handle was inlaid with a flawless panel of mother-of-pearl. It was a beautiful thing. An elegant thing. No doubt the beasts of Hergig had never seen such finery. It was worth more than their pox-ridden inn and all its contents.

But that wasn't the best part of it. Most importantly for his current purposes, the pistol was utterly deadly. The barrel had been ground by Boccherino himself, and dispatched shot as straight and true as a virgin's promise. Not that Silvio was worried about missing his target on this occasion. The brute was trapped like a pig in its pen, blinking and wondering desperately what to do.

'Now then,' said Silvio, calmly, relishing his control. 'I expect you're reconsidering your position. What was it you were going to do to me? Now I recall it. Drown my head into your... what you call it? That *firkin*. And hold me down while I died in the muck you people call *ale*. Doesn't look so likely now, does it?'

A line of sweat ran down the man's temple. From the corner of his eye, Silvio could see that the rest of the tavern's occupants were staying in their seats. Some looked transfixed. Others were merely enjoying the show. He let his finger run up and down the length of the solid silver trigger mechanism, savouring the power.

'As I see it, you have no idea what kind of gun this is,' said Silvio, sadistically. 'If you were forty feet away and running into the dark, still she couldn't miss. You're out of your depth, fat man. Count yourself fortunate I was only after your wife. If I wanted your hovel and your stash of coins, I could take them too. Any time.'

The brute was becoming enraged again, but held his position with difficulty. He knew that a single move would finish him. Silvio enjoyed watching the tortured expression on his face.

'So I tell you the truth,' said Silvio, toying with his prey like a cat. 'It's probably not so bad a thing that you found us when you did. I hate to tell it to you, but she's really not that good. I mean it, have you people ever heard of a *bath*?'

That was possibly taking things a bit too far. There was a low murmur of anger from the seated drinkers around them. They didn't mind one of their number being humiliated, but casting aspersions on all of them was dangerous. This thing had better be wrapped up.

'You're lucky I'm in such good mood,' he said, pressing the muzzle of the pistol more firmly against the man's flabby flesh. 'Another day, I'd leave a hole in your skull. Now, back away, slowly. You let my companion and me leave this place in peace. Come after us, I'll not be so forgivable. Do not forget, my aim is true, in shooting as it is with all things.'

His hands shaking, either from rage or fear, the drunkard slowly took a few steps backward. His tiny, piggish eyes blazed with an impotent fury. Silvio checked to see that Lukas was by his side before retreating towards the doorway. He kept the pistol raised, his eyes sweeping the tavern for threats. The natives seemed cowed by his display for the time being.

As he reached the door, Silvio allowed some of his customary swagger to take over. He bowed to the assembled gathering in mock salute.

'Thank you, fine sirs, for your most exquisite entertainment,' he said, his voice silky. 'I am overjoyed to learn that men of Hergig are as hospitable and accommodating as their wives and their daughters. When this silly business is over, we may think of coming to visit again.'

That final insult lit the fuse. Chairs were kicked over and tables rammed to the walls as the tavern rose up in a wall of rage. Silvio turned to Lukas, a wicked smile on his lips.

'Run!' he shouted.

The two of them turned and fled into the night, curses and bellows of spluttered anger following them as they went. Thankfully, the pursuit did not last long. The denizens of the tavern were mostly too drunk to stand, and those with some sense were wary of the pistol. After a show of chasing them from the inn, they gave up the hunt, grumbling and muttering as they returned to their lukewarm drinks.

Once they were sure the last of them had stumbled off, Silvio and Lukas stood panting under the eaves of a half-derelict town house. Silvio felt a thrill run through his refined body. This was why he loved being a mercenary. There was nothing quite like the rush from taking advantage of the stupidity of the locals. And if things ever went wrong, his most loyal companion, the esteemed Boccherino pistol, was always there to ensure a hasty exit.

He turned to Lukas, and grinned.

'This is life, eh?' he said, his teeth flashing white in the dark.

The sandy-haired youth from Averland didn't look too sure. He was still too timid, too green. Like all the men of the Empire, he didn't have enough imagination.

'You're a madman,' said Lukas between breaths. 'We could've been killed.'

Silvio laughed.

'By that rabble?' he said, disgustedly. 'By Luccina, I'd have been ashamed to have been *scratched* by one of them.'

'You're right,' came a voice. It wasn't Lukas's. 'That would have been sloppy.'

Silvio whirled around, raising his pistol quickly.

'Declare yourself!' he hissed.

A man's shape emerged from the shadows. He was as dishevelled and grimy as the wretches they had left behind in the tavern. He was heavy-boned, and wore a long leather overcoat. His greying hair hung in lank curls to his shoulders, and the stench of drink hung around him. Only his bearing gave him away. He might have looked like a vagrant, but Silvio could see he was nothing of the sort.

'Put your gun down, lad,' the man said, walking towards them casually. 'It's a nice piece. A Calvasario?'

Silvio kept the pistol raised, watching the newcomer with suspicion.

'Close,' he said. 'You know your marques. How does man of Hergig acquire such knowledge?'

The man laughed, a strange, bitter sound.

'I'm no man of Hergig,' he said. 'So it's a Boccherino. Very nice. Though I dislike Tilean pieces. Flashy, but temperamental.'

Silvio kept his aim steady.

'I told you declare yourself,' he said in a low voice.

The man shrugged.

'You don't scare me, lad,' he said. 'You put on quite a show back there, but you were never going to shoot. I'll give you a name, though, for what it's worth. Ironblood. No doubt you've heard of it.'

Silvio frowned. It was familiar. Where had he heard it? Somewhere back in Tilea, perhaps. He had an image of a pistol. An outrageous, three-barrelled monster. A work of genius. Surely, it could have nothing to do with the man before him. The man looked little better than a wandering savage.

'It means nothing to me,' he said. 'What do you want?'

Ironblood shrugged.

'Have it your way,' he said. 'As for what I want, that should be obvious. You're here to fight. I'm here to hire. You've worked in an engineer's company before?'

Silvio nodded cautiously.

'Many times. In the Border Princes, Ostland. I had given up on work here. The Hochlanders don't seem to know what any one of them is doing.'

Ironblood smiled grimly.

'Then we're agreed on that, at least,' he said. 'They have guns, though. Heavy cannons, mortars, some lighter pieces. And they have handgunners. Some of them are very good. Huntsmen, mostly, drafted in by Ludenhof from the countryside. They just need someone to lead them. Someone who does know what they're doing.'

Silvio let his finger relax on the trigger. Beside him, Lukas stayed mute. This was interesting.

'Can you afford me?' said Silvio, letting his habitual confidence bleed into his speech. 'You'll not find a better master of handgunners. I can shoot golden tassel from Karl Franz's nightcap at hundred paces. What's more, I can teach the others to do the same. If these Hochland guns are all they're told of, of course.'

Ironblood shrugged.

'Some of the older ones are,' he said. 'What can your friend do?'

Silvio started to reply, but Lukas spoke over him, the words spilling out in his enthusiasm.

'I've studied at Nuln, sir,' he said in his young, high voice. 'Under Captain Horgrimm. I can handle a long riflegun, and man a standard mortar battery too. I know the theory of the volley guns, and have been second in command of a rank of cannons. Big siege cannons, they were. I even took over once, when one of the recoils caught the captain.'

Ironblood looked at Lukas with a mix of scepticism and amusement.

'Can you command men, boy?' he asked.

Lukas looked downcast.

'I'm learning,' he said, weakly.

'The boy's new,' said Silvio. 'I teach him what he needs to know. His family is Herschel. He comes with me. But I'll say again, how much are you offering? We are not some flea-infested dogs of war. I'm not so sure you can pay our price.'

Ironblood laughed at that, and his heavy body shook with mirth.

'Don't try to bargain with me, lad,' he said, grinning. 'If you weren't for sale you wouldn't be here. And you'll get no better offer. Unless you fancy joining the flagellants or the halberdiers. I can't quite see that, looking at your fine clothes.'

His expression became more serious.

'Listen, the money's good,' he continued. 'I'm under commission from the count's agent, and you won't want for payment. We'll be a small company. Half a dozen men, at most. There'll be little glory in this messy campaign, but there will be gold. So what will you say?'

Silvio thought for a moment. The man Ironblood spoke the truth. It was probably going to be the best offer they'd get. Slogging along in the mud with the regular state troops was not something he was prepared to do, even for a generous share of the bounty. As he looked into Ironblood's eyes, Silvio could see that the man was used to command. If he and Lukas weren't going to leave Hergig and look for some other fight to take up, this was the obvious thing to do. And once on the road, there were bound to be possibilities. There always were.

'How long do we have?' he said, retaining his sceptical expression for the sake of form.

'The army leaves in four days,' said Ironblood. 'You'll need to give me your answer in the morning. You'll find me at the Grand Army store yards. Ask for me by name.'

'Very well,' said Silvio, keeping his voice neutral. 'So we'll think about it.'

Ironblood nodded.

'You do that,' he said. 'But don't take too long. And for the sake of Sigmar, stop pointing that pistol in my face. You look like a fool.'

Silvio bristled a little, but lowered the weapon. As he did so, Ironblood bowed to take his leave, and retreated back into the night. Silvio watched him walk off, consumed by his thoughts. This looked like a good bet, but it never paid to be hasty.

'What are you doing?' said Lukas urgently, once Iron-blood was out of earshot. 'We should be jumping at this! It's why we're here, after all.'

Silvio looked at him wearily. He liked Lukas, and the boy was a good engineer. But he would have to learn some guile, or his career would be short and painful.

'We'll do it, don't worry,' said Silvio, casually extinguishing the taper on his pistol and sheathing it in its holster. 'But I don't want him to think we are too keen. That is fatal.'

He took a deep breath, and looked around him. The dark streets were nearly empty. Lukas waited expectantly.

'Come on,' said Silvio at last. 'There will be another inn open somewhere. If we're going to join this strange thing, we'd better make most of what's on offer.'

He looked down at Lukas. The boy was as eager as a puppy.

'Just don't embarrass me,' Silvio said, stalking off with Lukas in tow. 'I still haven't given up on finding wench. You make them nervous.'

CHAPTER THREE

These are nice drawings. They are by your children, yes?

Reputed remarks of High King Thorgrim Grudgebearer, on being presented with a copy of the Notebooks of Leonardo da Miragliano by the Emperor Karl Franz

HERGIG WAS POOR, and it showed. The thoroughfares were narrow, the buildings old and shabby. Most were made of wood. Aside from the imposing Kristalhof, there were few stone constructions. Even the city walls seemed in poor repair, despite the fact they had been necessary for the city's defence many times in living memory. The skulls of slaughtered beastmen still hung over the main gates, presumably intended as a warning to their kin not to come back. Magnus didn't blame them for staying in the forests.

The morning had dawned cold again. He had a hangover again. It was thirsty work, recruiting. His mood was dark. Why had he come to such a place? What had possibly drawn him to this Sigmar-bereft wasteland? The people were stupid and superstitious. There were more temples to Shallya and Taal than to the divine protector of the Empire. Perhaps it had been the reputation of the gunners. The Hochland long gun was undoubtedly a piece of engineering mastery. Even the gunsmiths of Nuln admired the best examples. But when Magnus had arrived in the city, he had been disappointed. There were few smiths left. Many had fled south to escape the endless wars. More had been poached by richer employers in the lands to the south, their secrets scattered across the Empire and feverishly copied by less-skilled hands. A genuine Hergig piece was now a rare and precious thing. Magnus wondered if there was anybody left in the city who really knew how to make one.

Even if there had been, there was still more talent in his own bloodstream than in the whole province. The Ironblood pistol was whispered about reverentially in the corridors of the College of Engineers. True flintlock, a rarity in the Empire. Three barrels. Exquisitely bored. The cleanest workings you could imagine. Nearly impossible to fire without igniting truly. And the deadliest aim of any gun he had ever used. The very fact that his name was associated with such a masterpiece occasionally filled him with a terrified awe. Only three had ever been made. Now two were lost, and the third was in a crystal casket deep within the college vaults. He had heard rumours that a second was still in use somewhere in the Empire. A witch hunter. A woman. From time to time, he pondered trying to track her down.

The same thing stopped him every time. Shame. He had not made the guns. His father had, the great Augustus Ironblood. The old White Wolf of Nuln, so-called because of his mane of ivory hair, sweeping down from his severe, lined face. At one time Magnus had wanted nothing but to follow in the old man's footsteps. And he had started well. Too well, perhaps. And then…

Magnus looked down at his filth-spattered coat. He held his hands up. They were dark with long-ingrained grime. His nails, once worn to the quick by honest work, had grown effeminately long. Frau Ettieg was right. Augustus would have wept.

He took a deep breath. Such thoughts depressed him. There was no use dwelling on them. Nothing could change what he'd become. He was the product of fate, like everyone else.

Magnus stepped around a pool of something foetid and unidentifiable. On the far side of the street, it looked like a fight was breaking out. A man in ragged robes broke from a crowd and tore off towards the poor quarter. He was followed by a scrum of angry townsfolk. Some were newly-arrived mercenaries, by their look. No doubt they'd been trying to buy luck charms or some other nonsense. Paying for a bundle of crow-bones from a street wizard was stupid and dangerous. Trying to cheat your customers was even more stupid. From behind a row of houses, the man's voice rose in panic. It looked like they'd got him. He wouldn't last long.

Magnus sighed, and pressed on. Soon he had reached his destination, a low-beamed house on the fringes of the Hofbahn. The door was open and light streamed from the room within. There was the noise of a man's laughter, and children squealing, and a woman's high voice chiding them all mockingly. Magnus smiled in spite of himself. There were some things in life he couldn't be cynical about. He smoothed his hair down again and brushed some of the muck from his coat. Knocking on the door frame to announce himself, he ducked under the lintel and entered.

The doorway led straight into a kitchen, warm with the smells of cooking. A vast man sat at a long wooden table. His beard was a fiery red, just like that of a Bright wizard. His girth was enormous, and he seemed to fill half the narrow chamber by himself. When he saw Magnus enter, his smile froze for a second on his lips. Then he recovered himself, and let out a bellow of delight.

'Ironblood!' he roared, and rose from his seat.

Magnus smiled, and stood patiently to embrace the bear hug.

'How are you, Tobias?' Magnus said, feeling his ribs groan under the pressure.

Tobias Hildebrandt stepped back, still grinning.

'As well as ever,' he said. 'Life is good. And you?'

Magnus ducked the question, and turned to the woman.

'Anna-Liese,' he said, bowing his head politely.

Hildebrandt's wife looked back at him guardedly. She was a pretty, brown-haired woman in the prime of life. If she looked a little tired and distracted, then she had every right to be. There were four children clustered around her, staring at Magnus with alarm. They knew who he was, but they had never seen him looking quite so shabby. He suddenly felt self-conscious. He should have made some effort to scrub the worst off. Perhaps the smell of beer was still on his breath.

Magnus looked at Hildebrandt, not enjoying the awkward silence.

'Could I speak with you?' he asked.

Hildebrandt shot his wife a glance. She understood at once.

'Children, come,' she said in her gentle, remonstrating tone. 'Your father has business to discuss.'

Quietly, efficiently, they slipped out of the room. Anna-Liese closed the door behind her. With a pang, Magnus realised he'd broken up a precious family moment. He envied Hildebrandt. The man had achieved everything that Magnus had been unable to. In a dark and brutal world, there was still space for the simple pleasure of hearth and home. That, Magnus thought dryly, was what they were all fighting for, after all.

'So,' Hildebrandt said, in his rumbling voice. 'What's all this?'

Magnus sat down at the table, and Hildebrandt resumed his seat.

'A commission,' said Magnus. 'I've had a look at the documents. It's worth a lot. It could wipe out our losses. Interested?'

Hildebrandt looked at him warily. Magnus could see the indecision. He understood the man's doubts. About everything.

'What kind of commission?' asked Hildebrandt.

Magnus explained the story of the margravine.

'We'll have several companies of gunners,' he said. 'There are some big pieces too. Cannons, some mortars. Ludenhof's been something of a collector. There's a Helblaster or two, maybe some rocket batteries. They're serious. They have the ironwork. They just need crew to man them.'

Hildebrandt took a deep breath. As he did so, his massive lungs slowly filled, and took just as long to slowly empty. His face was marked with doubt.

'I thought you weren't–' he began.

'I don't have a choice,' said Magnus, cutting him off. 'Ludenhof found out I was here. They're short-handed. And anyway, I need the money. I'm going to do it. Are you with me?'

Hildebrandt sighed again. He was beginning to resemble a bellows, sucking in air and expelling it again.

'It's not easy,' he said, grudgingly. 'There's Anna-Liese. She'd hate for me to leave again. We've not been in Hochland long. And the children. I don't know, Magnus.'

Magnus knew his old friend better than that. Anna-Liese would miss him, to be sure. But he would miss her more. Hildebrandt had always been a family man. For him, the fighting had always been about the money. Money to secure their future, to pay for an education at the temple, to lift them out of the gutter. Unlike Magnus, he hadn't drunk it all away. He could afford a modest house, to keep his children in clothes, to put meat on the board and ale in the cellar. What reason could he have to go back to it all?

'You don't have to decide now,' said Magnus, trying to keep the disappointment out of his voice. 'I can come back later.'

Hildebrandt looked torn.

'We're getting older, Magnus,' he said. 'There comes a time in a man's life when he's no good on the field any more. We've done our bit for the Emperor. Do you have to take this commission?'

Magnus felt a sour taste form in his mouth. It was all very well for Hildebrandt to talk of picking and choosing commissions. He didn't have Grotius on his shoulder, nor a pile of debt on his back. The man had become comfortable. Soft. Perhaps this had been a bad idea.

Magnus rose.

'Think about it,' he said. 'I've got things to see to. You know where I am.'

Hildebrandt stayed seated. His face creased with concern.

'How much are you drinking, Magnus?' he said. 'You don't look well. Why not come and stay with us for a few days? Just until you get things back in order. I have connections. We could keep it quiet.'

Magnus stopped in his tracks. For a moment, for just a moment, he had a vision of what that might be like. Laundered sheets. Hot water in the copper. A warm hearth. Evenings surrounded by a proper family, rather than the transient scum he associated with. The vision was uncomfortable. Painful, even. He shook it off.

'I'm expected in the Kristalhof,' he said, gruffly.

Without waiting for Hildebrandt to reply, he turned and left. From within the house, there came a sound of a long, final sigh.

* * *

THE WEATHER LIFTED slightly, but not enough to drive the chill from the air and the damp from the walls. A steady drizzle had been falling for two days, turning the normally muddy streets into teeming rivulets. The inhabitants of the city went about their business with hoods drawn tightly over their heads. The heavy swell of the Talabec glinted dully under the grey sky, and the ravens stayed gloomily on their branches.

Gradually, painfully, Ludenhof's army had taken shape. Money had changed hands, and more mercenaries had arrived. The inns and brothels of Hergig found their takings rising sharply, as did the cutpurses. Honest residents of the town stayed behind locked doors after dark, nervously watching the columns of staggering soldiers reel through the streets, carousing as they went. The songs were a weird mix. Reikspiel was blended with Tilean, Estalian, Bretonnian, even the harsh tongue of Kislev. Wherever there was fighting to be had, the jackals would cluster from all over the Old World. They were never short of work.

Not all the recent arrivals were dogs of war. Outside the city walls, a ramshackle camp had been erected. The sound of tolling bells could be heard emanating from it at all hours of the day and night. A crude representation of the twin-tailed comet, hewn from old, rotten wood, stood lopsidedly in the centre of the settlement. The inhabitants had grown quickly from a few dozen to over a hundred, and still they came. The folk of Hergig shunned these newcomers even more than the mercenaries. They could hear the crack of whipcord and the shrieks of pain. Flagellants were seldom welcomed by the ordinary folk of the Empire.

The wretches had come to Hergig to do the only thing they still knew how to do. Labour, fight and die.

Magnus lifted his head from the pitcher of water, feeling its cold touch revive him. From his garret room vantage point, Magnus could just about see the edge of the camp beyond the city perimeter. It had been positioned on a marshy curve by the riverbank. No doubt the mud and mosquitoes would be seen as more blessed penitence from Sigmar. He felt nothing but disdain. However far he fell, he would never be as bad as those foam-mouthed fanatics. Magnus shook his head.

Behind him, the door suddenly slammed open. Magnus's heart sprang up into his throat, and he whirled around. He clutched for a sword at his side, but it wasn't there. He was barely dressed.

In front of him, there was a bearded man. No, too short for a man. A dwarf. He stood with his legs apart, arms by his sides. A huge axe was clenched in his right hand. Magnus's eyes flicked over to the nearest chest. Too far. He'd be dead before he could get halfway.

He looked back at the stranger. With effort, he forced his heart to stop hammering. If the intruder had wanted him dead, he would be so already. He calmed himself down, and waited for what was coming.

'Very wise,' came a low, rumbling voice, seemingly aware of his thoughts.

'Who are you?' said Magnus, struggling to keep his voice steady. His mind was working quickly. He had no weapon to hand, but he was a big man and knew how to use his fists. But a dwarf was something else. They were like a ball of solid granite, bound with iron and crested with something sharp. He'd never seen a man take one on by choice.

'Thorgad Grimgarsson,' came the answer. The voice was harsh, scraped raw by a life spent fighting in the deeps of the earth. 'You, I know. At least by reputation.'

Magnus took a better look at the intruder, feeling his thumping heart begin to return to normal. Thorgad looked like all the other dwarfs he'd known. There was the unnatural stockiness, the exposed arms of pure bunched muscle, the heavily decorated beard with its elaborate plaits and rings of iron. Thorgad's hair was a dark, deep brown, almost black at the lips and eyebrows. His squat nose and cheeks were heavily tanned, and the ink-blue shapes of old tattoos ran across every inch of exposed skin. He wore a heavy leather jerkin and a round iron helmet. His boots had iron tips, and were covered with old, dry mud. He had a bandage around his thigh, and there were other fresh wounds. Like all of his kind, his expression was hard to read, and his origins hard to guess. To the extent he could tell, Magnus thought he looked old. His hands were laced with scars, and his eyes bore the confident glint of a seasoned warrior.

Magnus leaned back against the wall. The dwarf didn't look like he'd come to fight. In his heavily indebted situation, though, you could never be too careful. Bounty hunters were not unknown in Hergig. He kept his fists bunched, and his eyes open.

'Well then, Master Grimgarsson,' said Magnus. 'You've come into my room and given me a scare. Well done. There was a time when that would have been an achievement. Now you're here, you'd better tell me what you want.'

Thorgad fixed his steel-trap gaze on Magnus. He didn't smile.

'You're mixed up in this new army,' he said in his growling voice. 'That's what I heard, at any rate. Ludenhof has got this damn-fool idea into his head, and he's trapped you in it.'

'It's a commission,' said Magnus, guardedly. 'I'm a master engineer. I choose the ones I take and the ones I don't.'

Thorgad raised an eyebrow.

'So you say,' he said. 'Or it might be that you've run out of money and luck, and this is all that's left.'

Magnus felt his temper begin to rise.

'Watch your stunted tongue,' he said, conjuring as much menace as he could, given the situation. 'State your business, or get out.'

Thorgad ran a thick finger along the edge of his axe.

'Get me out?' he said. 'And how would you do that? If you fancy your chances against a dawi, then bring it on. I won't stop you.'

Magnus scowled impotently. The dwarf might have been shorter than him, but Magnus knew from long experience that an experienced warrior like Thorgad was a match for all but the toughest of human fighters. It was not for nothing that the dwarfs looked down on men, despite the height difference. For a moment, Magnus pondered rushing him, trying to knock him off balance before he could get hold of the axe properly. It was futile, and they both knew it.

Thorgad scowled.

'Enough of this stupidness,' he said, hefting the heavy bronze-inlaid axe head as if it were made of straw. 'I'm not here to kill you. Or even to make your life more difficult than it already is. You haven't worked it out yet? I want to join you.'

For a moment, Magnus couldn't believe what he was hearing. A dwarf joining an engineering company wasn't unprecedented, but it was rare. The stunted folk believed themselves the most accomplished engineers in the Old World. Magnus had known many of them from his long years studying at Nuln and fighting in the Emperor's armies. If a human created a faster-loading gun, a dwarf would look down the barrel and sniff at its inaccuracy. If a human made a cannon capable of smashing ten-foot-thick walls apart, a dwarf would ask why it couldn't demolish mountains. For all he respected their achievements, Magnus mostly found dwarfs insufferable. They were arrogant, prickly and far too easily angered. Having one along with him on the campaign, all things being equal, would not be a good idea.

'You've a strange way of asking for a favour,' Magnus said.

Thorgad frowned. Or, at least it looked like frowning.

'A favour?' he said. 'If you think going on this journey will be a favour, you can't know the land around Mor-gramgar.'

He leaned forward. Under his bushy eyebrows, his deep-set eyes glinted brightly.

'I guess you haven't been told much about this campaign yet,' Thorgad said. 'That's no surprise. The count doesn't know what he's doing. No one here does. I've seen cack-handed umgi campaigns before, but even by your standards this is bad. You've already had one army destroyed. Sending another one into the mountains before finding out what happened is stupid. Really stupid.'

Magnus tried to interrupt, but was halted by Thorgad's stare.

'Let me tell you about Morgramgar,' said the dwarf. 'It is old. Very old. The battlements may be the creation of your Empire, but the foundations are not. It has been built to survive, carved from the living rock by folk who knew what they were doing. It stands on a spur of solid stone, and its dark walls rise a hundred feet from the plains below. Water bubbles from the deeps beneath, shielded by solid stone, impervious to spoiling. There are storehouses hewn from the earth within capable of holding months' worth of food. An unprepared army would break against those walls like the tide while the defenders drank and ate their fill within.'

Magnus looked doubtful.

'I've seen some drawings,' he said. 'It doesn't look that big. I've run sieges before.'

Thorgad shook his head.

'Size is not the issue, manling,' he said, scornfully. 'You're twice my height, but I could stand you on your head before you could reach for your sword. The point is this. Morgramgar is nigh-on impregnable. You won't break it without help. You need me. I can deliver the citadel to you.'

Magnus saw that the dwarfish sense of modesty was still much as it had ever been.

'Oh yes?' he said, unconvinced. 'And you're prepared to prove it, I suppose. Talk is common, particularly from your kind.'

Thorgad's eyes darkened at the insult, and Magnus saw his hand grip the axe more tightly.

'Don't mock me, manling,' he growled. 'I travelled far to find you. You should listen to wisdom when you have the chance. Don't become more of a fool than you already are.'

Magnus sighed inwardly. This was why dwarfs were so wearisome. They handed out insults like cheap coins, but could never take one back. He'd never met a stunted one who didn't have a rampaging sense of personal pride. Perhaps it was a height thing.

'I've worked in the mines under the Worlds Edge Mountains since before your esteemed father was alive. I've marched in more armies in the dark places of the world than your race will ever know. I have hewn stone apart like flesh, tunnelled under sheer mountainsides, brought down centuries of labour with a single blow of an axe. It's in my blood. If you want to take this citadel, then I'll say it again. You need me. Take me with you. You need not pay me a florin. I scorn your gold. I just need to be there.'

Magnus raised an eyebrow.

'You scorn my gold?' he said, genuinely amazed.

Thorgad shook his head disgustedly, and said no more. Magnus looked at him intently. This was an unexpected development, albeit one with possibilities.

'Suppose you tell me why you're so keen to come along?' he said. 'I can believe you know what you are doing. I've never met a dwarf yet who didn't know the right way to point a cannon. But you're not in it for the money? That I find hard to believe.'

Thorgad still didn't reply at once.

'My reasons needn't concern you,' he said at last, the words dragged from his lips. 'My task in Morgramgar is my own. But I will swear loyalty to you and your company. If you know anything of the dawi, then you'll know what that means. My oath will bind me until the task is accomplished and the citadel is broken. Then I will go my own way. All debts paid. That's the offer. You would do well to accept it.'

Magnus silently weighed up the options. Although the dwarf wasn't to know it, the company at present still consisted solely of himself and the Tilean. Hildebrandt might waver, but Magnus hadn't found any other engineers of adequate quality. To turn down a concrete offer would be difficult. The fact that Thorgad would work for free was incredible, if troubling. But he knew the value of a dwarf oath. Whatever reason Thorgad had for wanting to get inside Morgramgar, it was clearly powerful.

Magnus ran a weary hand through his unkempt hair. Thorgad waited patiently.

'Very well,' said Magnus at length. 'I'll take you on. But if you're going to do this, then be aware that I command this company. I don't care how things are done in Karaz-a-Kazoo, or wherever you're from, but we do it my way in my command. That goes for you as much as the other lads. Can you do that?'

Thorgad looked sourly back at Magnus, clearly not relishing that prospect.

'You have my oath, manling,' he said, grudgingly.

Magnus spat on his hand, and held it out.

'Then we'll seal it,' he said.

Thorgad spat a thick gobbet of phlegm onto his own palm, and walked towards Magnus. The two clasped hands tightly. Magnus felt the iron-hard grip of the dwarf fingers, and spasms shot through his arm. Taking on the dwarf in combat would have been madness. It was lucky Thorgad had intended him no harm.

'When do we leave?' said Thorgad, releasing Magnus's hand and wiping his own on his jerkin.

'There are a few things still to do,' said Magnus, truthfully enough. 'Scharnhorst aims to leave tomorrow. The muster will be at dawn, in the shadow of the Kristalhof.'

'I will see you then,' said Thorgad, and started to walk from the room.

'Wait!' said Magnus. 'There is work for us to do. I know nothing of what your skills are.'

Thorgad shrugged, and kept walking.

'That can wait,' he said, flatly. 'I have business elsewhere. I'll see you at dawn. Look for me at the castle.'

With that, he was gone, clumping down the stairs in his heavy iron-shod boots. Magnus stood for a moment, unsure of what to do with himself. From downstairs, he heard Frau Ettieg's squeal of alarm, followed by a door slamming.

Eventually, Magnus walked over to the bed and sat down heavily. That had been unusual. The disturbance had upset his rhythm. Normally, he might have had a drink to calm his nerves. But he was trying to cut down. Scharnhorst's words had hurt him more than he liked to admit. He needed to clean himself up. Perhaps this was a chance to turn things around. Or get killed. One of the two, certainly.

Magnus sighed. He'd rather have had Tobias beside him. But Hildebrandt would have to make up his own mind.

CHAPTER FOUR

Forget all you have been told about the heroic legends of the Empire. Forget tales of bravery and sacrifice. Forget the legends of the rune-fangs and Ghal Maraz. Do you really think that we would remain the mightiest realm on the earth if we relied on those magical trinkets in battle? I will tell you the truth. Every battle is won or lost before a sword is even picked up. The real glory of the Emperor's armies lies in one simple, mundane thing. Planning. If you have no stores of blackpowder, no ledgers for payment, no lines of supply, no schedule for armaments, you are doomed. I will also tell you the most potent weapon in all the armies of men. Though you may not believe me now, you will when the time of testing comes. Curb your

*laughter, and listen to me. It is the baggage
train.*

From an address given by General Erasmus Jasper von
Mickelberg, Chief Instructor at the Imperial College
of Arms, Altdorf

THE NEW DAY dawned, cold and wreathed in rain. Heavy
clouds were being driven south-east by winds from the
far steppes of Kislev and the gloomy plains of Oster-
mark. The rain-bearing palls were piled up on the
northern horizon, discharging their load in heavy,
lightning-laced storms against the flanks of the distant
mountains. The bleak forests of Hochland were damp
and sodden. The worst of the winter chill was leaving
the lowlands, but the spring rains had been quick to
take their place.

Ludenhof's army had been assembled on a wide area
to the north of the city. Normally the space was flat and
dry, kept free of farms and woodland for the purpose of
mustering soldiers for the endless wars of the north.
Now it had been turned into a vast pool of slick mud,
churned up by the ceaseless movement of men. Horses
laboured and whinnied as they were whipped to their
stations. The infantry hauled their wargear through the
mire, cursing as the grime clutched at their boots.
Dampened by the incessant drizzle, drained by the filth
underfoot, the army presented a dismal aspect.

The count himself was nowhere to be seen. Members
of the nobility had ridden out at first light to inspect
the progress of the campaign. Otherwise, it had been
left to Grotius and Scharnhorst to ensure that the men
were put in order. The Imperial agent sat on his horse

atop a low rise, impassively looking over the mass of striving figures beneath him. All across the open plain, the shouts of sergeants and the groans of their charges filled the air.

Despite the short time given for preparation, Grotius had performed his task well. There were nearly four thousand troops assembled, organised in rows of companies according to their function. The bulk of the men were state troopers and drafted militia, arrayed in the Hochland colours of red and forest-green. Some attempt had been made to impose a modicum of uniformity on them, but for every smartly arrayed soldier in well-kept hauberk and helmet, there were a dozen wearing hastily dyed rags and clutching pitchforks rather than halberds. Alongside the regular troops were the mass of mercenaries, some decked out in a close approximation of Hochland livery, most wearing whatever they had come to Hergig in. They were under the command of their own captains, grim-faced men bearing the scars of battle. Most had better weaponry than the state troops, and knew how to use it too. The dogs of war sharpened their blades with expert relish, no doubt eager to spill the blood that earned their keep.

Set aside from the great bulk of troops were the more accomplished elements of the army. There was a small company of knights, clad in dark armour and mounted on heavy chargers. They were not enough to form a proper cavalry charge, but looked well-equipped and practiced in the arts of combat nonetheless. There were no pistoliers or outriders alongside them, but several companies of handgunners had been assembled. These were composed of hunters and trappers from the highlands, drawn into the army with the promise of gold and the threat of the gaol. They were tall, bearded men, uncomfortable in the squalor of the city but deadly in the harsh wilderness. They spoke little, and cleaned their prized guns with quiet dedication. Of all the native soldiery, they looked the most efficient.

And then there were the artillery brigades. Several dozen large items had been prized from Gruber's store yards. In pride of place were the iron-belchers, the huge siege cannons. They were drawn by teams of two carthorses each on great metal-framed wagons. Each was massive, forged in the furnaces of Nuln or Middenheim and decorated with the devices of those cities. Benedictions to Sigmar and Karl Franz had been draped across them by the superstitious crews, which now hung limply in the rain, the ink running down the parchment in rivulets. Other, lighter cannons were drawn in their wake, their slender barrels raised into the air like the snouts of beasts. Behind them all were more canvas-covered carts, each hauled by fresh teams of horses. Within them was stored the shot, the balls of iron grape, the kegs of blackpowder, the rams, the tinder, the spikes, the hammers and all the other equipment needed to keep the mighty machines of war firing true.

But the conventional cannons were not all. Despite Gruber's slovenliness, there were also carts laden with other artillery pieces of arcane design. Most were covered in waxed sheets to keep them from the rain, but here and there outlandish muzzles poked from their shielding. A practiced eye would have seen the telltale outlines of mortars, squat and wide-bellied in shape. They would also have spotted two large machines, tightly bound with rope to their platforms and weighed down with lead balls. The Helblaster guns, as volatile as a Marienburg fishwife and almost as deadly. Non-engineers steered well clear of such contraptions. Even before battle had been joined, their fearsome reputation went before them. Just as dangerous, and as unpredictable, were the Helstorm rockets, of which there were also a couple of examples amidst the artillery column.

As in the case of the cannons, these engines of war were attended by horse-drawn carts laden with ammunition, parts and supplies. Getting them all to the battlefield in one piece was a minor miracle in itself. Together, the massed ironwork had the potential to devastate an opposing force, whatever its origin. Cannons feared no monster of Chaos, and were indifferent to the horror inspired by the rampaging greenskins. Their deadly cargo was as effective against the sorcerer and the heretic as it was against mortal soldiers. And yet in the wrong hands, such mighty engines could wreak havoc amidst the ranks of the faithful too. Not for nothing did the ordinary infantryman look on them with a mix of respect and revulsion. Only the wizards inspired greater feelings of ambivalence amongst the ordinary folk of the Empire.

On the edge of the massed ranks of soldiers, the final contingent of troops lay. The flagellants had grown in number considerably, and now formed perhaps a tenth of the entire complement of infantry. They had made no attempt at all to don the colours of Hochland, and were arrayed in their usual batch of rags and tattered cloaks. Some were naked to the waist, their chests laced with self-inflicted wounds, daubed slogans and tattoos. They seemed impervious to the biting wind and driving rain, no doubt sustained by their endless chanting to Sigmar. Cowled priests went among them, sprinkling holy water from great brass censers and leading the liturgy. They were a breed apart, the flagellants, looked on with uncomprehending eyes by the bulk of the troops. Hochland was no centre for the cult of Sigmar, and the zealots were often seen as little better than madmen.

From his vantage point close to the army commanders, Magnus gazed over the ragged host. He was surprised that so much had been accomplished in such a short time. No doubt it was mostly down to Grotius. The man may have been a slimy toad, but he was clearly an astute one. As he pondered how such a creature had risen to his current position of power, the man himself came riding over.

'You're still with us, then,' he said from atop his horse, giving Ironblood a supercilious smile.

'It was too good an offer to turn down,' said Magnus, dryly.

'Very wise,' said Grotius, bringing his steed to a standstill. 'And I hope you're impressed with what's been accomplished. The count's army would not disgrace any battlefield in the Empire.'

Magnus wasn't sure about that. A massed charge of Reiksguard would make short work of the little cavalry they possessed, and he'd seen much tougher-looking ranks of state troopers from other provinces. But he did have to admit that the number of halberdiers was impressive, as was the artillery train.

'Shame the count's not here to see it himself,' said Magnus.

Grotius's face registered a faint flicker of disapproval.

'The count is detained with many matters of state,' he said. 'I'm sure he would be here if he could.'

'The elector's place is with his men,' came a new voice from behind them. It was harsh and grating, as if scarred by a lifetime of barked orders.

Magnus turned, and saw a warrior priest standing before him. The man was tall and powerfully built. Like most of his order, his head was bare. His torso was encased in thick plate armour, and dark red robes hung to his ankles. He carried an iron warhammer in his right hand, crowned with spikes and engraved with passages from the holy books. His eyebrows were low and dark, causing shadows to bleed across his eyes.

'Ah, Kossof,' said Grotius. 'This is Herr Magnus Ironblood, our master engineer. I assume you've not had the pleasure of each other's acquaintance.'

The two men looked at each other darkly.

'Why we tolerate the blasphemy of the new science in the Emperor's armies I will never understand,' said Kossof in a low voice. 'If Holy Sigmar had sanctioned the use of such infernal machines, he would have written of it.'

Magnus snorted derisively.

'I don't think there were many great cannons around when Sigmar was on earth,' he said, keeping the contempt in his voice to the fore.

Kossof scowled, and looked as if he had discovered a new and disgusting kind of beetle on the underside of his iron-tipped boots.

'I have come to expect such disrespectful blasphemy from those of your twisted persuasion, Ironblood,' he said. 'One day you will realise the folly of your pursuit of knowledge. If we did not live in such craven times, I would be empowered to show you the error of your ways.'

Ironblood took a step forward, reaching for the short sword at his belt.

'Oh, really?' he said. 'And how would you do that?'

'Gentlemen!' said Grotius, in a weary-sounding voice. 'As entertaining as your little disagreements are, this is hardly the place for them. You should continue your theological discussions some other time. Preferably after your task is accomplished and your orders have been carried out.'

Magnus looked between Grotius and Kossof, unsure which of them he found the most objectionable. In their own very different ways, they embodied everything he hated about the Empire.

'I'll leave you to it,' he growled, turning on his heel without giving Kossof a second look.

Behind him, he could hear the two men start to confer. He ignored them. Grotius was not coming on the campaign, so if they had some petty conspiracy between them, it mattered not.

As Magnus walked somewhat aimlessly in the direction of the artillery train, he saw a familiar shape come up the hill to meet him. At once, his mood lifted, and Kossof was forgotten.

'Tobias!' he cried, and ran over to the huge man. 'It was good of you to come. Anna-Liese has given you the afternoon off, then?'

Magnus found himself grinning as he spoke, but he meant no disrespect. Hildebrandt's well-ordered family life was what made the big man so admirable.

'Something like that,' said Hildebrandt, looking sheepish. 'Magnus, I'm coming with you. I've thought it over, and we could do with the money. Anna-Liese has come round. She doesn't like it, but a man has to be master in his house.'

For a moment, Magnus stood stunned. He had resigned himself to a long, dreary journey with the inscrutable Thorgad and the untried duo of Messina and Herschel. Hildebrandt coming with him was a completely unexpected boon.

He clasped his old friend's hand, speechless for a moment.

'That's… *good*,' was all he could muster. 'Really, that's good. I thought you'd decided against it.'

Hildebrandt looked pleased, but there was something else behind his expression. Worry, perhaps. Or maybe regret.

'I couldn't let you go on your own,' said the big man, not entirely convincingly. 'You'd blow yourself up. Or someone else. And it's been too long since I did some real work. Got my hands dirty. You know what I mean.'

Magnus looked at him closely. There was something the man wasn't telling him. But he was in no mood to inquire too deeply. The fact that he had an ally, someone he could rely on to get things done properly, was more than enough. He smiled again, uncaring of the rainwater running down his lank hair.

'There'll be five of us,' he said. 'Two men I've hired, and a dwarf who's coming for his own reasons.'

'A dwarf?' said Hildebrandt, eyebrows raised. 'I thought you hated dwarfs.'

Magnus shrugged.

'I'm not paying him,' he said. 'And there's been little enough time to arrange anything else. Come, I'll take you to meet the others. We'll have to divide up the workload differently now, but another pair of hands will help.'

Hildebrandt looked across the plain, his expert eyes picking out the heavy guns and already making an assessment of their best deployment.

'Let's go then,' he said. 'I don't like the way those volley guns have been stowed, for a start.'

The two men walked down the hill briskly, over to the staging area for the gunnery crews. As they went, they were soon lost in a technical discussion of firing rates and powder delivery.

All around them, men marched with growing purpose, their faces set grimly against the drizzle. Horsemen rode between the milling companies, delivering messages and carrying orders. Everyone could sense that matters were nearly set in place. Whispers had gone round that Scharnhorst was on his way. The signal to break camp, a series of braying notes from the horns, would soon sound. The preparation had been done, the gold had changed hands, the men had been found.

The wait was over. Hochland was going to war.

ONCE THE ORDERS to move out had been given, the army roused itself like a massive, sluggish animal. The knights had ridden out first, along with the commander's retinue. Scharnhorst rode at the head of the line on a giant black stallion. It was a fine-looking beast, stamping and shaking its head as it walked, and it wouldn't have looked out of place in the stables of the Knights Panther. His retinue was composed of the usual senior officials, clad in the finest armour and draped in the red and green of Hochland. Despite their impressive appearance, most were there to oversee the distribution of food, the maintenance of discipline in the ranks, and the protection of the army's chests of coins and other things worth stealing. Scharnhorst's most useful captains marched with their men.

All in all, Magnus thought Scharnhorst's commanders looked pretty competent. They shared their commander's savage demeanour, and spoke little as they rode. That was good. Having been commanded in the past by effete sons of the urban nobility, Magnus could appreciate when the conduct of the campaign was in the hands of proper soldiers.

After the captains came the small company of knights, followed by rows and rows of marching infantry. The state troopers went reasonably quickly, cheered by the prospect of getting under way at last. Though few of them relished battle, standing around in the rain waiting for their orders had blighted their spirits. It was better to be moving, whatever that entailed in the future.

Despite their size, the formations moved from the staging area and on to the main road north with little fuss. Magnus watched the outriders move up and down the columns of men, barking orders and dragging the serried ranks into a close approximation of good order. Things had started well enough. The army looked like it could fight. He'd been in many that had never looked like that.

Finally, behind the last of the swaggering lines of mercenaries, the artillery train was given leave to pull off. Magnus shouted out a series of orders to the drivers of the carts. Ropes shivering, the horses leaned into the task. Gradually, with much swearing and beating, the heavy wagons broke into movement. Gouts of mud were thrown up from hooves and wheels, but the big guns were under way. Magnus walked over to his horse, a lumpen, dull-eyed creature with a shaggy mane and matted coat, and mounted expertly. He cast his eyes across the slowly moving column of wagons, and felt a glow of satisfaction. He had the tools with which to work.

A sudden craving for a drink came over him. Magnus swallowed, feeling the rise of the nausea within him that always accompanied periods of sobriety. Not now. Things were just getting going. He had to stay clean.

He kicked his steed into a steady walk, and rode over to where the rest of his company were mounted, waiting expectantly for him.

'So here we are,' Magnus said, putting a brave face on his craving. 'Back in the saddle. Anything to report?'

'Food's lousy,' said Silvio. 'Hochland troops smell worse than greenskins, and those guns won't fire without much of my work.'

Lukas grinned.

'At least we'll be kept busy,' he said, brightly.

Thorgad looked up at Silvio. Unlike the others, he went on foot. He'd been offered a mountain pony, but that had met with nothing but scorn. So the dwarf laboured in the mud, his cloak already stained with the filth of the road. Magnus knew from experience that dwarfs could march a long way before they became weary. But still, Morgramgar was many miles distant. A strange race.

'If you keep complaining,' Thorgad said to Silvio darkly, 'I might come up there and give you something to complain about.'

Hildebrandt looked at the wagon train with concern, ignoring the bickering between the Tilean and the dwarf.

'Messina's right, sir,' he said to Ironblood. 'I've not been here long, but we've pieces here that'll shatter when we put the fire to them. This won't be easy.'

Magnus sighed, and let a tolerant smile spread across his face. The guns he had were faulty, the rain was incessant, he felt terrible, and his men were already arguing amongst themselves. In Scharnhorst and Kossof he was surrounded by officers who would rather he wasn't there at all. All things considered, that wasn't bad. At least no one had tried to kill him yet.

'All right, lads,' he said, raising a hand to silence the squabbling from Messina and Thorgad. 'We'll take another look at the cannons when we reach camp. For now, I don't want to lose our place in the column. There's plenty here who'll rejoice to see us fall behind, so I don't want them to have the satisfaction. Keep an eye on the ironwork. Don't let any of those damned zealots near the blackpowder. Otherwise, relax and enjoy the journey. We'll be busy soon enough.'

He kicked his horse again, and shoved his way to the front of the artillery column. Hildebrandt followed him, while the others spread out along the lines, watching the swaying wagons carefully.

Magnus felt the pleasure of command dilute his lingering nausea. No one had called him 'sir' for a long time. Not since...

But it was better not to think about that. He drew in a long draught of cold, rain-laced air, and looked up at the distant northern horizon. Even so soon into the campaign, his heart had begin to beat a little faster, and some of the sickly pallor had left his cheeks. They were under way, and battle would not be long in coming.

THE ASCENT FROM the plains around Hergig to the highlands was tortuous. As a province, Hochland was covered in mile upon mile of dark, twisted forest. Some called it the Eastern Drakwald, an offshoot of the mighty woods that cloaked Middenheim in fear and mystery. Others called it the southern edge of the Forest of Shadows, the Hochland Deeps, or simply the Dark Country. Even more so than the rest of the sparsely populated Empire, the depths of the Hochland forest were unexplored and untouched by the hand of man. Mighty ravines scored their way across the tumbled landscape, draped in grasping ranks of sleek-barked trees and tangled undergrowth. At the base of those ever-shadowed gorges, barely lit by the shrouded rays of the sun, all manner of primordial beasts dwelt in a perpetual twilight realm. Only the foolish or the mad sought them out. Every child in Hochland knew the dangers of the deep forest.

The beastmen were the most feared and hated. Some said they were the changeling children of impious parents, left to fend for themselves amongst the crushing briars. Others said they were the true soul of the forest, remnants of a time before Sigmar when men lived in scattered bands and feared every fleeting shadow. Yet more said that they were a portent of the future, a grim warning of the End Times when the final hosts of Chaos would rise up again and mankind would fall before the limitless legions of the damned.

Whatever the truth, it seemed that the numbers of beastmen rose every winter. At night, their bellows and whinnies could be heard in outlying villages and towns, causing grown men to pull their bedclothes over their ears and women to weep into their nightdresses. And all sensible folk knew that there were worse monsters lurking in the forgotten places. Tales were told of the creeping dead, limping through the marsh gas when the fog rolled down from the high peaks. Whispers ran through Hergig of skeletal witches, summoning all manner of foul sorcery over their bubbling cauldrons of maidens' blood. There were legends of fey elven spirits flitting between the boughs, spiteful tree-sprites conversing in forgotten tongues under the sickle moon, and scuttling giant spiders ridden by their cackling goblin masters in the endless, cloying gloom.

In the past, when the Empire had been stronger, perhaps not all those stories had been believed. Now, as the enemies of man multiplied once more and the undergrowth was alive with scurrying horrors, there were few who did not place credence on the old tales. The most outlandish myth of all, that the very cities themselves were riddled with the warrens of warp-spawned rat-men, sounded less crazy than it once had. They were truly dark times when such madness was believed even by learned men.

Chris Wraight

Every so often, the terror would be banished for a time. A crusade would be launched, and pious men of the Empire would sweep into the dark places with cleansing flame. Priests of Sigmar would banish the horrors, and the blood of the beastmen would stain the earth. The famed Boris Todbringer was still worshipped by the far-flung folk of the northern Empire. Whenever there was a break in the endless warfare on his northern borders, he would muster companies of his grim-faced Knights of the White Wolf, and the creatures of darkness would cower in their forsaken hollows. And yet, once the slaughter was over and the proud warriors of Ulric had returned to their homesteads, the shadows would lengthen once more. No living man had penetrated the heart of the forest, and none would ever do so. The Empire could limit the spread of the ancient woods, but it could never hem them in entirely.

Magnus reflected on that as the army wound its way north from Hergig and began to climb up into the highlands. They went by the ancient forest roads, the highways of the Empire in the north. The trees had been felled far from the trail, and the surviving trunks lurked sullenly in the distance on either side. All knew that such ways had not been made by men. Older hands had carved them from the living forest, and strange spells had been placed on them in time immemorial to ward off the throttling branches. Men were only the latest to make use of them, ignorant of their origins.

As the ranks of men passed through the trees they sang bawdy songs of waylaid virgins and genial foresters, swinging their packs with abandon. The humour was forced, however. All stayed wary. The army was large, but not powerful enough to scare off all denizens of the woods. They all knew the beastmen were there, watching, waiting.

As they passed through a particularly deep gorge, its sides rising high and jagged into the pale air, Lukas came alongside Magnus. His face was still cheerful, though the edge had been taken off it by the bleak country around them.

'This place is like nothing I've seen before,' he said, looking at the dark eaves of the trees doubtfully.

'No place for men,' agreed Magnus, avoiding peering too closely at the shadows. 'You're from Averland, yes?'

'Right,' he said, unable to keep his eyes off the forest. 'We keep the land tilled there. I never thought I'd wish to see another farmstead again in my life. But after this...'

'Don't look too closely, lad,' said Magnus. 'We'll be out of it in time. The mountains have their own dangers, but at least the air is pure and the stone is clean. This is cursed country.'

The army went quickly, perhaps part-driven by some vague sense of fear, but mostly by Scharnhorst's iron will. They set up camp infrequently, and only when the trees pulled back and the air was free of the rustle of hostile branches. Even then, at night there were howls from the tree edge. Some of the scouts, foraging far ahead to pick out the best route north, never came back. None asked after them. The men pressed on, hands on pommels, eyes flickering back and forth watchfully.

Despite the clipped pace, it took them several days of marching for them to clear the bulk of the forest. Whenever they camped for the night, they piled the fires high. Tired limbs made for heavy sleep, but only the bravest slumbered completely through the strange calls and shrieks from the darkness. Just once did they come into the open, bellowing and whinnying. The first engagement of the campaign was short and vicious. The beastmen were routed quickly, driven back by a hail of arrows and shot. After that there were no more raids. But the songs ceased. The soldiers kept their eyes on the northern horizon, desperate to leave the oppressive, endless ranks of trees.

When the breakthrough came, it was surprisingly sudden. The columns of men had been toiling for hours up a sharp defile, choked with roots, boulders and brambles. The horses were skittish, and the wheels of the carts fouled and needed to be freed often. For the first time since leaving Hergig, the pristine ranks of marching men broke into confusion, and the shouted orders from the sergeants and captains were abrasive and replete with curses. But then, just as the ascent seemed destined to go on forever, the vanguard broke into easier ground. The rest of the army coiled up after them. Rank by rank, company by company, they left the forest and marched into the open.

At the rear, behind the long trail of infantry, the engineer companies were last to climb the steep ascent. Magnus had remained at the very back, marshalling the route of the heavy guns as they crawled up the treacherous ground. By the time they had reached the final ridge, the flanks of the horses were shiny with sweat, and the axles of the carts groaned under their load.

When the last of them had crested the rise, Magnus looked up and surveyed the scene. The land yawned away in gentle curves of steadily rising wilderness. The peaks of the hills were bare of trees and covered in a dense carpet of gorse and heather. A mournful wind scraped across the open country, rustling the grass and sedge. After the close air of the forest, the highland seemed both severe and fresh. The army spread across it, grateful for sight of the horizon once more.

And then, far in the distance, Magnus saw their destination for the first time. On the northern edge of his vision, the mountains rose, grey and purple against the haze. They looked impossibly far. The margravine had chosen her bolt hole well. Climbing through the passes to Morgramgar would be a trial for the best of commanders. Magnus could see that others in the army thought the same thing, and low murmurs of discontent rippled through the infantry companies.

But Scharnhorst was in no mood to indulge petty gossip. Within moments of the last carts breaking into the highlands, the horns were sounded. Whips cracked, and the steady beat of hide drums started once more. Like a sullen beast of burden, the army started to march again. There would be no rest until the walls of the citadel stood before them. And then the real work would begin.

CHAPTER FIVE

After the slaughter at Skaalgrad, General Horstmann was taken before the Grand Council of Enquiry in Talabheim. He was unrepentant, despite losing the field and over half of his men to the foul Norscans. When asked what had precipitated his downfall, his answer was simple. Division in the ranks. He seemed to think that no further explanation was required.

Record of the trial and execution of Alberich Horstmann
Talabecland State Archives

FOR A FEW days, the rain had held off, and the worst of the stink over the soldiery ebbed. Clothes dried out, and rust was cleaned from the blades of weapons. Morale was high. But then the clouds closed once more, and the weather turned. Rain fell in steady streams without break or let. It got everywhere, into the kegs of dried food, into the crates packed with straw and iron shot, even through layers of wood and waxed cloth into the powder stores. It was relentless, an endless torrent of grey, cold misery, hammering on the downcast heads of the army as it toiled across the highlands. The ground became boggy and treacherous, and the horses stumbled as they went. In every direction, the sky was low and dour, mirroring the spirits of the men.

Hildebrandt wiped his brow clear again, watching as the water slewed from his shoulders onto the ground below. He was relatively lucky, with a stiff leather jerkin and heavy hood. The ordinary infantrymen trod sullenly in their inferior gear, moving onwards only to keep the chill from their breasts, soaked to their hides.

The big man looked back over the row of lurching carts. The going was tough in the mire. Axles creaked, and lashings came loose. Trying to keep such temperamental machinery on the road was worse than keeping a woman happy. At least women gave you some reward for your pains. The guns were fickle mistresses indeed.

Not for the first time, he wondered whether he'd done the right thing in taking up Ironblood's commission. Hildebrandt was old enough to escape the Imperial draft, and could have been expected to live the remainder of his days out in relative peace. It was not so much that he was too old to serve, but more that he'd done his time. There were only so many dead bodies a man could see before his mind began to turn. He'd witnessed old soldiers in the gutters of Nuln and Hergig, wedded to the bottle, dousing their self-pity in strong ale before the cut-purses finished them off. That was no way for a man to go. Not when he had a brace of children waiting for him by the hearth and an honest woman to warm his bed.

Despite all of that, the decision had not been hard to make. He owed it to Ironblood. The man had saved his life in the past, and they had fought like brothers when they were young. Hildebrandt had watched the man's descent into squalor with alarm. Now that Magnus seemed to have rediscovered a spark of self-command again, Tobias had a duty to see him through the campaign. One more failure would finish Ironblood. That could not be allowed to happen. Once this campaign was over, they could both think again. For the moment, cracking Morgramgar open was the only thing they could look forward to, the sole object of their attention. The alternative was to repeat the past. Hildebrandt knew some of what had happened back then, but not all. What he did know was enough to make him want to ensure that it never took place again.

He raised his eyes from the slow-hauling carts and squinted up the trail ahead. The land was rising rapidly. They were passing into a narrow gorge at the foot of the peaks. On his left, the earth was gradually falling away as the trail rose. On his right, the cliffs were soaring into sheer walls of striated stone, as sharp as teeth at the summit and flecked with sparse vegetation. The road wound between the extremes. Soon it would be little more than a ledge between the mountain's shoulder and the chasm to the left.

Hildebrandt pushed his horse into a canter, and joined Magnus further up the column. He looked grey and tired. An empty gourd flapped at his side. Hildebrandt could smell ale on his breath.

'This is dangerous,' he said, grimly. 'Wide enough for the guns?'

Magnus nodded. He seemed alert enough.

'I was thinking the same,' he said. 'We'll have to go in single file. Carefully. Is everything lashed securely?'

Hildebrandt looked back at the ramshackle caravan.

'Aye,' he said. 'But the rain plays havoc with the bearings. Some of these carts would come apart at a sneeze.'

'Get Messina, Herschel and the dwarf to spread out down the train,' said Magnus. 'First sign of trouble, shout. I don't want to see Gruber's precious machines at the bottom of the gorge, and neither will Scharnhorst.'

Hildebrandt pulled his horse round, and trotted back down the line of heavy-laden carts. The drivers looked nervous, and kept tight under the shadow of the cliff on their right hand. The horses knew the danger, and their eyes rolled as they strained. The creatures were tired, and their spirits looked fragile. After several days in the wilds, Hildebrandt knew how they felt.

The column crawled on, climbing ever more steadily into the heart of the mountains. The rain fell remorselessly, scything through the gusting wind as if it wasn't there. Streams formed along the rock-strewn passage, gurgling and bubbling down the trail, making footing treacherous. Men swore under their breaths as they hauled their gear. No songs were sung, and the only speech was the hoarse yelling of the captains, urging one more push before they laid camp for the night.

Hildebrandt rode ceaselessly up and down the train, watching the progress of the wagons intently. Messina and the boy did the same. As the path narrowed and the drop to their left became more sheer, the tension mounted. It would only take one wheel to go.

After another hour of solid, nervous progress, at last the landscape seemed to relent. Ahead of them the path widened as the gorge closed, and they reached the head of the pass. Hildebrandt felt his fingers loose their clamped grip on his reins, and he let a low sigh of relief escape his lips.

An axle snapped. It sounded like a tree falling. With a heave and snap of splitting wood, the wagon in front of him lurched drunkenly to its left. The horses reared in their tethers, and the wheels ground down into the soft earth. Shouts of panic came from up ahead. The wagon veered near the cliff edge, only pulled back by frantic hauling on the reins from the driver.

'Cut the harness!' came a desperate cry.

The horses had got trapped, and were going mad. One of them reared again, fighting to get loose of the cart. The waterlogged earth seemed to dissolve under it. It was carrying one of the siege guns. Tobias heard the snap of leather stays going, and the cart slid further towards the abyss.

'Cut the damn harness!' came the cry again.

The horses were scrabbling in the mud, unwittingly pulling the cart nearer to disaster. Tobias saw men leap from the wagon. The driver was still fighting to keep it on the path. He was going down.

Hildebrandt knew what he had to do. His heart beating powerfully, he leapt from his horse and ran up to the stricken cart. The ground beneath his feet was liquid. It felt like the entire hillside was sliding. If the cannon took the whole ledge down with it, there would be no hope of getting the other wagons past the breach.

Tobias sped past the reeling wagon and under the flailing hooves of the terrified horses. He was a big man, but under their flanks he felt little more than a child. He pulled his sword from his belt and slashed at the leather harness. Two swipes, and the straps sprung free, whipping at his face as they did so. One of the horses bolted up the path, neighing frantically, rearing afresh as its path was blocked by the men ahead.

Everything seemed to be in motion. The earth was slick and wet, the cart was churning its way closer to the edge, the second horse was prancing jerkily in its harness. Tobias felt his nerve nearly go. In an instant, he saw a vision of himself being dragged over the edge. The cannon was huge. Getting caught up in the cart's demise would be fatal.

Hildebrandt cursed, and plunged towards the tethered horse.

'Jump, man!' he yelled at the driver. The man was still trying desperately to right the wagon. 'Get away!'

Tobias had a vague impression of a white-faced, terrified figure pulling at the reins, and then it was lost in a whirl of movement. He felt the rock give way under his feet. With a lunge, he managed to cut the final cords of the harness, and the foam-flecked horse bolted. Its legs buckled on the edge of the precipice, and it went over. The animal screamed, an unearthly sound, before being dashed against the rocks below.

The horses had been cut free, but it was too late to save the wagon. The momentum of the cart was carrying it past the edge. Even as he tried to scramble out of the way, Tobias could see the heavy iron muzzle of the cannon leaning over the brink. The driver of the cart, still trapped on the swaying wreck of twisted wood, was shrieking like a woman. He was lost. There was no way back.

'Leap!' cried Hildebrandt one more time, though he knew it was hopeless. He was in danger himself. His boot caught in a rope trailing from the broken cart. He felt the sudden tug on his thighs. For a second, pure panic gripped him. He could feel himself being pulled over. Frantically, Tobias hacked at the rope. He was dragged along, hauled from his feet. His free arm hit the ground heavily. His fingers scraped across the loose earth, tearing through the mud.

His sword bit home. The rope snapped, and with a sigh the entire cart seemed to collapse in on itself. The lip of the path crumbled, and the broken structure swung over the edge, trailing rope and twisted planks of wood. The driver, still caught in the mechanism, let out a strangled scream as he was borne over into the gorge. His voice trailed horribly for a moment, echoing up from the chasm, until it was obscured by the crash of iron against rock. Then nothing.

The danger wasn't over. Hildebrandt was still on the edge, and the earth continued to slide. He was on his stomach, trying to pull himself free of the landslip. It wasn't enough. He was falling. It was like trying to swim up a waterfall. For a moment, he saw Elena's face, staring at him with reproach. Then the last rock disappeared from beneath his boots. He was over the void.

A hand grasped his wrist. The grip was firm and unyielding.

'Help me, damn you!' came a gruff voice, full of fear. 'He's heavy as a bear!'

More hands pulled at him, dragging him from the brink. Tobias looked up, his heart still pumping. He was surrounded by men. Ironblood was there, as was Thorgad. Shakily, he pulled himself to his knees. The ledge had held.

'Mother of Sigmar,' said Magnus, looking pale. 'I thought we'd lost you.'

Hildebrandt took a look over his shoulder. The cart had caused ruin on its descent, and a jagged gouge had been cut into the edge of the path. Stones still clattered down the slope. All along the surviving portions of the ledge, men stood, mouths agape, looking with horror at the broken cannon in the chasm below.

Tobias felt his arms begin to shake uncontrollably. With shivering hands, he made the sign of the comet across his breast.

'Thank you,' was all he could say to Ironblood, his voice thin and weak. 'By all that's holy, thank you.'

SCHARNHORST LOOKED COLDLY at the engineers. They presented a sorry aspect. Ironblood's appearance had improved slightly since Hergig, but the man still looked slovenly and grime-covered. His company were little better. The big one, Hildebrandt, seemed to have lost his nerve entirely, and stood silently to one side. The others, a Tilean and a young lad from

Averland, were withdrawn and mute. Worst of all, there was the dwarf. It was embarrassing to have one of them witness this shambles. Though many commanders considered it an honour to have dwarfs marching alongside them, Scharnhorst was a Hochlander. He had little dealing with the dwarfs in the province, and he distrusted anything unusual.

Scharnhorst sighed.

'So you got the rest of the guns up the hillside?' he said.

'Yes, sir,' said Ironblood, looking almost belligerent. His eyes were rimmed with red. 'Despite the landslide, we drew the remaining pieces through. It was hard work. We had to shore up the left hand of the ledge. That's why it took so long.'

The men were all in Scharnhorst's canvas tent. The day was waning, and candles flickered in the half-light. All around the camp, fires were being kindled. The troops were exhausted after the climb. Aside from Ironblood and his motley company, Scharnhorst had his senior captains with him, including the leader of the flagellants. They all sat in the shadows, regarding the engineers darkly.

Scharnhorst sighed.

'Herr Ironblood,' he said, wearily. 'You seem to think that losing one cannon is little cause for concern. And yet, if I understand it correctly, the one we let slip was one of our largest pieces. If we lose many more of them, getting to Morgramgar will be a waste of time. What do you expect me to do? Go up to the doors and knock?'

Ironblood remained impassive. The man looked

tired. That wasn't surprising. They were all tired.

'It's a matter of regret,' said the engineer, keeping his voice steady. 'But we couldn't account for the ledge giving way. We did all we could. Without Hildebrandt here, it would have been much worse.'

Scharnhorst sniffed. He was unimpressed.

'From what I was told, the spark that set this off was a broken axle,' he said. 'On a baggage cart in your care.'

Ironblood visibly bristled at that.

'I can only work with the material I'm given,' he said, and the insolence in his voice was evident then. 'If I could have chariots of iron to carry our guns up the mountainside, then I would use them. I remind you, sir, that everything we're using comes from your store yards.'

The warrior priest Kossof hissed from the shadows. In the flickering candlelight, his face looked like a mask.

'Perhaps it is a shame that the whole train didn't fall into the abyss,' he said, his voice a sibilant rasp. 'Then there would be nothing to blast apart our brave troops from behind our own lines.'

There was a murmur of assent from some of the other captains. Thorgad took a step forward, his face glowering with scorn. Scharnhorst fixed Kossof with a withering look.

'Enough,' he said. 'Don't be a fool. We need as many gunnery pieces as we can get.'

He turned back to Ironblood.

'When Grotius told me we needed a master engineer to oversee our artillery, I was hardly persuaded,' he said. 'He assured me that one of your sort was necessary. To ensure that there were no mishaps with the great guns.

Needless to say, I am hardly reassured by your progress so far.'

Ironblood looked like he wanted to interject, but Scharnhorst talked over him. The little man would have to wait for permission to respond.

'According to the plan, we should be coming to the approaches to Morgramgar soon. We're now far behind, held back by your antics in the passes. It's not good enough, Ironblood. I won't tolerate another delay at your hands. Is that clear?'

Ironblood had by now gone red with rage. Scharnhorst could see the man clenching his fists, trying to suppress the protests that were undoubtedly building within him. The general didn't care to hear excuses. It was results that mattered.

Eventually, Ironblood controlled himself.

'I understand, general,' he said. He looked like the words were being dragged from his mouth. 'I'll speak to the men. We'll look at the carts again. We'll make any repairs necessary tonight.'

Scharnhorst nodded.

'Good. See that you do. Now go. I have matters to discuss with the others.'

Ironblood baulked at that also. No doubt he thought of himself as a senior commander. The man would have to learn his place. He was a technician, nothing more. If he couldn't look after his own little realm, then he could hardly be expected to take his place at the high table of command.

The engineer bowed stiffly, then turned on his heel and left the tent. Awkwardly, the others followed him without a word. The flaps fell back into place, and the candle flames guttered.

Scharnhorst looked around at his advisers. They looked half-drowned. The rain continued to fall, drumming on the tent roof, and their spirits had sunk.

'Anything to say?' he snapped, trying to rouse some response from them.

Johann Kruger, the captain of the Knights of the Iron Sceptre, looked up. His lean, aristocratic face looked less lined with fatigue than some of the others.

'The engineer Ironblood spoke the truth,' he said, calmly. 'The artillery train is in bad shape. Your man Gruber gave them little of quality to work with.'

Scharnhorst sneered.

'You're defending him, Kruger?'

Kruger shrugged.

'We'll need those guns when we reach Morgramgar,' he said. 'Don't make an enemy you don't need.'

Only one of the noble blood would dare speak so freely to a general, Scharnhorst thought. Kruger was bound by allegiance to himself and Sigmar only. Scharnhorst despised the attitude, but needed the man's expertise. One of the wearying aspects of command.

'The same advice goes for you, master knight,' said Scharnhorst, adopting a warning tone. 'I'll heed your advice, but remember who's in command.'

Kruger looked unperturbed by the admonishment, and sank back into contemplation. In his place, Kossof spoke again.

'Is this not a sign, general?' he said, making an effort to knock the rough edges from his normal harsh speech. 'We can bring this heretic to heel without the use of the new science. Why else would Sigmar send the rain? Why else would our prized gun be the first to fall?'

Scharnhorst didn't like the look of smug triumph in the man's eyes. Something about Kossof turned his stomach.

'I won't tell you again, Kossof,' said Scharnhorst. 'The plan of campaign calls for artillery, and as long as we arrive with any pieces intact, we'll use them.'

He leaned forward, and pointed a lean finger at the priest in the half-light.

'And I warn you,' he said, 'don't pursue your superstitious vendetta against Ironblood behind my back. If he rectifies his error and proves himself on the field, I'll bear the man no ill will. You should do the same. There'll be no dissension in the ranks of this army.'

Kossof glared back at Scharnhorst for a moment, clearly taken aback. No doubt the man had thought he was reinforcing the general's own views. The priest would have to learn otherwise. Scharnhorst was a fair man. Hard, perhaps, but fair. The only thing he didn't tolerate was failure. Beyond that, there were no favourites.

'I understand,' said Kossof, bowing slightly. 'Herr Ironblood needn't fear interference from me.'

'I hope not,' said Scharnhorst, putting feeling into the words.

He reached for the charts and ledgers. There was much business to get through before he would let the officers back to their beds. The start of the campaign had been bad enough. If they were going to get to Morgramgar without some serious infighting breaking out, things had better improve soon.

THE DAWN BROKE. The rain had stopped falling at last, and a frigid wind tore across the highlands, freezing the sodden troops as they huddled together in the mud. Only the officers and knights had tents to shelter them from the elements. The ordinary soldiers slept in thin blankets, wrapped tightly around them to ward against the worst of the chill. Many of them had stacked their wargear on top of them as they slept, partly to keep it out of the mire, partly to add a little more protection from the knife-sharp wind.

Magnus woke suddenly, his body somehow remembering the routine of battle from all those years ago. His head was sore, buffeted both by the cold and the iron-hard ground. Every muscle ached from shivering, and his joints were as stiff as an elector's starched collar. He opened his eyes and looked around. The fire had long gone out, and there was just a meagre patch of damp, charred earth where it had been. The other engineers lay huddled around it, still asleep.

Hildebrandt snored loudly. The man had hardly spoken since his encounter with the cliff edge, and had drifted into a deep slumber as soon as he'd hit the ground. Magnus had never seen him so scared. There was a time when both of them would have laughed at a brush with death. Maintaining a front was all-important. It would not do for the men to think you were weak. But Tobias seemed to have forgotten that. He'd been shaken, and badly. Perhaps he now had more to lose. Whatever the truth, he hadn't spoken to Magnus about it, and Magnus hadn't asked.

Messina and Herschel slept also. The two of them had worked hard the previous night, checking the gun-hauling wagons and making minor repairs. Ironblood had been impressed by the Tilean. Despite his raffish appearance and superior bearing, he knew what he was doing. He was strong, too. The boy Herschel had been keen, and worked hard under Messina's direction. Any misgivings Magnus had about bringing him along looked like they'd been misplaced.

Groaning slightly from the effort, Magnus hauled himself from his tangled cloak, and stood up. The wagon nearest him was piled high with crates and tarpaulin-covered chests. Just to be safe, Magnus went up to one of them and pulled the material back. His own collection of ancient chests were still there, all still locked, all still safe. He gazed at the ornate metalwork of the nearest, and let his finger run down the side of it absently. Had he been foolish to bring all the gear along? Probably not. In his absence, Herr Ettieg would no doubt have tried to break into the stash. Safest to keep it by his side, however expensive and difficult it was.

'There's something special in there, no?' came a familiar voice from a few yards away.

Thorgad was sat on a pile of sacking, puffing on a long clay pipe. He was looking at Ironblood steadily.

'None of your damn business,' said Magnus, irritably. He pulled the tarpaulin back hurriedly, and walked away from the cart. 'How long have you been up?'

'A few hours,' said the dwarf. 'I'm amazed at the sleep you umgi need. I can remember campaigns under the earth where we went without sleep for days at a time.

None of us suffered from it.'

Magnus ignored the boast, and came over to sit by the dwarf. His bones felt like their marrow had been replaced with rods of ice.

'Got any food?'

Thorgad handed him some strips of dried meat. The donating animal was unidentifiable, and they were almost black with age. Magnus took one, and ripped a corner with his teeth. It was like biting into cured leather, and he felt his jaw ache with the effort.

'Traggot,' said Thorgad. 'Broiled wolf hide. Dried over peat. Not many umgi get to try it.'

Magnus grimaced.

'They're missing out,' he said, still chewing.

'We're nearly there,' said Thorgad, letting gouts of smoke drift up into the grey air. 'Whatever your general says, we haven't lost much time. The loss of one cannon will mean little when we get to Morgramgar.'

Ironblood gave the dwarf a sidelong look. Was Thorgad trying to make him feel better? That was out of character, and something to worry about. When a dwarf turned his hand to sympathy, then things were truly bad.

'Let's hope so,' said Magnus, attacking the chunk of meat. It remained solid and unmoving in his mouth.

'Tell me,' said Thorgad. 'Your name is a famous one among your people. I've asked around. Ironblood brings respect. And yet, when I met you, you looked like you were ready for the dung heap. What went wrong?'

Ironblood looked at him sourly, swallowing the meat at last with some difficulty. It had been hours since he'd allowed himself even a sniff of ale, and his mood had soured.

'Are you always this direct?' he said.

Thorgad smiled bleakly.

'Aye, manling,' he said. 'No point in beating about the grobi nest.'

Ironblood felt the lump of wolf gristle slide down his gullet slowly. He'd be digesting it for the rest of the morning. Dwarf stomachs were strange and terrible things.

'I'll say it again, then,' said Ironblood. 'Mind your own damn business.'

He pulled his cloak tight around him, feeling the blood beginning to pump back into his feet and fingers.

'We'll be on our way soon,' Magnus said, changing the subject to something more immediate. 'And I'm glad it's not far. This whole campaign can't end soon enough for me.'

Thorgad spat on the ground, and looked disdainful.

'You really don't understand, do you?' he said, his voice growling with displeasure. 'You and that idiot general think you'll arrive at the citadel, lob a few pounds of iron at the walls and then come merrily home again when they fall down. Believe me, it's not going to be that way.'

Ironblood felt sure he didn't want to hear what was coming next, but kept listening. The dwarf seemed to know what he was talking about. You could never tell when one was just boasting for the sake of it, but Thorgad had an air of casual knowledge that held his attention.

'You've forgotten a whole army's been lost up here

already,' said the dwarf. 'That doesn't happen by accident. Even an umgi general couldn't massacre the men
under his command single-handedly.'

The dwarf's eyes shone. He seemed to be taking a
kind of sadistic pleasure in recounting the tale of
human weakness.

'This country will get very hard. Very hard, very soon,'
he said. 'We'll be passing through the perfect terrain for
an ambush. Do you think this von Kleister will let you
walk up to her gates without a fight? No. She's not stupid, that woman. I'll wager she's got more sense than
your man Scharnhorst, at any rate. Expect an attack,
and soon. Her troops know the country. They'll strike
by night, or when we're breaking camp. When we're
weak.'

Ironblood looked sceptical.

'There are four thousand men in this command,' he
said. 'It'd be brave to attack us in the open. We have
archers and handgunners to guard the flanks. Some of
them know this country too.'

Thorgad shrugged.

'So you say,' he said. 'We'll see what happens.'

Then he leaned over to Ironblood, and fixed him
with a level stare.

'But just remember,' he said, and his voice was low.
'I'll say it again, so the importance of it isn't lost on
you. There was a whole army sent up here ahead of
you. None of them came back. None of them. Does
that sound like something to take lightly? You should
be more afraid, master engineer, and not just for the
axles on your precious carts.'

Thorgad sat back, looking grimly satisfied. Magnus

wanted to say something to puncture the dwarf's insufferable pride, but nothing came to mind. If he was honest, Thorgad's words had unsettled him. The mountains were a cold, unforgiving place. He looked up at the peaks around them, pale in the morning air. Mist rolled lazily down their flanks, wreathing the valleys in shadow. They were silent, cold, inscrutable.

Then, just as he began to feel the full effect of the dwarf's portentous warning, the horns sounded to rouse the sleeping army. All around them, men groaned, and rolled over in their cloaks. In an instant, the sergeants were on their feet, wiping their eyes and barking out orders. Irritably, blearily, the camp began to rise. Magnus's thoughts were broken, and the harsh reality of the present rushed in to take their place.

He took a deep breath, and looked down at Thorgad. 'So be it,' he said. 'One more march, and we'll be right under Anna-Louisa's petticoats. And then we'll really see what's been going on up here.'

With that, Magnus got up and stomped off to wake the others. As he left, Thorgad stayed seated, gently smoking his pipe. His expression was hard to read, but his eyes glittered like flints.

CHAPTER SIX

The engineer can create machines to counter all foes. From the precision fire of the master-crafted pistol, to the massed volleys of the handgunners, there is little that can stand against the effective deployment of blackpowder weapons. But there is one thing he cannot counter, no matter how skilled he is with iron, steam and steel. That is fear, the devourer of men. Let terror enter the hearts of your troops, and all the guns in the Old World will not be enough to ensure victory.

Master Engineer Lukas Grendel
Address given at the College
of Engineers, Nuln

As the army climbed ever higher, the weather became steadily colder. While the lowlands around Hergig were enjoying the first few days of spring, the mountains remained as hard and cold as marble. The snowline was still far above them, but the biting wind made the air frigid. Men, shivering in their damp clothes, bent their heads low and gritted their teeth as they marched. Several had fallen sick in the grinding conditions. There was little to be done for them. Those that could still walk were given such crude potions as existed and propped up by their fellow soldiers. A few poor souls, lost in fevers or defeated by the high airs, had been left behind. They would either have to find their way back to Hergig somehow or die out in the wilds.

For those that had made it up into the Middle Mountains, the white summits now rose around them on all sides. The army had reached the heart of the high country, and the road rose and fell constantly, winding and diving around great outcrops of grey-banded rock. The few trees that grew in such places were dark pines, grasping on to the edges of the mighty cliffs with gnarled roots. Thin grey grasses rustled endlessly in the wind, a constant susurration that set even the most experienced soldiers' nerves on edge.

As he rode, Magnus found himself drawn to the high peaks, now ringing the horizon. The mountains gazed down at the massed columns of men as they toiled up towards their goal. They looked pitiless and bleak, crested with glittering crowns of rock-broken ice. There was an air of menace emanating from them. Every so often, as the wind moaned and eddied against the raw, jagged rocks, Magnus thought he caught the echo of

116

fell voices, whispering malicious words just beyond mortal hearing.

There were tales about the mountains, just as there were tales about the forest. Strange things gnawed their way under the rock, it was told. All knew that high up in the snow-covered heights, far beyond the reach of mortal men, ancient creatures lived. Armoured dragons, crouching over their hoards of ice-crusted gold. Fur-covered monsters in the shapes of men, howling their loneliness to the glittering stars. Magnus had never really believed such stories. But now, looking up at the sheer flanks of the great mountains, he felt his nerve begin to fail him. He had been dry for almost two days, and it played havoc with his nerves. There were surely secrets hidden in those terrible heights, secrets that mortal men were never destined to discover. This was not their place, no more than the deep forest was.

Suddenly, his thoughts were interrupted by shouts from the men in front of him. Something was going on further up ahead. Magnus rose in his stirrups, trying to make out what was happening. Bugles had been sounded, and captains of the handgunners were riding up towards the vanguard of the army.

Magnus turned in his saddle, and called over to the others.

'Hildebrandt, Thorgad, you come with me,' he said. 'Messina and Herschel, stay with the guns. We'll be back soon.'

He kicked the flanks of his horse, and broke into a canter. Hildebrandt was soon at his side, lumbering along on his giant carthorse. Thorgad broke into a run, cursing as he tried to keep up with the horses. A low stream of obscene Khazalid pursued them as they rode up through the ranks.

Magnus was soon joined by other company captains, summoned by the call of the horns, each with the same look of consternation on their faces. The signal for battle had not been given, so the massed ranks of foot-soldiers stood down, grateful for the rest. For some reason, Scharnhorst wanted his commanders to come together at the head of the army. That was unusual, and whatever was unusual was a cause for concern.

Passing four thousand men took some time, even on a fast horse. Eventually, Magnus and the others reached the vanguard. Thorgad arrived some time later, his cheeks blood-red. No one dared so much as smile at him.

The army had halted at the entrance of a sheer-edged valley running roughly north-west. Its flanks rose like the inside of a clay bowl, smooth and free of vegetation. The road at its base ran swiftly into shadow, for the sun failed to penetrate far down into the deep gorge. It was hard to make out much beyond the first few hundred yards, but it seemed from the curve of the rock as if the valley continued for at least a couple of miles.

Magnus looked at it with distrust. A natural place for an ambush. The enveloping cliffs could hide a whole regiment of archers. Once within the welcoming embrace of the slopes there would be little an army could do to defend itself. Within the bowl-shaped depression, the wind moaned and echoed mockingly, as if daring them to enter.

'What is this?' asked Magnus, bringing his horse alongside Kruger, the captain of the Iron Sceptre knights.

'The scouts have returned,' said the knight, peering into the valley beyond with a grim look. 'The enemy is nowhere to be seen. But there's… something else.'

Magnus didn't like the expression on the man's face. He was about to quiz him further when Scharnhorst came riding up with his retinue. He looked even more sour than usual. The cold air and dry wind suited his personality perfectly.

'Kruger, Kossof, Ironblood, Meckled-Raus, Harrow-grim, Halsbad,' Scharnhorst said perfunctorily. 'Come with me. There's something you should see.'

Without waiting for them to reply, he pulled his horse round and rode up towards the maw of the valley. The named captains broke into a canter and followed him. Many of their retainers did too.

'You should come,' said Ironblood to Hildebrandt and the dwarf. 'I don't like the look of this, but we should all see it.'

They rode swiftly from the head of the pass and into the long shadow. Once out of the light of the sun, the temperature plummeted even further. The sheer sides of the chasm soared into the pale air like battlements, cutting off the sunlight and amplifying the scraping sigh of the wind. Within those terrible walls, everything became bleak and colourless. The few trees clinging to the rock were small and stunted, their bare branches groping up into the air like crone's fingers. Aside from clatter of the horses' hooves, there was almost no sound at all. It felt as if they were riding into the mouth of the underworld.

Magnus looked up at the rock around them warily. He could see no sign of movement up above. It was the scouts' task to make sure that such places would be free of snipers or longbowmen, but you could never be sure. He half-expected a hail of arrows to come spinning down from the bleak heights at any moment.

They kept riding. They had gone nearly a mile when Thorgad noticed the stench.

'Grimnir's beard,' he spat, shaking his head with disgust. 'That's as foul as a slayer's gruntaz.'

Soon afterwards, Magnus realised what he meant. A familiar aroma wafted up from the valley before them. For an old soldier, it was as commonplace as the smell of sour beer and sweat. Death. The reek of death. It was everywhere. His heart began to beat more heavily. There could be only one explanation.

The company rode on, eventually cresting a narrow ridge across the valley floor. Only then did Scharnhorst give the signal to halt. The captains formed a line on the rise, looking ahead with grey faces. None of them spoke. None of them needed to. They had found the army that had gone before them.

Strewn from one side of the valley to the other, corpses lay in twisted formations on the ice-hard ground. Old blood, brown and cracked into flakes, was streaked across the stones. Swords lay where they had been dropped, wedged between rocks or half-buried in loose gravel. One of Hochland's battle-standards still stood, its tattered flag fluttering in the wind. The insignia of Count Ludenhof had been replaced by a crudely daubed death's head. Obscene insults had been scrawled across the rocks around it.

Many of the bodies had been stripped of their armour, their boots and even their clothes. Some were headless. A few had been cruelly hacked apart, their limbs lying like discarded toys amongst the carnage. The icy air had preserved the corpses from decomposing entirely, but the steady onset of putrescence had turned the scene into a stinking, rotting charnel house. Magnus saw Hildebrandt pull a piece of cloth to his mouth, trying not to gag. Thorgad looked on impassively, his snub nose wrinkled against the foul odour.

So this was what had become of them. Killed to a man. No survivors.

'I don't want the men to see this,' said Scharnhorst. His voice was thin and unforgiving. A kernel of anger underpinned it. It was the first time Magnus had heard emotion in his speech. 'We'll find another route to the citadel. But we cannot pass without finding out what happened here.'

Kruger raised an eyebrow coolly.

'We can see what happened,' he said. 'What good will it do us to linger over it?'

Scharnhorst continued gazing over the scene of desolation before them, as if by boring his eyes into the rocks he could bring the silent corpses back to life.

'Look again, master knight,' he said, coldly. 'How many battlefields have you ridden across? When did you ever see one like this? Do not look for what is there before you. Look for what is not.'

Mutely, Magnus turned back to the ranks of broken cadavers along with Kruger and the others. To look on the scene for more than a moment was hard. It seemed somehow disrespectful. Though they were now grey-skinned and hollow-eyed, the victims had once been men like him, full of blood and clothed in flesh. For a moment, Magnus couldn't see what Scharnhorst was going on about. He resented having to peer at the dead for longer than was necessary. Then, gradually, he began to understand.

All of the stricken men were wearing the colours of Hochland. The first army had clearly been more organised than the second. There were no mercenaries among them, and no livery from other states of the Empire. As Magnus's eyes swept across the benighted scene, his suspicion was confirmed. There were no enemy troops there at all. All the corpses were clad in the remains of Ludenhof's colours. It was as if an invisible enemy had come down from the heights and struck them as they marched.

Though some distance away, Magnus could still make out the look of terror and amazement on the dead men's faces. He'd never witnessed a battlefield like it. Even in the most heinous one-sided slaughter, a few troops from both forces ended up lying in the blood-soaked mire. Here, it looked as if the wind itself had borne death on its wings. The steady thump of his heartbeat began to quicken again. This was a silent horror beyond anything he had encountered. He reached for his gourd. It was empty. If the mountains themselves had risen up and destroyed a whole army of men, what hope did they have? They would be dead before a single shot was fired on the walls of Morgramgar. There was some bestial presence in the peaks, something they could never hope to resist.

They were dead men, just like the ones lying in the dirt before them.

Magnus could sense that others were thinking the same thing. A shiver of unease passed along the line of commanders. One of them, a lieutenant of Kruger's, started to retch dryly into a rag.

'Do not forget yourselves, men,' said Scharnhorst, sternly. His voice still had an edge of anger in it, and trembled as he spoke. 'These were good folk of Hochland once. They deserved better than this, a cold grave in the mountains with no blessing or hope of burial.'

He looked at his men on either side of him, and a frown of disgust passed across his features.

'For anyone thinking that this is the work of some unnatural spirit or vengeful shade, forget that now. These men have been killed with steel and shot, just like any other troops. The battlefield has been cleared. They've done it to unnerve us. Do not let them have this victory. You are men of the Empire. Find your courage.'

As Scharnhorst spoke, Magnus recovered himself. Of course, that was what had happened. The awful smell, the moaning wind, it was beginning to get to him. He shook his head, trying to shrug off the persistent feeling of doom and hopelessness.

'It's not a pleasant task,' continued the general, looking back over the corpses with distaste, 'but we have to do it. There will be clues. Things we can use. I'll give you an hour. Move amongst the dead. Find out what happened. Then we'll ride on by another path. Whatever happens, we must not repeat their mistakes.'

Magnus exchanged glances with Hildebrandt. The huge man clearly wanted nothing to do with the fields of slowly rotting cadavers. Magnus wasn't too keen on the idea himself. The captains hesitated, regarding the mangled limbs with revulsion.

'Damned weaklings,' muttered Thorgad, and unbuckled his axe from its leather ties. He stomped down the ridge towards the battlefield. That was enough to shame the others into action. With a sigh, Magnus and Hildebrandt did likewise, following the dwarf down into the stinking pit, their faces pale.

'I saw a tapestry like this once,' said Hildebrandt, clasping a scarf to his face as he walked. 'In the Temple of Morr in Wurtbad. A vision of the afterlife.'

'Something to look forward to, then,' said Magnus. Everywhere he looked, the glassy eyes of the dead stared back at him. Those which still had eyes, that was. The crows had been busy at the sockets, and every exposed flap of dead flesh was scored with peck-marks. The smell was overpowering.

'What does he expect us to find?' grumbled Hildebrandt, picking his way through the decaying ranks. 'These bodies are weeks old. The battlefield has been cleared.'

Magnus shrugged, and looked up again at the steep defiles on either side of them.

'They were ambushed,' he said, grimly. 'Volleys of fire from up there would cause havoc. Block the valley at either end, and you have a massacre on your hands.'

'Why don't they try it on us?' he said, following Magnus's gaze into the heavens.

Magnus shook his head, trying to avoid breathing deeply of the noxious air around him. He remembered Thorgad's words. They'll come at night, or when breaking camp. When we're weak.

'Maybe they lost more men than they'd hoped for,' he said, knowing his words sounded hollow. 'But I don't trust our scouts. This place feels wrong. There are eyes on us, or I'm a greenskin.'

Hildebrandt didn't reply, and started kicking away some of the discarded blades that littered the ground. The two men were in the thick of the ruined army, and the piles of bodies lay almost on top of one another.

'There's nothing to see here but death,' he murmured, bitterly. His great face was heavy with grief.

Magnus lifted his eyes from the ranks of bodies and looked at Hildebrandt with concern. The man was in a bad way. The fall had knocked some of the spirit from him. This field of decay was doing the rest. Perhaps it hadn't been right to bring him along. The man's courage was not what it had been.

Magnus was about to tell him to return to the ridge when a hoarse shout came from Thorgad. The two men hurried over. Unlike the others, who had trodden lightly and with distaste through the sickening scene, Thorgad had rummaged vigorously amongst the bodies. Any remaining gear had been rifled through. The enemy had looted most of the objects of value, but such had been the scale of their victory that the defenders' weapons lay where they had fallen. Clearly, the rebels had had no great need for more swords or spears.

'I've found something,' the dwarf said, gruffly.

125

Thorgad had a sliver of metal in his palm. It was about five inches long, curved like an elongated *S*, and artfully carved. He gave it to Magnus.

'A serpentine,' Ironblood said, turning the object over in his hands. It was the device used to lower the burning match into the pan, employed in long guns to detonate the blackpowder charge.

Thorgad nodded.

'Aye,' he said. 'The only piece of gunnery I've found. Whoever stripped this place has done good work. They might have had a dwarf's eyes. There's nothing left of them. Nothing at all. It's as if they were never here.'

'Apart from this,' said Magnus, thoughtfully. He pulled a monocle lens from his jerkin, and fixed it to his right eye. He drew the sliver closer, and peered intently at it. The mechanism was familiar, and yet unfamiliar. He could clearly see how it fitted with the rest of the gun, but the shape was more angular than was common in Imperial weaponry. It was not from the north of the Empire, that was for sure. Hochland guns had their own unique workings of which their gunsmiths were fiercely proud. It might have come from Nuln, though there were also subtle differences from the products of that city's great schools. The serpentine wouldn't have fitted any of the guns in his handgunner companies. It was too big, and too bizarrely shaped.

Magnus paused, unsure of himself.

'This is new to me,' he said at last, putting the eyeglass away and holding the metal up to the meagre light. 'There was a time when I could have told you where every bearing from every working in the Old World came from. Now I'm no longer so confident. But I'd say this is new. From a new mechanism, too. I've never seen its like.'

Hildebrandt took the serpentine and examined it intently. Thorgad nodded his squat head in agreement.

'You should ask yourself something, Ironblood,' the dwarf said. 'Those peaks on either side of us are high. Very high. Could your gunners hit a target from there? If the ambush was raised from those cliffs, their guns can shoot a long way. I don't think any umgi weapons are that good.'

Magnus squinted as he gauged the distances. The dwarf might have been right. If they had fired from so far, the range of their weapons must have been good. Worryingly good.

'There's something else,' said Thorgad, taking the piece back from Hildebrandt. 'This design has something of the dwarfs about it, or I'll shave my beard off. Your race would never carve something this way. You don't have the tools for it. See the angle here, where the pin is fixed? That's dawi design. I'd stake my hold on it.'

Magnus took another look. He was no expert on dwarfish manufacture, but Thorgad had a point. It had the mark of the stunted folk. The quality, too. He frowned, thinking hard.

'Are there dwarfs in these mountains?' he asked.

'There are dwarfs all over the Empire,' said Thorgad, dismissively. 'But in numbers? Not here. There's nothing of value to us in these hills. In any case, my people wouldn't be getting involved with your fights. Why would they risk their necks for Anna-Louisa when there are grudges to avenge in the east?'

Thorgad stowed the serpentine safely in a pouch at his belt.

'No,' he said. 'If dwarfs are involved, then there are few of them. Perhaps some smiths, working for hire.'

Thorgad didn't look at Magnus as he spoke, and Ironblood thought the dwarf wasn't telling all he knew. He pondered pressing him for more, but decided against it. If Thorgad had his secrets, no amount of cajoling would prise them from him. They would come out in the end, one way or another.

'So we know this,' said Magnus, resignedly. 'They have good guns. Of their own design, by the look of it. I don't like that. You're right about their range. We have nothing to match it. I should tell Scharnhorst.'

'He won't be happy,' said Hildebrandt.

'Have you ever seen him happy?' asked Magnus. 'I'll tell him myself. The scouts must be forewarned.'

Magnus looked out over the scene of desolation. Whatever guns the enemy possessed, they had wreaked terrible destruction. The thought of it sent a tremor down his spine.

'They're not perfect,' he murmured, thinking of the serpentine. 'They didn't erase all the evidence. That's something.'

As he spoke, Magnus found that he didn't believe his own words. The more they discovered about the unseen enemy, the more Magnus found himself full of misgiving. Why hadn't they shown themselves? Were they tormenting them? Letting the army exhaust itself in the ascent before letting their full force loose on them? He felt his stomach begin to rebel. The noxious odour of death was intensifying. There was little more they could do in such a place.

'Come,' Magnus said to Thorgad and Hildebrandt. 'We should go back. This battlefield sickens me. We'll think more on it once we're marching. Messina might know more – it could be a Tilean design.'

Thorgad nodded curtly, and the three of them began to pick their way over to the ridge, stepping around the forests of warped and mangled limbs as they went. Far above them, the cold wind whined. The stone itself seemed grim and hostile. This was a cursed place. The sooner they were out of the valley of the dead, the better.

WITH THE VALLEY route denied them, the army had to take a circuitous path to their eventual destination. They had been barely a day's march from Morgramgar on discovery of the site of the massacre, but Magnus guessed that the detour would take them at least twice that. With no sign of their goal, the men had become fractious and restive. The endless cold, poor diet and lack of decisive action were all playing their part. Fights broke out for the smallest of reasons. The harsh regimen of the sergeants was redoubled, and it became common to see soldiers dragged from their companies to face the lash for insubordination. As with all the campaigns Magnus had ever been on, the longer it lasted without combat, the more the cohesion of the army was put under strain.

If Scharnhorst realised the scale of the unrest, he gave no sign of it. The pace remained punishing. Kruger and his Knights of the Iron Sceptre rode ceaselessly along the flanks of the marching companies, urging greater efforts for the glory of the Emperor. The captain and his men became hated by the common infantrymen, who had little in common with the noble riders on their powerful steeds. At the rear of the entire host, the trail of carts and wagons crawled onwards painfully slowly. No matter how hard the drivers whipped and goaded the straining horses, there was only so much progress the beasts could make. Several of them had collapsed from the strain. When resuscitation proved impossible, their necks were cut, and they were left for the wolves. There were now no spare horses to pull the great guns. If any others failed to make it, the engineers would have to commandeer replacement steeds from the cavalry units. That would be neither easy nor popular.

The day waned to dusk. In the far north, strange shapes could be seen flying low on the jagged horizon. Birds, perhaps. But they were big ones, and their wings were like those of a bat. As the light died, they passed from view.

Scharnhorst's men cleared a series of rubble-choked gullies and emerged onto a wide plain several hundred feet above their starting position. The land was flat, stony and scored with great cracks. Little grew on it but lichen, clinging to the underside of great boulders. With nothing to break its path, the wind tore across the bleak landscape, whipping at the clothes of the soldiers and making the standards snap and ruffle. When the order to cease marching and form camp was given, men fell to their knees with exhaustion, heedless of rank, deployment or the need to organise sentries. As the heavy wains were hauled up the last few hundred yards, campfires were lit on the bare stone, and thin gruel slopped into tin pails. The dark was coming quickly, and the shadows were long.

Magnus and the engineers were, as ever, busy with the rearguard. Corps of handgunners had been called back to assist the safe mooring of the gunnery train. Messina and Herschel rode amongst them, threatening and encouraging as necessary. There was work to be done before night fell, but few of them could think of anything but their bellies and a snatched night's sleep. The gruel was little better than water, but at least it was hot.

As the sun sunk towards the serrated west, Magnus looked at the scene before him wearily, feeling a heavy tiredness eke away at his bones. It had now been days since he'd had a proper drink. Up in the barren wilderness, even the sparse comforts of Frau Ettieg's homestead suddenly took on a strangely wholesome aspect. He found himself salivating at the prospect of a tankard full of frothy, well-drawn beer. Once, it had been such a common pleasure. Now it had become the stuff of dreams. For a moment, just a moment, he forgot about the burden of command, the endless complaints of the wain drivers, the worry over the state of the big guns, and imagined sipping a warm, thick, foamy draught of properly bitter, malt-soaked home-brewed ale. Magnus half-closed his eyes, and let the reins of his horse fall slack. His fingers crept towards the gourd.

The first shot rang out.

'Cover!' came a panicked voice, and immediately the camp burst into action. Men scrabbled for their guns.

't move. The shots

no sign of them. This was bad. The troops were exposed,
and the light was almost gone. Picking out the enemy
snipers was going to be difficult.

Keeping his body low, Magnus ran over to the nearest
company of handgunners. Several of them had been
felled. The rest were frantically pulling their long guns
from leather holsters and striking flints to light the
matchcord.

'Keep calm!' cried Magnus. 'Remember your training.
They can't fire again for a moment. Load your guns and
wait for my signal.'

As the words left his lips, the dusk was lit with a barrage of light. The sound of blackpowder cracked in the
air. On Magnus's left hand, a man crumpled heavily,
clutching his eyes and screaming. He rolled away, blood
pumping from the wound. Magnus looked down in horror, transfixed.

'That's impossible,' he breathed. 'No one could reload
that quickly. How many ranks have they got?'

His mind was racing. This was dangerous. He turned
to the handgunners.

'Form a line!' he shouted, seizing the stricken gunner's
weapon from where he'd dropped it. 'Wait for my mark!'

The men around him hurriedly finished loading their
guns, blowing powder from the sealed pans and replacing the scouring sticks. They crouched down in a long,
ragged line facing away from the lines of carts. Elsewhere

132

in the camp, the sound of gunfire echoed. Shouted orders and screams of pain rose up from the length of the column. It sounded disorderly. This was a shambles.

Magnus rammed the shot home, checked the burn of his matchcord and hoisted the gun to his shoulder. He was lucky. It was a genuine Hochland long gun. It would fire true.

'Raise your weapons!' he shouted. On either side of him, muzzles fell into line. It was slow, though. Far too slow.

There was nothing to aim at. Nothing to see. The shots had come from the murk beyond the camp perimeter. They would have to shoot blind. It would be a miracle if they hit a thing.

'Fire!' cried Magnus.

The guns recoiled as the serpentines snapped back and blackpowder burst into flame. With a ragged snap, a volley of shot was sent sailing into the gloom. Smoke from the ignited powder floated across the camp. There were similar jarring cracks from elsewhere in the camp. The defenders were slowly responding. Magnus wondered if any of them could see more than he could.

'Reload!' he yelled, knowing that time was of the essence.

He crouched down low. The matchcord was taken off and pan exposed. He spilled a leather pouch of iron balls into his palm, drew out the scouring stick and rammed one into the barrel expertly, keeping a close eye on the spare powder. This was complicated, dangerous work. If something hit the stores, they would all be immolated. Best not to think about it.

Magnus raised himself to one knee.

'Quicker, damn you!' he growled. The handgunners were taking too long, fumbling as the light failed. This was going to be a massacre. He remembered the grey faces in the valley. They never stood a chance. 'Sigmar flay you, load the damn guns!'

There was a flash of light from far off. Magnus ducked. A fresh volley of shot slammed into the camp. Men were hurled from their feet. Shot ripped through leather and ricocheted off iron. Fresh cries of sudden agony rose up. The lines were wavering. To their left, the defence was broken, and men were fleeing from the danger. Magnus pushed himself back into a crouch. How in the name of Morr were the attackers loading so fast? They'd released three heavy, disciplined volleys so far, and the defenders had barely got one away.

'Raise your guns!' he shouted. 'Aim for where the powder flashes!'

It was almost useless advice. They were firing blind, hoping against hope that their shot would somehow hit the right target. The enemy had no such worries. They knew where to aim, and their target was huge. Every volley would hit something or other. The dark was their ally.

Slowly, clumsily, the handgunners assumed the firing position. There were fewer of them. Some of the gunners' matchcord had extinguished, some had shattered scourers, others lay face down against the rock, blood pooling.

'Fire!' bellowed Magnus.

The guns cracked once again, sending the iron balls screaming into the dusk. It wasn't clear that they'd hit anything at all. The position was hopeless. Where was the cavalry? Why hadn't the scouts secured the area?

'Reload!' croaked Magnus, his voice breaking and going hoarse. With trembling fingers, he reached for more shot. The barrel of his gun was hot, and the stench of blackpowder was close in his nostrils. He kept low, heart beating hard. At the rate the bastards were firing, it couldn't be long before…

The muzzle flashes came again, and more shot whined over his head. With terrible repetition, more men cried out in pain as the shot found its targets. The rate of fire was unbelievable. How many attackers were there? Were they advancing? How far away were they? It was impossible to tell. It was a fiasco. They were being picked off like grouse.

At last, Magnus heard the bugles ring out. Someone had taken charge. The order to advance was given. There was no option but to take the fight to the enemy. Torches had been hurriedly lit, and Magnus heard the thunder of hooves as the knights charged in the direction of the incoming fire. Kruger was there, his voice raised in dreadful anger. It was horribly dangerous in the low light, but it was the right tactic. The only tactic.

'Take up your guns!' cried Magnus, lifting his own to his chest and cradling the all-important cord. 'Follow me!'

At last, the men had some direction, something to get their teeth into. With a roar of aggression and rage, they rose up as one and charged across the broken stone. Magnus was at the forefront, eyes wide, sweat starting from his skin, expecting to hear the blast and whine of gunfire at any moment. He muttered a quick prayer to Sigmar. All there was now was luck, or grace. The light had almost gone entirely, and every black shape against the earth looked like an enemy soldier. His heart banged in his chest, his lungs laboured. Battle had come at last.

They kept running. No shots echoed. The bugles rang out again. Some of the knights had overshot, and were cantering back. The air was filled with the shouts and war cries of the defenders, but no guns fired. It was as if the enemy had never existed.

A cold shiver passed through Magnus's stomach. They should have been hard upon them by now. They were being drawn out. The snipers had withdrawn. It was a trap.

'Hold fast!' he screamed, juddering to a halt and holding his hand up. All around him, men ran heedlessly onward, consumed with the desire to spill blood.

Finally, the guns rang out again. The noise came from further away. Magnus flung himself to the ground. Hot blood splattered across him. The handgunner on his right side slumped to the rock, scrabbling at his torn stomach, squealing like a stuck pig.

Magnus rolled away, sick with rage and impotent fury. They were being played for fools. It was the oldest tactic in the sniper's manual. Hit hard, withdraw. Hit hard, withdraw. The defenders were being strung out in an attempt to engage an unseen foe. Soon the light would fail entirely, and shooting would become impossible for both sides. Their only hope was to keep together, keep their volleys disciplined.

'To me!' Magnus roared, standing up. He cared nothing for the danger now. Their only chance was to stop running after shadows and stay in formation. 'Form a line! To me, men of Hochland!'

The survivors heeded his call. Soon he was surrounded by a dozen men. In the low light, their faces looked bewildered and angry.

'Raise your guns and aim for the flashes!' bellowed Magnus, trying to instil some sense of purpose. 'Fire on my mark, then withdraw. Damn you all, this is a bloodbath!'

The men crouched down, and long guns were prepared. On Magnus's mark, the entire line let off a rippling wave of fire. Once again, the shot whined into the dark. Whether it hit anything, no one could tell.

'Withdraw!' cried Magnus, pulling at the handgunners nearest him as he fell back. 'Don't go chasing phantoms! We must keep our shape!'

Gradually, the rest of the army seemed to be adopting the same strategy. The ranks of gunners were holding now, retreating step by step. Every so often, the crack of detonation would echo into the darkening air from the lines of defenders. There were no more volleys from the hidden snipers. They had gone. Like shades of death, they had retreated back into the shadows. As the night fell, even their guns would be no use. Somewhere in the night, the knights were riding hard, trying to find them.

'Mother of Sigmar,' breathed Magnus, feeling disgusted and dejected. He and his men retreated back to the camp perimeter. There were bodies everywhere. Some moved weakly, crying in pain. Others were as still and cold as the rock around them. The toll had been dreadful.

Gradually, the sounds of battle ebbed. Once Scharnhorst's commanders realised the attackers had fled, they reined in their men to conserve ammunition. Chasing after them in the dark would be suicidal. In any case, it was clear that the attackers had planned to strike and then retreat. The defenders had been out-thought, out manoeuvred and out shot. It was a disgrace.

Magnus reloaded, just in case, and sat heavily on a wooden crate. There were no more shots from the dark. Around him, handgunners stood stupidly, wondering whether to fire blindly or just hold their position. Magnus ignored them. They would have to absorb this lesson in tactics, and learn from it. There was nothing they could do now until the morning.

From the gathering darkness, a man walked towards Magnus. It was Messina. He had his flintlock pistol by his side, and the muzzle still smoked. A smouldering fury was in his eyes.

'Where were damned scouts?' he spat. 'It was like trying to shoot *fantasmi*.'

Magnus looked up wearily. The man was right to be angry.

'The knights might catch some of them,' he said, though he knew it was unlikely. 'We can't chase after them in this light.'

He looked at the handgunners. They were still waiting for orders. Now that the short, vicious firefight was over, many looked shocked.

'Make sure you're loaded and ready to fire again,' said Magnus to them, testily. 'We'll organise patrols, and get proper sentries for the camp edge.'

The gesture would give them something to do, but Magnus knew it was futile. The enemy wouldn't be back tonight. They relied on surprise to offset their lack of numbers. It had been a devastating tactic. He spat on the ground, got up and started to walk off towards the centre of the camp. All around him, torches were being lit and men were running to their stations. Too late. All much too late.

'Where you going?' asked Messina, looking exasperated.

Magnus turned to face him, his lined face lit up by the dancing flames.

'To Scharnhorst,' he said, his voice flat. 'We've got some talking to do. If he still doesn't think he needs a proper strategy for the guns, then he's a bigger fool than I thought he was.'

With that, Magnus turned and stalked towards the general's tent. His mood was black. All around him, the night was filled with the cries of the dead and the dying. The first encounter had come and gone. And they had lost.

CHAPTER SEVEN

Never forget that behind the sights of the gun there lies a man. He must be trained to use his weapon, just as he would a pike, a broadsword or a loom. The tools of war are dangerous and fragile things, and blackpowder makes them more so. The mastery must be taught slowly. Repeat the lessons, and repeat them again. Once on the battlefield, it will be too late for further schooling. If they enter battle not knowing how to kill, all they will learn is how to be killed.

Heinz-Karl Fromann,
Chief Instructor, Stirland
State Gunnery School

MESSINA WAS FUMING. The campaign was turning into a dangerous and exhausting farrago. A half-competent general would have laid in precautions for a raid against their position, especially as they were now closing in on Morgramgar. The scouts and outriders had been dispatched far too easily. Even now, far into the mid-morning, several were still missing. Scores of soldiers had been killed before they'd even had a chance to pick up their weapons. For an army the size of Scharnhorst's, the casualties were bearable. But the blow to morale was real. The men were already teetering on the edge of fatigue and disrespect. Now that the incompetence of their masters had been fully exposed, they were even more so.

What made it worse was that the attackers had all used long guns. There was not an arrow in sight amongst the bodies of the slain. The ordinary halberdiers now looked askance at the engineers. Messina knew exactly what they were thinking. That the enemy was being better led, and was better equipped. And that their own commanders were arrogant fools.

'Again,' snapped Messina, looking down the line of handgunners. 'We'll do it again until you get it all right.'

Under Ironblood's orders, he had taken several dozen of the best troops in the gunnery companies, and was now drilling them mercilessly. Their performance had been sloppy. Damned sloppy. Whatever training they must have had in the past was clearly poor. While the bulk of the army was busy putting the camp into some kind of order, Messina and Herschel had been trying to instil discipline into the Hochlanders' firing. If they were attacked again with such rates of fire, they would lose as many men again. Speed of reloading was everything.

In front of his unforgiving gaze, the state gunners filled the pan, charged the barrel, loaded the shot, rammed it down, replaced the rods, fixed the cord, raised their rifles and fired into the distance. Their movements were getting better. The shame of the debacle the night before had driven them to improve. Some of the Hochland hunters were good shots. But they were slow, terribly slow.

After releasing their flurry of shot, they stooped quickly and reloaded their guns. A second volley cracked out across the echoing plain. That was better. Not as good as the enemy had been, but better.

Messina felt a presence at his shoulder, and turned. Herschel was observing quietly. The boy looked like he hadn't slept much. For all the Tilean knew, it might have been his first taste of real combat, and Messina could imagine that it hadn't been what he'd imagined.

'Keep it up, *ragazzi*!' he shouted to the handgunners. 'I want twelve more before you return to camp.'

He turned away from them, and walked slowly back to the wagons. Herschel came with him.

'How's it going?' said the young man.

'They are not bad soldiers, I think,' said Messina. 'But their training has been poor. I don't have the time to turn things upwards. We must accept they are the better shots.'

Herschel nodded. He looked worried.

'Herr Ironblood took some men out this morning,' he said. 'To see where the attackers had come from. We found footprints. They'd been taking aim from an incredible distance. There's no way we can compete with that.'

Messina stroked his elegant chin thoughtfully. Despite everything, he still took care over his looks. He was clean-shaven, and his clothes looked almost clean. That marked him out from the bulk of the officers, let alone the average infantryman.

'So they can fire further as well as faster,' he said. 'That is unfortunate. I'd put my money on these Hochlanders to hit their targets, but they have to get into their position first.'

Herschel took a deep breath, and the worry remained heavy on his face. The lad was inexperienced, but was still nobody's fool. In the short time Messina had known him, he'd been impressed by the boy's knowledge of ballistics. When he spoke, the men listened to him. That was no easy feat.

'Can I ask you something, Silvio?' Lukas said, cautiously.

Here it came.

'Of course.'

'You've been on many campaigns,' said Herschel. 'You've served under many master engineers. What do you make of Magnus Ironblood?'

Messina drew in a breath of cold air. This was delicate. Unity was a virtue. But the truth was even more valuable.

'I have heard the name, of course,' he said. 'I am sure you have too. But names don't command armies. You remember how he looked when he found us? Something made him into that state. He has fallen. Perhaps he can't get it back. I don't know.'

Herschel looked pensive.

'I don't mean any disrespect,' he said, keeping his voice low. 'But we were badly beaten last night. There should have been plans in place. Any rabble could have attacked the camp. There was nothing arranged. Frankly, I could have done…'

He trailed off, and gave Messina a worried look.

'Don't worry, lad,' said Silvio. 'You can speak freely with me.'

Herschel shook his head, clearly full of doubt.

'I know how to fire a long gun,' he said. 'I know all the technical matters. But commanding an army… Perhaps I should keep my mouth shut.'

Silvio smiled at him.

'Perhaps you should,' he said. 'But not with me. I think that you are right. We've got to get things up together, and soon. We're nearly at the place, but there's time for more of those attacks. Ironblood thinks we'll just have to put them up, hold formation and suffer the losses.'

Silvio glanced over his shoulder at the practising handgunners. The volleys were still erratic. They were up against a foe they couldn't hope to match.

'Luccina only knows why we're so outgunned,' he murmured. 'These places should be home to nothing more than bandits and sheep. There is something strange going on. If we're going to think it through, we'll have to be creative.'

He clapped his hand on Herschel's shoulder and drew his face close to the boy's.

'I have some ideas myself,' he said, in little more than a whisper. 'Ironblood won't like it, but he'll never have to know. Are you in the mind for some danger? If we carry it off, there might be money in it.'

Herschel looked uncertain.

'What do you mean?' he asked. 'Ironblood ought to know about anything we're doing.'

Silvio smiled tolerantly. The lad was young. He'd have to grow up quickly.

'You may have noticed that our captain is not as respected as he would like,' he said, keeping his voice to a confidential murmur. 'Now, I do not suggest that we do anything disloyal. He is paying us, after all of it. But reputation is everything. If we were to do something by ourselves, something that might turn things just a little in our favour, it would do no great harm. To catch a general's eye is never a bad thing. We have to think of our own position.'

Lukas still looked unconvinced.

'What do you have in mind?' he said eventually, his mind clearly working through the possibilities.

Messina grinned.

'I thought you might never ask me,' he said. 'Come with me. But keep it to yourself. We've a lot to gain, and a lot to lose. And that's just how I like it.'

HILDEBRANDT WATCHED MAGNUS walk heavily back into the camp and collapse onto a pile of old sacking. The man looked spent. He'd been busy most of the night organising watches to prevent a repeat attack, and most of the morning leading search parties to track down the snipers. Both efforts had been unfruitful. The attackers weren't fools. They would choose their moments, sweeping down when they weren't expected, and retreating as soon as the army could respond. It was a dirty kind of fighting, but effective nonetheless.

'Did you find much?' asked Hildebrandt, warily.

Magnus snorted.

'More of the same,' he said. His voice was thick with tiredness. Magnus looked almost as bad as he had done in Hergig. His hair was lank, and there were hollows of grey under his eyes. 'They'd slit the throats of the outriders. Crept up as the night fell. Nothing left behind. Just some powder-burns on the rocks, the odd piece of shot. Like ghosts. Damned ghosts.'

Ironblood sighed, and let his powerful shoulders relax. Hildebrandt looked on with concern. The big man was feeling the effects of his brush with tragedy still. The entire army was strung out on its feet. There were whispers amongst the soldiers. Most of them didn't bear repeating.

'Their guns are better,' said Hildebrandt, simply.

Magnus rolled his eyes.

'You think I don't know that? What are we supposed to do about it?'

Hildebrandt paused.

'You brought the chests with you,' he said. 'The machine from Nuln. I saw it. Do you plan to use it?'

Magnus sat up sharply, his eyes flat with suspicion.

'Have you been spying on me, Tobias?' he said.

Hildebrandt sighed with irritation.

'Of course not,' he said. 'It's there for all to see. But I know what's in them. The others don't.'

Magnus scowled. When he was tired, he became belligerent.

'You have no idea what's in them,' he said, scornfully, hauling himself to his feet.

Hildebrandt felt his own anger rising. After being persuaded to come on this terrible campaign, the least he deserved was some respect.

'It's the Blutschreiben, isn't it?'

There was a smug note of victory in his voice. He was closer to Ironblood than anyone. Despite all that had happened, Hildebrandt knew he wouldn't have left the past entirely behind.

Magnus didn't reply at once. He had a dark look in his eyes.

'It's locked away,' he said finally. 'That's how it'll stay.'

There it was. That old defiance. That old pig-headedness. It would be the death of both of them.

'Morr rot your bones!' spat Hildebrandt. 'How long are you going to let it hold you back? It's brilliant! Your father never got it right. You were almost there, Magnus. Almost there!'

Magnus took an angry step forward, his hands trembling.

'Almost!' he cried. 'How good is almost? It wasn't good enough for us last night. It won't be good enough if the siege guns crack when we roll them up to Morgramgar. And it wasn't good enough back then either.'

His voice wavered. Old memories were rising to the surface like oil in water.

'It wasn't good enough for him,' he said, softly, withdrawing, his eyes losing their focus. 'There's been enough death. It's not ready.'

From the shadows, Thorgad emerged. He was carrying a huge pile of cannon shot, half his own height. The dwarf had been working flat out since the attack. His axe had been little use in the fracas, and he seemed ashamed not to have contributed more. When he saw Hildebrandt and Ironblood in conference, he put down his burden and came over to them.

'A damn mess this has been,' he growled, rubbing his beard.

At the sight of the dwarf, Hildebrandt felt his own anger ebb. The strain was getting to all of them.

'I'm sorry, Magnus,' he said, bringing the debate to an end. 'I shouldn't have spoken. But it's frustrating, knowing…'

'I know,' said Magnus, quietly. 'They're out shooting us. But we can weather the storm. They're only coming at us now because they fear the siege. Once we have the heavy iron lined up, then they'll be in trouble. We have to hold our nerve.'

Ironblood looked at Hildebrandt directly. Amidst all the sullen weariness, there was a spark of defiance left. Not much of one, but it was there nonetheless. The old man was hard to grind down.

Thorgad spat on the ground.

'So what's next?' he said.

'We'll keep drilling the men,' Magnus said. 'They've got to get their rates of fire up. As for the rest, the knights and the lunatics, that's not our task. Scharnhorst can look after them.'

Hildebrandt nodded. The knowledge that the Blutschreiben still existed, albeit packed away and dismantled, was tantalising. But now was not the right time. He could return to the subject later.

'Very well,' he said. 'Messina and the boy have been busy with them all morning. I'll lend them a hand. We'll be at Morgramgar soon enough anyway.'

Thorgad looked doubtful, but said nothing. Magnus let out a deep, shuddering sigh, and sat back down again.

'By Sigmar, I hope so,' he said. 'When those cannons are delivered and we're sending death at them from a safe distance, then I'll relax. Until then, we've got a contest.'

AT NOON, THE army moved onwards once more. The dead were disposed of quickly and with little ceremony. There was no time for burial, and the bodies were merely piled together and thrown into a crack in the granite plain. Lime was thrown over them, and Kossof gave a blessing. As he spoke to the assembled ranks, hostile eyes were directed at the engineers. Whispers had spread throughout the troops that Ironblood was still drinking, that he had spiked the defenders' guns to make them fire more slowly, that he was somehow in league with the enemy. It was wild talk, and baseless, but fatigue and fear did strange things to the men's minds.

When they returned to the march, they made slow progress. The land wound inexorably upward. The path passed between two mighty shoulders of hard, tumbled rock. It was dark and scoured of all but the hardiest grasses by the wind. The wains struggled, the men laboured, and the chill air bled the last of the energy from tired legs.

The very landscape seemed set against them. But there was more than cold stone to contend with. In the constant moan of the wind, there were fragments of fell voices. It might have been imagination, might not.

High up in the crags, there were definitely things moving. Stones would skitter down slopes, clattering into tired ranks of infantry. Echoing roars sounded from far off in the peaks, and were answered by distant hammerblows. These were not portents of Anna-Louisa's men. They were the noises of the unknown mountain reaches, far above the tolerances of mortal men. Whatever dread sentience dwelt in those terrible extremes, it did not descend to trouble them. But all were aware of its presence, and the knowledge added to the febrile atmosphere in the army itself.

Throughout all of this, Ironblood rode ahead of the gunnery companies, keeping himself to himself. He spoke rarely, and solely to Hildebrandt. Tobias was similarly quiet, locked in thought. Thorgad seemed utterly content in his own company, and strode tirelessly alongside the straining horses. Only Messina and Herschel still kept up something approaching banter with the men. They had been the most heavily involved with the punishing rounds of firing practice, and were looked on by many of the troops as their real mentors.

The warrior priest Kossof made the most of the situation. He and his acolytes had become the most animated of the army's many ranks. Every fresh adversity seemed to swell their sense of righteous fury.

'Trust not in the new science, brothers!' Kossof cried cheerfully, as the snap of whips and shrieks of the faithful rang out into the air. 'Keep faith in Holy Sigmar! The sword and the spear are the blessed weapons! The time when we will use them is coming! Keep faith!'

The gunners looked darkly on him as he passed them, but the words found resonance with the halberdiers and pikemen. They had been largely redundant on the journey so far, unable to respond quick enough to the night-time raid. Their skills would only come into play when they arrived at the citadel, and until then they looked restive and surly.

The other component of the army which retained its vigour was the Knights of the Iron Sceptre. They had the luxury of superior rations and the best equipment. While the bulk of the men shivered in the biting wind, they still rode up and down the lines, secure within heavy suits of armour. Though they were resented, they were also admired. The knights had done more than any others to chase down the night-time attackers, and they were trusted far more than the flighty bunch of engineers and their drunkard commander.

Despite the harshness of the terrain, they made steady progress. Scharnhorst had sent many men ahead as scouts on the few remaining horses. They patrolled in groups of six, mindful of the possibility of ambush. The rest of the army kept as bunched together as they could, all eyes on the shadows in the rocks.

After another day of heavy toil, the men crested the last of the great ridges before the valley in which, so the charts said, Morgramgar lay. The citadel itself was some miles distant, and the depression was wreathed in a heavy fog. Mindful of the mistakes of the past, Scharnhorst called a halt as the sun began to wane. They were in a shallow, wide valley surrounded by broken country. It was the only location wide enough to accommodate the whole army, but it was hardly ideal. There were vantage points in the hills around.

All knew what that meant, and the men's eyes flickered nervously up at the jagged rocks enclosing them.

With an hour to go before nightfall, the camp was rigged properly, and sentries were posted on the high ground beyond. Fires were lit all around the perimeter, and gunners placed on every vantage point. They knew the enemy would come again. This was the rebels' last chance to strike before the siege was laid. At least they would be prepared this time.

As the final glow of the sunset ebbed behind the mountains to the west, Magnus sat on his horse, staring moodily at the dying of the light. Thorgad stood alongside him, scouring the mountains ahead.

'Tough country,' he muttered, seemingly to himself.

Magnus paid no attention. He knew his mood was weakening his authority with the men. They were looking for a decisive sign, and he was giving them none. His whole body ached for a drink. The scale of his dependence had begun to frighten him. Had he really sunk so low? How close had he been to losing himself entirely? It was a frightening prospect. And yet, despite knowing how ruinous it had been, how close to the edge it had taken him, every fibre in Magnus's body yearned for one more swig.

His sombre gaze swept across the ranks of gunners. They were primed and ready, muzzles arranged in long rows, ready for the assault. Their faces were grim in the failing light. They knew that they presented a big target. The enemy would not have to be accurate. Somehow, the defenders would have to pick their opposite numbers in the murk. What was worse, their guns were inferior. Magnus wanted to offer some words of comfort and encouragement. He couldn't think of any. His mind was sluggish and morbid. They would just have to cope as best they could.

Just as before, the attack came without warning. Scharnhorst's extra scouts had clearly not done their job. The night was suddenly lit from all around with muzzle flashes. An instant later, and the harsh sound of the blackpowder igniting echoed from the mountain flanks. Shot spat into the close-packed ranks of men. The sickeningly familiar cries of agony rose into the night.

'Keep your formations!' cried Magnus, suddenly galvanised into action. 'Remember your training! Return fire! Aim for the flashes!'

The response was less chaotic than it had been. Despite their losses, the lines of handgunners held their shape, and a disciplined volley whined off back into the night. Some of them might have even found their mark. It was hard to tell. Seeing anything in the gloom was nigh on impossible. As long as they retained their positions, though, they would get through it. The temptation to go charging off into the foothills was strong, but it must be resisted. The enemy would just draw them on, picking them off as they stumbled up the slope.

A second wave of incoming shot slammed into the defenders' lines. So quick. Most of the handgunners were still reloading when it impacted. Magnus saw one man take a musket-ball in the face as he stooped to pick up fresh shot. He spun round from the force of the blow, his skull caved in. The gunner fell without making a sound, and lay immobile. On either side of him, his comrades worked grimly to prepare a second volley.

'Keep your shape!' yelled Magnus again, knowing they would be itching to run. It was hard to fight the instinct. 'Fire in rounds! Hold your positions!'

Then, without warning, something new happened. From the far side of the camp, there were three mighty crashes. There was a high whine that slowly disappeared into the night. Something had been launched. There was a trail of smoke just visible against the darkening sky. Magnus followed the curve of the projectiles, his mouth hanging open in surprise. They were rockets. But he hadn't ordered any fired. They were for the siege. How had they been found?

'What in Sigmar's...' he began.

Then they detonated. The explosions were massive, and the earth seemed to vibrate under his feet. Three huge blooms of red cascaded over their heads, fizzing and drifting to earth slowly. These were not his rockets. The entire space was lit up with a lurid illumination. The outlines of men were suddenly visible on the ridges around them. The light didn't die away, but kept burning in the air. Spinning sparks flew from the floating shards, picking out every detail of the rocky hills above them in stark detail.

There was a roar of excitement from the men in the encampment. This was what they needed. From somewhere amongst the press of troops, orders were barked. Infantry began to swarm up towards the rocks. Kruger was at the forefront, his armour still glinting in the poor light, his charger labouring up the slope.

'Keep your formation!' shouted Magnus again to the gunners, but his words were ignored. More rockets screamed into the sky, bathing the land around them in fresh layers of harsh colour. The attackers were exposed. With all the energy born of days of pent-up frustration, the defenders broke out. Murderous oaths were sworn, and a savage light was in their eyes.

Powerless to prevent it, Magnus spat a curse and joined the surge up the shallow slope. He kicked his horse viciously. He must have presented a tempting target so high above the shoulders of his men, but he didn't care. Someone had usurped his authority and fired rockets. He didn't know whether to feel angrier with himself for not thinking of it, or his subordinates for going behind his back.

'Messina,' he hissed to himself. 'Those are Tilean flares. No one makes them like that.'

Then he was amongst the fighting. The snipers on the ridges had been surprised. The enemy. Face-to-face at last. They hastily tried to withdraw. With their positions exposed, retreat was impossible. The knights had been primed, and were heavily engaged, hacking and slashing from their steeds. The halberdiers, desperate for a fight, had joined the fray. In the blood-red light, the combat was murderous. Men grappled against each other like daemonic creatures, their eyes staring with hatred. The chance for revenge had come, and they were seizing it with both hands.

Magnus drew his sword, and rode into the morass of grappling bodies. A man leapt up at him, using his long riflegun as a club. Magnus swung the blade, feeling its keen edge snag on flesh and bite deep. Blood spat up, smearing across both him and his steed. It was hot and thick. The smell was overpowering. It took him back instantly to the battles he'd fought as a young man, back when he'd still eagerly rushed into combat, the thrill of it running through his veins. Before he'd lost his nerve.

Magnus ploughed onwards, swiping with his sword like a harvester in the fields. The snipers were pitifully unprepared. They'd expected to release a few rounds of shot into a supine enemy, then shrink back into the darkness. Many of them didn't even have swords with them. Just guns. And they were next to useless in a close press.

More rockets screamed into the sky above them. Fresh explosions detonated, showering the scene with more light. It looked as if blood was raining down from the heavens. Magnus pulled his horse round, facing a terrified enemy gunner. The man dropped his weapon and raised his hands. He was unarmed. Scared. Alone. For a moment, Magnus met his gaze. The gunner was a Hochlander, just like the ones running amok amongst his comrades. For this evening at least, he'd picked the wrong side.

Magnus rode him down, blocking the screams from his ears as the horse's hooves trampled the man into the ground. Another sniper emerged, and he cut him down too. There was no honour or glory in it. The tables had been turned, and the hunters had become the prey. As Magnus hacked and stabbed with a vicious fury, there was one nagging thought at the back of his mind. The victory hadn't been his doing. When this was over, there would have to be a reckoning.

THE FIRES STILL burned. Some of the knights had yet to come back, and were pursuing their prey as far as the rockets would allow them. In the rest of the camp, raucous songs rose bawdily into the night. Ale had been released from the supply wagons, and the officers let their men indulge in it. After so many days of hardship, a victory, even a minor one, was worth celebrating.

Scharnhorst sat on a low stool by his tent, feeling a cold satisfaction within. They were nearing the end of the long trek north. After so many days in the wilderness, Morgramgar was now in range. Their losses had been serious, but not out of the ordinary for a major campaign. Perhaps two hundred had been slain in the raids, mostly gunners or poorly armoured flagellants. More had died on the ascent, and there had been some desertion. They could absorb that. More importantly, they had struck back at last. The price in dead was immaterial. It was the effect on morale that was important. When the morning came, they would march to the citadel walls, knowing that the enemy was vulnerable.

His captains stood around him, sharing in the satisfaction. They had all been involved in the rout. Many had flagons of ale in their hand, and blood on their tunics. Now they looked like real soldiers. The Tilean engineer, Messina, held pride of place amongst them. He had drunk deep, and had a ruddy glow in his lean cheeks.

'You did well,' said Scharnhorst, allowing a thin smile to crack across his stern face. 'If I'd known your rockets were so potent, I'd have ordered them used before.'

Messina grinned back, his eyes shining with pride and ale.

'They're of my own design,' he said. 'Brought specially in private stores. You won't see flares like that just anywhere. The recipe is a secret.'

'How many are left?' asked the general.

Messina shrugged.

'Not many,' he said. 'They will be less good when we lay siege. But they did the job I asked of them.'

Scharnhorst nodded.

'That they did. You are to be commended. I take it that your superior officer approved these plans?'

'He did not.'

The voice was Ironblood's. Magnus pushed his way to the front of the charmed circle of men. His leather coat was streaked with mud and gore. In the flickering light, his face was terrible. His sword was still naked in his hands, and it dripped steadily. He had been drinking. He looked worse than he'd been in Gruber's yards.

'Put your weapon away, man,' hissed a voice. It might have been Kruger's. Ironblood ignored him.

'I authorised no use of rockets,' he said, staring at Messina with fury.

Scharnhorst rose from his seat. His satisfaction turned instantly to irritation. The man was a liability.

'You have some nerve, approaching me like this,' he said, his voice low. 'You would do well to remember your place, Ironblood.'

Magnus looked up at him. His eyes were wild.

'Yes, it *is* important to respect rank, it is not, general?' he said. 'If your subordinates start to act without your explicit orders, then there'll be no discipline left. Isn't that right?'

Messina said nothing, but his face was disdainful. At his shoulder, the young Herschel stood, hovering uncertainly.

Scharnhorst took a deep breath.

'If you'd run your company with more competence, I'd have some sympathy,' he said. 'Your men have had to do your job for you. Your comrade has dipped into his personal stores for the cause. As a result of his actions, we have had a victory. Perhaps you should learn from his example.'

Magnus's eyes circled around the gathering of captains. He looked like a trapped beast, surrounded by hounds. Messina met his stare with a blank insolence. Herschel lowered his gaze. Ironblood looked like he was about to speak again, but then his colleague, Hildebrandt, came bursting out from the circle of men.

'I apologise, sir,' he said to Scharnhorst, bowing quickly. He grabbed Ironblood's arm, and began to pull him away. 'The battle has been hard. He doesn't know what he's saying. He needs rest.'

Magnus briefly resisted, sullenly snatching his arm back. But then the fire left his eyes. He looked defeated. With one last poisonous glare at Messina, he let Hildebrandt draw him away. The two of them stalked into the darkness, and were gone.

For a moment, no one spoke. Even Kossof seemed embarrassed, and stared intently at the ground. The fire crackled. The sound of singing rose into the air from elsewhere in the camp.

At length, Scharnhorst sat down again.

'A volatile man, that Ironblood,' he said. 'Perhaps we will have to look at the division of responsibilities again. Maybe Grotius was wrong about him.'

Scharnhorst looked up at Messina, who hadn't moved.

'You seem like an enterprising young man,' he said. 'We're nearly at the point where our engineers will be most useful. Do you have any more ideas for taking the fight to the enemy?'

Messina smiled, and his eyes glittered darkly.

'Indeed I do, sir,' he said, his voice glossy with satisfaction. 'Indeed I do.'

CHAPTER EIGHT

Do not trust the seeker after knowledge! The boastful mind is the most dangerous enemy of man. Our proper task is to till the earth and guard the hearth. Those who seek truths amongst the stars or dabble in the new sciences are at the root of our downfall. Whenever a man of learning turns to the dark powers, then the Ruinous Gods laugh at our folly. Each time a child opens a book and is taught to read the signs within, the day of destruction looms nearer. Forget what you have been told by the foolish and the worldly! Ignorance of forbidden knowledge is power. Shun the wizard, the seer and the engineer. Only in faith and labour shall we be preserved!

Luthor Huss
The sermon at Erengrad

IN THE HEART of the mountains, a wide valley had been carved from the sheer rock by millennia of scraping ice. Like the rest of the highlands, it was bleak and barren. The rock was grey-banded granite, abrasive to the touch and tough as the bones of dragons. On all sides of the valley, the cliffs rose up tall and sheer. Their summits were jagged and impassable. Snow still clung to the uttermost peaks. The wind tore through the narrow gaps and skirled across the valley floor, tousling the few plants that grew and scraping the rock ever drier.

At the southern end of the valley there was a break in the otherwise perfect wall of cliffs. From this gap, the trail to Morgramgar wound steadily, picking its way across the desolate valley floor and looping around the many piles of boulders and mighty stone formations. The outcrops of rock were massive, and stood like the statues of some long-forgotten race of giants amidst the emptiness. An observant traveller, if any had existed so far into the wilds, might have picked out strange shapes on their flanks, almost like carvings. No doubt he would have put them down to the wind. In such a barren place, what else could they be?

The path ran for three miles before it reached the head of the valley. There, the mighty cliffs rose up once more, sealing the enclosed space in a circus of stone. Beyond those vast ramparts, there was no more travelling. The peaks piled up on top of one another, rising ever higher, until the land and sky seemed to meet in a haze of distant whiteness. The road ended.

At the point where the trail gave out, a mighty spur of black rock jutted out from the base of the towering cliffs. Unlike the dove-grey stone around it, the spur glistened darkly from many chiselled facets. It didn't belong. It looked like it had been hurled down from the heavens in some ancient war among the gods. It was shaped like the prow of a ship, sloping upwards and into the air of the valley. The wind broke across it, and no snow marred its surface. It was cold, hard and as slick as glass.

On top of the spur, a hundred feet above the valley floor, rose the isolated citadel of Morgramgar. The point where its dark walls met the stone below was indistinct. It seemed to loom from the cliffs around it, like some spell-induced growth from the roots of the mountains themselves.

Its base was solid and angular. The walls were arranged in a star shape with five points facing outwards. The blocks of stone were massive, each one the size of a peasant's hovel. They were rectangular and smooth, fitted together so perfectly that the joins were barely visible. The windows in that sheer surface were few. Every so often, a narrow shaft could be seen, set back far into the heavy stone and lined with iron. Pale illumination shone from some. In others, a deep red glow bled out into the cold air. Near the base of the citadel, the noise of a low throbbing could be made out, as if some vast machine was turning in the stone beneath. The rocks reverberated with it, sending a faint hum out into the valley beyond.

Further up the flanks of the citadel, the walls became taller and thinner. A cluster of towers burst from the foundations. They were slender and angular, clad in the same dark stone and topped with razor-sharp turrets. Flying bridges and twisting balustrades ran between them, fragile and perilous-looking in the high airs. Where there were windows, they glowed an eerie pale green. The narrow slots had glass panes in them, and strange shapes were carved around the frames. The stone was scored and pitted with age. Drab banners hung from the highest balconies. Once, the emblem of Hochland had been displayed proudly by loyal margraves. Now new insignias had taken their place. A long sable standard hung from the highest tower. It was unmarked, save for a grotesque death's head etched in crude lines of white. The hollow eyes gazed back down the empty gorge, daring any intruders to approach it.

At the top of the central tower, a soaring pinnacle which reached several hundred feet above the plain below, a large chamber had been constructed. It was too big for its base, and sat awkwardly atop the dark and forbidding citadel. More pale green light leaked from its many windows. More so than the death's head below, the chamber gave off the aspect of a terrible, sentient awareness. It was as if the windows were eyes and the jagged roof above it the horns of some ossified daemonic entity. Chains hung in great loops from beneath its overhanging eaves, clanking and swaying in the ever-present wind.

Within that chamber, Anna-Louisa had set her seat, and peered south across the valley. Her mighty armies were housed below, stationed in the vast halls that ran beneath the walls. The real glory of Morgramgar was not in its jagged pinnacles and towers. Deep within the foundations, ancient workings scored their way into the shadows beneath. There were massive chambers in the stone. Over the centuries, they had been allowed to fall into disrepair. That had changed. Now they were full of provisions, armaments, billeted men and, so rumour had it, deadly machines of war. Morgramgar had been restored, turned into a place of death, a citadel against which armies would break themselves like stones under the hammer.

On a narrow balcony overlooking the plain, set halfway up the sheer walls of the central tower, two men stood. They were both clothed in black, and their hair rustled in the chill air.

'They will be here soon,' said one of them.

He was a high-browed man with receding dark hair. His skin was pale and his eyes had deep bags under them. He looked like the kind of man who spent his days in the dark, by the forge, or in long-forgotten subterranean chambers. He wore a heavy amulet of silver around his neck. His cloak was of fine quality, and a collar of ermine trimmed his neck. He would have passed for a noble-born in many cities of the Empire, but some features of low birth gave him away. His gnarled hands spoke of manual labour, and he stooped as he stood, almost as if he expected some blow to rain down on him from a superior. Despite this, his gaze was proud. His lips curled around the words as he spoke.

'Indeed so, Rathmor,' said the second. 'But they've been blooded. We could have hoped for little more.'

Rathmor's companion was cut from different cloth. Though he wore the same dark robes, his frame was heavy. He had a neatly clipped silver beard and a mane of white hair to his shoulders. His features were blunt, and his skin was tanned and weather-beaten. Like

Rathmor, his hands were scored by years of labour, but from wielding swords and shields rather than the machines of the forge. He bore himself proudly, leaning into the wind, his wide shoulders set back. He had the look of a man who feared little and ran from nothing. A warrior, then. Unlike his companion.

'I do not like your complacence, Esselman,' said Rathmor, pursing his thin lips distastefully. 'We don't have unlimited resources, despite her largesse. We lost too many of our men when you persuaded her to march against the first of these armies. I still think that was a mistake.'

Esselman sneered at the smaller man, not bothering to hide his contempt.

'What would you have done?' he asked. 'Stayed here, crouching behind your walls as they came to get you? You're a coward, Rathmor. I can't fathom what the lady sees in you.'

Rathmor took the insult in his stride, as if he was quite used to it.

'What she sees in me is my incomparable genius,' he said, unselfconsciously. 'If I weren't here, you'd be nothing more than a rabble, squatting in the mountains waiting for your mistress to drag you out to your deaths. Admit it, Esselman. Without the modifications to your guns, you'd never have crushed Ludenhof's men.'

Esselman shrugged.

'We had the advantage of surprise,' he said. 'But I admit you've improved our range. Which is why we should have ridden to engage them again. This hiding and fleeing is hateful.'

Rathmor let a superior smile creep across his features.

'You're a warrior,' he said. 'All you think of is standing up and fighting. If the Empire were run by the likes of you, we'd be little better off than the beastmen.'

He leaned over the edge of the balcony, peering down towards the outer walls, far below. The sound of the muffled workings wafted upwards. A faint tremor could be sensed in the stone itself. It was as if all Morgramgar was a giant machine, and they were merely passengers on it.

'You're backward-looking,' said Rathmor, looking at the iron and stone around him. 'You belong to the past, when men hid from monsters in the shadows like children. The new science is everything. Blackpowder machines. With such tools, we could banish the scourge of Chaos forever. Even the elves would sit at our feet as slaves, and man would be master of the world.'

There was a strange light in the man's eyes as he spoke. Esselman looked weary. He had heard the speech a dozen times.

'Your toys are useful,' he said, grudgingly. 'The lady likes them. That's why we tolerate you. But they'll never replace a good man with a sword. Don't get carried away.'

Rathmor's expression wasn't dented. He was lost in a reverie of his own.

'A man with a sword?' he repeated, mockingly. 'Can a man with a sword fell a marauder at a hundred paces? Can he tunnel down to the deep ores and extract gold from the roots of the world? Can he throw fire into the air and immolate whole companies of our enemies?'

He laughed scornfully.

'Your age is passing, old warrior,' said Rathmor, gleefully. 'A new time is coming. The time of steel and steam. All it takes is vision. The Emperor will never allow it. There are too many in Altdorf with closed eyes and slow minds. But they'll see. When the spring comes and we sweep down from the mountains, then they'll see. The Empire needs shaking to its rotten core.'

Esselman's face remained impassive.

'So you keep saying,' he said. 'You've convinced von Kleister. How you did it, I'll never know. But you have, and so here we are. Stuck in a hold in the mountains. We've turned Ludenhof against us, and if we ever escape Hochland we'll have the armies of three more states hard on our heels. Your strategy's worked a charm so far.'

Rathmor's laugh was replaced by a scowl. His expressions changed quickly, like a child's. On the fringes of his wizened, clever face there was an air of petulance.

'Things are just as they should be,' he said. 'Our strength is still growing. The machines aren't complete. We just need time. Morgramgar is impregnable. We'll wait out the siege, hold for our moment. This army will be destroyed, just as the first was. The rumour of our success, and the gold beneath our feet, will spread. When the time is right, we will march south. But only then. Not before.'

Esselman gave the man a warning look.

'Remember your place, Rathmor,' he said. 'The lady tolerates you, but I'm the master of her armies. I need your machines, but I won't be dictated to. We'll march when I say so.'

Rathmor gave a mock bow, his sardonic smile returning.

'Of course, my lord,' he said, silkily. 'Yours will be the word of command for the men. But we still need more time. The forges are busy, but we cannot rush the work. There is still much to learn, much to discover.'

Esselman turned back towards the empty valley stretching before them. There was still no sign of the approaching army. No living creature stirred against the bleak backdrop of granite.

'Is the infernal engine ready?' he asked. 'That's the one thing I'm interested in. That's something I could use.'

Rathmor gave Esselman a knowing look, almost a leer, and shook his head.

'Patience, my good general,' he said. 'It needs more work. I would not send it out against such a rabble. Its time will come when we are fully revealed at last. Then the whole Empire will see the greatness of my work. Just as they should have done, all that time ago. They were fools then, and they're fools now. We have nothing to fear from any of them.'

Esselman didn't share Rathmor's look of confidence. He squinted his eyes against the pale southern horizon, scanning carefully for any sign of movement.

'You can keep it under wraps for now,' he said, gruffly. 'The lady agrees with you. But if it's needed to break this siege, I'll call on you again. I won't stay cooped up in here forever. A man should take the fight to the enemy when he can.'

Rathmor didn't like the sound of that, and said nothing. He flexed his crooked fingers against the stone balustrade and rocked back on his heels. He seemed ill at ease standing still. His whole body itched for some kind of activity. He cut a nervous, strained figure next to his more assured companion.

'Your impatience will ruin everything,' he muttered. 'We have all we need. Gold, men, the citadel and the support of the lady. I'll say it again. All we need is time. Time to perfect the machines. Hochland has no engineers capable of breaching these walls. They're a race of goatherds and drunkards. Wait a little longer. When all is ready, I will give you your war.'

Rathmor's speech became more excited. He was drifting into a reverie again.

'You will ride into Hergig at the head of an army the likes of which the world has never seen. If you think the weapons I've given you so far are good, wait till you see what's coming from the forges. If I could somehow do without the necessity of flesh to man my creations, I would. That's the only weak link. Otherwise my machines are perfect.'

Esselman recoiled slightly from Rathmor. The two men clearly had different philosophies.

'I sometimes wonder,' he said, slowly, 'why you didn't stay at Nuln. If your genius was so evident, they would surely have made some use of you.'

A look of aversion filled Rathmor's eyes, and he rocked back away from the balcony's edge.

'Everything has its price!' he said, his voice rising in pitch. 'What does it matter that a few men died? That's the price of progress!'

A sneer crept across his womanish lips again.

'They couldn't pay it,' he said. 'We had to leave. Me, and the other one. We both had to leave. All the visionaries did. They're as blind as their masters in Alt-dorf.'

Esselman looked at Rathmor with distaste. The little man was consumed by a sudden vitriol. His hands shook, and spittle flew as he spoke.

'That, my friend, will be the sweetest moment,' Rathmor said. 'Only when the walls of Nuln are besieged with ranks of the infernal machines. Only when the college is wreathed in fire, flames they cannot put out, will I return. Only when they're on their knees, begging for forgiveness and to recognise my genius, will I deign to speak to them again. The dogs. The damned, blighted dogs! Only then will I go back.'

Rathmor's speech had become shrill and repetitious. He shook slightly, and the strange rocking motion started up again. Esselman stepped away from him, looking revolted.

He was about to speak, when a chime sounded deep within the tower behind them. Both men froze. Rathmor's face was already pale. It seemed to lose even more blood in an instant.

'What does she want?' he hissed, looking at the skull-like chamber suspended above them. The light from the stained-glass windows was green and sinister.

'Who knows?' said Esselman, taking a final look down the valley. It remained empty. 'But I'm not going to keep her waiting. You'd better come too.'

The echoing chime sounded again. It was strangely redolent of a child's toy. A glockenspiel, or a clockwork model. And yet its effect on the men was immediate. With a look of extreme reluctance,

Rathmor smoothed his dark clothes over his chest, and steadied his shaking fingers.

'Damn her,' he whispered, looking extremely perturbed.

'Don't let her hear you say that,' replied Esselman. 'Genius or not, you'd better keep that tongue under control.'

Slowly, with reluctant steps, the two men withdrew from the balcony and retreated into the tower behind them. Unseen hands slammed the doors shut. The chill breeze wafted across the vacant platform.

With their passing, no other movement was visible on the spiked battlements. No watchmen patrolled, no scouts rode from the gates, no defenders paced across the bleak courtyards. But from deep below, Rathmor's engines continued their ceaseless grinding. The chains below the high chamber swung in the wind, and the hidden forges burned. Like some nightmare creation suddenly bereft of human controllers, Morgramgar waited for the coming battle, its mysteries hidden for the moment, its depths uncovered, its terrors veiled.

CHAPTER NINE

What limits their powers, these engineering geniuses? I am not sure that anything does, apart from the moral law given us by Sigmar and Verena. If the engineer was allowed to indulge his every speculation without constraint, then the race of man would soon descend into barbarism. There are sketches of machines in the vaults of the college that defy belief. I have been shown them. Unholy amalgamations of human flesh and iron workings. Mixtures of steam technology and the art of the wizard. These things must never be allowed to see the light of day. You have my word that I am a supporter of the new science, but perversion is perversion, wherever it is found, and a matter for the witch hunters.

Elector Emmanuelle von Leibwitz
XVth Report of the Imperial Commission
on the College of Engineers

AT LAST, MORGRAMGAR had come into view. The vanguard climbed the final few yards up a slope of loose scree, and the valley unfolded before them. The citadel was a mere speck of darkness against the distant cliffs. Only as the army marched down the bare valley floor did its true scale become apparent. The fortress was small only in comparison with the gigantic cliffs behind it. An observer on the ground could see its titanic scale well enough.

Scharnhorst maintained his habitual pace, and the road was traversed quickly. The victory against the snipers had restored the spirits of both men and commanders. Half a mile from the enemy ramparts, the general called a halt. The various companies spread out across the plain. All eyes were fixed on the dark, strange edifice before them. Morgramgar was a twisted construction. In the harsh mountain light, it looked almost as if it had been forged from iron rather than built up from stone. There was no sign of movement anywhere near it. The road leading to the gates was silent. The massive entrance was shut. Doors of age-stained wood were enclosed in a frame of black metal. The portal was carved into the shape of a gaping wolf's mouth. Two eyes burned above the lintel with some strange fire. Even in the harsh daylight, the effect was unsettling.

Bugles sounded across the army, signalling the deployment pattern for the siege. State troopers fanned out, led by their captains. The halberdiers, pikemen, swordsmen and mercenaries, by far the largest component of the army, arranged themselves in a long line facing the enemy walls. The knights were deployed in the reserve, far out on the right flank. Their cavalry charges would be little use unless a sortie emerged. Scharnhorst and his retinue took up position on a broken rise, well behind the bulk of the army. The flagellants were deployed in a ragged group on the left flank. They were kept well away from the main soldiery by Scharnhorst, a situation which pleased everyone. As soon as the deployment was complete, the fanatics started their imploring benedictions to Sigmar, and their thin, warbling voices drifted over the empty plain.

Once the last of the carts had been hauled up, Magnus, Hildebrandt and Thorgad began to oversee the unloading of the heavy guns. Most had survived the journey in more or less one piece, but several had suffered damage and needed running repairs. The dwarf seemed to take this personally, and spent his time tutting with disapproval. Herschel and Messina were nowhere to be seen. They had become increasingly a law unto themselves since the last attack.

If anything, Scharnhorst seemed to be encouraging the split in the corps of engineers. Magnus had seen the Tilean ride closely alongside the general's staff on the ascent. It put his teeth on edge, but there was little he could do. In the cold light of day, he was ashamed of his performance. The outburst had been an

177

aberration, even for someone in his weakened state. For so long, he had held out against the lure of drink. His one slip had carried a heavy penalty. The only response was to make amends on the field. He found some comfort in the heavy, repetitive work of deploying the guns and organising the crews. There was much to do before all would be ready, and it was in such situations that the art of the master engineer came into its own.

He was marshalling the unloading of one of the huge iron-belchers, a massive piece with the fanciful name 'Brunhilde' engraved on its iron barrel, when Hildebrandt rode up towards him.

'Why are you here?' the big man said, looking exasperated. 'Scharnhorst's called a council of war.'

Magnus's heart sank. He hadn't even been informed. Messina had replaced him in the general's estimation. Magnus carried on with what he was doing, tightening a series of thick leather straps around the unwieldy machinery to allow it to be lifted down.

'I guess I wasn't required,' he said nonchalantly, concentrating on his work.

Hildebrandt dismounted heavily, and strode up to him.

'Listen to me,' he said, pulling Magnus around to face him. 'This is pathetic. You've given up. Messina's a pushy bastard, but he's half your age. He hasn't served as long as either of us. If you let him walk over you, you'll become a laughing stock.'

Magnus smiled wryly.

'Am I not already?' he said, looking around at the busy gunnery crews. 'The men are whispering behind my back. They think I can't hear them. Perhaps it's best to let the young blood take over.'

Hildebrandt looked disgusted.

'When I knew you of old, you'd never have let things come to this,' he said. 'Mother of Sigmar, Magnus. You've changed. It's humiliating, watching you like this.'

Magnus failed to respond to that. He felt as if all the fight had been beaten out of him. He had returned to the shell of a man he'd been in Hergig. Whatever Grotius had roused in him, it hadn't taken long to die.

'What does it matter?' he said. 'We'll be paid in any case. I'll clear my debts. You can put your children into a trade. Everyone's happy.'

Hildebrandt shook his head.

'Not if that preening fool gets us all killed. He's no idea what he's doing. Scharnhorst is impressed with his rocket trick, but Messina has no idea how to deploy the heavy guns. And if you think the boy Herschel will do any better, you're madder than he is. You need to put a stop to this, Magnus. Morr's blood, man. You're being turned into a fool by your own crew. I never thought I'd live to see it.'

Finally, Magnus felt the sting of shame. Hildebrandt stood before him, his face torn between accusation and pity. That was hard to bear. He could take anything from Tobias, even contempt. But not pity. They had come too far together. Even after his fall from grace, the bond of friendship and respect had never completely severed. It would break his heart to see it snap now.

'Where are they placing the wall-breakers?' asked Magnus. He was too weary for another battle with Messina and Scharnhorst, though he knew it had to come.

'Messina wants them over on that ridge,' said Hildebrandt, pointing to a shallow hillock directly in front of the first ranks of handgunners. 'They'll be close enough to send shot over the lower battlements. He's got some Tilean contraptions. He says they'll kindle fire once they land.'

Magnus frowned.

'That's too close,' he said. 'For all we know, they've got guns on those walls with a greater range than ours. I wouldn't put anything past them.'

Hildebrandt let out another infuriated breath.

'Exactly!' he cried. 'You need to tell Scharnhorst that. Messina's all over him. If the defenders get their own shot amongst our cannons, we'll have hauled them up here for nothing. You're still in command. Put an end to this madness.'

Magnus looked back towards the distant walls of Morgramgar. There wasn't any sign of gunnery on the walls. But that meant nothing. It was already evident that the enemy's artillery commander was highly skilled. It wouldn't be hard to conceal barrels behind those massive walls. The more he looked, the more sure he was that there was something hidden behind the blank, dark facade. Some of the openings below the battlements looked very strange indeed.

'I'll have a word with the general,' said Magnus at last. 'He's got to have forgiven me by now, hasn't he?'

Hildebrandt clapped him on the shoulder.

'I'll oversee the rest of this,' he said. 'Just make sure these pieces get put in the right place.'

SCHARNHORST GAZED AT Magnus with his familiar expression of wary disregard. The general was standing amidst the command retinue in his full ceremonial dress, a brass spyglass clutched in his hand. Kruger, Kossof and the other commanders were with him as always. Towards the rear of the group, Messina lurked, keeping his head down. Magnus had no doubt that he'd been active in talking to Scharnhorst behind his back. For the moment, Ironblood chose to keep his thoughts to himself. After his outburst the previous night, his position was precarious to say the least.

'And what, may I ask, is the point of bringing our big guns all this way, if we can't place them within range of the castle walls?' said Scharnhorst, his tone sarcastic.

Magnus worked hard to keep his voice respectful.

'I'm not sure who advised you to do that, sir,' he said. 'Of course we need to place our artillery pieces in range of the walls. But sending shot high over the battlements will require them to be moved too close. We need to proceed with caution. We've already seen that the enemy possesses handguns far superior to ours. It is reasonable to assume they've prepared heavy artillery too. If we rush into this, we'll lose our advantage.'

Scharnhorst pursed his lips.

'What would you suggest?' he asked.

'Deploy our guns immediately in front of the ranks, with companies of halberdiers on hand to defend them against raids. They won't be able to lob shot right over the battlements from there, but they'll be close enough to blast at the foundations. That's all we need to do. One crack in the walls, and we've got our entrance.'

Kruger turned his aristocratic head towards the citadel. 'I don't know, Ironblood,' the knight said. 'Those walls have been designed to withstand punishment. I think we should be aiming higher. I've seen the effect of fire within a closed space. We'll cause panic. We should aim to make this siege as short as possible. I don't want to be here longer than I have to.'

Magnus stifled some smart remark about needing to head back to the estate to oppress the serfs. No one here knew anything about ballistics. Apart from Messina, that was.

'I could be wrong,' Magnus said, speaking slowly and carefully, trying to stay humble. 'I'm aware we haven't exactly covered ourselves with glory. But I've got a strong feeling about this. We've been drawn up here by them. They wanted us to come to them. If they were worried about us deploying our cannons so close, they'd have tried to frustrate us. But they're waiting. They want to make it look as if we can just walk up and start firing at them. I don't believe it for a second.'

Scharnhorst was listening carefully. Magnus had to give the man his due. He was sceptical, but he was paying attention.

'You asked me to run your gunnery for you, sir,' Magnus said, completing his case. 'That's my advice. Deploy as far back as you can. It'll take time to find our range in any case.'

Scharnhorst rubbed his chin thoughtfully, looking back and forth between the ranks of his own men and the silent walls of the citadel in the distance.

'Messina,' he said, sharply. 'What do you think?'

Silvio came forward. He at least had the decency to look abashed, and didn't meet Magnus's eyes.

'Herr Ironblood is master engineer,' he said, disingenuously. 'His view carries the most weight. With all respect, though, I disagree.'

His shifty eyes flickered around the assembled men nervously. Magnus could guess his predicament. The man's stock had risen after the deployment of the flares. But those around him were officers, to whom the chain of command was near-sacred. Kruger looked at him suspiciously. The Tilean would have to play his hand carefully. Magnus kept silent, waiting to see how things would unfold.

'Those walls are thick. They are designed to take our heavy shot,' said Messina. 'You can see that from here. I've seen stone like that before. The shape of the star makes it strong. If our shot is just hitting the base of walls, we'll be here for weeks. We don't have unlimited cannonballs, and our lines of supply are long.'

For a moment, Silvio's gaze alighted on Magnus. Ironblood stared back at him implacably. Messina's eyes quickly moved back to Scharnhorst.

'We have explosive charges,' he said, quickly. 'Like mortar rounds, but lighter. They're an invention of mine, and I've used them before with success. They're caskets, tied with steel wire and capable of surviving a detonation in the barrel, but full of quick-fire which explodes on hitting. *Fuoco del muerto*. An apt name. Once it is lit, it's hard to douse quickly. If we keep up a volley, we can clear the walls. Maybe even in hours. They'll be so busy running after those fires, you will be able to attack the gates in safety.'

Scharnhorst remained silent, pondering the options. Kossof, standing at the rear of the captains, muttered to himself.

'What does it matter which of these heretics we listen to?' he said under his breath. 'They're both as bad as each other. We should be storming the gates!'

Scharnhorst ignored him. The general looked supremely irritated. Magnus felt an acute sense of shame begin to creep across him. This situation should never have arisen. If he'd been a proper master of his company, Messina would never have been able to undermine him so completely. Now that it had happened, he would just have to wait on the general's decision.

'We'll deploy on the forward ridge, as planned,' said Scharnhorst. His voice had a tone of finality about it that brooked no disagreement. He turned to Magnus. 'This is nothing personal, Ironblood. But I can't see any ordnance on those walls, and the scouts report nothing either. You've been too cautious all through this campaign. If we can get those lower levels on fire, our task will be made that much easier. And if we end up spending weeks up here waiting for the walls to crack, we'll start running low on supplies.'

Magnus felt his heart sink. The final humiliation. His command of his men had been undermined again. He pondered protesting, but then saw the implacable expression on the general's face. The man wasn't going to change his mind.

'I want you to oversee the deployment as soon as those guns are unloaded and prepared,' said Scharnhorst. 'You're the master engineer. Make sure that they can clear the battlements.'

The general turned to Messina.

'Take your orders from Ironblood,' he said, though his voice didn't quite carry the conviction it had earlier. 'He's the superior officer. Remember that.'

The two men bowed, and left the group of commanders together. As they walked down from the retinue, the remaining captains fell into discussion about other aspects of the siege. There was much to organise, and the day was waning fast.

Magnus gave Messina a hard stare. The Tilean said nothing, and had trouble meeting the older man's gaze. It was the first time they'd spoken since Magnus's performance in front of Scharnhorst. As they walked on, there was an uneasy silence.

'Why are you doing this, Messina?' said Magnus at last. His voice was neither accusatory nor whining. He just wanted to know. 'We'd be better working together. You can't hide behind the general forever.'

Messina kept his eyes on the floor.

'I do not know what you're talking about, sir,' he said. 'General Scharnhorst asked for my advice.'

Magnus laughed, a bitter sound with no mirth in it.

'So you're playing that game,' he said. His pained smile left his face. 'Listen, lad. You're young. You know how to fire a pistol, and you're good with the machinery. That's why I hired you. But don't play politics. You may think you can run with Scharnhorst and come away with something extra from this, but you'll burn

185

your fingers. I've served with his sort before. He doesn't think much of me, and that's given you your chance. But overplay your hand, and you'll regret it.'

Messina remained stony-faced.

'Where do you want me starting on these guns?' he said.

Magnus sighed. There were fights he enjoyed, and fights he didn't. This was one he didn't.

'The iron-belchers are ready,' he said, motioning towards Hildebrandt and a gang of gunners. 'I'll look to the lighter ordnance. If I'm right, and I hope I'm not, it's all we'll have left in a few hours anyway.'

BY MID-AFTERNOON, THE guns had been hauled into position. Crews milled around them, piling shot in neat pyramids behind the heavy iron cannons and laying out the rest of their equipment on sheets of leather. The artillery pieces were the largest in the army's arsenal, designed to break down castle walls or send heavy shot hurtling into massed enemy formations. Magnus had seen similar guns in action on many battlefields in the past. Used rightly, they were devastating. Used wrongly, they were expensive, dangerous follies. It all depended on who was in charge.

Each cannon had a crew of up to half a dozen men attached to it. The most important member was the master gunner, responsible for sighting the gun. This was an inexact science, mostly involving ramming wooden wedges under the great wheels to raise the barrel to the required angle. The master gunners had travelled with the same weapon for years, though, and knew all its idiosyncrasies and kinks.

The master was accompanied by a gunnery crew who had responsibility for loading, sponging and firing the mechanism. One man carried the heavy ramrod used to thrust the shot and cartridge of blackpowder deep into the barrel, while another had a stave-mounted sponge of rags covered in wool used to clean the interior after a detonation. There were pails of dirty water next to every piece, needed for when the iron barrel reached dangerous temperatures. During a heated exchange, this could happen with unnerving speed.

When the shot was loaded and rammed, the gun aimed in the right direction and at the right elevation, the gunnery master would step forwards with a lighted wick. The flaming kindling would be dropped into the pan, filled with blackpowder. All being well, the detonation would be immediate. The blackpowder would cause the cartridge within the iron shaft to explode. The cannon would rock back on its wheels, slamming against the back of the chassis and jumping like an animal. With any luck, the crew would have got out of the way in time, cowering behind whatever shelter they had to hand. Gunnery hands soon learned to move quickly.

With a well-bored piece, the shot would be sent high and true, and the cannon would come back to rest on its chassis, ready for reloading. But such was the way of things that the cartridge was perfectly capable of rupturing the shell of iron around it, or blasting the breech out backwards, or shattering the wooden framework beneath, or a dozen other calamitous things. Not for nothing were prayers whispered to Morr every time a great cannon was deployed. They were ferocious devices, but also capricious. If the barrel exploded, the worst of all the things that could happen, then there was little hope for the crew.

To his credit, Messina worked hard on the deployment. Magnus watched him closely. In another situation, he would have agreed with the Tilean's strategy. But this was different. Having been stung once by the range of the handguns, he had a deep-seated feeling that their deployment was ruinously close. Something about the enemy's equipment scared him. The serpentine was part of it. For all Thorgad's words about dwarfish design, there was something familiar about it. Nothing he could put his finger on, just a vague recollection of something from the far past. He took the shard of metal out of his pocket and looked at it again. It winked in the sunlight, looking as innocent as a lady's necklace. Only an engineer would know it for what it was, the trigger that ignited the destructive power of the weapon. It was a piece of exquisite, and dangerous, machinery.

Magnus sighed, and put it away. Messina and Herschel were coming towards him. The Tilean had recovered most of his habitual self-assurance, but the lad from Averland looked uncertain whom to defer to. Ironblood almost felt sorry for him.

'We are in place, sir,' said Messina. 'Will you give the order to fire?'

Magnus looked along the line of cannons. The crews gazed back at him expectantly. The fuses had been lit, and the first volley of Silvio's strange shot had been loaded and rammed. Thorgad and Hildebrandt stood some distance away, looking unconvinced. Neither spoke.

'Very good,' said Magnus, and glanced up at the silent walls of Morgramgar. There was still no movement visible on the high walls. The dark citadel remained entirely silent, entirely still. Only the slight movement of the death's-head standard and the swaying of the strange chains broke the impression of implacable hostility. It was an unnerving construction. The walls looked as smooth and unbroken as ever. If he didn't know that the citadel was swarming with troops deep inside, Magnus might have presumed it had been abandoned.

From several yards away, Scharnhorst stood peering at the ramparts through his spyglass. All other eyes were on the artillery rank.

Magnus pushed that out of his mind, and raised his hand.

'On my mark!' he cried.

The master gunners shuffled to their positions. Magnus could feel his breathing begin to speed up. There was an air of stifled expectation across the whole army. This was what they had come for.

He muttered a brief benediction to Sigmar, then raised his eyes to the walls once more.

'Fire!' he cried.

The wicks fell. Almost immediately, the cartridges in the cannon exploded. In a ragged line, the great guns leapt back on their chassis, and the air was filled with the noxious stench of blackpowder. Messina's ingenious shells were blasted high into the air.

Magnus followed their progress intently, shading his eyes against the white of the sky. The master gunners had done their job well. Only one shell spun off target, smashing into the rock in front of the gates. It exploded messily, spreading an orange carpet of flames across the stony ground. The rest sailed over the tops of the ramparts. They ignited against the dark walls, spreading their deadly cargo across the battlements.

There was a roar of appreciation from the men of the army. Fists were raised. Lines of ink-black smoke began to coil from the citadel's lower levels. Still there was no sign of movement from within.

'Reload!' cried Magnus.

Messina was standing close to him, watching the progress of his inventions with concern. Thorgad and Hildebrandt came closer, each staring intently at the walls.

The gunnery crews worked quickly. Sponges were loaded with cold water and rammed into the smoking barrels of the guns. Men slopped more water over the ironwork, watching anxiously for any signs of overheating. Fresh cartridges of compressed blackpowder were delivered, and hastily thrust back against the breeches. Then more shot was delivered. The men carried Silvio's bundles of death warily, walking slowly across the uneven ground and taking care where they trod. The loads were placed in the cannons, and the crew pressed them against the cartridges gingerly.

Magnus stole a last look at the walls of the citadel. The fires did not seem to be catching. There was some smouldering somewhere behind the towering walls, but not the inferno Messina had promised. He didn't know whether to be pleased by that or not.

He turned his attention back to the row of artillery. They were ready to fire again. One by one, the gunners finished their preparations and looked up at Magnus, waiting for the word.

'Fire!'

Again, only one misfire. One of the cannons recoiled too heavily, spinning on its axle and slewing to the left. A young lad was caught by the rebounding iron. His scream was drowned by the heavy detonation along the line. Fresh shells soared into the air. They were well aimed. All cleared the first line of battlements, and the sound of their explosions cracked across the valley. The men cheered again. More smoke rose.

'Reload!' cried Magnus. 'Get that man out of there!'

Something was wrong. The fire wasn't kindling. Morgramgar remained defiantly unharmed. The fires were being put out as soon as they started. There was still no visible movement on the walls.

The crews worked hard. The man who had taken the brunt of the misfire was dragged back from the ranks. His leg was a mangled mess of blood and tendons. His screams continued, only ebbing as he was pulled away from the vanguard and towards the makeshift apothecary's tent.

Messina was looking worried.

'The lower levels should be now on fire…' he muttered, looking at the walls with suspicion. 'Why isn't it catching?'

Magnus ignored him, and prepared a fresh volley.

'Fire!'

The shells rose up once more. No misfires. All found their target. Briefly, flames licked the flanks of the citadel. Smoke rose. Then it died, extinguished by the ever-present wind. The cheers lost some of their vigour. The troops could see that the volleys were having little effect. Still Morgramgar remained implacable. The standard still hung. The chains still revolved. The silence was unnerving.

Magnus looked over at Scharnhorst. The general gave no sign.

'How many of these things do you have?' Magnus hissed to Messina.

'As many as we have need of,' said Silvio, looking distractedly at the fortress. 'Keep it going! It only takes one to catch.'

Magnus doubted that. It wasn't working. He considered ordering a halt, drawing the cannons back to a safe range. He dismissed the idea. One more round. Scharnhorst would expect him to give the strategy a fair shot.

'Reload!' he shouted, feeling his voice begin to hoarsen.

As he did so, something began to change on the walls of Morgramgar. A sick feeling took hold of him. He knew it. There was machinery there, embedded in the stone. Plumes of steam escaped from the ramparts, billowing into the air and drifting across the battlefield. The red fires in the wolf's eyes burst into a full blaze. The unnatural light in the citadel windows glowed more fiercely. Massive clangs echoed from deep within the fortress. Signals, perhaps. Or maybe the operation of giant machinery.

'Hurry it up!' bellowed Magnus, not liking the look of what was happening at all. The crews rushed to comply. The rest of the army, lined up some distance behind them, had ceased making any noise. They were looking at the walls.

There were resounding booms from the citadel. High up in the outer ramparts, stones suddenly seemed to withdraw and slide to one side. The scrape of wheels against iron was clearly audible. From the gaps in the wall, round muzzles were thrust forward. There were over a dozen of them. They were huge. Sculpted wolf's heads and skulls had been placed over the cannon shafts. From the holes behind them, smoke boiled and ran down the walls, collecting at the base of the citadel. With more grinding, the guns were run out. The largest extended at least six feet over the plain below, hanging precipitously.

Magnus knew at once that they were within the range of such monsters. The guns were a third bigger than his own largest iron-belchers. Not only were their own guns within range, but the rest of the army was as well.

'Get back!' he cried, hoping Scharnhorst would hear him. 'The troops must withdraw!'

The crews around him kept working. They had little choice. There were more ominous rumbles from Morgramgar. There was still no sign of any human activity. The terrible row of wall-mounted cannons seemed to operate as if possessed of a morbid will of its own. Smoke continued to pour from the gaps around the barrels, draping the walls in a curtain of foul-smelling gloom. Echoing booms sounded from within the structure. Whatever had been unleashed was coming to fruition.

'Fire when ready!' yelled Magnus, desperate to get the shot away.

From behind him, he could hear men scrabbling to retreat. The troops weren't stupid. They knew they were in too close. Messina's strategy was unravelling fast.

In a ragged, undisciplined sequence, Ironblood's cannons fired again. Just as before, their deadly cargo hit the target. The flames recoiled from the dark stone as if it were glass, cascading back to earth in rapidly cooling gouts. The plan had failed.

'That's enough!' cried Ironblood. 'Pull back! Get those guns moving!'

It was an impossible task. The cannons took time to move. Even working flat out, there was no hope of getting them all away. The crews complied as best they could, dousing the steaming barrels, kicking the wedges from the wheels, dragging horses over to haul the guns from danger.

Messina's eyes were staring. The man was losing his composure.

'What are you doing?' he hissed. 'We can still make it all work!'

Ironblood gave him a weary look.

'Forget it, Silvio,' he said, curtly. 'I counselled against this from the start. We're exposed. Help me withdraw, or get out of the way.'

Messina hesitated for a moment, clearly torn. But the crews needed no urging. They were working hurriedly, shouting orders to one another, desperately trying to pull back before they were covered in shot.

Magnus stole a look towards Scharnhorst's position. Even the general was pulling back, surrounded by his escort of knights. Only the flagellants were staying put. Their leaders were hurling invective at the citadel, utterly undaunted by the bizarre mechanisms being unveiled before them.

Then, it happened. The entire valley was rocked by a huge row of explosions. Men fell to the ground, covering their ears. The blasts echoed from the rock around them, booming and amplifying. The air was filled with the screaming sound of iron tearing through the air. Magnus fell to the ground immediately.

The shot impacted. It was grape, bags of leather stuffed with twisted fragments of iron and bursting gobbets of blackpowder. When it hit, storms of metal flew through the air, tearing apart anything it passed through. Men screamed, clutching faces and torsos. Blood stained the rocks.

The retreat instantly became a rout. There was no standing up against such a withering volley. The front ranks of the army were sliced apart, their ordered ranks dissolving into ruin instantly.

Magnus got to his feet shakily. If the enemy cannons were as quick-loading as their guns, a second round would be imminent. His palms were sweaty with fear. He should have withdrawn sooner. The signs had been there.

He took a hurried look around him. Some of the cannons had been hitched to their steeds, and were being dragged back. Others had been abandoned. There was no hope of retrieving them. They would be isolated, free for the enemy to pound into scrap at their convenience. Even as he ran from the scene, Magnus's fists balled in frustration. After so much effort, so much time, to lose guns in such a manner was a bitter blow.

The booms rang out from Morgramgar again. The grape fell shorter. They were going for the artillery lines. There were fresh explosions as the shells of the cannons, still hot and steaming from their bombardment, were blasted apart. The acrid stench of burned metal and blackpowder wafted from the ridge, mixed with the sickening aroma of roasted flesh. Not all the crew had got away.

The army continued to withdraw. All across the plain, the bodies of the slow and the unlucky were strewn, twitching weakly or torn apart. Gradually, the range of the defenders' guns was exceeded. Even the flagellants were forced to flee from the scourging grapeshot, screaming curses incoherently as they staggered from danger.

More booms rang out from Morgramgar. The echoing blasts were like nothing Magnus had come across before. Even seasoned warriors cowered under the resounding report. The waves of noise rebounded staggeringly from the valley walls around them.

Magnus stopped running. Like the bulk of the men around him, he knew he was now clear of the enemy guns. He turned, watching the grim evidence of the botched deployment. The abandoned artillery pieces were being turned into worthless shards. As the defenders' cannons found their range, every last item was pounded into the hard ground. The approach to the citadel was turned into a pitted morass of blood and churned earth.

It seemed to go on forever. Even once the army had been driven away, the bombardment continued, ramming home the message of their inadequacy and futility. The surviving troops looked on, horror-struck. Any satisfaction in their minor successes had been entirely erased. The scale of the task now became horribly apparent.

Magnus limped across the ranks of disheartened men to Scharnhorst's retinue. The expressions of the captains were grim. Kossof had been silenced by the thunder of Morgramgar's arsenal. Kruger's face was pale.

Scharnhorst saw Ironblood approach, but said nothing in greeting. He looked shaken by what he had seen. Magnus waited for him to speak. He felt little emotion. Vindication had arrived, but at a terrible price.

'How many pieces did we lose?' Scharnhorst said at last. His voice shook, and this time not from anger.

Magnus took a deep breath.

'By my reckoning, half the big guns,' he said. 'Those we salvaged don't have enough range to hit the walls without being blasted apart. If you want to break this citadel, general, we're going to have to think of something else.'

Scharnhorst pursed his lips, and his gaze passed back to Morgramgar. The guns had fallen silent at last. The fortress returned to its air of horrifying stillness. Smoke idly drifted across the pockmarked battlefield. The moans of the wounded and dying rose weakly into the air. None ventured forth to try and retrieve them. For the time being, the battle was over.

CHAPTER TEN

*Gah! The umgi have never understood warfare.
They think the whole world is flat. Their minds
work in two dimensions. If they had ever defended
holds from grobi and thaggoraki, they would know
that battle may be joined from above and below. I do
not ever expect them to master mechanical flight, for
their minds are weak and limited. But I cannot
understand their aversion to tunnelling. Perhaps
they are afraid. Yes, that must be the explanation.*

Hadrin Yellowbeard
Ironbreaker Champion,
Karak Azgal

THE SUN SET. Scharnhorst withdrew the army back
down the valley, and a guard was set on the approaches

to Morgramgar. Sealing the citadel was easy. There was only one way in and one way out. For as long as the besiegers stayed out of range of the monstrous guns, they were masters of the land around the fortress. Mindful of the possibility of a sortie, Scharnhorst trained his remaining cannons on the land immediately before the gates. Companies of halberdiers and handgunners were rotated regularly, keeping a close watch on the eerily quiet walls.

Quiet they were, but not silent. As the evening darkened into night, men became aware of the low hum emanating from the dark towers. Some even felt the earth drumming under their feet. The series of throbbing vibrations was not always audible. It ebbed and flowed. But when the muffled rhythm made itself known, a sense of dread filtered across the entire army. The noise was unnatural, like massive wheels turning endlessly down in the roots of the mountains. Combined with the strange, glowing lights high in the topmost pinnacle, it was enough to make the hardest hearts quaver. Some openly questioned whether Morgramgar was inhabited by humans at all, or whether some other nightmarish force had taken roost in its angular towers. Few of the soldiers planned to sleep much during the night, whatever their superiors instructed them to do.

Once the wreckage of the initial bombardment had been cleared away, Scharnhorst called a fresh council of war. By the light of huge bonfires, the captains of the army gathered together. The mood was grim. They had been given a lesson in the power of the cannon. Hundreds had been killed by the whirling grapeshot.

Several battalions had lost nearly all their men. The flagellants had been decimated. The largest guns had been
destroyed. What was left was clearly incapable of breaching the walls.

All sat around the fire outside Scharnhorst's tent with
slumped shoulders, speaking little. Tensions between the
various factions within the army had subsided. Now that
the scale of the task before them had been made clear, the
mood for infighting had dissolved.

Eventually, Scharnhorst himself arrived. He had been
touring the defences on the perimeter of the camp.
Despite the long, grim day, he looked as vigorous as ever.
Unlike some of his commanders, his bearing remained
proud and upright. He still wore his ceremonial dress,
and the iron symbol of the Grand Army was displayed
prominently on his breast. All could see that he was angry,
though the rage was buried deep. When he spoke, his
voice was as controlled as ever.

'So,' he said at last. 'We have come through peril and
extremity to this. The enemy is content to remain in the
citadel. We do not have the guns to trouble him. Is there
any way around this?'

Kruger spoke first, as always.

'We don't have the means to break the walls,' he said,
simply. 'Our only option is to starve them out. We do
have the numbers to ensure than none within can escape.'

Scharnhorst shook his head.

'Did you not listen to Grotius's assessment?' he said.
'Morgramgar has its own sources of water which we cannot interfere with. They have stores for months. How will
we keep ourselves supplied? It would be ruinously expensive.'

Kruger looked a little stung.

'We have to show them we're committed to the long haul,' he said. 'A siege will be drawn-out and difficult. But the count has resources. He must raise more money, send more supplies.'

Scharnhorst let slip a thin smile.

'You do not know the count as I do,' he said, 'nor the state of the Hochland gold reserves. We're on our own, at least for now. If all else fails, I will send to Hergig for aid. But don't expect to hear anything more than expressions of regret.'

Kruger stood down, unsatisfied. The warrior priest Kossof spoke next.

'Can we not assault the walls directly?' he said. 'There would be losses, of course. Those unholy guns have already slain many of my men. But the bulk of our infantry is still intact. A sustained charge against the gates would surely force them in. And once we're inside, we can bring our superior numbers to bear at last.'

One of the captains of the halberdiers, a tall, blond man named Dieter Halsbad, shook his head scornfully.

'Haven't you seen those gates?' he said. 'We'd need a heavy ram to break them down. All the time, we'd be under attack from those cannons.'

Kossof snarled at him.

'Of course I've seen them!' he snapped. 'But those cannons are high on the walls. Once we're under their range, we'll have a free hand.'

Kruger shook his head.

'I don't think so,' he said. 'We don't have siege engines. Those walls are too high for grapnels, and they

202

look stronger than many I've seen. If the order's given, then I'll ride with you all the way. But it would be a bloodbath. We aren't equipped to storm that place without a breach from the guns.'

Kossof scowled, thought for a minute, then withdrew, glaring at Ironblood and the engineers. Magnus, who was tired after another long day restoring the surviving guns back to working order, felt his temper rise.

'Don't blame the engineers,' he said, hotly. 'We work with the materials we're given. There are no cannons in all of Hochland capable of matching theirs. Sigmar alone knows how they've come by such machines. If you want more siege engines, then look for them yourself. I'll wager there's nothing between here and Talabheim to match their defences.'

Scharnhorst raised his hand impatiently.

'Enough,' he snapped. 'Arguing will get us nowhere. We have what we have. And I do not intend to go back to Hergig while Morgramgar remains intact. If any of you have any better ideas, now is the time to speak.'

Halsbad spoke up again.

'If we can't assault them directly, nor bring down the walls with cannonfire, can we not get at them from below? What are our engineers for, if they can't undermine the foundations? There are more ways than one to topple a rampart.'

All eyes turned to Magnus.

'You're asking more than you know,' he said. 'That place is built on solid stone. There's not a patch of honest earth in this whole valley. It's all damned granite. But if a weak point could be found, then maybe we could do something. I don't have answers for you now, but I can study the possibilities with my men.'

Scharnhorst looked at him slightly less coldly than usual. Though he would be the last to admit it, the general was no doubt aware that his judgement over the placing of the great cannons had been faulty. Magnus's stock had not exactly risen, but that of his main rival had fallen, leaving them more or less where they had been at the beginning of all this.

'Very well,' said Scharnhorst, curtly. 'We'll adjourn to let the engineers do some work. We'll convene again at dawn. Whatever answers we have then, we'll need to make a decision. I'll not waste my men away on this Sigmar-bereft plain while the margravine mocks us from the comfort of her perfumed boudoir.'

He turned on his heel, and stalked back to his tent. Slowly, and without speaking, the commanders rose and returned to their companies. For once, Kossof had little to say. He seemed to have been taken aback by the slaughter of his followers. The flagellants had been the slowest to pull back, and had suffered terrible losses. The crack of the whip had been savage in penitence since.

As Magnus walked back to the gunnery companies, Hildebrandt came alongside him. His hands were black from working on the guns.

'What did Scharnhorst have to say?' asked the big man, bristling with curiosity.

Magnus shrugged.

'Not much,' he said. 'The man has no ideas. Those Morgramgar guns have surprised everyone. Including me. They're monsters.'

Hildebrandt looked like he was angling for something.

'And have you come up with anything yourself?'

Magnus shook his head.

'Not yet,' he said. 'I played for time. There are some tricks I can remember from the old days. We might be able to do something with the Helstorms. Or a tunnel. I need to think about it.'

Hildebrandt lost his patience.

'You know what I mean, Magnus,' he said. 'The Blutschreiben. You can't keep it hidden any longer. It was designed for a situation like this.'

Magnus looked at Tobias in frank amazement.

'I told you it wasn't to be used,' he said. 'Do you know nothing of me at all? I haven't kept it hidden out of spite. It doesn't work! Let that be an end to it!'

Hildebrandt let out a frustrated breath.

'Then why have you still kept the components, stashed away in those crates of yours? It could be reconstructed in a day. With the barrels of the guns we have left, we have something that would make those great cannons look like ladies' pistols.'

Magnus turned on Hildebrandt, his gaze low and threatening.

'Enough,' he said, his voice flat. 'It will not be used. I won't debate with you. We'll have to find some other way to solve this puzzle.'

Magnus didn't wait for a reply, and stalked off into the darkness. After letting a long, weary sigh escape his lips, Hildebrandt did likewise. His huge shoulders were slumped in resignation.

Only after they were gone did two more figures creep from the shadows.

'Sounds interesting, wouldn't you say?' said Messina coolly.

Herschel gave him a warning look.

'I think we've done enough,' he said, his voice full of worry. 'We're just making things worse.'

Messina glared at him.

'You're in this already, Lukas,' he said, his voice harsh. 'Come with me. I've an idea what they're talking about.'

The Tilean strode confidently off towards the baggage train. Only later, and reluctantly, did Herschel follow him, looking over his shoulder as he went.

WHEN MAGNUS RETURNED to his place in the camp, a fire had already been lit. Sitting next to it was Thorgad. He was smoking again, and rings of vapour were floating gently into the night air.

'Where've you been?' growled Magnus. The dwarf had been missing for some time. His help would have been invaluable when reconstructing the damaged artillery pieces.

'You haven't done well, Ironblood,' said Thorgad bluntly. 'I've not seen a campaign run this badly since my youth. And that was many lives of men ago.'

Magnus scowled. He was in no mood to indulge the dwarf's insufferable arrogance. Despite Thorgad's eagerness to join the company, he had done little enough to justify his place. He was becoming a liability, just like that snake Messina and his lapdog.

'Watch your tongue,' Magnus said sullenly. 'This is not a good time.'

Thorgad snorted. It might have been a laugh. Or perhaps just an expression of contempt.

'There hasn't been a good time since we left Hergig,' he said, his eyes twinkling with malice. He hefted his axe lightly in his left hand. In the firelight, the keen edge sparkled. 'This is Glamrist. As old as that citadel over there. I brought her with me to cleave heads. She's thirsty, but there's no blood to drink. I'm beginning to wonder why I bothered.'

Magnus knew he was being goaded. He was almost too tired to care.

'Then go back,' he muttered. 'You seem to know your way around here.'

'Maybe I will,' Thorgad said. 'But that would be a shame. Because then you'd never find your way into Morgramgar. Which is what I'm here to show you.'

For a moment, Magnus felt his heart leap. So the dwarf knew the way in. But then scepticism rushed back in. If this was some kind of sick joke, then the stunted bastard would feel the force of his bunched fist, and damn the consequences.

'All right,' he said, warily. 'You've got my attention. Now I suppose you're going to tell me the solution's obvious, and only a thick-headed umgi could have missed it.'

Thorgad placed Glamrist down beside him, and beckoned Magnus to come closer.

'You remember that I told you Morgramgar was old,' he said. 'I doubt the humans in there have any idea how old. These mountains have seen many inhabitants come and go, and few remember them all. There are strange places under the earth here. Rock halls, glittering with amethyst. Mighty caves worn by the ever-grinding of unseen rivers. All of them overlooked by your folk. You've never been much interested in what's beneath your noses, always chasing after the next flashy thing on the surface. Just like the elgi, curse them.'

Magnus had to work to conceal his impatience. Like most dwarfs, once Thorgad got going with a story he was hard to rein in.

'The point of this, as you'll have grasped if you had any wit about you, is that if you can't get into a place by going over ground, then you'll have to consider going under it. It's that simple.'

Magnus felt his earlier excitement ebb. The dwarf was proposing nothing he didn't know about. But delving into the solid rock around Morgramgar would take a legion of men, and equipment they didn't have. He felt sarcastic and disappointed.

'So what do you suggest?' he said. 'Start digging from here? We should emerge under the citadel in, say, a few months. Perfect. I can already see the look on Scharnhorst's face when I tell him this.'

Thorgad didn't reply for a few moments. He looked like he was weighing up whether it was worth going on. His face was openly scornful.

'There are times when I can't guess what other men see in you, Ironblood,' he said at last, his voice dripping with irritation. 'Your men have made you look a fool, and you're no closer to finding a way to break the citadel open. If I were you, I'd listen to good advice. I'd say you need as much of it as you can get.'

Magnus felt his temper bubble up within him. Days of setbacks and humiliation had taken their toll. He was near the end of his strength. He could see himself reaching out to knock the smug stunted one from his complacent perch. He hadn't been in a fight since Hergig. Perhaps it would do him some good.

Thorgad must have noticed the murderous look in his eyes. Maybe for the first time in his life, he backed down. Clearly, there were more important things at stake than pride. And, for a dwarf, that said a lot.

'Enough of this,' Thorgad said, shaking his head. 'While we bicker here, time is being wasted.'

He leaned forward, his face now deadly serious.

'You took me on this campaign with nothing but my word,' Thorgad said. 'Never let it be said that a dwarf doesn't know how to repay his debts. Come with me. I'll show you a way to the heart of the citadel.'

Magnus was about to pull back, but something in the dwarf's eyes held his attention. Thorgad was in deadly earnest.

'How do you know this?' said Magnus warily.

'You don't need to know,' replied Thorgad. 'But you're in need of something. I'll take up less than an hour of your time. Can you afford to pass the chance by?'

Magnus thought for a few moments. His body ached. His mind was sluggish with fatigue. A large part of him wanted nothing more than to roll himself up in a blanket and fall into a deep sleep. Thorgad could have been talking rubbish. But, once again, the dwarf's eyes held him. They were deep, set under protruding eyebrows, and caught the glint from the firelight. Thorgad's gaze didn't waver.

'Very well,' said Magnus, half-cursing himself. 'Show me what you're talking about. But it had better be worth seeing.'

Thorgad nodded, and got up laboriously.

'You'll need to come with me now. There's some walking to do. Take a weapon.'

The two of them walked across the camp swiftly. Around them, men were settling down for the night as best they could. It was still bitterly cold, and the harsh terrain offered no respite from the chill. The bonfires burned all across the plain. Above them, in the distance, the unearthly illumination from Morgramgar stained the crisp night air. The towers were black against the black of the night, punctuated only by the shining windows. At the very summit of the central tower, the glowing lime-green glass leered out across the plain like a collection of deathly eyes.

'You're not taking us anywhere close to that, are you?' said Magnus. He was no coward, but the citadel had an unclean, unnatural aspect. Under his feet, he could still detect the constant hum of something working.

Thorgad smiled grimly.

'Close,' he said. 'But not so close that we'll be seen. You asked me where I'd been. Scouting. I need to show you what I've found.'

They crept towards the edge of the camp. When they reached the perimeter, the watch challenged them. Ironblood's face was recognised, as was the dwarf's. They were waved through, though they were watched long after they had passed from the glow of the massed fires and into the dark of the night.

It took Magnus's eyes a moment to adjust to the darkness around them. The stars were out, but the sickle moon threw little light across the barren landscape.

Thorgad went surely and swiftly, but Magnus found himself tripping over every rock on his path.

'Slow down!' he hissed, as the dwarf threatened to leave him far behind.

Thorgad waited for him to catch up, drumming his fingers against Glamrist with impatience.

'How long do you want to be out here?' he said, irritably. 'You've longer legs than me. Use them!'

They carried on walking, Thorgad leading, Ironblood traipsing along behind. From the camp edge, they struck out east towards the nearest valley wall. When they reached it, they turned left and followed the sheer rising cliff for some distance. Morgramgar was ahead of them and to their left, its lights shimmering in the deep dark of the cliff base. They were edging closer, creeping along the extreme right hand of the valley floor. In the dark, the going was slow, but soon the far end of the valley was nearing, and the citadel loomed massively to their left.

'Won't they have watchers on the walls?' said Magnus, looking up in fear. The fortress ramparts were altogether too close.

'They'll struggle to see anything down here,' said Thorgad, looking unconcerned. 'We're just two black specks against the black rock. They'd have to have the eyes of a daemon to see us.'

Magnus found himself wishing Thorgad hadn't used that word. There was something strangely daemonic about Morgramgar. He looked over his shoulder. In the distance, the lights of the camp twinkled. With any luck, any watchers in the citadel would have trained their eyes on that.

'Where are you taking me?' he whispered, feeling altogether too exposed. The unnatural throbbing was stronger the nearer they came to Morgramgar. The mountains themselves seemed to be alive with a faint, repetitive movement.

'We're almost there,' said Thorgad, curtly. 'Stop asking questions, and hurry up.'

They crawled on, heads low, hugging the shadows of the steep rise to their right. The further they went, the closer they came to the mighty cliffs at the very end of the gorge. The spires of Morgramgar were now visible in some detail, their edges sharp against the starlit sky. The citadel gave off an aura of palpable dread. Magnus found his eyes repeatedly drawn to it. He was both repelled and strangely attracted to the cluster of green windows at the summit. In his weariness, it was easy to imagine that the structure was some massive, primordial beast, hunched up against the mountain and staring balefully out at the valley beyond.

Magnus blinked, trying to retain his concentration. He was losing his grip.

Finally, thankfully, Thorgad halted. They were several hundred yards from the right-hand flank of the citadel, wreathed in darkness and hard under the lee of the valley wall.

'Here it is,' said Thorgad.

He was pointing to a deep cleft in the stone to their right. It was hidden on either side by massive outcrops of granite. Perhaps only a dwarf would have noticed it. To the casual eye, it looked just like a thin shadow against the endless screen of stone. But, as he came closer, Magnus could see that the cleft headed swiftly downwards. Just beyond the lip of the entrance, the space rapidly expanded.

Thorgad crept up to the narrow chasm, and stepped inside. There was a spark, and the dwarf held a small lantern above his head.

'You'll need this,' he said, beckoning to Magnus.

Ironblood followed Thorgad into the opening, squeezing through the tight gap and grazing his shoulders against the rough edges. The light of Thorgad's lantern bounced and reflected off a dazzling wall of smooth, dark chinks. The chamber was little higher than a man, and not much wider either, but it ran off into the distance ahead. As far as Magnus could make out, it went steeply down, before veering suddenly left. Beyond that, Thorgad's light didn't penetrate.

'I followed the fissure for some distance,' said Thorgad. 'It runs deep into the mountain root. Further along, there is a vaulted cave. You could house a dozen men there in comfort. The air is pure, and the earth solid. It can't be more than five hundred Imperial yards from there to the foundations of the citadel.'

Magnus looked around him, suddenly seeing the possibilities.

'This rock is like iron,' he said, doubtfully. 'We don't have a team of miners with us. As for me, it's been years since I oversaw anything like this.'

Thorgad snorted derisively.

'What do you need umgi miners for?' he scoffed. 'You have me. And if you have blackpowder for blasting, and axes and hammers for gouging, then you'd be able to delve this stuff. It's not as hard as the bedrock under a Karak, not even close. We would set our young ones on such stone to test their arms.'

For the first time that evening, Magnus's mood had improved sufficiently to appreciate the dwarf's boast. A team of men, working in shifts, could carve a tunnel under the foundations of the citadel. It would be hard work, but he'd seen such things done in sieges before. The fact that the cleft existed made it possible. They could work in secret, and far underground. If done right, the defenders would know nothing of it.

'I take back my earlier words, dwarf,' said Magnus. 'Once a tunnel runs beneath the foundations, every-thing changes. We have charges for detonation. Or perhaps a way could be made for a raid. In either case, we'll be safe from those guns.'

Thorgad frowned.

'Don't get carried away,' he said. 'This is difficult and dangerous work, particularly for you. You won't seize the citadel this way.'

Magnus nodded, his spirits undiminished.

'I know,' he said. 'But it's a start.'

He turned to face the dwarf, the first genuine smile on his face since the discovery of the stricken army in the vale below. At last, there was something for him to begin proper work on. Messina would be kept away from this. He would need a few dozen men, no more. And Scharnhorst would have to hold it secret from the others. It could be done. It just needed planning.

'That's all I need,' said Magnus, his voice quickening with excitement, considering the possibilities. 'A start. My friend, I believe our luck has changed at last.'

CHAPTER ELEVEN

You fear the monsters of Chaos, mortal? Well you should. They will shrive your soul before the altar of their infinite lust. They are powerful, and terrible. But, and here is the root of all forbidden knowledge, even such creatures as these are nothing but the creations of the minds of men. Without our dreams, they are mere phantasms. It is our thought that conjures them into the world of flesh. And so this is the most dangerous lesson of all. There is nothing so perilous in all the world as the unlocked mind of a man. There is no escape from the consequences of our nature. In our unfettered imagination, the very thing that makes us great, lies the seeds of our ruin and damnation. Fear the learned man!

The Proscribed Scrolls, Folio XIV
Mavolion, The Heretic of Framburg

THE EARTH WAS riven by torment. Deep under the mountain, mighty machines toiled. The rock chamber was lit by dozens of braziers, and blood-red light swam across the stone. The space was vast, supported by massive columns. Flames burned in sunken channels scored across the floor. Booming, repetitive drum-rolls echoed through the cavernous emptiness. The voices of men rose in labour. There were hundreds of them, black shapes against the firelight, hammering at anvils, or tending the huge mechanical devices around them.

Every so often, plumes of steam would spurt from some hidden pipe or valve. Pistons revolved slowly in brass sheaths. Metal was beaten against metal. Sparks skittered across the smooth floor. Furnaces roared insatiably, fed by lines of labourers bent double under their loads of wood. The heat was intense, the stench of burning heavy.

Far under the surface of the earth, down in the very bowels of Morgramgar, Anna-Louisa's forces were being armed. Wickedly curved spear-tips cascaded into waiting baskets and were dragged off into the armouries. Swords were drawn from the forges, still shimmering with heat, and plunged into water before being taken to the grinding stones. Iron crossbow bolts were sharpened and hardened, then added to the forest of shafts already fashioned. Deeper within the windowless chamber, more esoteric creations were being crafted. Strange pieces of metalwork were lovingly chipped and polished, then sent down along the lines of workers to be assembled into machines of war. Men pored over gun barrels, trigger mechanisms, blackpowder assemblies and all the other paraphernalia of the gunsmith's art. Master gunners walked up and down the rows of craftsmen, picking up components and staring at them through round eyeglasses. The slightest flaw was noticed, and the piece rejected. Under their exacting tyranny, the surviving pieces were flawless.

Further down into the mountain heart, right down in the very base of the castle's foundations, the armouries were full to overflowing. Anna-Louisa had more arms than she had men to bear them. Such was her policy. When the spring came, and the promise of endless gold spread across the impoverished Empire, then they would come. Mercenaries, state troopers, princes. All would flock to her banner, eager to use the tools of death her funds had created. Secure within the cold walls of her impregnable citadel, with every passing hour her store of deadly artistry grew. Soon there wouldn't be room for all of them, even in her near-boundless storerooms.

Rathmor looked over the scene with satisfaction. He stood on a narrow platform high up in the wall of the chamber. The balcony jutted less than four feet into the smoke-stained air, and an angular rail of iron ran around it. From the vantage point, he could see the rows of men work, the hammers rising and falling in rhythm. The sight enthralled him. At last, after so many years, he had a workshop worthy of his talents. Even Nuln, the centre of the Empire's industrial might, had nothing to compare to this. Nowhere in the lands of men were such weapons created. It was the start of a bright new dawn.

Perhaps this is how it had been in the glory days of the dwarfs, he thought. Maybe the old Karaks had echoed to the synchronised pounding of metal and the roar of fire once. No longer. They were half-empty now, and the oldest forges were cold. Only Rathmor, possessed of long-forgotten knowledge and a mind capable of using it, had grasped what needed to happen. The long years of ridicule were drawing to a close.

'Magnificent,' he breathed, his eyes sweeping across the nightmarish vista. 'Perfection. Excellence. Unmatchable.'

His thoughts were interrupted. From behind him, Rathmor heard the clatter of armoured feet. There was a narrow corridor leading up to the balcony, carved into the raw stone. It was filled with figures. One shadow was intimately familiar to him. Rathmor's heart sank. Esselman had come to monitor progress.

The warrior strode onto the balcony. He looked over the scene with distaste. His retinue stayed back respectfully. Rathmor nodded briefly in greeting. Esselman barely acknowledged his presence.

'You have turned this whole level into a smithy,' he said, coldly. His ivory hair was tinged with red from the fire.

Rathmor sneered.

'I was told to build you an army,' he said. 'You need tools. I merely provide.'

Esselman didn't look convinced. Something about the mighty contraptions of bronze and iron clearly appalled him. In the perpetual gloom, they hissed and pounded like unbound creatures from a nightmare.

'Where are the infernal engines?' he said, peering into the fiery murk below.

'Only one is ready,' said Rathmor. 'It will be many weeks before another can be completed. This is delicate work. We are on the frontiers of knowledge. I can't rush it.'

Esselman snorted.

'We may need them sooner than you think,' he said. 'Have you seen the size of Ludenhof's army? They're biding their time. We should have attacked them in the passes. Now they're encamped before us. We're hemmed in. I don't like it.'

Rathmor laughed, a scraping sound that was swiftly lost amid the pounding below.

'Why so scared?' he said, mockingly. 'It's not like you. There's nothing they can do to us in here. Their pathetic Tilean fire has been doused. It would never have kindled on this stone. Half their cannons have been smashed. The rest are barely capable of denting these walls, let alone break them. Let them starve in the open! After a few weeks of this, the machines will be ready. If they thought our earlier show was pretty, they'll love the encore.'

Esselman's severe face remained impassive.

'Perhaps you're right,' he said, in a tone that gave away his doubt. 'But it's a craven strategy. I'd rather strike now than later. It's been too long since I had a sword in my hand and some natural air in my lungs. Your filth poisons me.'

Rathmor smirked.

'Then petition the lady to let you go outside. I'd love to hear what she'd have to say.'

Esselman couldn't suppress a momentary shudder.

'Your case has been made now,' he said, turning away from the furnaces. 'We'll stay cooped up in here until our leashes have been removed. I'll not try to convince her again.'

Rathmor smiled.

'I'm glad you've seen reason,' he said.

Esselman gave him a dark look.

'I hope you're right about this, Rathmor. This is a fearful risk. Your contraptions are powerful, I'll give you that. But what we're doing hasn't been attempted for a generation. When the rebellion spreads from Hochland, there are mightier powers than Ludenhof to worry about.'

'So there are,' said Rathmor. 'But it can be done. Remember Marienburg. Where is your faith?'

As he spoke, the hammers rained down, the sparks flew. The flames leapt high against the chiselled rock face, and the giant cog wheels turned slowly in the darkness.

'If I had any faith, I wouldn't be doing this,' muttered Esselman. 'And that's what worries me.'

As he turned to face Rathmor again, Esselman towered over the hunched engineer.

'But, to give you your due, you've created all manner of toys down here,' he said. 'I know how deadly they are. And that's why I've come down. I want you to use them to make this place safe. Forget churning out more spikes for the lady. We need to make sure the citadel is secure.'

Rathmor's petulant expression returned.

'What do you mean?' he said. 'What more protection do you want? The walls are twelve feet thick.'

'I've conducted a siege before,' Esselman said. 'A castle is never as strong as your pride makes it. There are always weak links. You've boasted that your weapons are like nothing used before. Prove it to me. Lace this place with them. String your damned firecrackers from every archway in the citadel.'

He leaned over towards Rathmor, and the light of the fires below caught in his eyes.

'If they get in here, I don't want any of them to get out,' he hissed. 'Make this place into the father of all deathtraps. If those walls are breached, I want to hear them burn as they enter.'

A slow smile grew across Rathmor's lips.

'Traps?' he said, and his tongue briefly flickered with relish. 'I see what you mean. Well, a little extra security wouldn't hurt. And it would be a pleasant intellectual diversion.'

Esselman made to withdraw. It looked like he was keen to leave the foundry.

'Diversion or not, you'll do it,' he said. 'Just don't take too long about it. They'll come at us soon. I can feel it in my blood. I've seen the way you use fire. Start on the main tower, and work out. Everything needs to be covered. It may not come to it, but if it does, their flesh will be the fuel. We can't allow them to get this far in. There are secrets in the tower that would damn us all.'

Rathmor bowed his head. When his face rose again, it had a hungry look.

'I'll get right to it, general,' he said. 'It will be a pleasure. A genuine pleasure.'

MAGNUS SQUEEZED HIMSELF down into the tunnel once more. He didn't like working underground. The spaces were too confined. Whenever he descended into

Thorgad's workings, he couldn't forget the layers of stone pressing heavily down on the roof above. It wasn't natural. Not for a man.

Ironblood had never been one for earthworks. Many of his colleagues in Nuln had loved them. Those who had completed their training without being crushed or suffocated had found long and profitable service with the armies of electors, for siegecraft was highly valued. But for Magnus, the joy of his profession was the black-powder lore. That was where the childish excitement of the engineer really lay. He could still remember seeing the first demonstration given to him by his father, more than thirty years ago. Back then he could only watch, wide-eyed, his child's face lit with the sparking of the unnatural candles Augustus Ironblood had placed all around the floor of the forge. Only later had he been allowed to take the work on himself, to exper-iment with fuses, explosive charges and burn-times. That was where the magic was, in the unpredictable, capricious nature of the augmented fire, the plaything and the servant of the gunnery schools. And the danger too, of course.

Magnus pushed forward, past the narrow entrance and into the wider tunnel carved by Thorgad and his team of sappers. The work had been done brilliantly. Under cover of night, men had sneaked materials into the narrow cleft hard against the shadow of the valley wall. They had moved in small groups, taking as little with them as they could each time. All the tools, the gouges, axes and hammers, were kept underground. No wooden frame supported the fragile ceiling of the tunnel. Thorgad had insisted on this. It would be too easy for the enemy to spot large groups of men carrying heavy planks and beams into the rock opening, even at night. Instead, the dwarf had used his race's long knowledge of the bones of the mountains to direct the delving. The tunnel snaked through veins of solid, hard-wearing rock. The process made excavation dangerous and exhausting, but reduced the risk of collapse. Pillars were left standing at regular intervals, shaped into cunning forms by Thorgad himself. These columns carried the weight of the whole earth above. Every time Magnus brushed past them, he made the sign of the comet against his breast.

From the natural opening in the valley's side, the carved corridor ran steadily down into the heart of the mountain root. It didn't take a straight path, but ran unevenly through the most suitable rock. The gaps were just tall enough for a man to walk along, his body bent double. Thorgad stomped up and down the tunnel unhindered, but Magnus had to stoop low, his fingers inches above the floor.

After several days of unforgiving labour, the underground path now reached far under the valley floor, and drew near to the foundations of the citadel at its head. The men worked long through the night, relying on the ever-present hum of the fell machines in the bowels of Morgramgar to drown the noise of their hacking and chipping. Even in the face of solid rock, they used little blasting powder. On the few occasions when the only option was to crack open the rock ahead with a charge, Magnus had arranged for Scharnhorst to launch a volley of fire from the remaining iron-belchers. It was a crude tactic, for the cannons they had left were barely capable of hitting the walls at their current range. For the time being at least, though, it seemed to have worked. There was no sign that any of the defenders knew anything of the tunnelling going on beneath their feet. In fact, there was still no sign of any defenders at all. The citadel remained as chill and impassive as ever.

Magnus pushed himself into an even smaller gap, and felt his breathing grow more rapid. There were torches fixed to the walls of the tunnel. By some art of Thorgad's they burned brightly and with little smoke. But there was no escaping the cloying, deadening impression of being buried far beneath the earth. The air was hot and close. As Magnus neared the head of the workings, he could hear the men cursing. The smell of sweat was heavy. Iron clanged against rock, and the gloom was lit by sparks as well as fire.

'How goes it?' said Magnus, panting heavily and pressing his hands against his thighs. His palms were moist, and his linen shirt clung to him under the leather of his coat.

The dwarf turned from the rock face, and smiled. Thorgad was happiest underground. His mood was rarely as good in the sunlight.

'It goes well!' he growled, his eyes glittering with satisfaction. 'We're nearly through. Now all you have to do is work out what to do when we're in.'

Magnus sank back against the wall, letting his breathing ebb to normal. The tunnel was a hateful place.

'I showed your drawings to Scharnhorst,' he said. 'He's pleased. I think he might be starting to trust us again. That's good.'

Thorgad stomped over and leaned on Glamrist. The dwarf never used the axe to hew stone, but kept it by his side at all times. The ornate blade seemed to be some kind of talisman for him.

'So what did he say?' asked the dwarf.

'He wants the guns taken out,' said Magnus. 'The ones on the ramparts. With them out of the way, he thinks he can unleash Kruger, Kossof and the others on the gates. I told him I thought we could do it. What do you think?'

Thorgad blew out loudly, his scarred cheeks puffing out.

'Grungni's beard, human,' he said, shaking his head. 'How do you propose we do that? I can get into the lower levels, but what are you going to do after that? Storm the place yourself?'

Magnus smiled grimly.

'Not on my own,' he said, dryly. 'We have some tricks up our sleeve. Messina's not the only one with gadgets.'

He reached into his clothes, and withdrew a small metal sphere, studded with rivets and wrapped in a leather strip.

'Know what this is?'

Thorgad eyed the device warily.

'I've seen similar,' he said, distrustfully. 'Some kind of blackpowder weapon?'

Magnus nodded.

'These are charges,' he said. 'My own design. Small enough to fit a dozen on a belt, but nasty enough to clear a room of men. Pull the strap clear, and the wick ignites with a flint. Take care to get far enough away before it goes off, though. They're devastating.'

Magnus grinned, and tossed the ball lightly in his palm.

'These are from my own stash,' he said. 'The last I salvaged. They have a few extra tweaks.'

Thorgad frowned.

'Then stop throwing it around like a fool,' he growled. 'What's your plan?'

Magnus put the sphere away carefully.

'Two dozen men. Six armed with these, the rest with pistols and knives. Any more than that, and we'll need a bigger breach. Come out into the level immediately under the main walls, and we'll fight our way to the guns. We'll lace the lot of them with these bombs, shoving them into the breeches, and then withdraw. By the time they know what's going on, they'll have a brace of exploding barrels to contend with. Then we'll be out of the tunnel and away.'

Magnus sat back, satisfied.

'Scharnhorst liked the idea,' he said. 'He's asked me to pick the men.'

Thorgad glowered.

'That's a damn fool plan, if ever I heard one,' he muttered. 'You've no idea what that place is like inside. For all you know, we'll break into a guardroom stuffed with soldiers. Then your precious bomb-toys will be little use.'

Magnus looked at the dwarf tolerantly. He hadn't expected effusive praise from Thorgad. That wasn't really his way.

'We have old plans of the fortress,' he said. 'Scharnhorst and I looked over them. And you claim to know this citadel too, though Sigmar only knows how. If you can bring us up under the left-hand side of the main gates, we'll come through into one of the store chambers. There won't be guards there. Who'd expect an attack from beneath them? The soldiers will be up on the walls, and in the tower garrisons, and manning the forges. If we move fast, we can hit them hard and get out again. From the store levels, a spiral stair takes us up to the main ramparts. We'll need a bit of luck from there, but those gun platforms are big. We should be able to see them as soon as we're in range.'

Thorgad gave Magnus a sidelong glance.

'Your optimism commends you,' he said. 'But that's if all goes well. You're just as likely to be killed as you emerge, like rabbits from a warren.'

Magnus wasn't in the mood to be deterred. With war, there was always risk.

'They won't know a thing about it,' he said, confidently. 'We'll go in and then get out. Just as they did to us in the mountains. But they've got nowhere to go. Once those guns are out of action, we'll see how cocky they are.'

Thorgad frowned.

'I'll keep digging,' he said. 'If that's really what you want, then I can get you under the gates by dawn tomorrow. I don't like your plan enough to let you go in there alone, though. When the rock's breached, I'll come in with you. Glamrist is aching to cut flesh, and I won't dull its edge on this rock.'

Magnus grinned.

'That's good to hear,' he said, his eyes glinting in the darkness. 'They'll not expect to hear Khazalid, and an extra pair of hands will be useful.'

He turned around clumsily, and made to shuffle back down the tunnel towards the cold night outside.

'Send word when you're nearing completion,' Magnus said. 'I'm heading back to the camp to train up the attack party. Those bombs need some experience to handle.'

Thorgad nodded.

'I'll let you know,' he said, casting a critical eye over the men hammering away at the rock face.

When Magnus had moved back up along the narrow way and was beyond earshot, the dwarf shook his shaggy head.

'Damned fool umgi planning,' he muttered, walking back over to the head of the mine. 'This grudge had better be worth it.'

And then he was at the raw edge of the rock again, directing the work, striding back and forth like a general. Slowly, achingly slowly, hidden in darkness and sheathed in solid granite, the tunnel snaked on towards its destination.

MESSINA PLACED THE papers down on the table with a flourish. There were several sheets. Scharnhorst took his time to leaf through them. Silvio could sense Lukas's agitation from next to him, but paid it no attention. The boy was a sack of nerves.

They were alone with the general in his tent. From outside, Messina could hear the routine noise of the camp. Fires were being laid, weapons sharpened. Raucous cries and insults ran back and forth amongst the men. There was even the sound of an obscene song drifting across from the other side of the sprawling settlement. Messina, though he normally enjoyed such things, was glad that the words were impossible to make out. He doubted that Scharnhorst appreciated the finer points of the tavern singer's art.

Under the thick canvas sheets, the general's tent was as austere as his character. There was a thin roll of fabric laid on the ground against one edge, no doubt for sleeping on. A simple table next to it held a wooden bowl and a pitcher of water. There was a heavy iron-bound chest in one corner, and a simple desk and chair. Messina had seen generals' accommodation before, and most often it was like being in a temporary palace, stuffed with flagons of claret and barrels of fine meats. Scharnhorst, whatever his faults may have been, wasn't one of those gluttons. He slept on the stony floor like the rest of his men. Messina wondered if he even took off his sword belt.

The general sat at the desk, while Messina and Lukas stood before it. Herschel's head scraped the fabric ceiling. Like so many Averlanders, he was too tall for his own good. Scharnhorst took his time, turning the fragile sheets of parchment carefully. Some of them were very old, and flaked away in his hands as he did so.

'I won't pretend I can read all of these plans,' he said, lifting his severe face from the drawings. 'It looks to me like some kind of many-barrelled cannon. With wheels. No doubt you're here to tell me more about it.'

Messina nodded.

'It is a weapon, sir,' he said, 'but not like the ones you've seen deployed. You have heard of the steam tank of da Miragliano? This is a lesser device, though it operates on similar principles. But, if constructed right, has properties all of its own. It has two barrels, linked together and capable of being swivelled and targeted with great accuracy. It needs crew of only one to operate, although there is room for more. The gunner sits in this chair – here – and directs the firing mechanism. Loading of charges is automatic, performed by this hydraulic mechanism. I will not go into all the details, but the system is quite ingenious. The ammunition is fed in here, and the circulatory system channels it straight to the breech. Jams are prevented by means of the steel…'

Scharnhorst held his hand up impatiently.

'I don't need to know how it works, man,' he snapped. 'Just tell me what it can do.'

Messina felt his cheeks go hot. He had to remember than not everyone found the details of gunnery as interesting as he did. Even a first-year engineering student could have grasped how revolutionary the machine on the drawings was. Scharnhorst, however, like most men, had little patience for such things.

'It is battlefield piece,' said Messina, checking his enthusiasm. 'It cannot bring those walls down by itself, but it can bring havoc against enemy troops. The Blutschreiben, as I call it, can fire into massed infantry once every minute. The rate of fire is only matched by its power. The barrels are capable of tearing plate armour as if it were matchwood. With its unique targeting quadrants, it will hit even distant objects square on. Once the proper battle is joined, this machine is the one piece of artillery capable of turning the sea in our favour. Trust me, general. Whatever weapons they have hidden away inside that fortress, it is as nothing compared to this.'

Scharnhorst rubbed his chin absently, looking at the plans with care.

'And you say you can have this assembled soon?' he said.

Messina nodded.

'Very soon,' he said. 'Many of the components are prepared. They just need putting together, basic assembly and linking to the barrels of our cannons. Herschel and I have already identified two of our iron-belchers which we can use to construct the Blutschreiben. It will mean losing them, of course. But when you see the difference this machine will make, I tell you, you will never regret it.'

Scharnhorst looked up from the desk. His piercing eyes fixed on Messina firmly.

'What does your officer, Ironblood, make of this?'

Messina felt his palms quicken with sweat. This was where the deception lay.

'He is in agreement with me,' Messina said, working hard to keep his voice nonchalant. 'He is now fully occupied with the dwarf Thorgad on plans for the siege, and so delegated this task to me. Herschel and myself are quite capable of constructing the device. Once you give order to advance, it will be ready.'

Scharnhorst maintained his steady gaze, and Messina felt a trickle of sweat run down the base of his spine. Lukas's face was white. It had been a mistake to bring him along. The boy would ruin everything.

Eventually, Scharnhorst sighed.

'Listen, I don't care what politics are still brewing between you,' he said. 'If you think I've any interest in trying to sort out feuds within the gunnery companies then you underestimate how busy I am.'

The general rolled the parchment up and handed it back to Messina.

'You have my leave to construct this,' he said. 'If what Ironblood tells me is true, you have at most two days before the citadel is stormed. Make the most of it. If you haven't finished by then, I'll need you to marshal the artillery with the others. Can you do that?'

Messina swallowed. That was hardly any time. There were still aspects of the mechanism he didn't understand. But it was still possible. Everything was possible.

'Of course, sir,' he said, taking the roll of parchment from Scharnhorst's hand. 'So I'll deliver you a weapon the likes of which even your Marshal Helborg wouldn't dream of.'

Scharnhorst didn't look pleased by that. As ever, his expression remained thunderous.

'Get on and do it, then,' he snapped. 'When the time comes, report to my aide-de-camp. You'd better be right about this. You've already failed once. Don't let me down again.'

Messina bowed, and withdrew from the tent. Like a scared child, Herschel followed him, tripping over his feet as he stepped through the canvas opening. They hurried away from the general's quarters.

'I still don't think this is wise!' the boy hissed as they walked. 'You've no idea how to make that thing work.'

Messina rounded on him, jabbing a finger against Lukas's chest.

'Stop your whining!' he growled, his eyes savage. 'You did agree to work with me on this thing. If we get it right, we will walk away from here heroes. The mortars will be forgotten. We will have made our titles. What are you so worried about?'

Lukas looked daunted, but he held his ground. The men lounging around them on the rocks took little notice of the discussion. Arguments broke out all the time across the camp, and were hardly worth remarking on.

'There must have been a reason Ironblood didn't want it used,' Lukas insisted. 'You heard what he said to Hildebrandt. If Scharnhorst tells him...'

Messina laughed scornfully.

'Why would he do that?' he said. 'You heard the man. The sick blood between me and that *ubriacone* is none of his business.'

Messina felt his temper boil, and had to work to quell it. He stopped, took a deep breath, and some of the irritation left his face. There was no use getting angry with Herschel. The lad was just naïve, and he'd be needed to help build the weapon.

'Scharnhorst's no one's fool,' said Messina, more calmly. 'He will be happy to see rivalry between his engineers as long as it doesn't harm his own position. He will not tell Ironblood. And as for the danger, you must learn to live with it. Ours is a dangerous trade, *ragazzo*. Always it has been. If you can't live with that, you would be better off doing something less arduous.'

Lukas looked only half-convinced. There was still indignation in his features.

'Come on, lad,' said Messina, adopting a more fatherly tone. 'This will be good exercise for you. We will together see if we can make sense of Ironblood's plans. If we can't, then we must stop work. What do you say?'

Lukas hesitated, his open face clearly torn. For a moment, his eyes flickered over towards the edge of the valley, where Ironblood toiled under the earth with Thorgad. Then they flicked back to the rolls of parchment. His mind was being made up.

'We'll give it a go,' he said at last, though with no great conviction. 'But if we can't make it safe, we should stop. This is my first battle. I don't want it to be my last.'

Messina felt a wave of relief pass through him. Most likely the Blutschreiben would be mortally dangerous. But from the drawings he could see it would also be murderously powerful. Some gambles were worth taking.

'Of course,' Silvio said, comfortingly, putting an arm around Lukas's shoulder and steering him back towards the artillery lines. 'We'll take it slowly, checking every stage as we go. But remember – we have to keep secret from the others. Ironblood and Thorgad will not be a problem for us, but we'll have to stop that big man Hildebrandt from nosing around. He's too loyal to be brought along. Can you do that?'

Lukas nodded.

'I guess so,' he said.

Together, the two men headed across the camp, through the rows of idle men and towards the artillery pieces clustered at the rear of the army lines. There, Ironblood's stock of chests lay hidden. Once they had contained the plans and parts for the Blutschreiben. Now they held only straw and stones, the locks having been expertly picked and resealed. The prior contents were now in Messina's possession, carefully unpacked and ready for assembly.

With a sudden lurch in his stomach, Messina felt his earlier anxiety transform into excitement. The tools were all there. They just had to be put together correctly. And then the stage would be set for the entrance of the most devastating machinery of death ever to grace the battlefields of the Old World. It would be his name, Silvio Pietro de Taglia Messina, not Ironblood's, etched in the roll of honour in Nuln.

Messina smiled inwardly at the prospect, and felt a glow of pleasure. War could be a dirty business. But at times, just now and then, it was a thing of exquisite beauty.

CHAPTER TWELVE

It grieves my heart that the Church of Sigmar distrusts us so. While we remain divided, our enemies muster beyond the mountains, an everlasting tide of darkness that lusts for nothing more than our destruction. What more could we accomplish together! Perhaps the day will come. If the art of the engineer could be allied to the fervour of the noble warrior priesthood, I fervently believe that no force in all the Old World, not even the hordes of Chaos themselves, would be sufficient to stand against us.

*The Notebooks of
Leonardo da Miragliano*

THE TORCHES BURNED low. The atmosphere was close and stifling. Magnus, Thorgad and Hildebrandt stood with the other men of the raiding party just inside the entrance to the tunnel. There was barely room for all of them. Each could feel the breathing of the others. With the expectation of battle, all hearts beat a little faster.

Night had fallen once more, and Morgramgar was lit by its sinister green light. After driving the men hard for two further days, Thorgad had completed his excavation. Only a thin wall of rock now lay between the hidden workings and the foundations of the citadel beyond. Scharnhorst had given the order to conduct the raid, and now the infiltrators waited nervously, just inside the protective lip of the rock cleft, unwilling to go further. Down the tunnel, the lattice of charges lay.

'How long were those damned fuses?' hissed Magnus to Thorgad.

The dwarf scowled in the darkness.

'Long enough,' he snapped. 'Don't tell me my business.'

Down in the depths, at the rock face, kegs of black-powder had been laid against the remaining rock, and metal spikes had been driven artfully into the stone. Once the kegs went off, the wall of the chamber would collapse. Sigmar willing, it would also blow a hole in the adjacent citadel foundations large enough for them to enter by. If not, then all their work would be undone and the surprise would be lost. As he waited, Magnus couldn't help letting his nerves get the better of him. He knew that once the fighting began he would be fine. It was the hanging around that did for him.

He clutched his torch tightly in his left hand, took a deep breath and tried to calm himself. For some reason, he found himself remembering standing outside the college in Nuln, nearly a lifetime ago. The day before his entrance examination. Was that the last time he'd been as scared? Of course not. He'd been in many battles since. Every one scared him. He was no Helborg. Perhaps that was why he'd been attracted to engineering. You didn't need to be a hero, although there was a kind of bravery to it. The kind that let a man stand next to a lit iron-belcher and hold his ground. Or ram the shot into a long gun when the wind was blowing the powder across the matchcord. Many a knight would have refused such odds. It was a unique profession, and not without honour. So his father had always told him, anyway. Before he'd died.

Wincing, Magnus brought his thoughts back into the present. At his belt, the rows of little blackpowder charges clustered. In his right hand, his naked sword blade glinted from the flames. All the other men were arrayed in a similar way. The plan was simple. Once a way had been blasted in, they would burst into the fortress, find their way as quickly as possible from the deeps up to the gun levels, lay the charges and withdraw. If they did it quickly enough, they might escape with no need for fighting at all. Magnus knew that was unlikely. Morgramgar may have seemed silent and empty from the outside, but the place was stuffed with Anna-Louisa's soldiers. They were bound to run into some of them, even if they were quick. It was a fearful risk. Better than freezing to death out in the open, but still a risk.

From far ahead, deep down in the tunnel, the noise of fizzing suddenly echoed back up. Something was happening.

'Hold your positions,' he said in a low voice, bracing himself against the rock wall.

Around him, men gripped their swords more tightly, or adjusted their torches, or checked the leather straps on their charges for the final time.

When it came, the explosions were strangely muffled. There was a great boom, and the ground shook underneath them. The rock seemed to buckle, and some of the men briefly staggered. Lines of rock particles cascaded from the roof, making the torches flicker and gutter. But Thorgad's mining skills had been superb. The tunnel held.

From ahead of them, a wall of hot air and blackpowder-laced dust rushed upwards. More crashes could be heard rumbling deep within the earth. The dwarf's network of charges was going off, tearing down the remaining stone, blasting its way through the mountain like an animal. Only after several more detonations did the last of the crushing explosions die away. That was it. Now they had to trust to fate.

Magnus looked around his men one last time. In the flickering torchlight, their faces were tight with fear. But there was something else. Eagerness. The wait had been long. Now they needed to release their aggression.

'Remember your orders,' he said simply. He'd never been one for battlefield oration. 'Keep together. Sigmar be with you. Let's go.'

Magnus set off down the tunnel at a loping run, keeping his torch low against the ground and watching out for rubble in his way. The route was tight, and he had to stoop as he went. Behind him, he could hear Hildebrandt's heavy tread and the clatter of Thorgad's iron-shod feet.

They went down the winding corridor quickly, stopping only to squeeze past obstacles where necessary. The air was thick with dust and the stench of blackpowder. Magnus stifled a coughing fit as he went. There was no time to stop and cleanse his lungs. Everything depended on speed.

They arrived at the rock face. The air was hot. The final few yards of standing stone had been utterly destroyed. Thorgad's last chamber, lovingly hewn from the mountain bones, lay in ruins. Part of the ceiling had collapsed, blocking off a large area to their right. The torches had been blown out by the blasts, and the only light was from their own flaming brands. The air was thick with floating dust. It was hard to make anything out. For a terrible moment, Magnus thought that the blast had done nothing but close the end of the tunnel off for good.

Then, he saw it. High up on the left-hand side, there was a gash in the rock. A jagged slope of tortured and broken stone led upwards steeply. At its summit, the uneven surface of the mountain's innards gave way to the regular outline of walls. Thorgad had been right. The explosion had shattered the foundations of a storeroom right at the base of the citadel. The gap was narrow, but just wide enough for a man to slip through. They had their way in. The dwarf had been as good as his word.

'Follow me,' said Magnus, keeping his voice low. The enemy was sure to have been roused by the explosions, but there was no harm in keeping their presence hidden for as long as possible.

Magnus scrambled up the loose pile of rock. It was awkward work. He slipped several times, sending scree down behind him onto the heads of those following. Curses, and the sounds of men losing their footing, followed him up. Some of the rocks were still hot from the blasts, and Magnus felt the savage aftermath of Thorgad's fireworks even through the soles of his boots.

He crested the summit. The hole was dark, and there were no sounds from beyond. There was little time for caution. Magnus thrust his torch through the gap, and took a quick look. He'd emerged into a narrow room, walled with bare stone and piled high with crates of salted provisions. Some had burst open from the force of the blast, and there was a jagged crack in the wall on the far side of the chamber. Flagstones had been pushed upwards, and the footing looked treacherous. There was no sign of any resistance. The plans had been reliable. Either that, or they'd been very lucky.

Magnus pushed his way through the gap, and turned to haul Hildebrandt up. In a few moments, the raiding party had all squeezed into the chamber. From above, Magnus could hear footfalls. A bell was ringing far away, and its chimes resounded through the stone. The alarm had been raised. They only had moments.

'Come,' he said, and ran towards a doorway on the far side of the room. The door had been blown from its hinges and hung to one side. Magnus kicked it away, and burst into the corridor beyond.

There were torches still lit against the walls, and it became easier to see what was happening. The stone inside Morgramgar was dark and smooth, just like the exterior. Despite the noises from above, there was still no sign of any guards. For a moment, Magnus felt his nerve fail. This was too easy. Why weren't there any soldiers?

He pushed such thoughts to the back of his mind. The corridor led away in both directions. At the far end of the left branch, a narrow doorway led to a spiral stair. Just as the map had said it would. Magnus ran towards it, keeping his torch low and his sword raised. Once inside Morgramgar, the noise of the machinery was everywhere, making the walls vibrate with its constant presence. It was oppressive, and jarred his senses. No normal fortress should house such monsters.

The men came on behind him, keeping tightly together. Magnus reached the doorway, and plunged into the dark stairwell beyond. It was narrow and tight. He ran up the steps two at a time, hoping against hope he wouldn't meet a defender on the stairs.

A forlorn hope. He turned a corner, and ran straight into a soldier coming the other way. The endless grinding of the machines had hidden the sounds of his approach. For an instant, Magnus could see the staring eyes of the soldier, white in the darkness. The man fumbled for his sword. With a savage swipe, Magnus slashed across his neck, more by luck than judgement, spraying blood across the stairway. With a gurgled scream, the soldier collapsed, tumbling down at Magnus's feet, clutching at his pumping wound.

Magnus kicked him away with disgust. In the narrow space, he had to clamber over the still-hot body to keep going. Beyond him, the stair opened out into a larger room. He climbed up. Behind him, he could hear the rest of the men shoving the body of the guard unceremoniously down the spiral.

The room at the top of the stairs was large and better lit. The stone was black and as smooth as glass. It had a strange sheen to it. No wonder Messina's baubles had failed to kindle. There was nothing for them to latch on to.

Doorways led off in three directions. There was no sign of any more guards. Despite the rapid ascent, they were still down in the depths of the citadel.

'That one,' said Thorgad, pointing to one of the doors.

Magnus didn't wait to ask him how he knew. With the dwarf at his side, he ran towards the empty doorway. Hildebrandt and the others were hard on his heels. As they reached it, finally more guards emerged. One charged at Thorgad.

'Khazuk!' cried the dwarf, and hurled himself forward. Glamrist glittered as it was swung. Before he'd time to react, the soldier had his legs hewn from under him. He screamed horribly before Thorgad's second swing ended his agony. Magnus thrust his torch into the face of the other, briefly blinding him and sending him staggering back. The engineer stabbed his sword into the man's stomach. When he withdrew it, the blade was slick with blood. The guard slumped, his lips a red froth.

'There'll be more!' cried Magnus. 'Keep going!'

He and Thorgad raced through the doorway and up a second wide flight of stairs. These led to more corridors and more ascents. As they went, there was more sporadic resistance, but it was clear they'd surprised the enemy. The soldiers were disorganised, and came at them in twos and threes. They were all Hochland regular troops, just like the ones who'd attacked them in the mountains, and just as poorly prepared for a close fight.

After helping dispatch a scared-looking patrol of three more startled defenders, Magnus ran around a final corner and found himself in a long, wide gallery. They were making good progress. The company had climbed quickly, and was now well above ground level. There were windows high above them now, carved deep into the walls. From their narrow panes, starlight filtered down into the interior. Deep below, the machines continued to growl ominously.

'There,' said Thorgad, gesturing towards a narrow door. 'That's the way to the gunnery level.'

Magnus rushed over to the door. It was bolted. A heavy iron padlock hung from the latch. He shook the door on its hinges, but it remained fast.

'Stand back,' said Thorgad. Behind them, the rest of the raiding party clustered, looking over their shoulders nervously.

The dwarf swung Glamrist easily round his shoulders, building up momentum. He swung it hard against the bolt. With a flash of sparks, the metal severed cleanly. The door shivered, and swung open.

'Come on!' said Magnus, and plunged into the gap. He could feel his brand begin to flicker. They would not have light forever.

The band of men followed close behind. The door guarded another narrow winding stair, and soon their serried boots were thudding against the stone steps. As he sprinted up them at the head of the party, Magnus turned briefly to Thorgad.

'That's some blade,' he said, breathing heavily. 'Magic?'

Thorgad snorted a laugh.

'Not as you reckon it,' he said. 'Just sharp.'

The stair led out into a long, low chamber. It stretched off into the darkness, its far end hidden in shadow. More starlight filtered in from narrow windows. Magnus suddenly realised they were high on the south-facing walls, the ones that dominated the valley beyond. They'd come further up than he'd thought. They must be just below the level of those terrifying guns. There were no guards around, though the noise of commotion throughout the citadel was growing. They'd be discovered soon.

'Now where?' he said to Thorgad.

The dwarf grinned, and pointed upwards. Magnus followed the gesture, lifting his torch high. About six feet above their heads, massive gantries had been constructed. Mighty beams of steel-bound wood thrust themselves forward. Dimly, Magnus could see the dark barrels of guns laid over them. There were what looked like iron rails, wheels and chains looping below the huge mouths of the guns. Beyond the silent maws of cannons, there were hatches in the walls.

They were standing directly under the gunnery-level platforms.

'Majestic,' breathed Magnus, despite himself. The construction was awesome. To balance cannons that large over such a fragile-seeming mechanism was a truly marvellous feat. No doubt, when some signal was given, the doors in the walls would be opened and the huge weapons slid along the rails. Then the carnage would begin, just as it had done before.

'We don't need to climb up there,' said Hildebrandt, coming up alongside Thorgad. 'Destroy those rails, and the guns will come down sure enough. We can turn this chamber into a firestorm.'

Magnus drew a charge from his belt, and fingered the leather strap. A sudden, strange feeling had come over him. The artistry was too good. He could see the dull glint of hydraulic workings in the tangle of beams and ironwork above. It was a crime to demolish such finery. There were secrets here, secrets worth the lives of many men.

He hesitated. The bell continued to chime from far above. At the base of the stairs, he could hear the clatter of steel against stone. They were coming.

'Spread out!' he barked at the men. 'A charge under each gun, un-primed. Leave the rest in the chamber. Then get out! We'll have some fighting before we're done.'

The men ran down the chamber, torches held aloft, spreading out down the long, eerily silent space. As they went, their tread echoed strangely from the heavy iron frames above. It was an odd sensation, to have so many tons of metalwork hanging over their heads. Soon, if Sigmar so willed, it would be lying in a pile of twisted rubble and wood on the stone floor.

Thorgad, Hildebrandt and Magnus stayed at the near end of the chamber, guarding the entrance. No men came up the stairs. The dark was still their friend, and the soldiers were hunting in the wrong places. But it could only be moments before someone saw the broken doorway.

After just a few moments, the men came back. The charges had been laid, hurled up into the gantries and lodged against the bearings and hauling cables. Now they lay like eggs, nestled in the ironwork.

'Down the stairs!' yelled Magnus. 'Back the way we came! It's time to go.'

As he shouted the orders, he could hear the door being slammed open below. The guards had come at last. Without pausing, Thorgad charged down the steps ahead of the others, Glamrist whirling over his head, shouting curses in Khazalid. Hildebrandt followed close behind, his sword glimmering menacingly.

Magnus hung back, a blackpowder charge cupped in his palm. He unbuckled the remainder of the bombs from his belt, and sent them skittering across the stone floor. With one last regretful look up at the engineering above him, he tore the leather strip from the charge in his hand. The flint caught, and the wick sparked into life. This was the one, the flame that would ignite the rest in a frenzy of immolation.

'Burn well, little destroyer,' he whispered, and hurled it into the darkness above.

Then he turned and fled. From behind, Magnus heard the charge clang off the barrel of a cannon and come to rest somewhere in the gantry. He tore down the steps at the end of the chamber, knowing he had only moments. Before he hit the bottom, the bomb went off. There was a deafening crack, and the stairway behind him filled with flame and light.

That was just the beginning. One by one, the rest of the charges were kindled. Crushing booms blossomed, shaking the stone around them. There was the sound of tortured iron and snapping wood. The guns were falling. There were more explosions, and the acrid stench of blackpowder caught in Magnus's nostrils. Masonry fell down the stairwell after him. He was nearly caught by a heavy piece of stone tumbling down the steps. The blasts continued.

Magnus reached the bottom of the stairs, his breathing heavy and thick with dust. In the confusion, he'd lost his brand. He had his sword, and that proved well. The corridor at the base of the stairs was heaving with men. The citadel's defenders had found them, and now the raiding party was locked in a furious fight to escape.

'Sigmar!' bellowed Magnus. He launched himself into the press of men. His charge knocked a soldier from his feet. Magnus stamped on his neck and plunged his sword into his midriff, ignoring the strangled cry of agony.

Around him, the fighting was vicious. The raiders and citadel guards were locked together, grappling furiously at close quarters. Some had fallen already, though it was hard to make out from which side. Hildebrandt was in the thick of it, wading through the tangled mass like a giant, hammering at the hapless figures around him. Thorgad's voice echoed from the stone walls. The dwarf was clearly busy.

Magnus smashed his pommel into an attacker's face. He followed up quickly, ramming the man against the wall. The soldier had lost his helmet in the fray. His face was full of fear. In the flickering light of the torches, he looked young. Just a boy, like Herschel. Probably his first fight.

Magnus head-butted him savagely, and watched him slide down the wall, blood trickling from his ears. He didn't finish him off. There was little room for sentiment, but he was not quite lost in savagery yet.

He whirled round quickly, sword held high. Hildebrandt and Thorgad had turned the tide, and the fight was ebbing. The few remaining defenders were being driven off. Some of them were being pursued.

'Come back, you dogs!' yelled Magnus. 'Let them go! There'll be more. We need to get out!'

He set off at once, retracing the way the company had come just moments before. From above, the last few remaining charges were going off. A series of thuds shook the ceiling of the corridor, and a long crack snaked across it. The whole section of the citadel was being shaken. It could go down at any moment.

Aware of their plight, the company ran back hard through the network of corridors and stairways. Any resistance they met was swept away like chaff. A feral mood had kindled in Magnus's soul. His breeches were caked in blood. He could almost taste it. As he ran, he could feel his old heart pump powerfully within his breast. There were so few guards. They were going to do it. They were going to get out.

He ran down the last of the spiral stairways before the exit. The storeroom was just ahead, around the corner. Magnus made to cry out, rallying his men for one last dash, but the shout died in his throat. The corridor ahead was blocked with men. Enemy soldiers, standing in ranks of three deep. From behind them, there was the sound of more coming. At the last, they had been caught in a trap. The defenders had found the breach. It had been too good to be true.

Thorgad looked up at Magnus darkly as he loped along, not missing a stride.

'We nearly made it,' he said, dryly.

Magnus didn't stop running. He cast his flaming brand to one side. There was enough light from the wall-torches. He drew a long dagger from his side.

'We'll take some of them with us,' he replied, grimly.

Magnus and Thorgad ran headlong into the waiting rows of guards. The clash of steel echoed from the narrow walls. Hildebrandt was close behind, and he mowed his way into the combat like a harvester. One soldier was lifted from his feet and slammed into the wall. Magnus squared up to his opponent, blocking a hesitant sword thrust with his blade and stabbing back with his dagger. Thorgad was soon at his side, spinning and hacking away with Glamrist.

They were hemmed in. The corridor allowed no more than four men to stand shoulder to shoulder. The guards pressed against them, a wall of steel between them and the way out. When one fell, another took his place. Agonisingly close to the tunnel entrance, Magnus and his men were pushed back. There were too many of them.

With a cry of frustration and rage, Magnus smashed aside the man before him. Too slowly he saw the blade

251

flicker at him from the side. It pierced his flesh, digging deep just below his outstretched arm. Pain flooded across him, and he staggered, his vision cloudy. He had a dim impression of Thorgad at his side, and the blade was withdrawn suddenly. There were shouts and screams all around. In the half-light, it was hard to make out what was going on.

A man leapt over him. It was Hildebrandt. The big man had gone mad with rage. He was swiping wildly in every direction. For a moment, the soldiers were driven back. Magnus looked up, blearily. He could feel the hot blood, his own this time, slick against his side. Thorgad leaned down, his face lined with concern.

'All right?' he said, sharply.

Magnus nodded weakly. He was far from all right. He could feel his blood pumping strongly from the wound.

'I...' he began, but his voice failed him. He slumped further against the cold stone floor.

Even Hildebrandt was now in trouble. Many of the raiding party had now been cut down, and he was isolated. Thorgad sprung up from Magnus's side and raced to join him. Magnus could feel his vision darkening further.

So this was it. For some reason, amid all the carnage, he saw an image of his father loom up before him. It was as if his leonine head was leaning over him, looking at him sternly. That was too much to bear. The old man had always been disappointed in him. Magnus felt a strange kernel of determination harden within. If he was going to die, then it would at least be with a sword in his hand. He fumbled for the blade. Shakily, his head hammering and his hands cold, Magnus hauled himself upright.

The fight was almost over. Hildebrandt was trying desperately to hold three soldiers off at once. Thorgad had been backed into a corner, though it had taken a dozen guards to keep him there. Most of the other raiders were dead, and the few that remained were being butchered.

A guard, rushing to join the attack on the dwarf, suddenly caught sight of Magnus. He looked amazed, and then laughed.

'Not dead yet?' he asked, and walked casually up to him.

Magnus gritted his teeth, and held his sword in front of him as firmly as he could. In what seemed like the distance, there was the sound of fresh cries and shouts of anger. The fight was not quite over.

'Come and get me,' he said weakly.

The soldier laughed. He swung his blade at Magnus with a contemptuous ease. Magnus parried, and his sword was knocked from his numb fingers. It flashed as it bounced across the flagstones. There was a rapid movement, too fast for him to catch. His vision darkened, then cleared again. Everything was spinning.

Fighting the confusion, Magnus looked up. The soldier loomed over him. The engineer worked to keep his eyes open. He clenched his fists, determined not to flinch. But there was no killing blow. The soldier's face suddenly seemed familiar. There was a tattoo, and a bald head, and wild, staring eyes. And there was no sword, but a warhammer. In the flickering torchlight, it took him a few moments to work out who it was.

'Kossof!' he hissed, sliding back down against the wall.

Rough hands grabbed at him, pulling him back up. Magnus had the vague impression of more men running into the narrow corridor. There was a stench of incense, and ritual cries to Holy Sigmar. The flagellants. The place was full of them.

Kossof dragged Magnus from the front line of the fighting, away from the soldier, who lay on the floor, his neck broken. Kossof's own cloak was streaked with blood, and his eyes had a savage light in them. Magnus had to work to keep consciousness. He knew he'd lost a lot of blood. He was losing his grip on his surroundings.

'A bold plan,' said Kossof, pulling the engineer towards the storeroom door. 'But guns are no substitute for steel.'

Gradually, Magnus pieced together what was going on. The flagellants had come up through the tunnel. They had fought their way to his position. He looked over his shoulder. The remains of the raiding party and the flagellants were fighting a rearguard action, gradually withdrawing towards the breach in the foundations. He could still hear Thorgad in the thick of it. There was no sign of Hildebrandt.

'What…' he began, but his mouth was dry and his throat constricted.

Two of Kossof's men came up out of the darkness. The warrior priest handed Magnus to them, and he felt their rough hands prop him up. Kossof turned to head back into the fighting, hefting his warhammer with intent. Before he left, he fixed Magnus with a strange look.

'Perhaps I was wrong about you, Ironblood,' Kossof said. 'You started this. We will finish it. In all events, Sigmar will be honoured.'

Then he was gone, tearing back towards the press of fighting men, wielding his hammer like a scythe.

Magnus could barely see a thing. His vision was cloudy, and his whole side felt numb. He had the vague impression of being dragged into the darkness. The sounds of fighting died away. Around him, he could feel the swish of rough woollen cloaks. There were torches, and the noise of men rushing to and fro. Someone brushed past him, and the wound in his side sent out fresh spears of pain.

Then he was out. The night air was chill. Suddenly, his senses revived. Magnus shook off his helpers, and shivered weakly. He was back at the cleft in the rock, at the head of the tunnel. There were men milling all around. Kruger was there.

He looked up. The vast bulk of Morgramgar loomed up into the night. Its battlements were aflame. Great gouts of crimson fire soared up from the ramparts. Cracks had appeared in the walls. The green lights at the summit burned fiercely. The hum of machines still throbbed against the earth, but they sounded strained and labouring.

'What's happening?' Magnus asked, his voice cracking.

Kruger rushed over to him.

'You've been wounded, Ironblood,' he said, grabbing his arm to shepherd him away from the scene.

Magnus shook him off impatiently.

'Why's Kossof here?' he snapped, feeling the cold air restore his awareness. The pain in his side was crippling.

'He saw your handiwork from the camp,' said Kruger. 'Scharnhorst thought you might need some help getting out.'

All around them, men were being pulled from the tunnel entrance. Deep within the earth, the sounds of fighting continued, resounding outwards from the narrow cleft.

'Come with me,' said Kruger, taking Magnus's good arm again and dragging him from the tunnel.

'Wait!' cried Magnus, struggling weakly against the knight's iron grip. 'Hildebrandt's still in…'

Before he could finish speaking, there was a huge, thudding explosion. A mighty plume of smoke burst from the tunnel entrance, showering the men around with debris. Kruger was knocked from his feet. He dragged Magnus down with him, who fell painfully on his side. The shards of agony returned, and he almost passed out.

Desperately, filled with a terrible fear, Magnus pulled himself onto his hands and knees. The men around him were regaining their feet. The smoke from the tunnel continued to rise. There were further distant booms, and the sound of cascading stone. Magnus looked at the ruined cleft in horror. Whoever had been in the tunnel was surely dead. He felt sudden, fearful tears spike at his eyes.

'So you made it too,' came a familiar voice.

Magnus looked up. Hildebrandt was at his side, cradling a bleeding forearm and looking pale. Beside him, Thorgad was limping, as were several of the survivors from the raiding party.

A combination of relief and surprise washed over Magnus. He staggered to his feet. The pooled tears ran down his cheek. He felt himself becoming faint again. His left side was drenched in blood. Every time he moved he could feel it sticking against his flesh.

'What happened?'

'Kossof,' said Hildebrandt, his voice hollow. 'His men filled the breach. They pushed the guards back. That got us out. I saw him. He was like a man possessed. Then...'

He stopped speaking, and looked at the tunnel.

'They blew it up behind them, Ironblood,' said Thorgad. Even his stoic dwarfish face looked shaken. 'They sealed the breach with their own men, then set off more charges.'

Magnus followed Hildebrandt's horrified gaze. The last of the smoke curled lazily into the night air. The tunnel had become their rescuers' tomb. And they had done it deliberately.

Kruger came over to join them.

'We need to leave,' he said more urgently. 'It's not safe, so close to the citadel.'

Magnus ignored him.

'Of all the unexpected...' he started. 'Kossof.'

He shook his head. The pain was getting worse. He could feel the bleeding start up again. Somehow, it didn't seem to matter.

'Ironblood,' said Kruger again, his voice commanding. 'We need to leave.'

Magnus turned at last to face him. The knight was beginning to annoy him. He was tired, and good men had died. Even men he hadn't thought of as good had died.

But then the last waves of fatigue and pain came crashing down. When the end came, it was sudden.

Magnus fell back to his knees, barely feeling the sharp stone as it dug into his flesh. The whole world seemed to tilt on its axis, and his vision went dark. For a moment, he had the impression of falling, falling wildly, deep into a pit that went on forever. He thought he caught a last glimpse of Kossof's face, set grim against the light of torches, and then it was gone.

Magnus slumped to the ground, and knew no more.

CHAPTER THIRTEEN

What are the origins of the Engineers? None know for sure. It is true that the great Leonardo came from Tilea, as have many of the finest minds in our field. There are numerous others who could lay reasonable claim to founding the new science. But my judgement is that all of these are wide of the mark. There is little under the sun that men have truly created. We have learned our arts of magic from the elves. We have learned our ways of battle from our ancient enemies, the greenskins and the beastmen. If you ask me where the roots of our engineering lie, you must look under the mountains themselves. For the fathers of our art, there can be little doubt, are the dwarfs.

Some Principles of Battlefield Gunnery, as Observed by a Practitioner, Ludwig von Meinkopt

WITH THE COMING of the dawn, the fires on the ramparts had died out. The sun brought a cold, grey light to the dry valley before Morgramgar. The wind, the never-ceasing scourer of the land, continued to blast away at the thin grass and dry rock. The south walls of the citadel were dark and charred. Huge rents had been opened in the parapet. Thick black smoke continued to churn from some of the blasted holes. It drifted heavily from the damaged walls, before dissipating slowly into the pure, high airs of the mountains.

Magnus looked at the scene dispassionately. His side ached horribly. He shifted slightly to one side, and spasms of pain ran through him. He winced, and clutched at the bandages swaddling his ribcage.

'You've been lucky,' said Thorgad, munching on a cold chicken leg. Juice ran down his chin and into his voluminous beard. 'I thought you'd been stuck good.'

Magnus knew the truth of it. When he'd awoken with nothing more than a bad headache and a painful torso, the extent of his luck had become apparent. The apothecaries had done well, for once. He'd lost a lot of blood, but nothing vital had been pierced. If the blade had been just a few inches higher, then things might have been very different.

The engineer was sitting with Hildebrandt and the dwarf on the ground in front of the artillery train, enjoying an improvised breakfast of cold meat and stale bread. Before them, the whole of Scharnhorst's army was aimlessly preparing for the labours of the day ahead. There was little urgency about their movements. One of the great misconceptions about life in the armies of the Empire was that it was filled with constant action. In reality, most of the time was spent in either backbreaking labour or mind-numbing boredom. The moments of extreme danger or glory were rare. None of which made them less overwhelming when they came. And, as danger went, the raid into Morgramgar had been pretty extreme.

Magnus sighed, and chewed gingerly on the last of his bread. Every movement of his jaw seemed to create an echo of dull pain in his ribs.

'If it's luck,' he said, 'it doesn't feel much like it.'

He squinted into the distance. Beyond the ranks of slowly moving men and the half-mile of bleak, windswept valley floor, Morgramgar still lurked. If anything, the pall of smoke hanging over it seemed to amplify the sense of quiet dread that infused the place. After everything, all the bloodshed and explosions, still the citadel made no external sign of life. The battlements were empty. The chamber at the summit of the highest tower continued to glow a lurid green. The fires in the wolf's head over the gate burned. And beneath them, low and at the edge of hearing, the wheels still turned. It was impossible to escape that noise. The machines hidden deep within the vaults still ground and hummed. Their brief foray inside now seemed like a strange and unreal daydream. Even now, Magnus had trouble reconstructing what had happened.

Thorgad followed his gaze for a few moments, then lost interest.

'Gah,' he said, wiping his mouth. 'You're lucky you have me, for a start. You'd never have got in otherwise.'

Hildebrandt looked at Thorgad with disapproval.

'You should watch your mouth,' he said, spitting a knob of gristle onto the ground beside him. 'We did what we set out to do. The guns are silent. And some men didn't come back.'

Thorgad raised a bushy eyebrow, but didn't seem perturbed.

'I didn't say it wasn't a success,' he said. 'It damn well ought to have been, as well. That was a lot of digging, even for me.'

Magnus didn't join in the banter. He felt a conflict of emotions within him. It had been a long time since he'd been as close to death. He could still see the face of the arrogant soldier, his expected executioner. If Kossof had been a few moments later, then the result would have been different. He let a long, slow sigh escape his lungs, and tried to sit back on his hands. With difficulty, he managed it. Perhaps his ribs were knitting back together after all.

Of all the strange things about the assault, the role of the flagellants had been the most perplexing. Like all good folk of the Empire, Magnus had always looked down on them. Crazies, they were called. Morrslieb-touched, Sigmar's idiots, lash-lovers and worse. Kossof had seemed to Magnus just another in a long list of fanatics. To a man of science, the Sigmarites were the ultimate expression of the Empire's barbarism and backwardness. In every college of learning in the Old World, from Nuln to Wulfgard, they were regarded as little better than madmen and criminals.

Perhaps that view would have to change. In all his years as a soldier and engineer, Magnus couldn't remember anything braver. Now many of them lay dead, their bodies buried under the mountain. If any had been taken alive, their fate was probably much worse. Those that had not been part of the desperate rescue, the bulk of the many hundreds in the army, had taken the losses in their stride. They had appointed a new leader, Kossof's deputy, a man with bloodshot eyes called Johann-Mark Leibkopf. The sounds of whipcord and frenzy rose into the cold air of the camp just as they had done the day before. The regular soldiers still looked at the religious contingent with suspicious eyes, but there was less open scorn in their expressions now.

'We should have planned better,' said Magnus, a bitter tone creeping into his voice. 'It was foolish to think we'd get out on our own.'

Hildebrandt looked at Magnus carefully. The big man carried his arm in a sling. Just like Ironblood, he'd been lucky. The wound wasn't deep.

'Don't blame yourself,' Tobias said, his voice rumbling warningly in his barrel chest. 'Scharnhorst made the right decision to send them after us. And you delivered what you promised. The guns are silent.'

'Yes, so you keep saying,' said Magnus.

He found he couldn't stay bitter for long. The taste of fresh air and the knowledge that he'd cheated death once more was as effective a tonic as anything else. He reached down to pick up the iron tankard by his side. There was still a slop or two of small beer in there. He raised it in the direction of the tunnel, and saluted.

'I never thought I'd say it,' Magnus said. 'But thank Sigmar for Kossof and his fanatics. Who knows?

Perhaps they're on the right track with all that holiness. In any case, I'm glad they came along.'

Hildebrandt raised his tankard too, though with less conviction. Thorgad gave them both a contemptuous look, and shook his head. When he saw the dwarf's sour face, Magnus laughed.

The mirth didn't last long. His sides were too painful.

'So, what's next for this glorious campaign?' he said, changing the subject. 'We've bloodied them twice, but we're still no nearer taking the walls. Any news from our esteemed general?'

Hildebrandt tore off a fresh hunk of bread.

'From what I hear, the assault will be soon. Scharnhorst wants another council before letting the army loose. He's worried about how few guns we have. And the experience of being too hasty with the iron-belchers has taught him to take his time. You've got a day or two for your bruises to go down, I reckon.'

Magnus winced. He could already feel his stitches begin to itch.

'Well, if he wants someone to sort out the rocket launchers, he'll have to wait a few hours at least. After last night, I'm not moving, general or not. He'll have to come to me.'

Hildebrandt grinned. Thorgad squinted at him while eating.

'Not very wise, I should think,' the dwarf said. 'You've forgotten about your problem with Messina. He's been hanging around the general for a while now like a penniless harlot. I think Scharnhorst likes the idea of an engineer he can manipulate. You'd better watch your back.'

Magnus snorted bitterly, forgetting again how much it tortured his wounded flank.

'That womanish bastard?' he said. 'I'd forgotten all about him. Frankly, with all that's gone on, I don't really give a damn what he's up to. We've shown General Ironguts what we're made of, and he'll have to pay attention to rank from now on. As for that Tilean pretty-boy, he can hang himself up by his glossy locks and swing in the wind for all I care.'

Hildebrandt looked at Magnus, startled. Then his big face creased into a laugh, and it rolled out into the chill morning air. Even Thorgad was tickled, and his strange, gravelly chuckle joined Tobias's. It proved infectious. In the middle of the camp of war, surrounded by the weapons of death and the cries of the wounded, the three engineers gave up their habitual reserve, and laughed. For a moment, just a fleeting moment, the cares of battle lifted from them.

Magnus joined in, heedless of the pain in his ribs. It was good to feel the layers of care fall from his shoulders for a moment. Soon they would be back again. The assault couldn't be far away. And then all smiles would be banished, perhaps forever.

MESSINA CURSED FLORIDLY. A stream of Tilean expletives, most involving the parentage of the Empire's ruling class, emerged from the wooden framework around him. Lukas looked at him anxiously. This was not going well. The Averlander scratched the back of his neck, and stood away from the carcass of the Blutschreiben. It was still far from complete, and time was running out.

The two men were hidden under one of the larger canvas coverings at the back of the artillery encampment. Messina had hired several of the gunnery crews who had lost their great weapons to act as guards. A few pieces of exotic 'silver' pieces from Luccini had been enough to buy their loyalty. They would only discover the coins were a worthless tin alloy when the campaign was long over.

Under cover, and with a constant guard stationed outside to prevent casual spies, Ironblood's plans, long in the devising, were finally coming to fruition. The design was fiendishly complex. In essence, the Blutschreiben was a massively powerful mobile repeating cannon. It used two standard iron barrels, mounted on an elaborate wooden chassis. The genius of it, though, lay in three particular things.

First, the gunner was mounted on a seat on top of the structure and could direct the firing of the mechanism with consummate ease. A series of ropes, pulleys, brass dials and levers controlled every aspect of the gun's movement and detonations. The complicated and finely wrought gear mechanisms for this had been made by Ironblood himself. Like all the detailed sections of the machine, they had been taken from the great chests and bolted on to the crude wooden frame.

Second, there was an ingenious system for loading ammunition. Unlike the laborious process of sponging, ramming, firing and cleaning required for an ordinary cannon, in the case of the Blutschreiben everything was automatic. The complexity here was quite astounding, and the barrels of the cannons were surrounded with a lattice of greased ropes and linked chains, each with a specific function. Should any part of the system not work as expected, then the whole was liable to collapse. Given the amount of blackpowder contained within the machine's innards, a malfunction was not something the gunner would welcome.

Third, the barrels could be swivelled around on a great brass-lined turret. When the chassis had chugged its way into position, the gunner could dispense with any further movement, and spin his position around in a ninety-degree arc by using the steam-powered controls. A mighty furnace, perilously close to the blackpowder caches, provided the locomotive power for the pistons which drove the targeting. As ever, Ironblood's machinery for delivering such power was monstrously involved. A maze of copper piping sprouted from the rear of the gun platform. Only half of this had been connected thus far, and it already looked like a nest of baby snakes. The rest lay on the floor of the tent, jumbled in a heap where a frustrated Messina had dumped them.

Lukas looked over their handiwork so far, and sighed a weary sigh. He hadn't slept much since Messina had convinced Scharnhorst to let them build the damned thing. While Ironblood had been busy with the tunnelling, it had been relatively easy to keep the construction under wraps. Now that the engineers had returned, it was only a matter of time before they discovered what Messina and he were up to.

Though Lukas didn't know why Ironblood was quite so set against the use of his master weapon, he could take an educated guess. Like all experimental projects, the thing looked horribly dangerous. A standard cannon, with its relatively simple firing mechanism, was liable to blow up at any moment, scarring or killing its crew and showering debris across the battlefield. This monster, which could in theory hurl round after round of heavy ammunition through the air with barely a pause, using only the power of steam and mechanics, was liable to be an absolute nightmare to keep under control. And that was assuming they could put it together remotely correctly. As Messina's frequent cursing testified, that couldn't be relied upon either.

The Tilean emerged from under the chassis looking harassed. His normally glossy locks were matted and tangled. His olive skin was marked by blotches of grease and powder-burns. His fine clothes were ruined.

'How's it going?' asked Lukas, tentatively.

Messina gave him a dark look which spoke volumes.

'Have you deciphered secondary lubricant system yet?' he said by way of reply. His voice was tired and clipped.

Lukas pulled one of the many sheets of parchment from the jumbled pile on the floor. It was scored with notes and hastily scrawled diagrams. Deciphering it was like trying to read elvish. Not impossible for a human, but close to being a lifetime's work.

'I think so,' he said, cautiously. 'When you're finished working on the turret traction, I could attempt to fix it in place. We might be able to get shot-loading working then.'

Messina took a deep breath, and looked back at the half-finished machine. There was hatred in his eyes.

'By Luccina,' he spat, wiping his hands on his expensive clothes. 'If I'd known how complicated the damned thing would be...'

He didn't finish his sentence, but walked over to a low bench by the entrance to the tent. There was a flagon of watered-down wine. He picked it up and took a hefty swig.

'What time is it?' he asked, slumping onto the bench and looking exhausted.

Lukas shrugged.

'Mid-morning, I'd say. We've not got long before Scharnhorst'll want to know if it's ready.'

Messina shot him a poisonous look.

'Really?' he said, sarcastically. 'So that is news to me.'

He took another long swig. When he wiped his mouth, a long trail of some dark, oily substance was left against his cheek. Lukas kept a diplomatic silence.

'Do you think we'll make it?' the boy said, frowning as he looked over the semi-complete structure.

Lukas's moment of doubt seemed to galvanise Messina. He let out a derisive snort, and got up from the bench.

'By all the lawful gods, yes,' he said, putting down the flagon firmly. 'This is our chance, boy. He's had a success, that drunk man, with his tunnelling. We need one of our own. This will be it. When we advance, I will be sitting in that chair, sending death into the ranks of the enemy. There'll be no standing against us. That is all that matters.'

There was a familiar dark fire in his eyes as he spoke. Lukas knew better than to contradict him.

'Then we'd better get back to work,' he said, picking up his tools wearily. They had already been at it for hours. With a dreadful certainty, Lukas knew that the night ahead would be a long one.

* * *

RATHMOR WAS CONSUMED by a cold, malevolent rage. He stalked down the long corridors of the citadel, his black robes fluttering behind him as he went. His guns, his beloved guns, had been destroyed. There was no humiliation greater for an engineer. They should have been safe. They were within the walls. Someone would suffer for it. They would all suffer.

He pushed the door to Esselman's chambers open roughly. A startled guard standing in the antechamber raised his sword briefly in challenge before recognising who it was.

'Sir,' he said, nodding his head in acknowledgement.

Rathmor ignored him and ploughed on into the inner sanctum. There was a pair of metal-lined doors ahead of him. He pushed them both open, and they slammed back against the walls on either side.

Beyond was a large torchlit room. From far above, daylight weakly filtered down from windows high up on the eastern walls. Esselman's room was near the summit of the soaring citadel.

Only two men were in the room. One was Esselman himself. The other was one of the insurgents. A warrior priest. He was tied tightly to a wooden chair with leather straps. His robes were torn and singed. His severe face was bruised and lacerated. Either he'd picked up those wounds in the fighting, or Esselman had not been kind to him.

The captive priest barely seemed to notice Rathmor's entrance. His eyes flickered weakly towards him, then went back to blankly staring into space. He had a strange, resigned expression on his face.

Esselman slammed a fist against the wall in frustration.

'These damned priests!' he spat, and turned away from the captive. He walked over to a side table, and poured a tankard of dark ale. He drank deeply before lifting his head to acknowledge Rathmor.

'What do you want?' he asked.

Rathmor controlled his anger with some difficulty. After all that had happened, to be forced to treat with such insolent fools was almost beyond toleration.

'The lady is furious,' he snapped back. 'She's been tearing her chamber to pieces. Her staff don't dare enter.'

Esselman gave a hollow laugh.

'You think I don't know that?' he said, and a faint sliver of fear entered his words. 'By Sigmar, this is a damned mess.'

'Dare not take his name in vain, heretic,' hissed the priest, defiantly.

Esselman strode over to the bound man and struck him hard in the face. Unable to protect himself, the priest's head cracked sickeningly against the frame of the chair. For a moment, the man's eyes went glassy, and a trickle of blood ran down from the corner of his mouth. He recovered his poise with effort, and fixed a gaze of controlled hatred at Esselman. Even in his current predicament, the priest seemed unbowed.

Esselman cradled his fist in his other hand gingerly, and looked at Rathmor sourly.

'These damned priests,' he said again. 'I hate them. Ask any question you like, and all you get back are platitudes about the coming wrath of the comet. They disgust me.'

Rathmor looked at the priest with renewed interest, and a greedy look passed across his face.

'What do you want to know?' he asked, his mouth twisted into a leer. 'I have special instruments down in the forges. They would soon loosen a reluctant tongue, blessed by Sigmar or not.'

The priest gazed back at him fearlessly, as if daring him to bring on the tools of torture. Esselman regarded Rathmor coldly.

'What do you think I am?' he said, disdainfully. 'I'm a warrior, not a bastard witch hunter. There'll be none of your perversions while I'm in charge of the citadel.'

He rubbed his hands wearily across his face and took another long swig of ale.

'We'd learn nothing much in any case,' Esselman said. 'What's there to find out? That the army is intent on driving us out of here? That we know. There are no secrets in this war. They'll attack the gates soon. We have no guns to repel them. You'll have to trust to force of arms sooner than you would wish, Rathmor.'

The engineer shook his head reluctantly.

'It's still too soon,' he whined, looking at the priest with hatred. He would have loved to have spent some time alone with the wretched man, if for no other reason than to work out his frustration on some unwilling flesh. Esselman's warrior code could be inconvenient and frustrating.

Esselman spat on the ground contemptuously.

'You've run out of time, my friend,' he said. The word 'friend' was intoned coldly. 'She won't stand for it any longer. You've had months to get this army ready. Now we'll see how good it really is.'

Rathmor had to stop himself from bursting into an incoherent rage. It wasn't fair. Things were conspiring against him. Just as always, the ignorant were rushing his work. When it failed, as it always might, he would get the blame.

'You have no idea what's at stake here!' he cried, and spittle flew from his pale lips. 'There are still things I don't understand! The book…'

Then he stopped, as if an invisible hand had clamped itself over his mouth. Esselman looked at him warily.

'What book?' he said.

'Forget about it,' snapped Rathmor. 'That's not important. What is important is getting rid of this army of fools and fanatics.'

He shot an acidic look at the priest as he spoke.

'You know as well as I that the charade of gold will only last so long. We must move on. Von Kleister can keep the men fooled for a month or two, but it won't last. Everything depends on getting the machines together, and taking the fight to Ludenhof. Everything!'

Esselman gazed down at the hunched body of Rathmor with disgust.

'Don't try to tell me my duties,' he said irritably. 'If your precious guns had been less fragile, we wouldn't be in this situation.'

That was almost the final straw. Guarding the gunnery was Esselman's province. It was bad enough that the man's negligence had let a raiding party in to blow them up. To be blamed for their fragility was an insult too far. Rathmor's eyes bulged, and his thin fists clenched. He could feel his rage boiling to a climax. He tried to find the right words, but it was as if his jaw had been clamped shut. The veins on his temples bulged, and sweat broke out across his forehead.

Esselman must have seen the signs. He shook his head in resignation, took a final draught of beer, and some of the belligerence left him.

'Oh, don't get worked up, Rathmor,' he said disgustedly, walking over to the table and replacing the tankard. 'That'll do no one any good.'

Esselman leaned against the stone wall, and looked uninterestedly over towards the bound priest. Slowly, painfully, Rathmor suppressed his anger. One day, when he was at the head of a reformed New College of Engineers, his wrath would be feared across the entire Old World. He would be able to lash out, unrestrained, whenever the mood fell on him. For now, though, he needed men like Esselman. For now.

'We have things to do,' Esselman said, curtly. 'I don't care what the dangers are, we need your infernal machine. Now. And I want your traps laid, just as we agreed. If they'd been in place earlier, that little raiding party wouldn't have got far. You promised to turn the lower levels into a firestorm.'

Rathmor shivered with anger, but kept control of himself. Just.

'The machine will be ready,' he said, his voice shaking slightly. 'When they attack the gates, I'll let it loose. And fear not for the traps. If they breach the walls a second time, none of them will get out alive.'

Esselman seemed satisfied with Rathmor's vehemence.

'Good,' he said. He turned back to the warrior priest, who had been listening in silence, his eyes alert and his expression intent.

'Did you hear that, you damned zealot?' Esselman asked, a grim smile on his lips. 'I should have you killed. But I might just let you stay alive long enough to see your comrades burn. It'll be a fitting end to your doomed campaign.'

Esselman loomed over the warrior priest, his fists bunched. It looked like he might strike the man again, either out of spite or from simple frustration.

But then, a chime sounded. Just as before, the child-like noise echoed down the corridors. Both men froze instantly. Rathmor forgot his bubbling anger, and looked at Esselman, wide-eyed.

'What do you think she wants now?' he hissed.

Esselman swallowed, and looked suddenly uncomfortable.

'No idea,' he said, his voice quavering slightly. 'But we'd better not keep her waiting.'

The chime sounded again, quiet but insistent. Esselman looked at the priest sourly.

'We'll continue this conversation another time,' he said, and turned on his heel. He left the chamber, and Rathmor scuttled along at his heels. They were like curs summoned by their mistress. The door opened and closed with a slam. Their footfalls echoed through the antechamber and out into the corridor beyond. Then they were gone. With their absence, the room fell into silence.

Seemingly forgotten, the warrior priest Kossof sat as immobile as a graven image. Despite his ordeal, his body remained upright and his eyes glittered with a keen light. In the dark and the quiet, his lips began to move soundlessly.

'Vengeance,' he breathed, lips curling into a smile. 'Vengeance.'

THE SUN SANK towards the western horizon. The peaks began to cast their long, jagged shadows over the valley floor. Despite being wrapped in layers of clothing and encased in his long leather coat, Magnus was cold. His wound ached dully. The thirst had returned and every movement provoked a fresh spike of pain. It made him irritable and easy to anger. After the euphoria of the attack, the campaign, the lull before the storm. Though he could see the benefit of planning properly, he was itching to get back into the thick of things. The men were tired, driven into a sullen sluggishness by the endless cold, the moaning of the wind and that terrible, maddening throbbing that seemed to shake the very earth under their feet.

He wrapped his arms about himself, and stamped to try and generate some circulation. Perhaps he was still short on blood. He stalked off to find some more meat and drink. As he walked towards one of the provision wagons, he met Hildebrandt coming the other way.

'How are you feeling?' asked the big man.

'Not too bad,' Magnus replied. 'I've had worse.'

Hildebrandt looked preoccupied.

'Do you have some time to spare?' he asked, looking around him.

'Bags of it,' he replied. 'We're not doing anything until dawn.'

'Then come with me.'

Magnus followed Hildebrandt to the shadow of a row of artillery wagons, each still covered with canvas and kept under tight wraps. When they were out of sight of most of the soldiers, Hildebrandt took a bundle of rags from under his cloak and unwrapped it. Inside there were pieces of metal. They glinted weakly in the failing light.

'Recognise these?' said Hildebrandt, turning the fabric over and letting the pieces clink against one another.

Magnus took one and held it up, peering at the shard of steel intently.

'They're gunnery pieces,' he said, looking at it with expert eyes. 'Where did you get them?'

'One of the guards in the citadel had a pistol,' said Hildebrandt. 'I had time to take it with me when we left. I've been taking it apart.'

Magnus drew his eyeglass out, and studied the component carefully.

'Just like before,' he said, thoughtfully. 'This is good quality. Better than I've seen in a long while.'

Hildebrandt handed him some more. They were all of the same standard.

'What else do you see?' he asked.

Magnus pursed his lips. He handed the pieces back.

'They're dwarfish,' he said.

Hildebrandt nodded.

'Just like the one we found in the passes. They're all the same. We've got to face the truth, Magnus. These men are being armed by dwarfs.'

Magnus frowned, and took another look.

'I'm not sure,' he said. 'Thorgad thought they were dwarfish too, but only in origin. We don't know where these were made.'

Hildebrandt lowered his voice.

'Why's the dwarf here, Magnus?' he said. 'Something's going on in that fortress that he knows about. If his kind are arming our enemies, how do we know we can trust him?'

Magnus let slip a cold smile.

'If you fancy trying to prise the truth from him, you're welcome to try,' he said. 'I'll leave you to it, though. Thorgad's got no explaining to do to me. He's just one of the crew. And without him, we'd never have got inside the citadel.'

Hildebrandt looked unconvinced.

'He's got his own plans here, and you know it. It's no good. There's some secret about the weaponry in there, and he knows things he's not telling. We could be better prepared. I don't want to lead men into a bloodbath like we had in the passes. You should press him for what he knows.'

Magnus felt the smile leave his lips. He was loath to look into a man's secrets. He had plenty of his own. Sometimes he wondered if they were all that he did have.

'He'll tell me nothing. You know that. If I anger him, he'll leave. And then we'll never find out what reason he has for being here.'

Hildebrandt collected the pieces together, and wrapped them carefully up once more.

'So be it,' he said, looking disappointed. 'I can't force you. But I'm keeping my eyes open around him. Messina may be a rat, but at least he's a stupid one. There's something about Thorgad, though. I hope you don't live to regret not finding out what it is.'

Magnus placed a hand on his old friend's shoulder.

'We're nearly there, Tobias,' he said. 'They don't have the men to withstand a full assault. It won't be long before we're picking up our bag of gold and heading back to Hergig.'

Hildebrandt didn't smile. An unfamiliar look played out on his large, open face.

'Don't try to reassure me, Magnus,' he said. 'I've been in too many campaigns for that. There's something wrong with that place. Their equipment's too good. They have machines. Even the troopers can hear them working. I fear for you if you enter there. I fear for all of us.'

Magnus let his hand drop. Hildebrandt stowed the metalwork back under his cloak. Without saying anything more, he walked off into the gathering dusk.

Magnus watched him go. Then his eyes flicked up to the mighty citadel, still silent, still lit by the series of unearthly lights. The clouds of smoke had dissipated, and now it lurked like a shadow at the base of the distant cliffs. Hildebrandt was right. There was something unnatural about it. They would assault it soon. More men would die, just to satisfy the ambition of a distant count who barely left his summer palace. Such was the way of the Empire.

He sighed, and turned away.

CHAPTER FOURTEEN

Why are men so afraid of the power of artillery?
Because every state trooper knows that one day all
warfare will be conducted behind the barrel of a
gun. In the future, the sword and the spear will
disappear from our battlefields, and the ranks of
gunners will take their place. It matters not how
many nobles complain of this, nor how many witch
hunters confiscate our untried machines and
devices. Our day will come. History demands it.

Attributed to Frau Meikle
of Waldenhof

THE DAY DAWNED chill and grey, like all days in the high
peaks. During the night, high clouds had been driven
south, and now the sky was as clear and white as a

pearl. There was an ominous cracking from the far heights, as if mighty sheets of ice were grinding past one another. Down in the valley where the army still camped, the stones were as hard and pale as bone. It was a harsh place.

Though the sun brought little warmth, it did give light. As the first rays crept over the eastern line of mountain edges, trumpets were sounded by Scharnhorst's heralds. The time had come. Sergeants and captains sprung from their hard beds on the stone, and rushed to don their equipment. Soldiers were kicked from sleep. Cold fires were stoked into life, and pails of icy water were rushed from the stores. Reveille had arrived, and food was delivered swiftly to hungry mouths. The slop and meat stew had been made marginally thicker than usual. The men would need their energy for the fight, and even the flint-eyed, penny-pinching cooks knew it.

Magnus roused himself with difficulty. His wound had been plaguing him through the night, and his sleep had been fitful. For some reason, he had dreamed of his father again. The White Wolf of Nuln. For so many years that name had been both a blessing and a curse. A blessing, as it had got him into the college and secured his future in the trade. A curse, as he could never hope to live up to the mighty reputation. Even in death, the magisterial figure of Augustus haunted him. There was no escape, either at the bottom of a keg of beer, nor back on the hard road to war.

Magnus shook his head to clear it, and ran his fingers over his heavily stubbled chin. No time to shave. Things were moving. He pulled himself from the ground, wincing as his ribs creaked and the cold morning air flooded under the blanket. He reached for his overcoat with trembling hands, and wrapped himself in it. The mountains were hateful, and no place for honest men.

All around him, machinery of war was being pulled forward. The time for the great cannons had passed. Now the instruments of choice were the rocket-launchers, the volley guns and the other deadly tools of the battlefield engineer. Stomping to restore his circulation, Magnus walked over to the first wave of guns. The crews were pulling the covers from their pieces and dusting the fragile firing mechanisms down. When they saw him coming, they stood to attention and saluted. Magnus grinned wryly. Since the successful demolition of Morgramgar's heavy guns, his stock had clearly risen with the men.

'What do you call her?' he said, stopping by a Helblaster and its crew.

'Murderous Margrita,' came the reply, without a trace of irony. Crews often gave their artillery pieces names, and always those of women. For the men who knew they could lose a limb to the whims of their devices, it seemed appropriate.

'Very good,' said Magnus, casting his eye quickly over the machine. Helblasters were equipped with nine ironbound barrels. The top three fired in unison. Once the shot was clear, the whole edifice could be rotated on a central axis, bringing a fully loaded trio of barrels to play in an instant. In all, nine shots could be released before the contraption had to be reloaded. Magnus had seen them used many times in many campaigns. They were devastating, capable of cutting down entire ranks of oncoming enemy troops. When they worked, that was. Like all complex pieces, the mechanism had its flaws. Even the slightest misalignment could ignite the blackpowder charges too early. An exploding Helblaster was one of the most spectacular sights on the battlefield. Anyone within twelve yards of it would be lucky to escape with just his legs missing.

'Murderous Margrita' looked in good condition. Several days in the mountains had not obviously done anything to dent her martial prowess. The bindings looked secure, the breeches were clean and well-oiled and the wooden chassis was neatly painted. The wheels and axle were solid, and the ornate triggers gleamed proudly in the weak light.

'You should be proud of her,' said Magnus, with approval. 'Keep with the others, though. A massed rank of firing does more damage than a dozen individual volleys.'

The crew nodded respectfully, even the old master gunner. He looked like a veteran of the capricious ways of gunnery, with several fingers missing and a wooden pole in place of his right leg. When he smiled, Magnus noted that there were only two teeth left in his head and his nose had been badly broken. He shouldn't have peered into the breech, then.

Magnus kept walking, observing with some pleasure the efficiency with which the guns were being broken out and rolled into position. Things had come a long way since the store yards of Hergig. The men had been drilled hard, and they'd learned much on the job.

There was no greater tutor than the fear of death and dishonour. Every element of his command, from the ranks of the handgunners to the thunderous power of the heavy iron, was in better shape than when he'd found it. From what he'd seen of the enemy's capabilities, that was no bad thing.

Next in line was a slightly off-kilter looking Helstorm battery. These things were Magnus's pet hates. All knew that the design was an inferior copy of a template from the far-off East. Unlike the Helblaster, which was dangerous enough, the Helstorm had almost nothing to protect the crew should something go wrong. Like most examples of its kind, the Helstorm in front of him had a complement of nine rockets arranged on a fragile-looking frame. In theory, each could be fired independently. In practice, the fuses were so close together that several would often be unleashed at once. Given that the rockets were placed in different positions, this resulted in unpredictable behaviour. Magnus had seen volleys of rockets plough into the rear of lines of allied troops, causing huge bloodshed and confusion. He had also seen Helstorms literally launch themselves into the air when a rocket got jammed, taking their crew with them and hurling them across the battlefield. When Magnus saw a Helstorm, he had some sympathy for the ordinary soldier's dislike of war machines. They were devastating, in every sense.

Magnus looked at the example in front of him warily.

'Name?' he said, but without much enthusiasm.

'We haven't got one yet, sir,' replied a cheery-looking youth. The other members of the crew hung back. The master gunner wore an eye-patch. Never a good thing to see from the man responsible for aiming the thing. 'She's a new-build. Just out of the smithy in Hergig. We'll see how it goes, and name her when we learn her character.'

Magnus raised an eyebrow.

'This hasn't been fired?'

The crew looked sheepish, and said nothing. Magnus sighed, and looked at the mechanism. It all looked in order, but you could never be sure.

'Keep to the right flank,' said Magnus, sharply. 'Take double care over everything you do. If I see one of these rockets go into our own troops, I'll have you strapped to her yourself and fired into the ground.'

Without waiting for a reply, he stalked off further along the line. From behind him, there was a nervous muttering. There were a dozen or so more pieces all told, plus some mortars and the lines of handgunners. It was a good complement for an army of their size. More than enough to trouble whatever was in the citadel, certainly.

The light was growing rapidly, and around them the army was moving into position for attack. His inspection complete, Magnus called out down the line.

'All right, men!' he cried, standing on a shallow ledge overlooking the land in front of the fortress gates. 'You had your training. You know the plans. Keep disciplined, and keep together. We know the enemy has some tricks, but we've shown they can be beaten. Cover the infantry when they advance, and for the sake of Sigmar don't fire on our own people. Only advance when you get your orders. Good luck, and Sigmar be with you.'

It wasn't a very inspiring speech. There were a few half-hearted cheers from some of the younger crews. Most of the rest just got on with things, harnessing the horses and pulling their war machines into position.

'They're shaky-looking machines,' came a familiar voice next to Magnus. Thorgad stood next to him, looking disapprovingly at the devices.

'Glad you could join us,' said Magnus, dryly. 'This isn't really your sort of work.'

Thorgad shook his head.

'Agreed. I'll be happier when I've got flesh to cleave. But there's a place for blackpowder. I reckon you'll need it.'

Magnus looked up over the battlefield. Morgramgar stood on the far side of the wide open space, as dark and inscrutable as ever. The death's-head standard moved slightly in the breeze. The humming was still there, but it seemed reduced in volume. Whatever dark purpose the machines had been put to was clearly achieved. They knew battle was coming. On the tall ramparts, there was a telltale glint of steel. At last, there were sentries visible. Things were coming to a head.

'Have you seen Hildebrandt?' asked Magnus. 'We'll need him.'

Thorgad shook his head.

'He'll be along. But you should be more worried about your rival, Messina.'

A sudden feeling of uneasiness made Magnus pause. He'd almost forgotten about the wayward Tilean. The tunnelling had taken up so much time and energy that Messina's actions had seemed almost inconsequential.

'What do you mean?'

Thorgad shook his head dismissively.

'Too late to do anything about it now,' he said, looking over towards Scharnhorst's command retinue. 'Human business is none of my concern anyway. I think the signal's about to be given.'

As the dwarf finished talking, there was a loud blare of trumpets from the heralds. Riders broke from the cover of high ground, and began delivering sealed orders to the various captains arranged across the open ground.

From his vantage point at the rear of the entire deployment, Magnus had a good view of the preparation. Men were hurriedly taking their positions, rushing to form lines and complete detachments. Slowly, with some confusion and much yelling of orders from harassed sergeants, the familiar patchwork of an Imperial army began to take shape. Scharnhorst's forces were strung out in a long line facing Morgramgar's south-facing walls. On the left flank, the flagellants clustered. Heedless of orders, they feverishly banged drums and blew horns, chanting the name of Sigmar over and over. They had passed into their strange battlefield trance. Magnus had seen it before. They would be almost impervious to wounds once they were unleashed.

On the right of the flagellants were the first companies of halberdiers and pikemen. They were mostly composed of mercenary companies, and wore a variety of colours. Aside from the flagellants, they were the least orderly of the army's detachments, and Magnus could make out officers moving between them, trying to knock them into shape.

Beyond them, at the centre of the assault, were the Knights of the Iron Sceptre. Kruger was visible at their head, mounted on his giant sable charger. In their spotless armour and perfect formation, they were a formidable company, the iron heart of the entire army. On their right, the Hochland companies of halberdiers and handgunners had been arranged. They were kitted out in the red and green of their state, and stood silently in neat regiments. Unlike the flagellants, they made little noise. Most of them knew they would soon be fighting their countrymen, and there was little stomach for the forthcoming slaughter. Their commanders marched among them, trying to drum up some aggression. Magnus watched the spectacle grimly. When the blood started flowing, then they would remember how to kill.

On the extreme right flank of the army were the shorter-range artillery pieces, the Helstorms and the Helblasters. They were protected by a sullen-looking company of state troopers. Standing in front of a row of those monsters couldn't have been a popular assignment. Behind them on slightly higher ground were placed the long-range guns, the mortars and the surviving cannons. Their crews were still busy with the final adjustments to their range. All were pointed at the gates. With the removal of covering fire from the walls, they were now perfectly capable of hitting them. Once they were down, the charge would be ordered. For now, all eyes were on the guns.

Magnus looked back towards the centre of the deployment. As before, Scharnhorst stood on a low mound just behind the main companies of Hochland troops. He was peering through a spyglass, looking intently at the enemy fortifications before giving the orders to commence battle. Around him, his commanders shouted orders, which were quickly relayed down the lines. There were only three reserve companies held back. When the time came, the general clearly wanted a swift kill.

'Here he comes,' said Thorgad, motioning down the slope.

Hildebrandt was walking up to meet them, red in the face.

'Where have you been?' asked Magnus. 'This is about to begin.'

The big man looked worried.

'Your chests,' he said. 'They've been tampered with. The Blutschreiben components. They've been taken.'

Magnus felt as if the earth had been knocked from under his feet. He stared back at Hildebrandt stupidly for a moment, taking in the news slowly.

'How do you–' he began.

'I went to the wagon to retrieve the last of the ammunition for the big guns. We were unloading crates when a chest of yours was knocked from its place. The lock broke. There's nothing but straw in there.'

Magnus's incredulity turned quickly into rage.

'So that's what he's been doing!' he cried, his fists balling in impotent fury. 'The little bastard! He has no idea what he's doing. It doesn't work! If he tries to use it–'

His tirade was broken by a fresh blast of trumpets. Scharnhorst had given the signal. The barrage was to begin.

'Where is he?' hissed Magnus, his cheeks red with anger.

'You've got no time,' said Thorgad. 'The order's been given.'

Magnus looked around him. The gunnery captains looked back at him. For a moment, he considered leaving them in Hildebrandt's hands. He needed to track down Messina before he did anything stupid. But it was impossible. Scharnhorst's eyes were on him. His duty was clear.

'Damn it all,' he muttered. 'Messina can wait. He can't have done much with the pieces yet.'

He rose to his full height, and turned to face the waiting gunners.

'On my mark!' he cried, his harsh voice echoing down the lines of artillery.

The crews sprang forward, flaming brands at the ready. The spongers and master gunners stood back. Their work was done.

Magnus took a last look at their trim and angle of the guns, and the position of the barrels. There was nothing out of place. He looked up at the walls. They were as blank as ever, dark and sheer. Only the blast marks near the parapet gave away the effects of their raid.

'Fire!' he cried, and his voice bellowed out down the lines.

As one, the crews ignited the fuses. There was a short gap as the cord burned down. But then, one by one, the mighty engines let loose their deadly cargo. Mortars sent their charges looping high into the clear air. They rained down on the battlements heavily. There was no Tilean fire in them this time, but honest explosive charge and searing grape. Stone cracked and buckled under the onslaught.

With a screaming *whoosh*, the Helstorm rockets streaked towards their targets. Most hit the target, spinning into the gatehouse and exploding in a messy plume of fire. Only a few careered off course, slamming into the ground before the walls, or spinning wildly off into the skies before fizzling out and falling to earth in the far distance. The Helblasters joined in, sending ranks of piercing heavy iron shot against the distant gates, slamming into the stone and metalwork with a series of heavy, echoing blasts.

The ridge was engulfed with drifting smoke. Crews battled to reload their weapons amid the eye-watering clouds. Those soldiers closest to the artillery lines shifted away nervously, holding their ears against the splitting cracks and booms.

'Maintain your fire!' cried Magnus, though his voice was hardly audible in the cacophony. 'All guns to be aimed at the gates!'

Finally, as if held in reserve to remind all of their peerless power, the last of the great cannons were unleashed. Massive, ground-shaking booms rang out as the fearsome machines of war detonated, sending their iron shot spinning across the open ground. The noise of impact resounded heavily between the valley walls. Round after round slammed into the gates. Huge metal shot alternated with explosive rockets and dispersed grape. The citadel was being battered into submission.

Along the ranks of waiting soldiers, a low murmur began to pick up volume. There was no response from the fortress. It was as grim and unmoving as ever. But damage was being done. The rounds of stone-tearing ammunition kept hitting. The master gunners had done their targeting work well. Cracks began to appear in the masonry. The wolf's head lost its flame.

'Keep firing!' bellowed Magnus.

As he spoke, there was a shuddering crash to his right. He whirled around to see one of the Helblasters listing to one side, its barrels split open and steaming. A man was trapped under the wreckage, squealing in agony. Others rushed to pour water on the red-hot metal and haul the man free. Hildebrandt left his station to oversee the withdrawal of the piece. Magnus turned his attention back to the firing.

'Keep at it!' he cried again. 'No respite!'

The heat of the guns was now almost tangible, even in the ice-cold air. Another round slammed into the distant walls. All along the ranks of the army, men strained to see the results of the battery. Still there was no answer from the citadel. Their teeth had been drawn. The gate was defenceless against ranged fire. Magnus felt a grim sense of satisfaction. It was almost too easy.

Then, at last, it came. One cannonball, hurled far into the air and sent hurtling towards the gates, found its mark perfectly. The edifice, weakened by the ferocious waves of shot, crumbled. A huge cheer went up from the assembled ranks. Despite the drifting layers of smoke, they could see what was happening. The lintel had fallen. The arch was going down. The gates were broken.

More projectiles were hurled. Rockets spun into the ruin. Mortars sent their deadly contents into the breach. Flames sprang up as the entire gatehouse slid into rubble. On either side of its mighty frame, the walls began to splinter. All of a sudden, Morgramgar looked vulner-able. The way was open. The wolf had been thrown down.

Trumpets sounded once more from the command group.

'Cease firing!' cried Magnus.

It took a while for his order to be heeded. Some of the more enthusiastic crews managed to get another round away before they were dragged back by their counter-parts. The smoke rolled across the vista. Morgramgar was revealed again. Its walls were still smooth and unbroken. But where the gates had stood, there was now a gaping hole. The doors had been utterly destroyed, and the pillars on either side of them were bent and sagging.

Magnus smiled thinly. He had done what was asked of him. Now the army could be unleashed at last. He looked over at Scharnhorst, and nodded.

More trumpets rang out, and a series of signals passed along the ranks. With a roar, of relief as much as any-thing else, the long held-back ranks of footsoldiers were loosed. Like a herd of wild beasts, they rushed forward, brandishing their weapons in the harsh morning sun, yelling and shouting with abandon. At their side were the flagellants, outdoing all others in ferocity, scourging themselves into a frenzy even as they charged headlong towards the breach. The handgunners advanced too, keeping further back, held from the vanguard by their stony-faced commanders. Slowly, cautiously, Magnus gave the order for the artillery to be hauled to closer quarters. There was still work for them to do, but they would need to be nearer.

At the very centre of the huge mass of bodies, the Knights of the Iron Sceptre were the foremost. Their long black pennants streamed outwards as their steeds tore up the stone from under them. The noise of their massed hooves rivalled the blasts of the smaller guns. Magnus could see Kruger at the forefront, his standard held high, his black helm catching the sun and glinting like polished onyx. Despite himself, Magnus felt his heart surge. The sight was glorious. After so long trudging through the passes, hauling the machinery, putting up with one slight after another, the moment of release had finally come.

But just then, even as the vanguard thundered towards the gates and the hordes of men followed eagerly in their wake, there was a gigantic, resonating boom from the citadel. Silent for so long, it suddenly burst into life. Fires were kindled, and flames shot up from the battlements. Rows of archers appeared along the lower walls. From the gate there came the sound of brazen trumpets. Drums started up, beating wildly and echoing from the valley walls. As if waiting for Scharnhorst's men to commit themselves, Morgramgar finally stirred. The army it had been cradling within its deep vaults, so long rumoured, was finally disgorged from the broken gates.

With a blood-freezing shout, ranks of black-clad infantry poured from the breach to meet the onslaught. They kept coming. Rank after rank. There were gunners amongst them. The crack of their shots was audible even over the tumult. And there were mounted soldiers, armoured in plate and wearing black death's-head emblems. They looked as well armed as the Iron Sceptre knights, and charged towards the invaders with as much ferocity.

Still they kept coming. There were marching ranks of halberdiers, pouring from the shattered gates like ants spilling from a disturbed nest. The gap between the two armies narrowed. There was no let up. Each hurled themselves towards the other as if the End Times were upon them. Magnus narrowed his eyes. The vanguards would clash while still a long way from the gates. Had the enemy intended this? Why had his forces been kept in reserve for so long?

He turned back to the guns.

'Haul them faster, damn your eyes!' he bellowed, urging the men on. It took time to drag a whole artillery line into a new position. The guns needed careful handling. The barrels were red-hot still, and the horses were nervous and skittish from the explosions. The longer the crews took, however, the longer the footsoldiers were without heavy artillery cover.

Magnus looked back. Thorgad had scrambled on top of a pile of ammunition kegs to get a better view. He looked anxious to join the fray. The knights had reached the front lines of the advancing enemy. Behind them, footsoldiers piled in. Horses slammed into the front ranks, tearing a swathe through the oncoming infantry. Steel clashed against steel. The crack of long guns opened up from the right flank, and more men stumbled into the dust of the field. The pungent aroma of blood was mingled with the bitter stench of the blackpowder. The drums rolled. The fires burned. The war machines roared.

Battle was joined.

CHAPTER FIFTEEN

Guns! Explosions! The smell of fire and fear! Gentlemen, there is nothing better, nothing on earth. What sport would war be without it? They say that the age of Sigmar was the age of heroism. Don't believe a word of it! These are the days of glory, my friends! The time of blackpowder and steel! May it last forever!

Reported last words of Master Gunner Augerich
von Mettelblicken

MESSINA AND HERSCHEL were still working. The thunder of battle was all around, only slightly muffled by the thick canvas about them. The whine of rockets and the thud of the mortars broke the uniform clamour of arms. Below it all, the distant machines under Morgramgar still turned, and the heavy drums still rolled.

'Nearly there…' said Messina, clambering over the huge frame of the Blutschreiben. He had two different gauges of spanner in each hand, and was tightening the last of the bolts on the exterior of the wooden skeleton. Against all the odds, it looked like they would make it. The chassis was complete. The furnace was stoked, and thick black smoke was pouring from the rear stacks. It billowed out of the open tent doors. There was now no hope of secrecy, but the need had passed. The machine was functional. Its time had come at last.

'Is the locomotive bearing connected correctly?' asked Lukas, his voice sounding thin and scared. 'I don't think we're ready for this, Silvio.'

Messina laughed. His spirits had not been as high for days. Ironblood may have been a tyrant and a drunkard, but he knew how to build a war machine. The Blutschreiben stood nearly ten feet high at its tallest point. Its four massive wheels, adapted from the largest of their wagons and studded with iron spikes, turned effortlessly at the press of a lever. The enormous power of the furnace made the whole structure vibrate, like an animal eager to be released. Atop it all, the confusion of piping, bracings, gun housings, armoured plates, pulley mechanisms and gear chains, was the glory of the thing. A rotating chair, set on a ring of brass and festooned with controls of every sort. Though it was mostly constructed from wood taken from common wagons and iron stripped from existing artillery pieces, it was finer to his eyes than all the golden thrones of Araby.

Messina clambered into it, dropped the spanners and took control of the main set of levers. With a judder and a gout of soot, the machine rolled jerkily forward.

'She moves!' cried Messina, wild with triumph. He felt the same way he always did at the prospect of a fresh new conquest, of whatever sort. He could sense the enormous latent power of the machine beneath him. 'A work of genius! Why did the old fool not build it?'

Lukas hung back still.

'Are you really taking it out there?'

Messina looked down at him scornfully. He felt like some obscenely powerful potentate of the lands of legend, housed in his own steam-powered device of ruin.

'So what do you think?' he said, witheringly. 'Why would I build it, if not to use in battle? We aren't too late! This is our time!'

'There's been no testing!' cried Lukas, suddenly looking angry with his mentor. 'Ironblood knew there was something wrong with–'

Before he could finish, one of the gaskets within the maze of piping blew. A column of scalding steam shot backwards. The chains driving the wheels shuddered, then went limp. The smoke coming out of the main furnace began to splutter and spit out dark gobbets of oil.

'Shut it down!' cried Lukas. 'It'll blow!'

Messina, flustered, pulled a couple of levers in front of him and depressed a great brass-tipped column. The engine heaved and coughed, then went dead. Slowly, with a last parting shudder for good measure, the contraption came to a halt.

The air was thick with smoke. Soot had caked the entire rear end of the machinery. Steaming water leaked from the pipes under the chassis and pooled against the rock. The thing seemed to sink back a little into the earth.

Messina peered over the edge of the turret, his spirits still high. It was a setback, nothing more.

'It moves!' he said again, his face still filled with a childish delight. 'Help me get it working again!'

Lukas looked out of the tent entrance, clearly torn between making the machine safe and rushing to help with the fighting. For a moment, he hesitated, a sword in one hand, a wrench in the other.

'Come on,' said Messina, smoothly, knowing the lad was suggestible. 'We've spent days making this thing. All the problems have been solved. With this, we can turn tide of the battle. If we make a name for ourselves, what is the harm? We're so close!'

Lukas looked up at him, and his gaze was accusatory.

'This is all about the gold, isn't it?' he said, and he dropped the wrench. 'Enough. You've kept me tied up with this folly long enough. No more.'

He brandished his sword, and shot one last, dark look up at Messina.

'You've taught me a lot, Silvio,' he said. 'Perhaps in more ways than you know.'

And then he was gone, his blond head ducking under the tent flap and out into the camp beyond.

'Come back!' cried Messina, struggling to extricate himself from the narrow turret. 'Damn you, Herschel! It's not about the gold! It's about–'

His foot slipped. His hands scrabbled onto the brass lip of the chair, but missed their aim. For a sickening moment, he felt nothing beneath him. Then he was on the hard floor with a heavy thump, his head cracking against the near wheel of the Blutschreiben. His vision went black, and waves of blood-red pain started behind his eyes.

'Mother of Luccina!' he hissed, getting up with difficulty.

Messina staggered to the tent entrance. To their credit, the hired guards were still at their stations. They peered at Silvio as if he were some bestial creature from the wilds. The Tilean clasped a hand to his aching head, and scowled at them.

'Do not stand there stupid like Bretonnian pigs,' he snapped. 'There is three more silver pieces for each of you if you will come inside and help me get this thing working. Keep your mouth shut and don't ask questions, and I will make you all rich men.'

The venality of soldiers was always worth a punt. The three men looked at each other for a moment, then the most senior of them nodded.

'Very well. What needs to be done?'

Messina smiled through his rapidly developing headache. Who needed Lukas?

'Come inside, my good men,' he said. 'Steady yourselves when entering, and I will show you one of the wonders of the Old World.'

RATHMOR STOOD ON the balcony, high up on the leading wall of the citadel. He gazed over the battle, raging far below on the plain. The wind tore at his cloak, pulling it over his shoulder.

His expression was sour. There was no art in such warfare. The brutish clash of arms did nothing to stir his sensibilities. Only in the subtle arts of slow pain, or the mighty contest between machines, was there any glory. Above all, he valued the duel between masters of the single-shot gun. That was where the majesty of combat lay. To wield a true-firing pistol against one's opponent was the highest form of civilised conflict. Almost everything else was tedious barbarism. It was a pity that he'd almost certainly not have the opportunity to indulge his passion in this messy engagement.

He was shaken from his introspection by a familiar sound. Once more, like a recurring bad dream, Esselman had come to bother him. The man was irritating beyond words. His soldier's mind was pathetically limited, and his endless interference had become wearing. It seemed to Rathmor as if he'd never be left alone with his high, lofty thoughts. When all of this was over, he would really have to see whether the lady could do any better for her generals.

Esselman arrived on the balcony, stood beside him and looked over the same scene. His face was grim. There was a lurid weal on one cheek. The results of his last meeting with the lady, no doubt.

'You've set the traps, as we discussed?' he said, his voice clipped.

Rathmor nodded.

'All the inner levels have been rigged,' he said. 'If the need comes, we can turn this place into a pyre. But only if the need comes. The treasures in the forges are beyond price, even for the lady. We'll never see their like again.'

Esselman grunted in reply.

'Good,' he said. 'My place is on the field. I'll leave you to play with your toys.'

Rathmor bristled at the insult, but said nothing in reply. It was his 'toys' that powered the whole enterprise. Without them, Esselman would be nothing more than a provincial commander.

'There's one last thing,' said the general, curtly.

Rathmor waited. He knew what was coming, but Esselman would at least have to ask him outright.

'The infernal machine.'

Still Rathmor didn't reply.

'I know it's ready,' continued Esselman, his voice failing to hide a note of urgency. 'You told me yourself. Tell me where it is. I'll have a gunner assigned to it. They'll break against it like rain on the hills.'

Rathmor stayed unresponsive for a moment longer, but then his resolve failed. It was only a matter of time. He couldn't keep it safely stowed forever. This wasn't the proper moment for it, but the situation was difficult. He could hardly deny the man his tools now.

'Very well,' he said, turning to face Esselman and fixing him with as stern a look as he could generate. 'You can take it out. There are men in my retinue who know how to power it. If you truly need it to guarantee victory, that is. But I'd planned to unleash them all together. Alone, the infernal machine can cause havoc. In formation, they will be unstoppable.'

Esselman nodded. That was as close to thanks as he was ever going to get.

'It must be deployed now. They have the advantage of numbers. We need to break it.'

Rathmor looked back over the sea of men below. It looked like a tide of darkness, ready to wash against the foundations of the citadel. Much as he hated to see his beloved creations sent out prematurely, he couldn't help but suppress a smile at the thought of the carnage they would wreak.

'I'll come down with you. You will have your precious machine on the field in moments. Who knows? I may even join you out there. It's been too long since I tasted the aroma of blood on the air.'

The two men turned and walked back from the balcony. They disappeared into the tower behind, and the great doors were slammed shut. Far above them, the death's-head standard fluttered once, caught by the wind, and then hung still.

THORGAD HAD GONE. The dwarf could not be restrained, and had charged down the slope into the thick of the fighting. Even over so many other sounds, Magnus could just about hear him. His strange battle cries were like no other shout from the field. The engineer couldn't suppress a faint smile. Dwarfs were irritating and irritable in roughly equal measure, but they were peerless fighters.

He looked over his shoulder. The artillery pieces had been dragged forwards into their new firing positions. Hildebrandt had taken control of the longer-range pieces, and was already goading the crews to reload. Magnus turned away. That was no longer his job. He was with the handgunners. In a close melee, they were the ones to turn the battle.

'Form up!' he cried. The two detachments of Hochland handgunners under his direct command responded quickly. They were getting better.

The regiments were a few dozen yards from the press of the fighting. The battle was evenly poised. The enemy sortie had prevented the attackers from reaching the gates, but they had been unable to break through Scharnhorst's lines. Now the Hochland army had pinned the defenders back, and the hand-to-hand combat stretched in a long line before the citadel walls. For the moment, it was a stalemate. The conflict was ferocious, but it had yet to resolve one way or the other.

Some of the handgunners had already charged into the fray, dragged into it by their enthusiasm and foolish captains. That was not the way to conduct ranged battle. The guns were only effective at a distance, and could only bring their power to bear in coordinated volleys. The key was discipline.

'Keep together men!' bellowed Magnus, and looked down the lines of gunners severely. 'Fire, advance, then fire again. Any man who gets out of line will have me to answer to! And pick your targets. It's a mess out there.'

He raised his hand, and the gunners lifted their weapons to their shoulders. At the edge of their range, the boiling mass of fighting men struggled. It was hard to make out who was who. Then there was a break, and a contingent of Anna-Louisa's troops charged towards them. They were dressed in the black livery of the citadel, and were armed with swords and axes.

Magnus smiled. Fodder for his guns.

'Fire!' he cried, and there was a instant rolling crack along the lines.

Shot spun into the advancing attackers, felling a dozen instantly. The charge broke, and some even turned back.

'Reload!' shouted Magnus. 'Hold your positions! Quicker, you dogs!'

The men struggled to replace their shot. They were faster at it than they had been in the mountains, but still far off perfection. Anna-Louisa's men rallied, and the braver attackers started to advance again.

'Fire when ready!' said Magnus, seeing the danger. The gap was closing fast, and he drew his sword in readiness.

With a rippling series of detonations, the guns fired again. Their aim was good. The entire front rank of the oncoming troops collapsed in on itself. Men fell to the ground, legs cut from under them or torsos punctured. That was enough to break their spirit. The unit splintered, and began to stumble backwards.

'Do not run!' yelled Magnus, seeing some of the younger gunners eager to pursue. 'March forward, then fire on my mark!'

In a single, unbroken line of green and red, the Hochland men advanced, their guns held high. The enemy was melting away. There was no answer to the volley of concentrated fire. Nothing, not even the raving hordes of Chaos, could stand up to a properly commanded gun-line.

'Cease marching!' cried Magnus. 'Reload, and fire at will!'

The men applied more shot, and once more their deadly iron was unleashed. The solid core of handgunners became an island of order within the sea of confusion around them. Allied troops latched on quickly, and protective detachments were formed on their two flanks. The enemy attempted to charge again, but once more the withering fire cut them down yards before their goal. They advanced again. Once more, the defenders fell back.

Magnus stepped back from the lines of gunners, satisfied with his handiwork. They continued to advance
without him. He ran back up a shallow incline over to
his left to get a better view of the battle around him.
Some of the halberdiers from Halsbad's company had
withdrawn from the heaviest fighting, and were doing
the same.

'Going well, eh?' said Magnus, almost beginning to
enjoy himself.

One of Halsbad's troops looked at him coldly. He had
a jagged cut on his left arm, and his face and neck were
splattered with blood. The close-combat troops were seldom friendly with those who delivered death at a
distance.

'There's going to be another push,' the man said.
'Scharnhorst's throwing the reserves in.'

Magnus shaded his eyes, and looked out over the plain.
The enemy was being pushed back on all fronts. The
Knights of the Iron Sceptre could be seen in the very thick
of it. None were standing against them. Anna-Louisa's
men were better armed and equipped, but they were outnumbered. Far over on the left flank, Scharnhorst's
reserves were indeed mustering behind the disorganised
ranks of flagellants. Magnus could see what was happening. When the signal was given, they would charge
through their own men, their movements shielded by
the shrieking fanatics in front of them. If it worked, it
would break the enemy's far flank altogether. Magnus
looked over to Scharnhorst's command group, safely
removed from the fighting and standing clustered on a
ridge behind the reserve companies. The trumpets were
being raised. A thrill of anticipation passed through him.

The signal never came. As if to pre-empt Scharnhorst's manoeuvre, a tremendous roll of drums suddenly burst from the citadel. Fresh troops poured from the shattered gates. These looked like nothing Magnus had ever seen. They were clad in armour like knights, but the plates were dark and ornate. The helmets were carved in the likeness of the death's head, bone-white and gruesome. They carried huge double-bladed halberds, which they swung around them as they advanced. Unlike the ordinary troops, they didn't charge into battle, but advanced steadily and in formation. Magnus squinted to try and get a better look. They looked formidable.

But they were only the honour guard of what was to come. From behind them, a monster emerged. Huge plumes of ink-black smoke wreathed its passage. Six iron wheels churned the ground beneath it. Three tall ironbound chimneys belched vapours. The death's head was inscribed on its forward armour, etched in ivory against a black background. In front of its tall, curved fore-armour, massive iron spikes rose up cruelly. On every side, heavy plates had been riveted, inuring it to harm. As it rolled forward, a few arrows and shot clattered harmlessly from its flanks. More smoke billowed upwards as it laboured. Troops on both sides gaped at it open-mouthed. The momentum in Scharnhorst's men suddenly flagged. A ragged cheer rose from Anna-Louisa's.

Its progress was slow, like an insect steadily crawling towards its target. But Magnus immediately saw the danger. There was nothing on the battlefield to hurt it. It was smaller than the famed steam tanks of da Miragliano, but not that much. He had seen the devastation caused by one of those things many years ago. What was worse, there was something horribly familiar about the design of the war machine.

'Rathmor,' Magnus breathed, hardly daring to utter the words. 'Could it be?'

The machine ground its way forwards. No horse would come near it. Men fell back before it, unsure how to attack it. In their confusion, the dark-armoured halberdiers advanced unfought. A wedge was being driven between the attackers' forces. Heartened by the new arrival, Anna-Louisa's men renewed their attack. Scharnhorst's men, by contrast, were suddenly consumed with doubt. The charge of the reserves was halted. The knights rode back, rallying men around them as they did so.

Magnus suddenly realised he was standing transfixed, like so many others. He shook himself free of stupor, and ran down the rise, over to where Hildebrandt was frantically trying to aim his guns at the approaching behemoth.

'Have you seen that thing before?' Magnus said, urgently.

Hildebrandt, busy with fuses and quadrants, looked back irritably.

'Now isn't the time, Magnus,' he muttered. 'We need to take it out.'

'It's Heinz-Willem Rathmor's,' said Magnus with certainty, looking back at the machine grimly. 'We worked on it together. It's his Blutschreiben. He finished it. By Morr, he finished it.'

Hildebrandt brushed past him, a heavy round cannonball in his hands.

'I don't care,' he said, loading it into one of the iron-belchers. 'I don't care what you two worked on at Nuln, and I don't care what that thing is. We need to stop it.'

Magnus felt the blood draining from his face. It was getting closer.

'You can't,' he murmured. 'I know how it's built. We've got nothing to touch it.'

'Then get out of the way!' cried Hildebrandt. 'We've got to try.'

Magnus stepped back. Hildebrandt lit the fuse on the cannon.

'Fire at will!' the big man cried. 'Target the machine!'

His cannon, the largest they still had in operation, detonated. The iron shaft slammed back against its braces, and the chassis quivered. The shot was sent high and fast. Hildebrandt was a good aim. But cannons were not designed to hit precision targets. The ball thudded into a cluster of men advancing to the right of the infernal machine. They were scattered in all direction, stone and gore flying high from the impact and tearing a hole in the enemy formation. A good result. Not good enough.

More guns blazed. Rockets spiralled in on the creeping tank, mortars peppered its road, Helblasters launched volley after volley at its iron flanks. Some rounds hit. The monster shrugged them off, rocking slightly on its massive axles from the impact, but unhindered. Shrouded in smoke, it crawled on. Even the craters placed in its path by the cannons were no obstacle. Agonisingly, going at a slower pace than a man's walk, it kept coming, driving inexorably into the heart of the battle, striking the attackers down with fear and instilling new resolve into Anna-Louisa's hordes.

'Here it comes,' said Magnus, feeling hollow. 'It's moving into range.'

As it did so, two of the heavy iron panels at the front of the machine were drawn back. Just as had happened on the citadel walls, two gun barrels were thrust from the gaps. They were heavy and ringed with bronze. Wolf's heads had been carved over their mouths. From the gaps behind the muzzles, fresh smoke poured out, running down the sides of the tank and staining the ground as it came.

All could see what was happening. Those in the path of the machine scrabbled to race backwards. Formations were broken, and counter-charges were halted. The war machine halted. From its rear, bracing rods were extended. There was the sound of something being ignited.

Magnus threw himself to the ground. With a roar of fire, Rathmor's infernal engine let loose. Volleys of grape seared through the air. The twisted metal spun and bounced along the ground, slicing through limbs, armour and mounts. It fired again. A great channel opened up before it, cleared of men by the scourging power of its two cannons.

The retreat became a rout. Hildebrandt trained more guns on it. None were capable of breaking the heavy armour. The knights attempted to outflank it, perilously extending themselves by charging into the implacable armoured bodyguard on either side. They were repelled with losses.

Hildebrandt had joined Magnus on the ground. He looked shaken.

'Any suggestions?' he said.

Magnus poked his head up above the dirt. The machine was advancing again. On either side of it, Anna-Louisa's men were swarming around, preventing attack from close quarters.

'It's only a matter of time before it heads this way,' Magnus said, grimly. 'Let's use these guns while we've got them. Who knows? We might get a lucky shot.'

The two men sprung up and raced back to the line of artillery. Some of the machines had been abandoned. An air of panic had settled over the whole army.

'Get back to your positions, you fools!' cried Magnus, feeling a dark sense of resolve return. The shock of seeing the design he was so familiar with emerge from nowhere was wearing off. There were many questions to be answered. Right now, they would have to wait. Survival was the first priority.

The crews worked frantically to turn the heavy pieces around. The progress of the war machine was slow, but it still needed constant adjustment to keep up with. Gradually, the cannon barrels were trained on it once more. Wedges were driven under the wheels of the great guns, and master gunners took their last measurements. Time was running out. The infernal machine was closing. Even now its guns were turning in their direction.

'Fire!' cried Magnus. Despite himself, an echo of panic entered his voice. He could see the muzzles of the enemy guns train in on his position.

The cannons roared. The remaining rockets were dispatched in a flurry of smoke and blackpowder. Dozens of Anna-Louisa's men, advancing blithely in the lee of the war machine, were hurled to the ground, cut down by the hail of fire. The device itself was rocked, knocked back a yard by the ferocity of the rounds that hit. Some of the iron panels were knocked in, and one of the wheels shattered. Like a boxer reeling from a blow, the tank sagged in the ground.

'Mother of Sigmar!' exclaimed Hildebrandt. 'We got it!'

'No, we didn't,' said Magnus, his brow furrowed in confusion. 'We can't hit anything that hard.'

He looked back over the ranks of Scharnhorst's army. On the ridge behind the general's position, a new shape had emerged. It looked just like Rathmor's infernal engine, but without most of the armour cladding and decoration. It could have been designed from the same drawings, so similar was it in dimensions. There were only four wheels to the machine's six, and much of the chassis looked jury-rigged and liable to fall apart at any time. The guns were hastily bolted-together shells of cannons, held in place by an artful scaffold of iron bars and braces. Even more than Rathmor's machine, the newcomer was shrouded in thick black smoke. Naked flames coursed from the rear, licking the copper piping and sending plumes of steam far into the air. As it came forward, it wheezed and rolled, drunkenly heading directly into the path of the armour-clad monster.

'Messina!' cried Magnus, at last realising what he'd been doing. His stomach lurched with horror. All at once, nightmares from the past and present were converging. 'The madman! He'll kill us all!'

The flamboyant Tilean, exposed to the elements in his bare-bones contraption, took off his hat and waved it wildly over his head. Scharnhorst's men stopped in their tracks. Some of them stood stupidly, as if startled by the end of the world. Others roared with relief and raced towards it. For a moment, the broadsides from the first tank halted. Messina brought the Blutschreiben forward. As it came, the whole structure groaned and shifted. It looked liable to collapse at any moment.

'How did he–' started Hildebrandt.

'There's no time for that,' snapped Magnus, reaching into his jacket for the last of the blackpowder charges. 'He's doomed himself. But it'll give us the diversion we need. Gather the handgunners. We'll need to finish that monster off ourselves.'

Rathmor's war machine was turning, away from the ineffective lines of artillery and towards its new challenger. Like two great bulls, they squared up to one another.

Somehow, Messina was able to fire first. His two mighty gun barrels blazed. The whole shell of the tank rocked back, and several minor components spun into the air, knocked loose by the discharge. The volley hit home. Rathmor's tank was blasted sideways again. More of the iron panels were gouged inward, and several were ripped free altogether. The men around the tank were driven from it by the remorseless power of the impact. They scattered like children. The entire battle became focussed on the duel between the iron machines.

Magnus and Hildebrandt pulled together all the gunners who remained close to hand. The melee before them had become confused as companies from both armies scrabbled to get out of the way. Most of the enemy troops close to Rathmor's tank had been driven off, and the way through to the infernal engine was no longer barred.

'We're going closer!' cried Magnus to the handgunners Hildebrandt had gathered. 'We just need to get near enough!'

Some of the soldiers looked back at him as if he were mad. Others, inured to grim fatalism by long experience, picked up their guns and started to prime them for the attack.

'What are you going to do?' asked Hildebrandt, pulling his sword from his sheath and grabbing hold of two of the blackpowder charges.

'I know that machine,' said Magnus, taking up his own blade. 'The Blutschreiben's already blasted half its armour off. If it gets a shot of its own away, then Messina's a corpse. But he might have given us a way in.'

The gunners were ready.

'To me!' cried Magnus, and charged down the slope to meet the lumbering machine. The men followed him, fanning out on either side. Hildebrandt brought up the rear, as slow as an ox and already breathing heavily.

They descended into the heart of the battle. All pretence at ordered regiments and lines had been shattered by the arrival of Rathmor's war machine. Soldiers, heedless of orders, were grappling with each other, running from the scene, or merely trying to make sense of what was going on. Like so many battles, it had descended into a confused mess.

Magnus and the gunners kept together. Enemy troops in their way were knocked back with a volley of shots. The guns blazed, and swords flickered. Resistance was sporadic. All eyes were on the two war machines.

Messina had brought his machine into dangerously close quarters. Magnus risked a quick look over at it. It was trundling ever closer towards Rathmor's model, leaking oil, water, steam and smoke as it came. The first device was still crippled. Something had jarred with the drive mechanism, and three of its wheels spun uselessly. It lay heavily over to one side, and the choked wheeze of its steam engine was clearly audible.

Then, something seemed to click. The infernal engine righted itself, swaying on its wheels heavily, before turning to face the onslaught of Messina. The Tilean was less than twenty yards distant. He looked feral, his face fixed in an exhilarated mask of triumph as he worked the controls. His machine was still reloading. The infernal engine took aim.

'Merciful Verena...' breathed Magnus, hardly daring to look.

The guns fired. Rathmor's damaged machine shuddered as its payload was discharged. One of its other wheels shattered. Iron panels were shed from its side like scales. The machine had been badly damaged, and it showed. The wooden interior of the device was exposed, as was its lone crewman.

It mattered not. One shot was enough. The twin shells hammered into Messina's lumbering contraption. Already frail, the structure simply exploded. With an echoing smash, the entire frame blasted apart, throwing beams, wheels, barrels and chains high into the air. The furnace ignited with a thunderous boom, immolating the surviving shell in a ball of flame. Men too close to the impact fell to the ground, clutching at their faces or frantically trying to douse the fires kindling on their clothes. A second resounding blast swept across the battlefield. The Blutschreiben was gone, almost as soon as it had arrived. A spiked wheel came rolling crazily from the carcass, bouncing over the uneven ground, before clattering over. Then nothing. There was no sign of Messina.

Magnus turned his face away grimly. He had warned Hildebrandt it wasn't safe. Now Messina had paid the price.

'Keep going!' he yelled, urging the gunners on. Despite the jostling press of men around them, they had carved a route into the heart of the enemy ranks. Soldiers on both sides were still sheltering from the falling debris. Rathmor's monster was tantalisingly close.

This was the chance. Heedless of the danger, Magnus flung himself forward. One of the death's-head guards, turning slowly from the spectacle of the Blutschreiben's demise, spotted him. He swung a halberd. Magnus ducked under it, still running, not stopping to engage him. A gun fired from behind him, and the halberdier fell to the ground, a neat hole scored in his helmet. The handgunners were still close, then.

Only a few yards. The battered sides of the steam tank loomed up. Magnus could see the face of the man inside, white with fear, trying to bring it round. It was too late. The Blutschreiben had done its work. The armour hung from its flanks loosely, exposing the unprotected innards of the machine.

'For those who died in the passes,' muttered Magnus, bitterly, tearing the leather from the blackpowder bomb in his hand.

With all his remaining strength, he hurled the charge hard into the crippled tank. It lodged somewhere in the piping at the rear, deep within the remaining armoured shell and behind the pilot's head. The man inside stared at it, unsure what to make of the innocuous-looking egg.

Magnus turned away, only to see the gunners he'd brought with him either fleeing or slain. There were enemy soldiers all around. Hildebrandt had been tied up in combat some distance away and was bellowing with rage. The battle was closing back in around him. Magnus was alone, isolated and in the heart of the enemy ranks. Another of the machine's strange body-guards loomed up before him, halberd raised. The blade flashed in the morning light, ready for the downward blow.

The charge went off. Magnus was hurled forward, his head slamming against the rock. His side exploded with pain where his stitches dragged along the harsh stone floor. He had a vague impression of men being thrown around like dolls, and heavy objects whistling over his prone body. A scorching wind rushed past him, hot as a furnace.

His heart still hammering, Magnus looked up. The machine was gone, replaced by a crater of steaming, twisted metal. It shimmered with heat. Debris continued to fall, some of it heavy chunks of iron. Anyone within yards of the explosion had been knocked from their feet. Slowly, painfully, soldiers were hauling themselves up. Some lay still, blood seeping from their prone bodies. The explosion had caused carnage.

Magnus shook his head, trying to clear the black, spinning shapes from his vision. Dimly, he was aware of the still form of the enemy halberdier by his side. The man had fallen on his weapon, and a long trail of blood ran like a stream over the stones.

A shadow fell across him. Hildebrandt. The big man extended a hand. He was breathing heavily.

'We have to get back,' he gasped. 'They're regrouping.'

Magnus nodded weakly, feeling himself being pulled upwards roughly. His side felt as if it was on fire, and a line of hot blood dripped into his eyes.

Painfully, haltingly, barely aware of what was going on, he was dragged from the scene. Behind them, soldiers staggered back to take up their positions. Smoke drifted across the field from the source of the devastation. Trumpets blared from far away, a desperate attempt by the army commanders to marshal the troops again. They sounded thin and ineffectual after the echoing blasts from the tanks. The shock of the machines' arrival had knocked all shape out of the formations, both attacker and defender. Only slowly was the gap filled by fresh troops. The newcomers tore into one another once more, cutting the dazed victims of the blasts down where they stood. Amid them all, the two wrecks smouldered, surrounded by dozens of the slain.

As he was pulled away to safety, a dark thought entered Magnus's head. He had been responsible for both dreadful war machines. They were his designs. Now two other men had taken them and used them for their own ends. One was Messina, who had died for his ambition. The other was Heinz-Willem Rathmor, a name from the distant past. Suddenly, Magnus understood. The guns, the cannons, the cunning artistry of the weapons. There had never been a better mind than Rathmor. Even his father had said so.

'Tobias,' gasped Magnus, feeling the pain in his side begin to ebb. 'He's here.'

Hildebrandt finally halted, and set Magnus down against the charred ruin of a cannon housing. They had withdrawn behind their own lines. The battle still raged, but some way off.

'So you said,' replied the big man, collapsing heavily on the stones beside him. 'I thought he'd died.'

'So did I,' said Magnus, and a shadow passed across his features. 'If I'd known he were here, I might have told Grotius to stuff his commission.'

He felt faint. He'd been hit on the head by something, and his vision was still blurred at the edges. Every bone throbbed.

'Now that I know he's here, though,' Magnus said, his voice low, 'there's only one thing to do. I'm going to have to kill him.'

Hildebrandt looked at him. His face was drained of blood, and he seemed exhausted.

'Let it go, Magnus,' he said, his eyes almost pleading. 'There's enough for us to worry about here without making this personal.'

Magnus spat on the ground contemptuously. The spittle was laced with blood.

'You know me better than that,' he said, and his voice had a kernel of steel. 'Whatever else happens here, I'm going back in there. And when I do, I'll track him down. He'll know soon enough there's an Ironblood in Scharnhorst's army. I want him to know it. I want him to be afraid. He ought to be. I'm coming for him.'

CHAPTER SIXTEEN

So turns the path of war. The foolish commander is the one who trusts too deeply in his tools. Your wizards may falter, your artillery may misfire. Only one thing remains trustworthy, even when all else fails. The spirit of vengeance in men. When all other things desert you, rely on the capacity for hatred. That quality alone is what a wise commander cultivates in his soldiers, and no great battle has been won without it.

Grand Marshal of the Reiksguard Kurt Helborg
Memoirs, Vol. XII

RATHMOR STORMED DOWN the corridor. History was repeating itself. Once again, he felt the kind of anger and frustration that comes from a sudden bereavement.

He had never really cared for the loss of men he had known in life, nor even that of members of his own family. Esselman's entire army could be slain, and he would feel little emotion. But his machines, they were something else. Rathmor had an emotional attachment to each of them, from the lowliest barrel to the mightiest steam-powered monster of destruction.

The infernal machine had gone, laid low by the unlikeliest of chances. There should have been nothing in the enemy arsenal capable of piercing its armour. Even the luckiest of shots from a standard artillery piece should have been repelled with ease. But then the Blutschreiben had arrived. Against all hope, like a nightmare out of the past, a mere skeleton of what it could have been, the machine had appeared. Ironblood's machine.

Rathmor spat on the ground as he walked, heedless of the running men around him and the gongs echoing deep within the vaults of the fortress. Magnus Ironblood had come back. This put a whole new complexion to the campaign, and one that Rathmor didn't like.

They had been together in Nuln, the two brightest students of their generation. Ironblood had always been too cautious, but his mind was brilliant. Rathmor had taken up the mantle of creation for both of them. He had no illustrious father to dog his every move. He could indulge the wilder flights of his imagination with freedom. The pair of them, with Ironblood's rigour and Rathmor's powers of creation, had been an unbeatable team. Everything came easily, everything was enjoyable. After only a year at the colleges, poring over manuals of battlefield gunnery and the principles of the new sciences, their instructors were running out of things to teach them. The whisper had gone round that one of them would become Master of the College one day. The only question was which. Would the Ironblood name rise to even higher positions of honour and esteem? Or would the outsider, the hunched genius from Ostland, take the ultimate prize?

Rathmor felt his stomach clench inside him. Even to think of those days brought bile rising in his gorge. They were a long way off, those years of toil and humiliation, but the memory was still raw. The wounds had not healed.

The irony was that it had been Ironblood, usually so plodding and careful, who had created the Blutschreiben. Working alone and in secret, he had studied the forbidden drawings of the steam tank of da Miragliano. The secret of the massive war machines had long been lost, and even the most basic aspects of their maintenance had become a dark art in the fraternity. Only the sketches remained, recondite and incomplete.

That wasn't good enough for Magnus. Back then, he had believed engineering was the salvation of the Empire, that all problems were soluble. So he had spent long candle-lit hours in the deeps of the ancient library, squirrelling out facts from barely legible tomes. His reputation had granted his access to vaults normally hidden from students, and he'd amassed a huge stash of wondrous material. Rathmor could still remember the feelings of excitement when he'd seen them. A mobile gunnery platform, virtually invulnerable, powered by steam and hydraulics, capable of destroying almost any target with ease. The Blutschreiben was a marvel. Almost on a par with the steam tank itself. It promised to revolutionise the art of war and turn the Empire into the most powerful force in the entire world.

He carried on walking, oblivious to the commotion around him. He knew it wouldn't be long now before the enemy was in the citadel. He didn't care. With the destruction of the infernal machines, the way was now open. His plans lay in tatters. Another month, maybe two, and Anna-Louisa would have had her invincible army. Now it was wrecked, and by a man whom Rathmor thought had drifted into drunkenness and squalor. What was worse, the origin of his art was now at risk. Above all, even if von Kleister and her idiot general were slain, the secret in the depths of Morgramgar could not be discovered. There was too much at stake. He had to reach it before the invaders did.

Rathmor descended stairwells quickly, heading down level after level, leaving the inhabited parts of the citadel behind him. It got darker. The corridors got narrower. Soon the noise of the great wheels in the forges was ringing in his ears. They carried on churning out weapons blithely, oblivious to the coming storm. The air became hotter as the furnaces neared. The anvils were empty. The channels of fire were untended. All hands had been rushed to the defence of the walls. He was alone in his underground kingdom.

He looked up. Far away, high above the dark vaulted ceilings, the sounds of fighting filtered down. The invaders were inside. It would not be long now.

Rathmor turned, and slipped down the secret ways only he knew. He could still salvage something from this mess. The book was still there, and his drawings were with it. If he was careful, he could emerge unscathed, ready to try his designs somewhere else. He was still young enough, and the Empire was full of disaffected nobles with money to spend. He just had to retrieve the important things, and evade the hunters for long enough.

Deep down, though, he knew that there was only one man he needed to evade. Ironblood must surely know he was in Morgramgar by now. The design of his machines was unmistakeable, as good as a signature on a piece of parchment. And if Ironblood knew that Rathmor was here, then he'd be coming. Some crimes were too heinous to forget, and Rathmor knew that the passing years would have done nothing to heal the wounds.

With trembling hands, he withdrew his pistol from his jacket, and began to nervously clean the mechanism. Before the battle was over, he knew he'd be called on to use it.

LUKAS LOOKED UP, feeling the blood trickle down from his forehead and mingle with sweat. For a moment, he could barely remember where he was or what he'd been doing. Then it all came flooding back. The blasted crater before him was still smoking heavily. It was hard to make out anything within its rim. There were a few iron struts, bent out of all shape and blackened from the fire. Most of the wooden shell of the machine had been completely destroyed. Here and there, strewn all over the battlefield, a few pieces of the larger beams smouldered. It had taken days to build, hours of work both day and night working from plans neither he nor Messina fully understood. To have got it working at all had been a miracle. All for nothing. It had barely lasted minutes on the field.

Lukas pulled himself upwards, feeling his battered body protest. Though his memory of it was hazy, he could recall running towards Messina, desperate to stop him advancing. Then the opposing war machine had fired, and the Tilean had gone. All his flamboyance, his artistry, his arrogance and charm, lost to the world forever with a single blast of the device's guns. Messina had been exasperating at times. But he'd taken Lukas under his wing and given him a trade. Many fathers did less for their sons.

Lukas felt his senses returning. There was no time to mourn. All across the field, soldiers were recovering from the twin blasts, shaking their heads and gingerly getting back to their feet. Those who had been further away were closing in fast, advancing across the pitted earth, intent on closing the temporary gap in the fighting.

He clambered back up, legs shaky, and brushed himself down. He'd been hit on the head by something, and his left ankle was twisted and swollen. He'd been lucky, though. There were bodies on either side of him that still hadn't moved. The death of the steam tanks had taken many dozens of troops with them, from both sides.

Lukas looked around, and began to hobble back to the relative safety of his own lines. As he did so, he felt some strength return to his leg, and he picked up pace. The smoke was clearing, and the shouts of battle were rushing back in.

As he stumbled onwards, he was overtaken by a ragged-looking group of men. Their uniforms were torn, and they carried a mix of halberds and shortswords. Lukas suddenly realised he was unarmed. His sword must have been knocked clear when the Blutschreiben had exploded. He raised his fists desperately, aware even through his panic how futile and stupid the gesture was.

Then he saw the livery of Hochland, and a wave of relief washed over him.

'What are you doing here, soldier?' came a harsh voice from among them.

A burly man, the captain, grabbed him roughly by the shoulder and brandished a blade in his face. Lukas's vision swam. He was still shaken from the blast, and his grip on his surroundings was weak.

'You'll get yourself killed out on your own,' snapped the captain, taking a spare sword and pressing it into his hands. 'Stick with us. We're going back in.'

As the man spoke, Scharnhorst's trumpets blared out once more. From all along the lines of attackers, answering blasts rang. On either side of the halberdiers, ranks of soldiers began to advance. In the distance, on Lukas's left, disorganised bands of flagellants tore towards the citadel, shrieking and howling with incoherent rage. In their wake, rows of footsoldiers came onwards more cautiously. Some order had been restored to their detachments. Men who had been cut off from their companies like Lukas were absorbed into the oncoming formations and carried along with the advance.

There were none left behind. Scharnhorst had finally committed the reserves, and the entire army pressed forward, rank after rank of soldiers moving in concert.

Lukas grasped the handle of his sword, and gripped it tight. The feel of the blade in his hands was comforting. It was an honest weapon, not like the crazed constructions of his fellow engineers. For the first time in a long while, Lukas felt like he was among equals. The men on either side of him were from similar stock. There were no handguns, spy-glasses or mortars here. Just faith and steel, the bedrocks of the Empire.

Across the pitted battlefield, the enemy had formed up too. With a yell, Anna-Louisa's men rushed forward, their blades flashing in the sun. Lukas's company didn't hesitate. To a man, they let rip a ragged answering shout, and charged towards the approaching enemy.

Lukas was carried along. As he ran, a kind of exhilaration took hold of him. He joined in with the chorus of war cries, feeling his hot blood pound through his body. His blade felt light in his hands. His injuries were forgotten.

The lines closed in on each other. As the fighting broke out once more, the last thing Lukas thought was how simple the way of a non-engineer was. How much better it was to be amid a company of proper soldiers, shoulder to shoulder, wielding the weapons of Holy Sigmar, with only a natural and honourable death to fear. It was the life of an Imperial soldier. It was the life of a man.

Then the detachments crashed together. All was forgotten save the desperate struggle of arms. Lukas was lost in the melee, his blond head just one in a crowd of dozens, hundreds of others. Steel rang out against steel, flesh against flesh. The final push had begun.

SCHARNHORST SMILED. SLOWLY, bitterly, the defenders were pushed back to the citadel walls. Bereft of the imposing presence of Rathmor's war engine, they were beaten back by the Hochlanders' superior numbers. The close fighting gave no opportunity for them to bring their superior long guns to bear. Men grappled with men, fighting with swords, pikes, halberds, clubs, fists and teeth. There was little glory in it. Apart from the knights, who launched glorious charges into the heart of the boiling mass, the rest of the combat was brutal and ugly. Soldiers were dragged down to the ground by weight of numbers alone, throttled in the press and suffocated in the shadows. Eyes were gouged, fingers broken, scalps ripped, any mean or vicious trick to gain an extra yard of ground.

The greatest losses had been among the flagellants. They had flung themselves at the defending lines with utter abandon. Many had been mown down remorselessly with gunfire. Once they came too close for the enemy guns to be effective, they were sliced apart by the disciplined ranks of the defending halberdiers, working in concert like a team of harvesters before their crop. But it mattered not. Though the flagellants were slain in droves, they punched holes in the regiments of defenders through the sheer force of their charge. These were then exploited by the ranks of state troopers behind. Time and again the zealots would be hurled forward, only to be followed by orderly lines of soldiers ready to pile in and finish the task.

Across the rest of the field, the story was the same. Anna-Louisa's men, well drilled and superbly equipped, were borne down by the volume of bodies coming at them. The deathmask bodyguard of the war machine, the best close-combat troops in the defending army, cut down three men for every one of their number they lost. But it was still not enough. Inexorably, they were harried back towards the shattered gates of their citadel.

Watching all of this unfold with an expression of impassive flint, Scharnhorst stood with his retinue on the low mound that served as his outpost. Every few minutes, reports were brought to him by red-faced functionaries, detailing the progress of the assault. The news was mostly good. Where changes needed to be made, trumpets sounded in a series of signals, and the captains reassigned regiments and redeployed companies. Though every step was paid for in blood, the noose was closing in.

The Knights of the Iron Sceptre were continually in the thick of the fighting. On a rare lull between charges, Kruger rode up from the field and dismounted beside the general. His cheeks were heavily flushed from his exertions, and he wore a bloodied bandage on his left arm. Otherwise, he looked the same as ever. Haughty, aristocratic, implacable, deadly.

'We near the gatehouse, sir,' he said, pulling his helmet off and walking up to the command retinue. 'Your orders?'

Scharnhorst put his spyglass down. Though it was now almost imperceptible, the faint smile still played across his lips.

'They've been playing us for fools for days,' he said, a vicious edge in his voice. 'We've lost too many good men to their cowardly guns. Now they'll pay for every drop of blood spilled. Let us finish this. Take your knights and marshal the final charge. We'll assault the gates and push on within the citadel. Slay them all. We will make an example of this little rebellion, and the fear of it will resonate to the Talabec and beyond.'

Kruger looked over his shoulder at the battlefield. For a moment, he seemed hesitant.

'Are you sure?' he said in his unconsciously arrogant way. No other member of the army would have dared to question Scharnhorst. 'Ironblood thought there would be hidden dangers inside.'

Scharnhorst turned and made a signal to one of his aides. A horse was led up the hill, a huge chestnut stallion with an armoured faceplate and the colours of Hochland emblazoned on its tabards.

'The order has been given, master knight,' the general replied, reaching for the reins of his steed. 'I have been ordering the siege from the rear for too long. I myself will lead this charge. Muster your company. You will be my escort.'

Kruger bowed, and rushed back to his mount. In moments, the heavily armoured Iron Sceptre knights were assembled for another charge, their horses stamping at the ground and whinnying impatiently. Scharnhorst and his personal guard mounted. The finest armour Hochland could produce was on display. The general himself donned a heavy steel helm, emblazoned with Ludenhof's family emblem, the boar's head, and crowned with green and red plumes. He drew his broadsword, and its blade glinted in the sun. The day was waxing fast, and noon was now long past. The battle would be decided before it rose again.

'Men of Hochland!' the general bellowed, bringing his huge steed around to face the citadel. Before him, his entire army was laid out, locked in a pitiless battle with the beleaguered defenders at the walls. 'This is the turning point! Show no mercy! Death to the traitors! Forward! For Ludenhof, Karl Franz and the Empire!'

The men closest to the general cheered wildly, and surged forward. The knights kicked their horses. With a noise greater than the machines still churning in the bowels of the earth, the charge began. They swept down towards the gates, swords shining, hooves drumming. Behind them, trumpets gave the signal for the final assault, and fresh cheers rose from the furthest reaches of Ludenhof's army. The tide of men pressed towards the fortress. Notched blades rose and fell, throwing blood high into the air. The final push had begun.

MAGNUS AND HILDEBRANDT fought together, their shoulders touching, their weapons working in unison. The time for gunnery was long over. Artillery still fired sporadically from the ridge far behind them, but the combat was now so close that there were few clear targets for them. The handgunners had put down their long guns and picked up swords. The final hundred yards of ground before the gates were contested in hand-to-hand combat, close, visceral and brutal.

After the reserves had been mustered and all men had been thrown into the fray, the two engineers had ended up in the forefront of the attack on the right-hand flank. Around them were ranks of state troopers, most armed with halberds, swords and spears. The going was hard. The close press of men meant that swinging a blade properly was difficult. The fighting was a cramped, stabbing affair with little skill and plenty of trust to luck. Amid the grasping, thrusting morass, Hildebrandt towered like a giant. Men rallied to him, and he stood at the centre of a remorselessly advancing knot of soldiers.

Magnus was happy to fight in his shadow. The knowledge that Rathmor was in the citadel had thrown all thought of fatigue from him, and he hacked and stabbed at the men before him as if he were in the prime of his youth. His wits hadn't entirely left him, though. He knew he was wounded, and that he needed to conserve his strength. If Rathmor was the same man he had been so many years ago, he would have made precautions for an assault on the citadel. There would be devices in place to frustrate the attack. Even though the defenders of Morgramgar were reeling, there was still danger.

Hildebrandt roared like a bull, and ploughed on, bringing down two men in front of him with the sheer mass of his body. Magnus rushed to support him, thrusting expertly with his sword and parrying the return blows. The years of indolence and drunkenness were falling from him, and his muscles were remembering how to wield a blade once more. Though his arms ached, he carried on pounding and hammering at the defenders. It was as if they were pieces of metal on the anvil, ready to be smashed into shards. If Frau

Ettieg could see him now, his eyes shining with a grim ferocity, she wouldn't have dared to call him a disgrace.

The gate was nearing. Over to the left, the knights had almost fought their way to the shattered pillars. Scharnhorst was with them. Magnus caught a glimpse of the general's cloak rippling in the wind, surrounded by the glittering armour of his bodyguard. Kruger was wielding his mighty longsword with a roaring, concentrated fury. Few could stand against him. The end would not be long now.

'We have to be at the front of that assault,' hissed Magnus, pushing his hapless opponent backwards and head-butting him viciously.

Hildebrandt brought his blade down with a crunch on the shoulder of the soldier before him. He smashed another in the face with his free fist. He was splattered in gore, and his face was crimson.

'Morr's teeth, Magnus,' he muttered, his lungs labouring. 'We don't belong here. Leave the hacking to the knights.'

A defender crept beneath Magnus's guard and flashed his sword upwards. The man was felled by the spearman on Ironblood's left, skewered from neck to stomach, leaking intestines and gibbering horribly. Magnus nodded quickly in thanks, wiped the gore from his face and pushed on.

'He'll be down below. Down where those machines are. We have to find him.'

Hildebrandt grunted something inaudible in reply, and strode powerfully ahead. His mere presence seemed to daunt the defenders, and the lines wavered. Anna-Louisa's men were being pounded hard on every front, and now held only a small patch of land in front of the gatehouse. They were being driven in.

When the break came, it was sudden. The defenders' rearguard seemed to crack all at once, turning and bolting through the crushed gates. The ranks in front of them buckled. Scharnhorst saw the change, and the knights wheeled their horses around and hurled themselves directly at the breach. A fresh cheer rippled through the attacking forces, and the pressure built.

For a moment, Anna-Louisa's remaining men held the line, the heavily armoured bodyguards bellowing defiance. But it couldn't last. The ranks broke, and attackers poured into the breaches. Caught in the stampede, the defending troops were trampled underfoot or cut down where they cowered. Many of those fleeing were hacked apart by the knights. Kruger made the gates, and rode under them with a great roar of triumph. His fellow knights surged after him, Scharnhorst among them. The last defenders were swept aside, and the citadel was breached. With shouts of both scorn and triumph, Ludenhof's men piled into the gap.

'This is it,' said Magnus. 'Keep with them.'

Faced with nothing but fleeing defenders, Hildebrandt did his best to slow down, but the pressure of men moving all round them kept him and Magnus heading for the breach. It would have been near impossible to turn round, even if they'd wanted to.

'Back inside again,' he said, resignedly, wiping his sword blade as he pressed forward. 'This time by the front door.'

As they approached the gates, the ground became choked and pitted. The evidence of the earlier artillery fire was everywhere. The craters at the base of the ruined gatehouse were full of corpses, most of them still warm. Blasted remains of shot and cartridge casings were everywhere. It was hard to keep a secure footing, and Magnus felt himself stumble often as the baying crowds around him carried him onward.

The gate itself was the width of two carriages. Its span had been reduced by the piles of debris, and Scharnhorst's men had to squeeze themselves through at no more than four men abreast. From the far side of the walls, inside the citadel, the sounds of fighting could already be heard. The defenders may have been driven in, but there was clearly resistance still.

Eventually, after much shoving and cursing, Magnus and Hildebrandt reached the gates. On the far side, the first of Morgramgar's many courtyards opened up. It was hewn from the same dark stone that the walls were. Even full of clatter and noise, it was a mournful space. Dreary black walls enclosed the far three sides, each studded with narrow windows.

Beyond the opposing wall, the bulk of the citadel rose up imposingly. From ground level, the place looked like a vast cluster of broad-trunked towers, each connected to the others by a series of spiralling stairs and twisting buttresses. Everything was tall, narrow and tortured. The architects of the citadel, having had little space on which to build, had packed as much as they could into the few natural platforms. As a result, the whole place looked like a thicket of trees in a dark primeval forest, jumbled on top of one another and grasping upwards for light. Above them all, towering two hundred feet from the courtyard, the mighty central shaft rose. The summit of that tower was still crowned by the strange bulbous chamber, illuminated from within by the lurid green light.

The first courtyard was secured quickly. Scharnhorst and the rest of the knights dismounted. The winding stairs and narrow corridors would be impossible to negotiate on horseback. All of them knew that the rest of the fighting would be on foot, locked tight in the close halls of stone.

The few of Anna-Louisa's soldiers that had made it through the gates were now being beaten back into the interior of the citadel. A couple of narrow doorways were still held, and arrows had begun to spin down into the courtyard from windows high up in the towers beyond. It was a barely token effort. The retreat had been disorderly, and Scharnhorst was clearly keen to keep up the momentum.

'Spread out!' he yelled, brandishing his broadsword and looking murderous. 'Hunt them down! The traitors are up in the towers! A gold crown for the man who brings me the head of Anna-Louisa von Kleister!'

That ratcheted the frenzy up another notch. Soldiers, their faces distorted by bloodlust, tore across the courtyard, hammering down doors and crashing their way up the narrow stairs beyond and into the towers. There were more behind them, pushing from the rear for the chance of getting involved with the slaughter. Like the sea bursting through the breach in a tide-wall, Morgramgar was filling up with men.

'Are you with me?' cried Hildebrandt, carried along with the throng despite his vast bulk.

Magnus held back.

'Rathmor won't be up there!' he cried. Hildebrandt was already several yards away. Magnus kept his position with difficulty, ducking and shoving past the rows of rushing, eager bodies. Like some street urchin of Altdorf, he crouched down and scampered out of the main press. With much elbowing and jostling, he was soon at the right-hand edge of the horde, away from the main current of men surging ever upwards.

'I'll find you!' came Hildebrandt's roar, now some distance ahead. Magnus looked over to where he struggled. The big man had been pushed into the forefront of the assault. Fighting had broken out once more at the far end of the courtyard. A brief counter-attack from the tower beyond had been launched. The defenders weren't finished yet.

Magnus looked down to his right. There was a little door sunk far back into the wall. It led downwards, towards the lower levels of the citadel. The forges. If Rathmor was in the fortress, he would be there, down amongst his machines, cornered like a badger before the dogs.

Magnus looked back up for the last time. Hildebrandt was gone, caught up in the thick of the fighting. He knew he should go after him, stand beside him. Just as the big man had done for him, so many times. It was his duty.

But there was a stronger urge within him than duty. A cold flame had been kindled. He had long thought it extinguished, doused in ale and bitterness, but the sight of the war machines had brought it back.

Rathmor was here. His old colleague. The one who had stolen the Blutschreiben designs. The one who had built the experimental war machine in the foundries of Nuln, and paraded it as if the drawings were his. The one who had convinced that old man of engineering, the peerless White Wolf of Nuln, to pilot the first prototype. Rathmor had somehow convinced the magisterial figure that it was safe, that the flaws had been worked out of it. And he had then watched from safety as the magazine had exploded, cascading the watching professors with burning shards of iron and burying the dream in ignominy.

The memory was etched into Magnus's mind. He could remember his frantic last effort to halt it. On the day itself, he had come tearing into the parade ground after discovering the truth, too late to prevent it, but in time to witness the final explosion. His father, Augustus Ironblood, slain by a weapon of his own designing. From that day, from that moment, he had been doomed to live with the guilt. That was what had driven him away. The brilliance had gone forever. Never again did he innovate. He had lost his nerve. The drinking began. And there was never enough of it. Never enough to forget.

But guilt could be overcome. Revenge was the antidote. The man who had taken everything from him was near. Magnus took out the pistol from within his shirt, and began to prepare it. The time had come. He slipped from the ranks of the invading army, still heading up and into the heights of the citadel, and passed through the narrow door. The forges awaited, and vengeance.

CHAPTER SEVENTEEN

The engineers pride themselves on their scientific minds. But scratch under the skin, and you'll find them as passionate and irrational as the rest of us. They may claim to find pleasure in the mechanical workings of their machines, but put a pistol in their hand, and their blood will run as hot as any man's. Indeed, it has often been my supposition that the hearts of our famous mechanical scholars may be particularly prone to excitement in the heat of battle. Their imaginations are fertile, and their capacity for rage strong. If it were otherwise, how could they come up with such dreadful devices?

The Emperor Karl Franz

LUKAS DIDN'T LOOK back. He had been swept along through the gates like the rest of them, caught up in a tide of moving bodies. He still clutched his sword tightly, and the blade ran with blood. The spirit of exhilaration had ebbed slightly. He felt as if he had succumbed to a kind of madness during the assault. He had grieved for Messina with every blow struck. In a strange way, the fighting had been cathartic. No one noticed tears in the heat of battle.

The troopers around him pressed forward. The gates were coming closer. As Lukas passed under them, he marvelled at the destruction. The stone had been cracked and shattered. Metal bindings lay shredded and hanging. The ground had been turned into a morass of debris and churned earth. The blood had seeped into the meagre soil, and had been ground into a dirty slurry of deep red.

Beyond the gates, the courtyard was full of men. The knights had pushed far ahead, up into the towers. The last of the enemy soldiers had been driven up before them. Now the real fighting had moved upwards. But Morgramgar was a warren of passageways and corridors. There was plenty of opportunity to get your hands bloody if you knew where to look.

'Over here, lads!' cried the captain of the halberdiers. Lukas realised suddenly that he didn't even know the man's name. There was little enough time for introductions in the heart of the fighting.

He followed the captain's pointing finger. A door over on their left was still barred and locked. The main mass of the army had swept past it. The halberdiers broke from the ranks and raced over to it. One of the men, a brute with a swathe of tattoos on his exposed arms and a dark forked beard, slammed his shoulder into the wood. It shivered, and the hinges buckled. More men joined him. After several more heavy blows, the iron severed and the door fell open. A wide corridor stretched away on the far side. Noises of men running could be heard in the distance.

'That's our prey!' cried the captain, and tore down the passageway. His men were quick to join him. Like hounds after the fox, the halberdiers ran down the stone corridor, hollering and baying for more blood. Lukas went along with them, but remained quiet. He was no veteran of such assaults, but it seemed to him that things were a little too easy. Why were the enemy falling back so quickly? They had superior gunners. They knew the citadel better than the invaders. Doubt began to gnaw at him.

The corridor led up and round in a long curve. It was steadily climbing, heading from the cramped cluster of buildings at the base of the citadel to the higher levels. There were windows carved into the stone on their left. As they climbed, the west flanks of the citadel were exposed. Lukas gradually began to make sense of the place. It was built on a number of clear stages. Each one got narrower as they climbed. All ways led to the upper pinnacle, the strange emerald chamber.

They kept running. There was no sign of the defenders. Lukas felt his foreboding grow. They were being drawn onwards and upwards. He turned to catch a glimpse from the nearest window. As he did so, his foot caught on the edge of something, and he tumbled to the ground. He hit the stone hard, and was winded.

The rest of his company ploughed on upwards. There was the sound of coarse laughter.

'Catch up, youngster!' cried one of them.

Then they were gone, lost around the corner up ahead, the sounds of their footfalls and battle cries echoing into the distance.

Lukas shook his head and took a series of deep breaths. He looked down at his feet. He had tripped over a length of twine. He hadn't noticed it earlier. It ran the whole length of the passageway, shoved tight against the outer wall. It looked familiar. For a moment, he didn't know why. Then he recognised it. It was a long fuse. The twine was dry and quick to kindle. If lit, it would burn furiously. Its flame would travel up the corridor far more quickly than a man could.

Lukas's foreboding turned into a cold dread. They were being lured into a trap. The citadel had been prepared for them. He had to warn the others.

Still groggy from his fall, he pulled himself upright and broke into a halting run once more. The others were now far ahead of him. Lukas reached the end of the passageway, and entered a narrow chamber. From the sound of running and clattering, he could tell that the halberdiers had pressed on upwards. But there were other doors leading from the room. One was small and ordinary-looking. The length of twine ran directly under it. The fuse had been placed in the shadows between the stone flags. It was hardly visible even when he was looking for it.

Lukas stopped. He let his sword fall to his side. The sounds of pursuit died away, and the room became almost silent. His heart beating quickly, Lukas went over to the door. It was unlocked. He pushed at it, and it swung open easily. For a moment, he couldn't make out what was inside. It was growing darker outside as the day failed, and the light from the windows was weak.

Then his eyes adjusted to the gloom. It was a cache of some kind. There were objects piled up in the narrow space. To an ordinary soldier they might have seemed innocuous enough. But there were signs Lukas could read. Some of the objects had metal casings, studded with rivets. Some looked more like Messina's incendiary mortars. There were powder kegs amongst them. And more twine extended from the pile of explosive devices, some of it looping up to holes in the ceiling of the room, more leading off through narrow gaps back down towards the lower levels.

Lukas knew exactly what he was seeing. Just one node in a network. The citadel had been laced with such caches. There could be a dozen of them, or a hundred. It didn't matter. If the army continued to advance recklessly, they were heading for disaster.

Lukas left the chamber, and headed back down the corridor, his mind working furiously. He began to run back down, picking up speed as he went. He let the halberdiers carry on without him. There were more important men to warn. He had to find Hildebrandt. Or Kruger. Or even Scharnhorst. Someone had to be informed. Lukas fought to control the panic rising within him. As if blinded by their bloodlust, the army was rushing headlong into an inferno.

THE AIR WAS becoming hot. The torches had burned low, and many had gone out altogether. Deep in the vaults beneath the courtyard, the shadows hung from the stone. An eerie quiet had descended over the dark corridors. Every so often a rumour of the fighting above would filter down, echoing from wall to wall. The sound was distorted, twisted by its long journey from the far pinnacles of the towers. In the deep ways, the stone absorbed everything. Light and sound sunk into the black, smooth surface like water draining into a sponge.

Magnus went slowly, waiting for his eyes to adjust to the dim environment. His pistol was loaded and ready to fire. It felt heavy and reliable in his hand. An old make, a Gruningweld, one his father had recommended, years ago. One of the very first flintlocks. An exquisite piece. Magnus let his finger run along the trigger. One shot would be enough.

The floor of the corridor sloped steeply downwards. The blank rock walls were familiar enough from his last excursion into the citadel. Just as before, the throbbing of the engines in the foundations hummed through the whole structure. Magnus placed his fingers lightly against the wall. Faintly, very faintly, they were drumming with the vibration. Despite everything, the wheels still turned. Rathmor's forges had not yet fallen silent.

He crept on. The deserted passages were eerie and unnerving, much more so than they had been when enemy soldiers had run down them, hunting the infiltrators. Now all the guards were in the upper levels, grappling for control of the spires. All except one. With a dreadful certainty, Magnus knew that Rathmor was somewhere down below.

The corridor terminated in a small octagonal chamber. In the centre of it, a wide shaft had been delved and a spiral staircase wound downwards. The glow of flames emanated from the lip of the stairwell. There were noises too. Churning noises, like a vast beast bellowing in the far, deep forest. Magnus shook his head, and placed such thoughts from his mind. His senses were liable to play tricks on him. He felt alone, surrounded by the dark and the phantoms of the imagination. He gripped the holster of his pistol more tightly, and stepped down into the stairwell.

As he descended, the noises of battle died out completely. The black, steadily glinting stone was everywhere. It was just as it had been back in the tunnel. Close, cloying, heavy, oppressive. The walls lost the appearance of human construction. They looked like channels carved into the living rock by some awesome natural process. Magnus was no longer in the citadel. He was descending into the mines and tunnels below, the realm Rathmor had created for himself. As Magnus went ever downwards, the heat and noise increased. He was coming to the heart of it.

The stairway finally ended. Another long, winding corridor stretched away. There were a few torches still smouldering, but they weren't needed. At the far end of the underground passage, the stone was limned with crimson. There was an opening, and beyond it the play of flame was obvious. Firelight glimmered from the many facets of the stones. Magnus felt as if he had entered some replica of the underworld. He looked over his shoulder, back to the stairway he had come down. It curled off into the darkness. He looked back at the fires ahead. There was only one way.

He went on, feeling his heart thump in his chest like the machines below him. A thin layer of sweat collected on his brow, though his flesh was clammy and cold. Despite the heat, a chill had entered his limbs. The further he went, the more oppressed he felt.

The corridor came to an end. It opened out into another wide chamber. Just like the one on the level above, it was octagonal. That was strange. Imperial architects mostly disliked anything other than a crude rectangle. By the firelight, he could just make out markings on the walls. They were squat, angular shapes. Not human writing. These were the arcane symbols of the dwarfs. Runes. It was hard to see the detail in them, but they looked old. Very old. The edges were worn smooth. Only at the corners of the eight walls did enough depth remain in the scored characters to make out anything of their nature.

Magnus didn't stay to try and decipher their message. He knew no Khazalid. The dwarfs taught it to none but their own kind. At the thought of dwarfs, Magnus suddenly remembered Thorgad. Where was he? Most likely in the heart of the fighting, whirling Glamrist around his head and spitting obscenities. Then again, perhaps not. There was some strange connection with the dwarfs here. There had been connections with the dwarfs all along. Thorgad had said that men hadn't built the foundations of Morgramgar. Having seen them for himself, Magnus could see what he had meant. There were older delvings in the roots of the hills, perhaps even older than the kingdoms of men themselves.

He returned to the task at hand. There were two door-ways in the chamber, the one he had entered through and another set in the opposite wall. As before, a well lay in the centre, though there were no stairs leading further down. A bright red light burned from the edge of the octagonal stone lip. Magnus edged closer, and peered over the edge. Hot air surged up to meet him, singeing the tips of his straggling hair. The vivid light was blinding after the gloom of the descent, and his eyes watered. He stumbled onwards, over towards the far door. The noise of the machines was stronger. It came from beyond the narrow gap. Even before passing through it, Magnus could see that it opened into some kind of hall. The noises echoed and overlapped with one another, like ritual chants in a cathedral of Sigmar. The leaping light of great furnaces was visible, sending long shadows curling up the rock walls and flickering over the floor of the chamber.

Magnus pressed himself hard against the near wall of the chamber and edged towards the door. Slowly, care-fully, knowing he'd make a tempting target for any sniper lurking in the wide space beyond, he gingerly pushed his head around the stone doorframe. As he did so, he brought his pistol up gently to his breast, keeping his finger resting lightly on the trigger. The blood in his temples beat thickly, and a thin line of sweat ran down the small of his back. His eyes peered around the rough rock edge.

The vista beyond took his breath away, and for a moment Magnus forgot his danger entirely. The hall was vast. Vast beyond his imagination. He had come down to floor level, and a wide, paved surface stretched off into the distance. It looked like polished obsidian, and was marked by huge, intricate geometric patterns. In the flickering light, Magnus thought he could make out more runes, but their shape was indistinct and strange.

Fire was everywhere. It ran in long stone channels across the floor, hung in great braziers suspended on chains, was trapped in massive ironbound lanterns, rotating gently under the influence of some unseen force. The air was hot and thick, and the stench of tar and blackpowder was pungent. The noise was now ever-present. It filled every corner of the mighty arena, and the rock itself seemed to vibrate to the noise of the devices caged within it.

And what devices they were. The chamber rose to the height of a castle wall, disappearing into darkness before the roof came into view. Massive, vaulted pillars carried its weight, inscribed with great, jagged runes. Between them, huge wheels turned with a glacial slowness. They were fashioned of jet-black metal, hammered into a smooth surface and studded with iron rivets. They churned the channels of fire endlessly, and dripped with the liquid heat. From the wheels, heavy shafts turned. The flames glinted from their bronze flanks. At the end of the shafts, all manner of engines laboured, sending columns of thick black smoke, black even against the everlasting gloom of the high vaults, coiling upwards into oblivion.

Each of the machines was made differently. Some were for the smelting of metals, and the raw heat within their innards glowed brightly, ready to receive the next batch of unworked metal. Some were made for the forging of weapons, and their steam-powered hammers rose over anvils, poised to crash down and beat blades into shape. Others contained gigantic coppers in which strange liquids boiled furiously. Magnus recognised the process of blackpowder creation, but on a scale he'd never witnessed before.

The vast machines were far larger than their counterparts in Nuln. In forgotten Morgramgar, right on the edge of the Empire, deep within the frigid roots of the mountains, a factory of awesome power had been constructed. Despite his danger, despite the sense of latent fury which had been roused within him by Rathmor's presence, Magnus couldn't help but let a sigh of admiration escape his parched lips. It was a magnificent creation, the work of a masterful engineering mind.

Gradually, he forced himself to return to the reason for his being there. He was exposed, vulnerable. Magnus screwed his eyes up against the shadowy, shifting air. There was no sign of movement in the hall, besides the endless turning of the wheels and the flickering of the flames. The machines themselves lay idle, waiting for their crews to tend to them once more. There was no sign of any men among them. All had left, called away to defend their mistress high up in the towers.

Drawing a shallow breath and whispering a quick prayer to Verena, the protector of the settlers of debts, Magnus slipped out from the chamber and shuffled over to the nearest of the mighty pillars. As he went, he thought he heard an echoing movement from far down the hall. His eyes snapped round, but there was no sign of anything. Just flames and smoke. Magnus reached the shelter of the pillar, and pressed himself against the

hot stone. The girth of the columns at the base was easily the width of six men standing shoulder to shoulder.
Safe for the moment in its shadow, Magnus checked his
pistol over quickly. When the time came, it would have
to fire truly.

Rathmor had to be somewhere in the vast forge. This
was his place. Though not a superstitious man, Magnus
knew with a dreadful certainty that he'd be waiting.
There was a certain order to things. They had both been
summoned to Morgramgar for a reason. Now all their
affairs would be settled.

'Greetings.'

Magnus felt his heart leap in terror. He pressed himself hard against the hot stone. It was a voice from the
past, rebounding from the iron and stone around and
fracturing into echoes. He couldn't tell where it was
coming from. It might have been above him. It might
have been far away, past the rows of gently rotating
shafts. He gripped his pistol tight.

'I saw your machine on the battlefield,' came the
voice again. It had a strange, wheedling edge to it. 'So
you finished it, the Blutschreiben. I'm glad. It was a
worthy match for my own creations. They were all from
the same drawings. As you should know.'

Magnus made no reply. After so many years, to hear
Rathmor's voice again was a torment. In the shifting
light, just as he had before, he saw a sudden vision of
his father's face. He screwed his eyes closed.

'We needn't be enemies, Magnus,' came the voice. It
sounded like it was coming from somewhere different,
but it was unclear where. It was as fleeting and insubstantial as the leaping flames themselves. 'What

happened was years ago, and much blood and water has flowed since. You needn't hunt me like I was some kind of fugitive. We're the same, you and I. Cut from the same cloth. Will you listen to reason?'

For a moment, Magnus felt himself harking to the seductive words. They had been close, back then, the two of them. United against the ignorance and suspicion of the colleges. So long ago. It had seemed then that the new science would usher in an age of hope and progress. They had been at the forefront, the bright hope of the colleges, of the Empire itself.

But that was then. Too much had happened since. And some betrayals were too profound for forgiveness. He would not listen to reason. Not now. It was the application of reason that had led him to create the Blutschreiben. He didn't know who he hated more, Rathmor for building it, or himself for coming up with the plans.

Magnus took another deep breath, and felt the ash-flecked air fill his lungs.

'I'll not listen to your arguments, Heinz-Willem,' he said out loud. His voice echoed from pillar to pillar, and spun into the reverberating darkness. He knew he was taking a risk, and made his preparation to move. 'What would either of us gain? You've kept building them, kept working on the plans. You know I can't let you carry on. It's a monster. When would you give up on it? How many have to die first?'

He'd given away his position. Magnus looked over to his left. One of the huge machines loomed only a few yards distant. It rose, tall and dark, high up into the firelit vaults.

A thin laugh echoed down from the shadows. It seemed to come from everywhere and nowhere.

'That is the price!' cried Rathmor. His voice sounded on the edge of hysteria. 'You know that. Think what could be achieved, if we could perfect the designs. We'd surpass the art of da Miragliano. Princes would come and beg at our door, just for a glimpse at the power we could give them. That's what you're throwing away, Magnus.'

Ironblood tried to gauge the distance between the pillar and the shelter of the machine. Just a few strides in the open, then back into cover. He crouched low, tensing his muscles.

'Are these the words you used to convince my father?' Magnus said, letting the long years of anguish poison the words. 'Do you really think you'll make me follow him? If you'd had any shame, you'd have done what I did. Tried to forget. Instead, you persist in your delusions. It has to end, Heinz-Willem. It may as well be me that does it.'

Once again, the laugh echoed down from wherever Rathmor crouched.

'That's your final offer? There's nothing I can do to dissuade you from your pointless quest for revenge?'

Magnus tensed. This was it. Surely now the man had an aim. This was Rathmor's domain, after all. He knew all its ways.

'You know the answer!' Magnus cried. 'Never!'

As the words left his mouth, he pitched forward. He felt the shot as it whistled past his shoulder and cracked into the pillar. He kept going, legs pumping, until he was in the shadow of the nearest machine. He placed his hand on the metal housing, and snatched it back. It was fiery hot. Shaking, he crouched down, looking all around him, trying to see some clue in the smoky gloom. There was nothing.

Then there was the sound of running, far down in the vast hall, echoing into the void. Rathmor had withdrawn. To reload, no doubt. For a moment, Magnus's nerve failed him. He could still withdraw. He could run back up the winding stairs, up towards the light where his allies were fighting. He looked back over to the doorway into the octagonal chamber. It was still close. Tantalisingly close.

Magnus turned back to face the hall. He would only leave the forges when his task was done. Either that, or die here, the second Ironblood to be murdered by Rathmor.

Grimly, Magnus took up his pistol once more. Hugging the shadows, lurking like some creature of darkness against the heels of the churning machines, he crept forward. Step by step, he headed deeper into the heart of the mountain.

SCHARNHORST PRESSED FORWARD, a savage light in his features. Though few of his men would have guessed it, he hated standing safe from harm at the rear of his armies with his officers, ordering their movements through messengers and bugle-signals. For the most part, it had to be done that way. No commander could order his troops from the thick of battle. He had to have an overview of the whole, and a clear sense of which way the winds of fate and circumstance were blowing.

Not now. Thank Sigmar. The time for cold-blooded strategising was long gone. His men were running amok through Morgramgar, and the defences had crumbled. At last, he could take his proper place at the tip of the spear, sword in hand.

Scharnhorst swung his broadsword in a wide arc, and the defenders fell back again. On either side of him the heavily armoured knights rampaged, slicing their way through any resistance. Their armour was scratched and dented, their breastplates streaked with blood, their plumes ripped and tattered. They looked like death incarnate, tearing their way through the corridors and stairways of the upper citadel. None could stand against them.

They had fought hard up the many stairways and hidden chambers. Every bridge, every archway, every postern had been held against them. Each redoubt had been stormed, cleansed of the traitors who still clung to them. Anna-Louisa's men knew better than to expect mercy. The Imperial electors were not merciful men. Scharnhorst had his orders, and they all knew it. So they fought like ferrets in a trap, desperately clinging on to every slight defensive position, only ejected after all had been slain. It was dirty, tiring work. But it felt good. Scharnhorst was a patriotic Hochlander. The rebels were vermin. They had forgotten their allegiance, and in a world of war, that was all that mattered. Removing them from the realm of the living would make the remainder purer. Even in their deaths, they were doing Sigmar's work, after a fashion.

Scharnhorst looked over his shoulder. The vanguard was still at his heels. The knights clattered up the stone passageways to join him. Behind them, the state troopers clustered, baying for blood. He could dimly make out the vast shape of that engineer, Ironblood's deputy. The man looked good in a fight.

The general turned back to the task ahead. They had fought their way to the base of the central tower. The bulk of the citadel now lay beneath them. The valley floor was several hundred feet distant, and wreathed in the shadows of the gathering dusk. Fires had been started in the lower levels behind the walls, and their flickering light bled up the steep slopes of the inner walls. The first level of the fortress had been taken, and the last of the guards were being remorselessly hunted in the shadows. The second level was now contested. Knowing the value of striking at the heart of the contagion, Scharnhorst had not tarried, but had carried on upwards, fighting all the way, clearing the stairwells of Anna-Louisa's traitorous minions, pressing on to the central tower.

Now it loomed before them, stark and tall against the gloaming. There was a great courtyard set at its base, wide and paved with stone. At the edge of it there was an ornate parapet. The rest of the citadel was below that edge, and the stench of its burning rose above it.

In the centre of the courtyard, a wide stair rose. It ascended for many dozens of steps, and could have accommodated a whole company of knights. At the summit of the stairs, the huge tower soared into the air. Though only a single tower, it was larger than many small fortresses. The base was over forty feet wide, and the vast bole rose sheer and smooth from it. Studded into the courtyard-facing aspect were narrow windows, glowing with a lurid light.

Right at the top, leaning out over them, far above, was the final chamber. After everything, despite the ruins of the rest of the fortress, the windows of that bulbous pinnacle still shone with a bizarre green illumination. Far out into the gathering night they shone, staining the smooth stone with a sickly sheen.

Scharnhorst watched with satisfaction as his men cleared the courtyard of the final few defenders. His victory was almost complete. Only the tower remained. Its massive doors were barred, but that was of little consequence.

'Knights, to me!' he ordered.

Kruger and his company were immediately by his side.

'This is the final element,' said Scharnhorst coldly, gazing up at the tower. 'I will make the final kill. You will come with me.'

Kruger pulled his helmet off, leaned on his longsword for a moment, and wiped his brow. His face was flushed and ran with sweat, but his eyes were as piercing as ever. He looked at the doors doubtfully.

'We'll need a ram for those,' he said. 'Men won't bring them down quickly.'

Scharnhorst smiled grimly.

'I disagree,' he said, and turned around, back towards the press of men at his back. 'Where is the engineer?' he bellowed, his voice rising above the tumult. 'The man who was in Ironblood's company? I saw him.'

There was a brief commotion as the state troopers tried to find the man the general wished to see. After a few moments, Hildebrandt was located, and pushed to the front of the crowd. He emerged looking more weary than surprised, and bowed clumsily.

'What's your name, man?' asked Scharnhorst.

'Hildebrandt, sir,' replied the engineer, giving no hint of resentment at not being recognised. Both he and Scharnhorst knew that they had met and spoken many times on the long journey into the mountains, but it was not a general's responsibility to remember such things.

'Where's Ironblood?' asked Scharnhorst.

'Fighting in the lower levels,' replied Hildebrandt without hesitating.

Scharnhorst smiled. The man was loyal at least.

'Then you'll have to do,' he said. 'I know of the black-powder bombs. The ones you used to destroy the guns. There's one last task for them. Can you break down those doors?'

Hildebrandt looked over them, and nodded curtly.

'I can.'

He reached to his belt, and pulled two of the round charges from it. There were leather straps around them. In Hildebrandt's hands they looked little more than hens' eggs.

'Then do it,' ordered Scharnhorst. 'Blow them down on the first attempt, and I'll forget any harsh words I've said concerning engineers. And you shall have the honour of being in the vanguard for the final assault.'

Hildebrandt didn't need to wait for further instructions. He strode forward. Behind him, the ranks of men in the courtyard shuffled back. There was soon a wide gap between the doors and the first ranks of Scharnhorst's army. Hildebrandt ascended the stairs, looking up as he went at the strange, silent bulk of the tower. There was no movement from above. As the evening waned towards night, it remained implacable.

Hildebrandt reached the top. He placed both of the charges where the massive ironbound doors met. The man retreated down the stairs far more quickly than he'd ascended them, and came running back to the protective ranks of soldiers. As he reached the safety of the general's retinue, the charges went off. Two sharp cracks resounded across the courtyard, and twin orbs of fire rushed outwards. The doors rocked. One was blasted clean from its massive hinges. The flames and smoke cleared, and the damaged door swung open on one iron bracket. A dark green light leaked out from the interior.

For a moment, the men in the courtyard hung back. There was something unwholesome about the green glow coming from the shattered doorway. Scharnhorst himself felt an unusual pang of foreboding. What had been unleashed? Would a brace of daemons spill from the gap? Though the sounds of combat and looting still rose into the air from down below, the high courtyard was seized with a sudden hush. There was no movement from the tower. It stood darkly, looming over them like a noiseless portent of death.

Scharnhorst took up his sword, and was comforted by the weight of the steel in his hands. His doubts began to ebb away.

'Come,' he said, quietly but firmly. Around him, the knights raised their weapons as one. 'The bitch von Kleister is there. The one who has brought this bloodshed on our land. Follow me. The time has come to end this.'

As the last natural light bled from the west, the vanguard strode up the stairs, towards the ruined gates and into the last tower.

CHAPTER EIGHTEEN

I have learned, over long years of study, not to judge the exterior of any object without knowing the full details of its interior. The grandest building may conceal a rotten core, and the meanest-looking pistol may hide the finest rifling workmanship within it. That seems to me a good maxim for any engineer. We have often discovered that the way a device looks is no guarantee of its quality. In fact, though I hesitate to make the comparison directly, the same may too be said of men. Some of us who seem most fearful by reputation may turn out, on closer examination, to be nothing but weaklings and cowards. Conversely, even those who have sunk low, almost to the point of becoming nothing, may carry within them the smouldering spark of greatness, ready at any moment to leap once more into flame.

The Notebooks of Leonardo da Miragliano

THE MACHINES TOILED. Even after being abandoned by their makers, the valves and pistons still turned in the darkness. The channels of fire still burned, and the vaults still echoed. It was as if the place had a vital spirit all of its own, an animal awareness that filled its iron sinews and copper muscles.

Magnus steeled himself. The sound of Rathmor's footsteps had died away, and the cathedral-like forge was free once more of human sounds. Clutching his pistol carefully, poised to fire at the slightest movement, he crept free of the lee of the vast machine that sheltered him. Far ahead, the light of the fires seemed to ebb. Magnus went towards the end of the hall warily, keeping close to the cover of the mighty devices and hugging the shadows of the columns. Every so often he would jump as a sudden spurt of steam or belch of liquid fire caught him off guard. Then he would spin around, or flatten himself against the hot stone, his heart beating. But Rathmor had gone, fled into the lower levels, further into the dark heart of his kingdom. For the moment, Magnus was alone.

He took a deep breath. He could still taste the ash on his lips. He went on. The columns passed by in stately succession. As he padded silently, each fresh machine emerged from the fiery murk, and passed back into it behind him. He lost count of how many there were. Each one was more elaborate and heavily ornamented than the last.

Eventually, Magnus reached the end of the long rows of foundries. The final mechanical device in the hall had a great wolf's head carved from metal on its summit. Just like the gates. Thick brown smoke rose in a steady, boiling pillar from its central chimney. It smelled foul, and a brackish ooze lapped at its base. Magnus stepped around it carefully, knowing enough of Rathmor's ways not to get any of the strange liquid on his clothes. The pool looked poisonous in the gloom.

The light of the fires was losing its vibrancy. Most of the great channels of magma were now far behind him. Magnus began to descend again. He screwed his eyes against the perpetual murk. There were more chambers ahead, soaked in shadow, lit by measly, smoky torches. Their filth clogged the already acrid air. He had to stop himself coughing. Grimly, he pressed a rag to his mouth, and carried on.

It got darker, and lower. Magnus passed huge storerooms. Some of the contents of them could only be guessed at. They looked like they'd been bored directly into the rock. It was hard to gauge their size. In the gloom inside them, row upon row of weapons waited. Spears were piled in huge bales next to sheaves of swords. And there were guns, placed in racks and hanging side by side. They were long guns, the kind that had been used against the army in the passes. Even in the thick murk, Magnus could see the distinctive serpentines adorning their barrels. So they had been forged here, wrought using Rathmor's diabolical machinery. There were none quite like them in all the Old World. Dwarfish, and yet not dwarfish. There were still riddles to unravel.

The atmosphere started to cool. The fires were left behind. Magnus pulled his leather coat closer round his shoulders. The fine cloud of dust and soot lifted, and the air became sharper. It smelled dank. As the last of the fire-pits diminished into the distance, the light once more became dim. The few torches bracketed against the walls were scant compensation, and threw a thin orange light across the uneven floor. The elaborate paving of the hall was forgotten. The roof of the chamber had sunk to little more than a few dozen feet high. The magnificence of the forges was replaced by a cold, forgotten procession of dreary tunnels and storechambers.

In one of them, great dark shapes loomed in the shadows. They were covered in some kind of fabric. There were no torches flickering above them, but their outline was unmistakeable. Infernal machines. Rathmor's devices. A dozen more. It was hard to tell if they were finished, waiting for deployment at a moment's notice, or still in construction. All had the basic outline of the Blutschreiben. They were copies. Shams. But still deadly, for all that. Magnus shook his head in disgust. They were abominations. If Rathmor was allowed to complete his plan, it would spell destruction on a terrible scale for the Empire. Magnus felt the smooth weight of his pistol in his palm, and it reassured him. There was still time to halt it all.

He walked on further in the gathering gloom. He had begun to lose track of distance. The storerooms came to an end, and the darkness grew. Magnus stopped, and listened carefully. It was hard to make out much ahead. He felt as if he'd descended to the very root of the mountain. The shadows were as cold and ancient as any in the world. Going any further would be hard without a torch. But carrying a flame would make him an easy target. He decided to do without. It made his progress even slower. At any moment, Magnus expected to hear the report of a pistol. Even as he walked, his every muscle seemed to tense.

But there was nothing. Rathmor seemed to have shrunk back into the very rock itself. The more that Magnus crept onward, the more silent and ominous his surroundings became. The ceiling carried on descending. Soon he was walking down corridors not much taller than he was. The rock had been carved roughly around him, and there were faint track marks in the jagged floor. Every so often, he would pass some abandoned cart, knocked onto its side and left to decay in the eternal shadow. There were still torches, even so far down. They flickered and guttered. Some had gone out for lack of fuel. The others would follow them soon enough. Then the night would close over him, and he would be totally blind.

That thought was strangely terror-inducing, and Magnus pushed it out of his mind. He kept going, his feet treading silently on the unseen floor, his fingers running along the walls, tracing the serrated pattern of the stone under them. The churn of the machines was a distant whisper now. There were no other noises. It was as if he was lost at the centre of earth. The memory of light and wind felt distant.

There was a noise. Magnus pushed himself hard against the near wall, his pistol raised. His breathing quickened, and he strained to see ahead. There was no repeat of the sound. He couldn't even tell what it had been. But where there was noise, there was movement. And where there was movement...

Magnus waited for his breathing to calm, and set off again. It felt like he'd been walking for hours. Gauging time was near impossible. And then, he got the impression of space once more. The gloom around him was almost complete, but there was something in the air that told him the tunnel had opened out into a hall once more. Magnus slipped over to the near wall again, wary of the wide space. He paused, listening hard for any sound. There was nothing, except for maybe the slightest of moans as the air from above shifted down the miles of tunnel and chamber. No water dripped, no torch sparked. Something within Magnus told him that he'd reached the end. There were no chambers below this one, no more machines. Whatever had been done here, it was still a secret.

He looked down at the pistol in his hands. He could just make out its outline in the gloom. The last torch, some yards back, still lent a dim glimmer to things.

Then it went out. Caught by some freak gust of chill air, or doused by a malevolent hand, the light died. Magnus was plunged into complete darkness. He might have been swimming in the void before the creation of the world. Panic rose in his throat. He had been a fool. There was nothing he could do in such a place. He was blind, and alone. He had to get back, find a way towards the light.

Magnus whirled around, back in the direction he thought the tunnel lay. For a moment, he felt the urge to cry out loud, to scream, to do something to break the endless, terrible silent darkness.

Then he felt the cool metal press against his temple.

THE INVADERS CLIMBED the steps swiftly. Kruger and his knights were in the lead, powering up the twisting stairs even in their heavy plate armour. Hildebrandt struggled to keep up with them. Night had fallen, and he felt his fatigue latch on to him like a heavy cloak. The long, cold days in the mountains had taken their toll. His arms ached from wielding his weapon for so long, his legs ached from the endless climbing. It felt like they'd ascended halfway up the side of the peak itself. Only now were they nearing the uttermost pinnacle, the final chamber of the citadel.

Moonlight shone weakly through the windows of the tower, but there was little other light. The shadows clung to the walls like ink. Men's faces distorted in the murk, and Hildebrandt felt his mood become more febrile. The green tinge on the edges of the stone was growing. As they clattered up the narrow, twisted ways, it became steadily more intense. The nearer the summit they went, the more it looked as though the walls had been doused in some unholy alchemical substance.

There was no resistance on the stairs. The promised army of defenders looked to have melted away. Hildebrandt wondered if the strength of Anna-Louisa's forces had been overestimated. Certainly, since their initial setbacks in the passes, the battle had swung decisively their way.

The stairs went on, winding tighter and tighter as the tower drew towards its peak. Hildebrandt could feel his

lungs labour. His breathing began to come in shuddering heaves. He was too old and too fat for this. His
hands shook from tiredness. With a dogged growl, he
pressed on, determined not to be outdone by the
armoured men around him. Even after hours of fighting and pursuit, they still fought and climbed as keenly
as ever.

Just as Hildebrandt began to think that they'd be
plodding up the stairway forever, it came to a sudden
end. There was a narrow antechamber ahead. Three
iron lanterns hung from the ceiling. The glass in the
panes was lime-green. They threw a sickly light across
the stone. The walls were almost bare. Here and there,
a few gold trinkets had been hung. It was an incongru-
ous sight. In the eerie light, they looked strangely
sinister.

Scharnhorst was waiting in the antechamber, as was
Kruger and many of the other knights. There was space
for several dozen men, no more. At the far end of the
chamber, a large pair of doors was bolted against them.
There was still no sign of any guards. The room was
quiet. From down the stairs, the noise of men clattering to a halt on the stone echoed upwards. Hildebrandt
came to a standstill amid the knights, his chest heaving. It didn't look like Scharnhorst was in any hurry to
break the doors down.

'What's going on?' Hildebrandt asked a soldier next
to him.

The knight had taken his helmet off, and his jet-black
hair cascaded in curls almost to his shoulder. He
looked young. No more than twenty summers. The
battle hardly seemed to have touched him.

'Can't you hear it?' he replied in an aristocratic accent, inclining his head towards the doors. 'It's unsettled him.'

Hildebrandt paused, and listened carefully. For a moment, there was nothing. Just the ragged breathing of the men around him and the muffled sounds of soldiers coming up the stairs behind them.

But then he caught it. A high, wandering voice. Like a little girl's. It was some kind of whimsical tune. Hildebrandt thought he recognised it, but he couldn't quite place the name. Then it came to him. It was a lullaby. He'd sung it to his own daughter Hannelore. Beyond the mighty oak doors, right at the bitter summit of the dark citadel, in the heart of the pitiless mountains and surrounded by the dead and dying of two armies, someone was singing a lullaby.

Hildebrandt couldn't believe it. He looked over at Scharnhorst. For the first time Hildebrandt could remember, the general looked nonplussed. He stood by the doors, unmoving, his naked sword still in his hand. Around him, the knights waited for their orders. The assault had come to a grinding halt. Men waited on the stairs below, their vigour transformed into uncertainty. The singing continued, reedy and insubstantial. In the lurid green glow, the effect was more than strange. It was otherwordly.

At length, Scharnhorst turned from the doors. He had a strange expression on his face.

'There's some devilry here,' he muttered, before turning to Kruger. 'These doors are unlocked. We must enter and see this thing through. Come with me.'

Scharnhorst's eyes swept the assembled throng, and settled on Hildebrandt.

'You too,' he said. 'And bring one of those charges. Just in case.'

Without waiting for a reply, he turned and placed his hand on the doors. Kruger and Hildebrandt pushed their way through the crowd of soldiers to stand at his shoulder. The general hesitated a final time, and then pushed. With a long, sighing creak, the doors swung inwards. From inside, green light flooded the antechamber. The three men walked forward. This was the final room. There was nowhere else to go. They were at the pinnacle of Morgramgar. They entered the chamber.

MAGNUS FROZE, HIS OWN weapon by his side. He could feel the heat of another body close to his. A man's breath grazed against his cheek.

'Brave,' came a voice, close by. 'Very brave. But useless.'

The voice sounded sad, like a child who has had to put away his toys at the end of the day. Magnus stayed perfectly still. The gun's muzzle rested against his flesh. If he moved, he was dead. His mind raced, his heart thumped, but he resisted the urge to flail or plead. He would never plead.

There was a sigh from the darkness beside him.

'I really don't want to do this,' said Rathmor, resignedly. 'Do you think I desire the fate of two Ironbloods on my name? It's hard enough having responsibility for one. Though I don't feel I should share all the blame for that.'

Magnus kept his position with difficulty. His only chance lay in Rathmor making a mistake. If the man wanted to talk, so much the better. These moments were precious. He was painfully aware they could be his last.

'Why didn't you finish the Blutschreiben yourself?' the traitor engineer asked, and his voice became wheedling again. 'If you'd been open to persuasion, we could have completed it together. Then I wouldn't have had to go behind your back. You've seen that I've nearly perfected it. There are a dozen more down here, almost finished. Imagine them on the battlefield at once! Nothing could stop them. Even here at Morgramgar, the only thing that could break its armour was a half-finished machine of your own design. And I've improved it since Nuln. It's almost there, Ironblood.'

The voice broke a little. It sounded as if Rathmor was trying to convince himself.

'Almost there,' he said again, bitterly. 'I just needed a little more time.'

The pressure of the muzzle lessened. Rathmor was drifting into some kind of reverie. This was the moment.

Magnus spun round, wheeling in the dark, and knocked Rathmor back. There was a cry, and a dull thud. Magnus sprinted forward, blind and terrified, waiting for the blast to finish him. In the dark he ran straight into a wall, and fell heavily. Blood streamed from his nose. Frantically, he scrambled along the stone, certain to feel the explosion of pain at any moment.

It didn't come. Trembling, Magnus turned back. He could see nothing, just the endless black of the tunnel.

Rathmor didn't speak. He didn't fire his gun. It was as if he'd never existed at all.

Suddenly, a spark lit. A flame burst into being nearby. The mouth of the tunnel was illuminated, and Magnus could see how narrow it was. The walls of the subterranean cavern soared upwards into the preternatural gloom. The far end was lost in shadow.

His eyes adjusted slowly. Rathmor lay a few yards away, his limbs twisted awkwardly. His neck was severed nearly straight through. Dark blood still pumped down his jerkin and over the stone. His eyes were unfocussed, but his face was set into a mask of surprise. His pistol lay on the floor, forgotten.

The fire had come from a flint-strike onto a flaming brand. As the flame grew, the red light blossomed. The torch was held low to the ground. For a moment, it was hard to see who the bearer was. Then the dark shape of Thorgad emerged. The blade of Glamrist was red from the flame and from Rathmor's blood. The dwarf had a strange look in his eyes, at once full of triumph and emptiness.

'I told you,' he said gruffly, and his eyes glinted like jewels in the darkness. 'You'll be glad to have me along, I said. And I was right, was I not, Ironblood?'

HILDEBRANDT LOOKED AROUND him with amazement. In all his years of service, he had seen nothing like it. The room was circular, and huge. Great stained glass windows had been constructed on all sides. The moonlight streamed through them. Just as it had been outside, the glass was green. The panes were irregularly shaped, and threw odd patterns of emerald light across the floor.

Everything was bathed in the lurid glow. More lanterns hung from the distant ceiling, also throwing a green light across the space. Hildebrandt felt a tremor of nausea just looking at it all. There was no escape. The effect was sickening. He fingered the last of his blackpowder charges nervously.

The walls of the chamber were covered in paintings. They looked like the daubings of a child. In fact, crude representations of children were everywhere. There was a portrait of what might have been the goddess Shallya too, and another of some kind of Sigmarite betrothal ceremony. The brushstrokes were heavy and artless. Some images had been scored out with thick black ink. Others had been savaged, slashed apart, and from these the canvas hung down in tatters. Those that were left were bizarre and malformed.

Across the floor, wooden toys were scattered. Most of them lay forlorn in the sickly shadows, forgotten or broken. There were ceramic dolls with no eyes. Wooden soldiers were everywhere. All were mutilated in some way. Many had no heads. There was a wooden rocking cradle near the far side of the room. The sheets had been ripped from it, and several of the legs were broken. A music box lay next to it. It looked exquisitely made, with silver bindings on the rosewood case. But it too was broken. Shards of metal were scattered around it, and the lid was cracked. It would never play again.

Hildebrandt felt a horror well up within him as he gazed around. The men beside him said nothing. It seemed almost indecent to be there, as if they had intruded into some profoundly personal nightmare. Reluctantly, the big man let his eyes follow the sound of singing. Part of him didn't want to look. But it was impossible to avoid. In the very centre of the chamber, the margravine was sitting, staring at them.

She was in bed. Her huge four-poster bedframe dominated the room. It was lined with silk sheets and linen hangings. Once they must have been fine things, fit for a lady of noble birth. Now they were stained and tattered, and fluttered limply. The bedclothes were strewn with more dolls. One hung from the frame over the centre, a little noose around its diminutive neck. Others had been warped or disfigured.

Propped up by enormous bolsters, Anna-Louisa Margarete Emeludt von Kleister, commander of the rebel armies and mistress of Morgramgar, looked at them with glassy eyes. She kept singing, mumbling the words over and again. As she did so, she tugged weakly at her straggling dark hair. Strands of it lay all over the sheets in clumps. Her flesh was pallid. Dark lines had been scored under her eyes. What little she had left of her looks had been pasted over with heavy layers of rouge. Her lips were haphazardly painted. She looked a little like one of her own dolls. The stench of perfume was everywhere, powerful and pungent. It was a scene of madness and degradation.

She kept staring, but said nothing. Her singing petered out. The chamber fell silent. Eventually, Scharnhorst took a deep breath.

'Madam,' he said, falteringly. 'By the warrant of Count Ludenhof of Hochland, Elector of the Empire, I have come to end your treachery.'

Anna-Louisa didn't reply at once. It looked as if her mind, or what was left of it, was wondering. Then her eyes seemed to gather some focus. She gazed dreamily at the general.

'Have you come to marry me?' she said. 'It's about time. I've been waiting so long.'

A stray tear ran down her cheek, blurring the heavy make-up. Scharnhorst looked at Kruger, and his brow furrowed in confusion. The knight raised an eyebrow, but said nothing. Then Anna-Louisa shook her head, and laughed. It was a strained, gurgling sound.

'Of course you're not here to marry me!' she said, brushing her tear away. 'You're soldiers. They told me you would come. To take away my gold.'

She picked up one of her dolls, looked at it dispassionately for a moment and in a casual gesture twisted its head off. As she did so, a faint growl passed her cracked lips.

'My gold,' she said again. 'That's what they want me for. That clever man Rathmor. And my soldier man, Esselman. They told me they could buy men with it. And then we could break down the Emperor's palace, and he would have to marry me. And then I would have an heir. A little child. To play with. It's been so lonely here without one. So I gave them my gold. That's how it happened.'

A strange eagerness seemed to strike up in her eyes, and she leaned forward. As she did so, the blankets fell from around her. Hildebrandt could see that she was emaciated under her flimsy nightdress. Her movements were like that of a spider, stilted and creeping. Scharnhorst remained silent. He looked horrified.

'Do you know how much gold there is under these mountains, soldier man?' asked Anna-Louisa, looking suddenly delighted. 'Endless gold! The little men mine it for me, and then I buy more of them. Every day, more men come to serve me. Soon we will have enough, and Esselman will take them to break open the Emperor's palace. It won't be long now!'

Scharnhorst took a deep breath. Now that the shock of the sight was wearing off, he looked like he was tiring of the woman's babbling.

'My lady,' he said, choosing his words carefully. 'I fear you have been deluded. Your mind is deranged. Whatever plans you had have ended. Your armies are destroyed. Your citadel is taken. Any gold you have will be confiscated and withdrawn to the treasury of Count Ludenhof.'

As he spoke, Anna-Louisa's eyes seemed to lose their focus again. She started playing with one of her toys.

'My orders were to destroy your citadel and execute you for high treason,' said Scharnhorst, his expression full of doubt and his speech slow. 'Now that I see the truth, I must surmise that you have been misled. The real traitors are those who have told you such lies. I cannot judge this matter. I will take you to Hergig. Wiser heads shall determine what shall be done with you. You are ill, my lady. Very ill. Will you relinquish yourself to my stewardship? You will not be harmed. It may do your cause some favour, were you to come of your own free will.'

Anna-Louisa looked up vaguely.

'Give myself up?' she said, in her child-like, wandering voice. 'They told me you would say that. Let me think. My soldier man told me you would say that. And there was something I had to say. What was it?'

Scharnhorst looked sourly at the scene before him. Anna-Louisa was clearly too far gone in madness to debate with.

'Enough,' he said. 'Whatever your commander told you is not important now. The citadel is ours. At first light, you will come with me to Hergig.'

At that, Anna-Louisa suddenly leapt up from the bolsters. Her hair flew wildly, and settled in straggling lumps about her face.

'That's it!' she cried. 'I remember now!'

She giggled maniacally.

'There was something I had to tell you when you got here,' she said, in a girlish whisper, looking inordinately pleased with herself. 'That man said that you would come up the tower. Then I had to say that he is still on the second level, hiding. When you're all up here, he will come out. And there are special fireworks all over the second level. They were made by that clever man Rathmor. And he's going to set them off! We are all going to burn! Isn't that very funny? We're all going to burn!'

Scharnhorst looked at her intently, a sudden sharp concern in his eyes.

'What do you mean?' he snapped.

Before Anna-Louisa could reply, there was a commotion behind them. Hildebrandt turned round to see Lukas pushing his way through the crowded antechamber and into the room. The lad was dishevelled and panting heavily. He must have shoved and jostled his way up through the whole company of men lining the spiral stairs.

'Sir!' he cried, his voice desperate. 'You must withdraw! It's a trap! There are explosives lining the citadel! We've been drawn up here!'

For a second, panic rippled across Scharnhorst's features. He turned back to Anna-Louisa, then to Lukas again. He didn't know what to do. Despite the general's rank, Lukas looked exasperated. He was at the end of his strength, and a dreadful certainty was in his expression.

'Sir, we have to withdraw!' he cried again. 'There are enemy troops hidden on the second level. They will detonate the charges!'

Still Scharnhorst hesitated. The men looked to him desperately. Some began to shuffle back towards the stairway nervously.

'I–' he began, but he was cut off.

Deep below, a familiar booming had started. There was a distant crack of blackpowder. The green windows were tinged with the red of fire. Screams filtered up from the lower levels. Rathmor's final trap had been sprung. Down in the courtyards and armouries, the corridors and mess halls, the storerooms and cellars, the bombs were going off.

MAGNUS SANK BACK against the hard stone walls. His heart was still racing. His head was hammering from the impact of his fall. He felt as if his stitches had opened again. There was a sharp pain in his side, and a hot, sticky feeling of blood against his ribs.

Thorgad blew softly on his brand, and fed it some powdery substance. The flame flared up, throwing long shadows up the rock walls. The dwarf placed the torch against the wall, where it continued to burn.

The two of them were standing in a wide, tall cavern. Behind Magnus, the tunnel led back to the forge level.

On the far side of the chamber, more tunnels led off into the endless night beyond. They were roughly hewn from the bare rock, and showed signs of recent wear and tear. The stone floor was littered with rubbish. Old leather gourds, discarded rags, animal bones and broken tools cluttered the dark recesses of the cavern.

Thorgad looked at Rathmor's corpse dispassionately. Magnus felt his equanimity gradually returning. His heartbeat slowed to nearly normal.

'So, what are you doing down here?' he said at last, looking at Thorgad with a mixture of relief, fatigue and confusion.

Thorgad turned from Rathmor, and rested his gnarled hands on Glamrist. In the half-light, he looked like a graven image of one of the dwarf lords of old. He could have been made of stone himself.

'I might ask you the same thing, umgi,' he said. There was a resentful edge in his voice. 'Your people don't belong here. These are our delvings. The fortress above is a mockery of what was once here.'

Magnus leaned back against the rock, weighing the dwarf's words carefully. He had a feeling some truths were about to be revealed.

'You intimated as much when we met,' he said. 'So you wanted to revisit the place. I can understand that. A dangerous way to go sightseeing, though.'

Thorgad scowled. He looked in no mood to humour Magnus.

'Don't mock me,' he said, and his voice had a low, warning tone. 'These mines are older than your Empire. Older than your race itself, maybe. Do you think I would come here lightly? It has been many hundreds of years since the dawi dwelt here. Only in song do we remember this place. And many have forgotten even that. Shame on them.'

Magnus looked at Thorgad afresh. The dwarf spoke with a voice of reverence. The engineer said nothing in reply, but sat and listened.

'Perhaps you know something of grudges,' continued Thorgad, leaning heavily on his axe. 'They are debts of our race, to be paid in respect of some great wrong. They can stretch back for a thousand years, longer even than the long lives of my people. They are recorded with care, set down on tablets of stone and in the iron-bound books of the Karak archives. Though years may pass before they may be returned to, they are never forgotten. Such is the way of my race. We cannot let the debt go. Though the whole world may fall into fire and the Karaks sink into shadow forever, while there is still a single dwarf alive the list of grudges shall be in his mind, driving him to rectify the wrongs done to us through all the long bitter years.'

Magnus could feel his side spasm with pain. He stayed stock still and kept his mouth shut. Thorgad was eager to talk. That was rare for a dwarf. The opportunity might never come again.

'You asked me why I wished to join you,' Thorgad said. 'This is why. To fulfil a grudge held against my clan. In the past, long before the towers of Altdorf had been thought of or the foundries of Nuln first lit, one of my ancestors lost a thing of great value. A book. It is old beyond measure, and even my folk do not remember its origins. In the long years of war and strife, it was almost forgotten. But not quite. The record of grudges sets down that it was one of my blood who let the book slip through his fingers. Its whereabouts remained unknown, but it was enough that the deed had been done by one of my own kin. The shame has hung around my neck since I was a beardling.'

Magnus watched the dwarf intently as he spoke. Thorgad's eyes were not fixed on anything in particular. They seemed locked on something far away.

'Then, against all hope, there came word of an uprising in Hochland. A rebellion from the mountains. And it came to my ears that the traitors were using weapons of great quality. So good, in fact, that they surpassed the best that men could create. They were so good, I was told, that they even rivalled the guns of the dwarfs. And then a thought entered my mind, and it began to wear at me. These men were holed up in Morgramgar. I knew that the place had long ago been one of the halls of my people. It was called Karak Grimaz then, and its mines were famous. The name you give it is a corruption of its other title. The Morgrammgariven. The Halls of Silent Stone. Though the citadel above us was built by men, there were always the workings underneath, quiet and undisturbed. Umgi have never penetrated far into the deep places. Not unless driven there by some great need. But what if the book had been discovered there? I asked myself. And what if one of you man-creatures had the wit to use it? That fear wore at me, and I had no rest from that day onwards.'

'This book,' said Magnus. 'It had some secret techniques in it, then? It was a manual of some kind?'

Thorgad didn't reply, but unstrapped a large object from his back. It was nearly as big as he was. Carefully, his hands working with surprising gentleness, he unwrapped layers of sacking and soft fabric. Soon, in the gently burning light of the torch, a thick tome lay. The leather covers were black and cracked with age, and the spine and corners were studded with a tarnished bronze-like metal. A single rune had been engraved into the cover. The pages were bound closed with many straps, but the buckles on them had been broken.

'The Book of Khazgred,' said Thorgad, solemnly. 'In here are secrets no man has the wit to understand, even were he to spend a lifetime studying it. There are marvels inside beyond any of your short-lived kind. This Rathmor had barely scratched the surface of it. But what he learned was enough to make the long guns we found, as well as the cannons. He was clever. It was his cleverness that gave him away. How long had he had this thing? I do not know, but it must have taken him years to decipher the few passages which he did. He only gleaned a little, but even that was sufficient to make a leap into the unknown. The forges you see here, the machines, they are all but copies of the designs of Khazgred. In the days of our glory, we would have laughed at such follies. Even now, the great anvils of Karaz-a-Karak make them look like the work of children.'

Magnus leaned forward, ignoring the pain in his flank. His fingers crept gingerly towards the book, almost unbidden. So that was how Rathmor had managed to create such monsters. One of the fabled dwarfen manuals of arcane science. Just to peer inside for a moment would be the dream of a lifetime. He looked up at Thorgad, and an eager hope lit in his eyes.

Thorgad smiled grimly, and replaced the coverings over the book.

'This is not knowledge for you,' he said. 'Rathmor has paid for his insolence. I would not have Glamrist employed to keep your mouth shut as well.'

Magnus looked over at Rathmor's corpse, and shuddered. His spirits sank. Thorgad had spoken, and there was no point in arguing over it. The blade of the axe was too sharp, and he was too exhausted. He sighed. So he had just been a tool in Thorgad's long plan of vengeance.

'So you needed us to get you inside,' said Magnus, a little resentment creeping into his voice. 'That was your only purpose here.'

Thorgad nodded, and swung the tome onto his back once more.

'I never lied to you, Ironblood,' he said. 'Your war was your own business. It was merely my opportunity. You have my thanks, and that is not lightly given. But do not forget your debt to me, too. You'd have found it hard to scale these walls while the cannons were still blazing.'

Magnus hung his head. After all the anguish, all the labour, it seemed a bitter ending. An obscure book of the dwarfs. A human engineer with dreams of worldly domination. Both lost. Poor reasons to go to war.

'What'll you do now?' he said, his eyes still lowered.

Thorgad pulled his cloak about him, and hefted Glamrist in one hand.

'Go back to the east,' he said. 'The book will be returned to its rightful place in the archives. The grudge will be scored from the record. The honour of my clan will be restored.'

Magnus nodded resignedly.

'So be it,' he said. 'Then there's nothing more to do here.'

He felt battered, bruised and weary of the world. Slowly, awkwardly, he hauled himself to his feet.

'It must be night by now,' he said, wincing against the pain. 'As a last favour, can you help me find the way back up to the forge level? Your eyes are better down here than mine. I need to find Hildebrandt. The fighting in the citadel should be over by now. He'll want to know what happened to Rathmor. He knew him too, once.'

Thorgad gave him a strange look then, and his eyes glittered brightly.

'Don't be so sure the fighting is over, Ironblood,' he said cryptically. 'But I'll come with you, at least to the forges. Then you'll need to make your own way. Before we move, however, there's one last thing.'

He shuffled over to a small pile of rocks in the corner of the chamber. He filled both hands with small nuggets, and walked back to Magnus.

'These mines were the source of this von Kleister's wealth,' he said, disdainfully. 'It was with the promise of gold that she drew her mercenaries here. But that story had always seemed hollow to me. If there was still gold in these tunnels, there would still be dawi here. I've been exploring a little. This is what the woman has been building her army with.'

He emptied a pile of nuggets onto the floor at Magnus's feet. The last handful he gave to the engineer.

Magnus took them. In the gloom, they glinted and twinkled. He frowned.

'Gold,' he said.

Thorgad snorted with disdain.

'Grungni's axe!' he spluttered. 'Even now, you amaze me. Do you know nothing at all? This is kruckgol. Fool's gold, man. If this is what she's planning to pay her men with, they're in for a shock.'

The dwarf stood back, and let Glamrist swing in a gentle arc towards the ground. As it hit the pile of nuggets, they shattered, skittering off into the shadows. The ingots were as brittle as rusted iron. Magnus stared at the ones he held in his hand. They were worthless. Rocks, just like any other. The rebellion was built on sand. The final irony.

'We should go,' said Thorgad, sharply. 'This torch won't last forever, and even my eyes can't guide us quickly with nothing to see by. Come. But bring some of those nuggets with you. As much as you can carry. They may come in useful.'

Magnus did as he was asked. Then he and Thorgad set off, as quickly as the poor light would allow. Behind them, the cavern sank back into darkness once more. The shadows over Rathmor's body lengthened, then deepened, then closed over him for good.

CHAPTER NINETEEN

This is at the heart of all we do. The power of fire. Consider the irony of it. We rely on it for the most mundane tasks of the hearth and the kitchen. Without it, we could neither survive the winter nor feed ourselves in the summer. And yet, in the hands of a skilled craftsman, it turns into the direst of all our many weapons. Let that be the legacy of the engineer, if you wish to find one. That he turns the means by which we sustain ourselves into the great destroyer of men.

Ludovik von Rassingen
Professor of Engineering,
Imperial College, Nuln

MORGRAMGAR WAS AFLAME. The level behind the outer walls was a sea of fire. As the contagion spread, more blackpowder kegs ignited, blasting stone and tearing down walls. Some of the more slender towers collapsed entirely, falling in on themselves with an agonising slowness and showering the men beneath with charred masonry.

The roars of triumph and vengeance were replaced with screams of agony. Caught between the stone and the fire, Scharnhorst's army panicked. Men pushed past one another, trampling the weaker ones underfoot, pushing the slowest against the walls, desperate to find a way out. The flames leapt high into the night sky, bathing the mountainside beyond with a sheen of blood-red.

Scharnhorst finally reacted. Anna-Louisa was laughing uncontrollably, hugging her skinny sides and rocking back and forth on the bed. The general looked at her with disgust, then turned to Kruger.

'Rally the men at the courtyard below. Bombs or no, we'll have to cut our way down.'

The knight captain nodded curtly, and replaced his helmet on his head. His company began to head down the stairway. From below, the noise of men shouting and running could be heard.

Scharnhorst looked at Lukas darkly.

'How did you find out?' he asked.

Lukas was still out of breath.

'I found a cache,' he said. 'They've been well placed, and well hidden.'

Scharnhorst walked over to the nearest window, and gazed down on the levels below. The red glow of the fires mixed with the green sheen of the panes to create a strange muddy mixture of the two. The bedchamber looked more unnatural than ever.

'There are unharmed areas,' he muttered, looking over a trio of dark columns to the west of the central tower. 'They'll be there. Waiting for us to lose our nerve.'

He spun round on his heel, and his cloak swirled around him.

'Come,' he snapped, looking at Hildebrandt. 'This isn't over yet. The men must be rallied.'

Hildebrandt bowed, and the three of them went back through the antechamber and down the stairs. From behind them, Anna-Louisa's fey laughter degenerated into a series of sobs. Then she was forgotten. Scharnhorst's mind was working quickly. The situation was dangerous. But he still had the bulk of his army intact. The enemy commander had not been found, but even if he'd managed to hide some of his forces from the assault, they would still be outnumbered. It was all about holding the core of the army together. Once panic set in, the advantage would be gone.

Scharnhorst emerged from the tower at the summit of the wide leading stairway. Before him, a scene of devastation lay. The courtyard was high up on the southern face of the citadel, and it looked down over the valley and all the levels below. From beyond its wide parapet, huge flames danced like snakes. Smoke rose into the night air, blotting out the stars and polluting the light of the moon. Below, the rest of the fortress burned.

Lit by the firelight, his men milled around without direction across the wide expanse. For a moment, Scharnhorst couldn't see why they lingered. If they'd had any sense, they would have begun to descend into the lower levels and tried to find a way out. But the exits were blocked. From hidden passageways, Anna-Louisa's guards had at last emerged in numbers. They were all around the edge of the courtyard, and pinned Scharnhorst's men in and back towards the foot of the tower. There were many of them. They had gunners. The snap of blackpowder fire rang out in the night air. In their wake, Anna-Louisa's footsoldiers charged into the fray, bearing the look of men who had nothing to lose. To the east and west of the courtyard, where lesser towers reared their curved, spiked roofs into the air, arrows began to whine down. Scharnhorst's army was trapped, hemmed in on all sides. Any reinforcements must have been trapped further down. Scharnhorst shuddered. He didn't want to contemplate their fate.

'Men of Hochland!' he roared, swinging his sword around his head. He was heedless of the threat from the archers. The army needed leadership, or all would be lost. 'To me, men of Hochland!'

At his side, one of the Knights of the Iron Sceptre unfurled Ludenhof's standard. It rippled out in the fire-flecked wind, dark against the black of the stone behind it. A trumpet sounded. Slowly, with much confusion and labour, his men began to respond. Kruger strode down into the fray, barking orders and pushing troopers into position. Defensive lines began to form. The stream of arrows from above was met by a return volley from below. There were few archers in Scharnhorst's army, but at least it was a start.

The general remained at the top of the stairs leading to the tower, gazing at the battle intently. His soldiers had formed a wide defensive semicircle in the centre of the courtyard, their backs to the stairway. From the many steps leading up to the parapet from lower down, fresh troops poured in. They wore the black armour of all of Anna-Louisa's men. There were more than Scharnhorst had counted on. Where had they been hiding? It mattered little now. They were here, and a way had to be found to resist them.

His eyes swept across the scene. It was hard to make out any detail in the low light. The fires down below threw a red aura high into the sky, but against it the men were little more than grappling shadows.

Then, far off, he saw his adversary. A man, standing much as he was at the rear of his forces on the other side of the courtyard. He was on the edge of the parapet. His mane of silver hair was swept back and rippled in the wind. He stood with the confidence of a leader of men. Having seen the pitiful state of Anna-Louisa, Scharnhorst now knew who his real enemy was. He narrowed his eyes towards the unnamed opponent, and whispered a curse on him. Then he hefted his sword lightly in his right hand, and strode down the steps towards the front line. His bodyguard, a quartet of knights in the colours of the Iron Sceptre, fell in alongside him.

'Sir, is this wise?' asked one of them, his expression hidden behind his helmet.

Scharnhorst fixed him with a look of disdain.

'My place is with my men,' he said, curtly.

And then he pressed on, pushing his troops aside to get to the thick of the fighting. As he went, a shout went up from the knights.

'Scharnhorst!' they cried in unison. 'Scharnhorst for Hochland!'

The standard followed him into battle. When his men saw it, they seemed to garner fresh resolve. Scharnhorst took some comfort from that. The front neared. He whispered a prayer to Sigmar, and then hurled himself into the combat.

HILDEBRANDT AND LUKAS were together, fighting almost back to back. It was hard to make out what was going on in the dark, but they could tell things were going badly. The series of explosions below had turned everything on its head. The lower levels were lost, cut off by flames and the resurgent enemy. The tables had turned once again.

Still, Hildebrandt found that he preferred being in the thick of battle than being in that dreadful chamber up above. For all its horror, there was an honesty to combat with a sword. His opponents were men, just like him. They had the same aspirations as him, the same weaknesses and capabilities. But that horror in the upper room was like nothing he'd ever seen. Even as he swung his heavy sword against a row of desperate-looking attackers, he found himself chilled by it. There was something uniquely terrifying about the descent into madness of one who must have once been so privileged. Amid his revulsion, there was also a spark of sympathy. The carnage had been caused by other men. Anna-Louisa had just been a tool, a means for them to raise the money they needed.

Driven by outrage, Hildebrandt roared his defiance and lunged forwards at the advancing ranks of black-clad men. Lukas was at his side, fighting with considerable skill for a lad of his years. Just as before, Scharnhorst's men clustered around Hildebrandt's imposing presence. He became a focal point in the struggle for survival. On either side, a hundred similar little battles took place. No ground was given, no backwards step was taken. Though knocked off-balance by the lines of bombs, the men had recovered. For the last time, the forces clashed. This would count for all.

As he worked, swinging his blade with heavy strokes, Hildebrandt suddenly found himself wondering where Magnus had gone. A pang of worry hit him. He had been heading for the mines. Had he got back up before the bombs detonated? Even if he had, he might have walked right into the middle of the enemy. There was no telling where he'd ended up, or if he was even alive. The prospect of his old friend's death galvanised him even further, and he let slip a frustrated bellow of rage. Enemy troops scattered before him, and he waded forward, his sword sweeping in mighty heaves. The men beside him joined in, shouting with scorn and mockery as they pressed forward.

Then, something changed. A ripple of confusion seemed to pass through the soldiers on both sides. Orders continued to be spat out by the captains, but there was a distraction. The fighting became sporadic. Some detachments even disengaged entirely. The attackers in front of Hildebrandt seemed to lose heart, and hurried to withdraw. In the brief lull, Tobias looked around him. Lukas had turned from the fighting too. Others had done the same. Despite the urgings of their commanders, soldiers from the two armies were pulling free from the combat and looking up at the tower.

Twisting around awkwardly, unwilling to let his guard down entirely, Hildebrandt did the same. The smooth stone soared high into the air above them. Its flanks gleamed in the firelight. The pinnacle glowed brightly. Hildebrandt found the effect no less oppressive for knowing its cause. Now more than ever it reminded him of a cluster of eyes.

For a moment, he couldn't make out what the great distraction was. But others had seen it. Though some fighting continued, many men stood idly, looking up at the tower, mouths gaping. Hildebrandt screwed his eyes up against the night sky.

Then he saw it. She had emerged. One of the windows had been opened. Far up the tower there was a narrow balcony. Anna-Louisa stood against it, her skirts fluttering in the smoky air. She was too far away for Hildebrandt to make out much of her expression, but it seemed she was smiling. The effect was mesmerising. Soldiers of Scharnhorst's army who had been fed the story of Margravine von Kleister's power and majesty now stared at the frail woman standing over them. Her own troops were similarly transfixed. Many looked horrified, discovering for the first time the true nature of their dread mistress.

'O men of Hochland!' she cried. Her voice was high and fragile, but it carried down to the courtyard well enough. A crazed edge was still apparent in it. 'Why do you fight in my castle? Do you not know that soon we shall all march to Altdorf together? Put away your toys! It is time for bed!'

Her words had an instant impact. Soldiers of the citadel stood staring, or shook their heads in disbelief. From parts of Scharnhorst's regiments, a raucous laughter broke out. Commanders bellowed in anger, urging their men back to the fighting, but it was no good. Anna-Louisa had stolen their thunder. Like some grotesque ghost of childhood, she loomed over them. As her fortress burned down below, she let slip a giddy laugh.

'You look so funny down there!' she giggled. 'Stop your nonsense now. Where is my soldier man? He should have come to see me.'

More laughter broke out amongst the soldiers. Anna-Louisa's troops fell back, some openly disputing between themselves. The unveiling of their commander had broken their vengeful spirit. Hildebrandt could see the look of horror on the faces nearest him. He could understand it well enough. Many of them had died. They had been promised much. It would be a hard lesson, to learn how far they had been deceived. Some of the troops even put down their weapons, throwing their hands up in disgust. Their commanders began moving through the ranks, cursing them and ordering them to take up arms again.

They responded only slowly. The momentum of the battle had been broken, and it was slow to recover. The long days of fighting, the endless cold and privation, had broken the martial spirit of many of the men. It was not as if they were struggling for survival against one of the dread foes of mankind. They were all Hochlanders, all simple men of the Empire, locked in combat due to the whims and obsessions of their distant superiors. Like beaten animals, they were herded back into combat. The commanders barked orders, cajoled with promises of plunder, threatened with the prospect of punishment.

Slowly, unwillingly, the men took up their swords. Anna-Louisa continued to laugh and rave. The knights charged, and the spell was broken. Scharnhorst's troops reformed their defensive positions, and Esselman's contingents renewed the press towards the tower. Steel clashed against steel, and the cries of anger and agony drowned out the crackle and spit of the flames. The distant roar of the fires in the keep had grown louder, and the columns of smoke curling into the night were thick and dark. Anna-Louisa was forgotten, a pathetic figure railing from the balcony unheeded.

Then the assault stumbled again. A single shot rang out across the courtyard, echoing from the walls around it. Another voice was raised in a great, resounding shout. It came from one of the lesser towers on the east side of the courtyard. There was a balcony set high up. A man stood at it. He had long, grey hair and wore a leather coat. He leaned over the masses below, pressing against the iron railing just as Anna-Louisa had done. In one hand he held a laden sack. In the other he held a pistol.

'Men of Hochland!' he cried, and his voice echoed around the strangely quiet scene. 'You have been lied to! You were told there was gold for you at the end of your glorious campaign. You were told that your patron was a woman of power and wealth. All of these are lies. You can see with your own eyes that the margravine is mad. She has been used by evil men. Forget their stories! One of them is dead. The other still leads you. Reject him! He has nothing to offer you but this!'

At that, he swung the sack over his head several times, before launching it out over the heads of the two armies. It spun in the air, spraying its cargo in every direction. At first, it seemed as if the bag contained a collection of blood-red jewels. The nuggets rained down, bouncing from the stone and clattering across the flags. As they landed, the soldiers cowered, expecting some new engineering terror. But no fire exploded over their heads, and no strange blast kindled on the hot stone. The pebble-like projectiles lay against the flags, glinting in the firelight. Seized with a sudden realisation, men scrabbled after them.

'Gold!' came the cry. The scuffle became a frenzy. Fights broke out instantly. All discipline had been broken. The courtyard descended into confusion once more.

'My gold!' came a wail from the tower. Anna-Louisa had climbed onto the balcony edge, her face creased with distress. 'Do not take my gold!'

The man in the leather coat laughed, and the sound of it echoed even above the growing commotion below.

'Fear not, lady!' he shouted. 'It is worthless! Like your promises!'

The truth of it was gradually emerging. As men fought over the nuggets, they shattered and broke between their fingers. Greed turned to anger. A low murmur began to build across Anna-Louisa's forces. Hildebrandt, standing amid the ranks of Scharnhorst's troops, looked over towards the rear of the courtyard. The enemy command group was besieged by their own men, and had drawn arms.

'My gold!' shrieked Anna-Louisa, and stood, precariously, on the rim of the railing. She seemed to be stretched out into the void, desperately clawing at the air. Hildebrandt looked up. With a sudden feeling of nausea, he could see what would happen.

'Get out of the way!' he shouted. It was hopeless. There were dozens of men directly beneath her. They were squabbling over the fool's gold, all thought of the conflict lost.

There was a desperate, last flail before her balance was lost completely. Anna-Louisa grasped the railing, her eyes wide and staring. For a brief second, her gaze seemed to clarify. She looked out over the ruins of her fortress. The flames burned, licking even up the parapet of the courtyard. A wan smile crossed her ruined features. The madness in her eyes dimmed. Her features relaxed. For a moment, she seemed as she must have done, years ago. She lingered for a heartbeat longer. Then her fingers unclasped. Without a sound, she dropped from the balcony. Her nightdress flapping, she plummeted. Hildebrandt averted his eyes. There was a heavy crack, and then nothing.

THE FIRES WERE growing. The armies were seized by a dark and mutinous mood. The grip of the commanders was loosened, and murderous fighting broke out again.

Madness swept across the regiments, as the utter futility and desperation of their situation became apparent. They would get no money. There would be no plunder. All that remained was a blind rage, the fury of the mob. At the base of the tower, the storm of anger swirled. Hochlanders put down their long guns and picked up blades. Morgramgar had become a pyre, a gruesome monument to the folly of Anna-Louisa and the ruthless response of Ludenhof.

It seemed as if both armies would be consumed with the same primal rage. Once the lust for blood was kindled, it was hard to douse. But Scharnhorst was still at the heart of the fighting, and his knights were clustered around. The kernel of his army remained true, a fixed point around which the madness revolved. Slowly, his iron will began to exert itself. Regiments of Ludenhof's Grand Army were beaten into shape by their captains, and formed up to charge into the demoralised, shapeless ranks of Anna-Louisa's men. The Knights of the Iron Sceptre, noble warriors who had little need for more gold, kept their heads. Scharnhorst's army gradually recovered its poise, and began to push out from the steps around the tower. Slowly, and with each step contested, they pressed against the noose around them, driving the encircling ranks of soldiers back towards the parapet.

There was no disciplined response. Anna-Louisa's army had turned in on itself. It was an army of mercenaries, hired by the promise of riches. Seeing the ruin of their hopes, many of them tried to flee. Others went berserk in their frustration and bitterness, attacking anyone who came near them, friend or foe. Knots of desperate men dragged their own commanders down. Throats were cut in the dark, and scores settled.

The rot of mutiny spread fast. The most bitter of the fighters, professional murderers and brawlers, the dogs of war, needed a culprit for their loss. Too late did the command group see the danger. The rear ranks of Anna-Louisa's forces turned tail and surged towards Esselman. There was a murderous sheen in their eyes. Their swords dripped with gore as they came.

There was nowhere for the general to go. He was pinned at the back of the courtyard with only the sheer drop down to the next level behind him. One by one, Esselman and his commanders were set upon and pulled into the maw of the mob. Far from help, swords rose and fell quickly, and the cries of Anna-Louisa's captains were brief before being silenced. The orgy of rage was ratcheted higher. Soldiers trampled over their comrades, just for the chance to desecrate the corpses of the men who had betrayed them. Fists hammered down, feet stamped, fingers gouged. The stones were covered in a thick carpet of blood. With a roar of empty triumph, the mutineers dragged the corpses to the edge of the parapet. With little ceremony, the bloodied bodies were stripped of their armour and valuables, then hurled over the edge and into the inferno below. Esselman was the last. As his blackened, mutilated body sailed into the void, a huge cheer broke from the armies. Both of them.

Lukas looked at Hildebrandt, a mix of amazement and uncertainty in his expression.

'What is this, Tobias?' he said.

Hildebrandt leaned on his sword. He could see Scharnhorst and his commanders surging forward, slicing through the broken ranks of the enemy. The standard of Hochland was being carried into the heart of Anna-Louisa's forces. Their formations were broken, their hopes ended. All that was left was the final bout of killing, the final snuffing of the candle.

'This is the end, Lukas,' said Hildebrandt, wearily preparing to join the assault for the last time.

There was no triumph in his voice. All around them, Morgramgar burned. And in the firelight, crushed underfoot, the nuggets of fool's gold twinkled, a final mockery to heap insult onto the memory of all those who had died.

CHAPTER TWENTY

The fact that I have become, by dint of my skill and labour, one of the pre-eminent engineers in the Empire, is a matter of considerable pride to me. Not a day goes by without me giving thanks to Sigmar for his grace in granting me my gifts of invention and the moral character to use them wisely. And yet all these things pale into nothingness beside the greatest creation of my life, the one that fills me with joy beyond compare, and in earnest of which I would gladly give up all else. My son, Magnus, the priceless jewel for the sake of which all else has been done. I am proud of him, though he doesn't know it as he should. I am old now, and I write these words for posterity. One day he shall rise up and shake the Empire with his deeds. He has the skill. And, in time, if the fates are kind, he will discover the will.

Augustus Ironblood
Private diary. Recovered and preserved
in the Imperial College, Nuln

THE SMOKE DRIFTED down the valley, staining the clear mountain air. Dawn had broken several hours since, and still the lower levels of Morgramgar burned. Scharnhorst had long abandoned the attempt to save the citadel. The survivors of the assault had been withdrawn. Those who had fought for Anna-Louisa were disarmed and interned. Their trials, or what passed for them, would take place in Hergig. After a day of being near abandoned, the camp was inhabited again, and the men wearily went about gathering their supplies for the long march back to the lowlands. All were exhausted. There was no mood of victory. Morgramgar had held neither riches nor glory. It had been cursed, a monument to the madness and greed of the noble classes and nothing more.

Magnus sat on one of the artillery wagons back in the encampment, gazing over the ruins before him. They smouldered darkly under the shoulder of the mighty crag beyond. Every so often a muffled boom would announce that some hidden cache had gone off. The proud aspect of the fortress had been mauled beyond recognition. Many of the towers had fallen. Those that were left were charred and cracked. The forges, deep in the heart of Rathmor's conflagration, were lost forever.

Magnus thought of the rows of infernal machines hidden in those dark storerooms. And the ranks of forges, now silenced. Perhaps it was for the best that they were destroyed. There was some knowledge that the world was better off without.

His thoughts were interrupted by a massive, rolling blast in the distance. He lifted his eyes in time to see the central tower, the emerald-encrusted pinnacle, slowly crumble. With a muffled roar, it toppled over, throwing a cloud of dust high into the air. With it gone, the citadel lost its residual terror. It was now nothing more than a collection of ruins, high in the wastes of the Middle Mountains. They had done what they came for. Kleister's fortress had been razed.

There was a movement at Magnus's shoulder. Hildebrandt came and sat down by him. He watched the same spectacle grimly for a while.

'What do you think will become of it?' he said in his deep, rolling voice.

Magnus shrugged, not really caring.

'Who knows?' he said. 'Maybe Ludenhof will have it rebuilt.'

Hildebrandt turned away from the citadel, and looked at Magnus.

'You were in the vaults,' he said. 'How did you get out of there? The whole place was on fire.'

Magnus smiled weakly.

'It helped having a dwarf at my side,' he said. 'As ever, he knew all the hidden ways.'

Magnus sighed, and looked away from the wreck of Morgramgar.

'He's gone now,' he said. 'It turned out that this was more about him than any of us. He's happy, at least.'

Hildebrandt didn't ask what that comment was about. For a moment, the two of them sat in silence.

Two old friends, perched on a ramshackle cart on the edge of the civilised world. All around was wasteland, desolation and destruction.

'So was it worth it, this commission?' asked Hildebrandt, finally.

Magnus didn't reply immediately.

'Not for the money we'll get,' he said at last. 'And Messina's dead. I regret that, despite everything. I should have worked harder with him. He had no idea of the danger he was in. And the Blutschreiben has gone forever. I now know what Rathmor did after leaving Nuln. We've stopped him spreading his madness further. That's something, I suppose.'

Hildebrandt nodded, but without much enthusiasm. 'I suppose so,' he said.

Ahead of them, amongst the toiling ranks of men dismantling the camp ready for the journey home, Magnus suddenly caught sight of Lukas. The boy was laughing and joking with a band of halberdiers. In the sun, his flaxen hair looked bright and unsullied.

'The lad,' Magnus said. 'He was with you at the end, yes?'

Hildebrandt nodded.

'Will he make it, do you think? Will he become an engineer?'

Hildebrandt thought for a moment, before fixing Magnus with a level gaze.

'Maybe,' he said. 'But he's seen what can be done with the machines. He saw what it did to Messina. If that's the future, I'd wager he wants no part of it.'

'You sound like I did,' said Magnus. 'Back in Hergig. You don't regret what we've done, do you?'

Hildebrandt looked back over the smoking ruins of Morgramgar, and his expression was bleak.

'You persuaded me to come with you, Magnus,' he said. 'Truth be told, I came to protect you from yourself. Maybe this will be the saving of you. I hope it is. But there's nothing for me here now. A man grows sick of the killing. When we're back, that's it for me. No more campaigns. You'd do well to do the same. Find an honest trade. Leave the fighting to younger men. Our time has passed.'

Magnus said nothing, but followed his friend's gaze out towards the broken fortress. The smoke still poured out.

'The Empire will always need Iron Companies,' he said, though his heart was not quite in it.

'So you say,' said Hildebrandt, and neither was his.

In the distance, a series of trumpets were blown to mark the lifting of the camp. Horses were whipped into action, and the loaded wagons and carts began to move. Men shouldered their weapons and pulled their packs onto their backs. In the midst of them were the handgunners. Their numbers were sorely reduced. There were few cannons left too. Hochland's arsenal would take months to recover its strength. The entire state had been weakened, its strength sapped by the feuds between powerful men. Even as its armies were drained of their potency, the foes of mankind multiplied in the wastelands beyond. The whole affair had been dirty, vicious, demoralising and dangerous. If this was victory, it was a sour taste to savour.

Hildebrandt said nothing more. After a few moments, he got down from his seat and walked over to the remnants of the artillery train. His voice was soon raised in the distance, shouting orders to the men, getting the caravan into order.

Magnus watched him for a moment, before turning his gaze one final time back to Morgramgar. The thought that Rathmor, the architect of the disaster which killed his father, lay buried under the mountain was some consolation for all that had happened. And despite everything, there was a flicker of pride deep within his breast.

He reached down for his gourd. For the last few days, he had barely thought of having a drink. Now, with all the excitement over, he surely deserved a swig. As he drew the leather to his lips, he paused. For some reason, the smell of the ale repelled him. Perhaps it had finally turned. Of perhaps finally he had.

He let the gourd fall down at his feet. The beer ran from the neck, foaming brown. It seeped into the rock. There suddenly seemed so little point to it. He had drowned in drink to forget the past. Now the past had returned, and its horrors had been more fragile than he'd remembered.

Magnus took a deep breath, feeling the pure, cold air enter his battered frame. The craving had left him. Perhaps not forever, but for the moment. And as he had once said to Thorgad, a start was all he needed. For the first time he could remember since the accident at Nuln, Magnus reflected on the legacy of Augustus and felt no shame. He was complete. He was healed. All men had ghosts, but his were no longer vengeful. As the high clouds drifted past the ruined towers, he thought he caught the phantasm of his father's face one last time. The craggy features, the mane of hair. But no disapproval. Not any more.

Magnus sighed, and the daydream rippled out of existence. The wind was getting up again. He could feel his wounded side ache from the chill. He had to go. There would be plenty of time to decide whether he wanted to take on another assignment when he got back to Hergig. Perhaps Hildebrandt was right. Perhaps he should look to retire. And yet a part of him wondered if he would ever do it. The Empire would always need engineers. There would always be madmen like Rathmor to counter, always walls that needed to be breached. For all their dangers and temptations, the new sciences were still the future for mankind. For better or worse Magnus had always been a part of that. Maybe he always would be.

He turned his back on the smoking ruins, and headed back down towards the baggage trains. As he went, the cold air moaned across the stone of the valley. He passed the ruined iron of the cannons and joined the mass of men marching back the way they had come. For a moment his long leather coat was visible. Then Magnus vanished among them, just another face in the numberless armies of the Empire.

The campaign was over. They were going home.

ABOUT THE AUTHOR

Chris Wraight is a freelance writer. A long-time fan of Games Workshop background art and fiction, Chris is also into the novels of Patrick O'Brian, Philip Pullman and William Golding. He can occasionally be spotted running through the muddier bits of the country in training for some race or other.

His first novel, *Masters of Magic*, was published in 2008, followed by *Dark Storm Gathering* in 2009.

THE EMPIRE ARMY SERIES

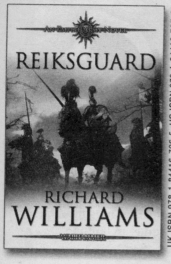

REIKSGUARD

RICHARD WILLIAMS

UK ISBN 978-1-84416-726-5   US ISBN 978-1-84416-727-2

IRON COMPANY

CHRIS WRAIGHT

UK ISBN 978-1-84416-778-4   US ISBN

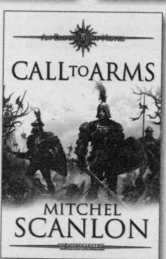

CALL TO ARMS

MITCHEL SCANLON

UK ISBN 978-1-84416-812-5   US ISBN 978-1-84416-813-2